OF IMPERFECTION

THE ALTERED EARTH TRILOGY

Of Friction

Of Abrasion

Of Imperfection

OF IMPERFECTION

ALTERED EARTH SERIES
BOOK 3

S.J. LEE

PEW BOOKS

Library of Congress Cataloging-in-Publication Data is available.

ISBN (paperback) 979-8-9892965-4-5
ISBN (ebook) 979-8-9892965-5-2

Cover design by S.J. Lee
Cover illustration by S. Scorpi

CONTENT WARNING

This book is meant for adults. Please continue with discretion.
A full list of content that may be sensitive to readers is
available at the back of the book.

CONTENTS

OF IMPERFECTION

CONSEQUENCE

THE BEGINNING OF THE END

FOR ONE MINUTE and forty seconds, Fury fell. She fell through silence and dark nothingness, and she clung to it, the illusion of stillness and liberation from everything.

The skull embed purred behind her left ear, and she ignored the flare of her HUD as numbers counted down in red digits. Her eyes closed, and the world drifted. The sedatives whispered through her bloodstream, slowing her heartbeat, cradling her nerves like a lullaby half-remembered.

She'd done this at least a hundred times in the past three and a half years—over two hours of chosen oblivion. But every fall became a little emptier, each time a little less freeing.

DEPLOY.

Fury opened her eyes.

No. Fuck off.

She blinked past the blaring red display to the widening lights below. City ruins stretched on, their expanse an open maw waiting to swallow her whole. Fractured skeletons of buildings glowed, and specks and shapes moved in the streets, unaware and unafraid of the real threat. If those specks and shapes looked up, they'd see judgment. A sentence already passed. An execution. Death.

But no one ever looked up.

Fury's visor flashed red again, faster.

DEPLOY. DEPLOY.

Fine.

She pressed the stimpad, and her helm filled with an invisible inhalant, the chill in her nostrils, her throat, then her lungs as she sucked it in. The calm was gone in two breaths, replaced by an itch, a burn, and a restlessness. That thing inside her that begged to run, rip, and tear.

The ground rushed up. The specks and shapes became heads. Shoulders. Bodies.

Targets.

Her HUD pulsed red.

CRITICAL VELOCITY BREACH.
DEPLOY. DEPLOY. DEPLOY.

Fury torqued hard, a ninety-degree snap against gravity. The propulsion pack kicked. Everything tightened and compressed, a violent jerk under her armpits, between her thighs, as the suit countered to keep her upright. She shifted. A small adjustment. Then her boots met the ground.

But they struck flesh and bone first, something soft and human that gave way like overripe fruit beneath reinforced soles, her drop armor absorbing the shock. She registered the uncanny crunch, a millisecond of noise, but she didn't feel the body pop like a blister, didn't feel the spray of guts as it exploded around and under her. Didn't feel anything.

She stepped out of the small crater of blood and shards, the pack thunking wetly behind her, its purpose used and abused. No hesitation. No ceremony.

Immune to the clotted viscera that clung to her exterior, metal fingers unlatched the long case attached to her right leg. A carbine rifle slid free with an elongated whisper. Its scarred grip fit into Fury's hand as though forged from her own marrow. Her arm and weapon synced, calibrating to their own rhythm. Metal and metal, fused by purpose, surpassing human matter.

Arm and rifle rose together in a smooth motion, and two tight, suppressed rounds tore through skull and brain as someone peeked from a burned-out chassis several meters away. Fury didn't need to confirm the target. Every unmarked person in this city was an Apostate. And every Apostate was an enemy.

Her device pinged, and guiding markers lit up in her skullhelm. In her peripheral vision, her radiation gauge ticked up, but she disregarded the soft reminder. Her armor could handle it. For now.

She moved up and over a fragmented foundation, past broken stone pillars, through the husk of what was once a skyscraper, until she reached another building with a wide, three-story base. Its twin squatted across the boulevard, one side caved in. A bridge that spanned the street joined the two, climbing into a single massive tower before sheared steel and pulverized concrete marked where the upper half had collapsed, toppling sideways and coming to rest upon the ground.

Fury's embed thrummed. She turned to the incoming ping and its directional marker, where a figure crouched outside the structure's door. It pinged twice more as additional individuals emerged, joining the first.

She lowered her rifle. Static spotted her skullhelm display as she approached. The interference was exactly as expected, but Fury paid no heed; she didn't need any of it to do what she and her squad were there for. In a world of countertech, jammers, and unreliable communications, all they trusted was muscle, metal, and instinct.

Her display blinked out before it folded back into her helm, silencing the buzz of warnings and alarms. Heavy air blanketed the exposed skin on her face, but she ignored the warm feeling, unconcerned. Her armor and stims would stave off most of the radiation, and any lasting damage would be addressed with more injections and concoctions. The ability to see and sense unhindered was worth it.

The first figure stood, rising two heads above her, his own skullhelm peeling back. Between heavy, dark brows and wide cheekbones, mismatched irises stared down at her, one blue, one green.

"The propulsion packs are not meant for late deployment," he said flatly. "How many times is this now? You are lucky you have not liquefied yourself."

"Oh, shut the fuck up, Boy Scout," groaned the stocky, armored individual next to him, a few centimeters shorter than Fury.

Alphabet.

"Ya gonna tattle to Sky-Eye?" he added in his gravel-thick voice. "It's one less fuckin' sod to chase down. I'd be more worried about the impact. Them knees." He twitched his fingers at Fury. "What took ya so long? Smellin' the roses?"

"Roses?" Boy Scout said. "There are no flowers here."

"Holy fuck." Alphabet groaned once more and disengaged his helm, revealing pitch-black eyes, a canyon of a scar across the bridge of a healing broken nose, and rough, dark stubble. He glared at their teammate. "It's an ol' fuckin' figure of speech, ya fuckin' plank. Two years together and still no bloody personality."

The last armored individual stepped forward, the same height as Boy Scout but leaner. She had already disengaged her skullhelm, and her short hair was slicked back, her blue and green eyes piercing her teammates. Her presence was the pause between lightning and thunder. "Are you done?" Vengeance asked.

Alphabet grinned. "Never."

"Remember why we're here."

"Hard to forget," he muttered, hitching his weapon higher onto his shoulder. "It's quiet." He wasn't referring to the ongoing klaxons that had settled into the background.

"They have abandoned him," Boy Scout said.

"Fat chance."

"Or it is a trap."

"More likely."

"Enough," Vengeance hissed. "The others are in position."

Fury's embed buzzed. Confirmation. The rest of their fireteam was across the street, unseen, but posted in the other building.

Vengeance pulled a thick rod from her back, and with a flick of the wrist it fanned wide. Plates unfolded and flowed down symmetrically until it was roughly the size of the Altered woman's torso. A shield.

She nodded. Fury fell in behind her, carbine raised. Alphabet and Boy Scout mirrored them on the other side of the building entrance. After another nod, Vengeance brutally stomped into the door. It exploded inward, and the squad flowed in two by two, clearing their arcs and sectors.

But only dense silence welcomed them. Inside, the foyer was slick with blood. Bodies lay in clumps, fresh enough that they were still warm. Fury nudged one with her heavy boot and scowled. There was no reaction. There was no welcoming party. No defenders.

The four continued on, pushing deeper toward the stairs. They climbed, weapons up and steps silent. On the second floor, skittering sounds of movement greeted them. Bodies—*enemies*—stirring just out of sight.

Vengeance's marker pulsed beyond the open doorway, and Fury's device purred with the internal signal. No one spoke. The Altered woman flowed through the door first, angled toward the threat.

A figure sprang up, rifle half-raised.

Too slow.

Vengeance's shield smashed forward, and reinforced metal shattered bone. Before synapses could fire, her blade found a throat. A smooth bayonet punch. A gurgle escaped the enemy's lips.

Fury caught movement ahead, a shape around the corner. She waited—only a second—until the silhouetted line of the wall broke with the curvature of a nose, a glimpse of an eye. She squeezed the trigger, and a body fell.

Vengeance coursed, and Fury moved with her. They didn't pause, didn't hesitate as they stepped over the corpses. Like outside, there were no friendlies here. Every life inside this building was marked for termination.

At the threshold, Vengeance held, listening. The others joined a second later, sweeping and covering their backs.

Silence.

They pushed forward and up. On the third floor, Boy Scout and Alphabet took point. Suppressed rounds stuttered in the air. A scream started and died.

With Fury close behind, Vengeance surged up the last steps, through the short hallway, and into a wide and high-ceilinged lobby, the fourth-floor nexus between the two buildings, a cathedral of disintegrated glass and fallen walls.

Fury counted at least a dozen outlines at the room's far end, tucked in as if the furniture and remaining wall between them signified safety. They were waiting. Hiding was their enemy's last refuge. Fury's muscles coiled, and the stims in her bloodstream yearned for motion. *Violent* motion.

With the coordination only time and blood forged, she and Alphabet wordlessly retrieved compact pucks from their armor. With a nod, they lobbed them into the open space.

The little contraptions bounced once. Twice. They were satisfying clinks against the once-expensive natural stone floor.

They wobbled, the metallic ringing pitching into a high whine that quickened, faster and faster, until it stopped.

Blasts tore the room apart. Sound and light bloomed like a second sunrise.

Fury and the others moved, two pairs split like dancers mid-turn. Bullets thundered, hissed, and whizzed all around them. Fury advanced on instinct, and her carbine spat holes the size of fists through armor. When her magazine ran dry, she fluidly drew her knife from her rig. Its blade was compact and cruel-toothed. Her right hand crushed while her left slashed.

Fist.

Knife.

Repeat.

At her side, Vengeance cleaved through her sector. Her shield was a battering ram, her blade an afterthought.

Their enemies didn't fight. They died.

In under forty seconds, the lobby was painted red. Near Fury, an Apostate choked, hands clawing at his ruined throat. She ended it with a downward strike through his thorax, cracking bone.

With the lack of movement that followed, Fury's breath calmed. She looked up as her embed thrummed. Their sister squad was on the third floor of their respective building. Blocked by a structural collapse.

Alphabet kicked a corpse away and dropped into the empty armchair it had guarded. "Fun," he muttered. He wiped the blood on his boots on the dead man's shirt.

A door creaked open, and Fury's attention flitted across the lobby. Two Apostates stood in its frame, half-armored and shoulders heaving. Fury could make out their eyes—large, dilated, and black as oil. The one on the left lifted his rifle. Barely.

His head jerked as bright red sprayed behind him. A hole had been punched below one dark eye, and a dagger was rooted above the bridge of his nose. The Apostate dropped, weapon clattering a meter away.

The other Altered froze.

"Got 'im first," Alphabet said, still seated. His finger popped from his rifle's trigger and wagged.

Boy Scout straightened from his throwing stance and reached for another dagger tucked into his armor.

"No, no. This one's Fury's." Alphabet tutted. "It's her turn."

The remaining Apostate's eyes darted toward his comrade's dropped rifle.

Alphabet tutted again, louder. "Ya don't want to do that." He whistled. "Feelin' like some samba? Mambo?"

Fury resheathed her blade.

"We do not have time for this," Boy Scout said, but he stood, waiting.

"X-Ray's en route, and Sky-Eye says Big Tango's not movin'. We have time. Let the woman work her feelin's out."

Boy Scout looked to Vengeance, but she only muttered, "Make it quick."

Fury set her rifle down. She palmed her skullhelm, and it fully collapsed into its default square panel. As she strode forward, she clipped it to her rig and shook out her mussed hair.

The Apostate's eyes widened, then narrowed. He glanced at her metal arm then back to her face. His lips moved. A whisper. "斷血者."

Duàn Xiě Zhě in the old Altered language.

In hers, *Sun-Killer*.

As Fury took another step, he dove. But not at her. He was going for the dropped rifle. Too slow.

Fury surged. Her boot thrust out, but the Apostate twisted and slid away. He was fast for a low-tier Altered bastard—still genetically engineered to be better than the average human.

And the stims he had taken made him more volatile, more dangerous.

But Fury had taken her own. Her stims weren't enough to give her the advantage, weren't even an equalizer, but she also had something he didn't. He wanted the weapon; he depended on it. And that was where he'd fail.

Fury was a weapon. She'd been shaped and molded since she was young, hardened by blood, sweat, and death. Once upon a time, she'd questioned her purpose, but then the Apostates rose, overthrew the Altered government, and attacked. Losing her limb had been a curse, but the evolved replacement had been a blessing, an added edge. Fury's rage sharpened into a point.

The enemy pivoted, one hand into his kit, the other reaching for her metal arm. She let him grab it, but before he could pull, she shot forward, her forearm ramming into his jaw. He staggered. Fury spun behind him, a fist of flesh and sinew burying into the meaty part of his lower back. He grunted but kept coming.

They moved in a blur. He lashed out, his fists wild but trained. One blow landed beneath her ribs. She felt the hit. Blunted, a padded hammer. She let it ride.

Her body shifted with the momentum, and she snapped an elbow back, then rocketed her palm like a piston into his chest. He flailed. Fury stepped in. Close. Too close for him to swing with any weight. Her right hand latched onto his jaw. Gripped. She parried another blow and climbed her fingers up into pliable skin, sank them into his cheeks. And squeezed.

She waited for the brittleness before the crack. The crack before the pop. But it didn't come.

The Apostate floundered his hands at her, one at her wrist pulling and the other pushing. But it was the pumped knee that interrupted her stance and balance. His face pulled out of her grip, but with a swift swipe and a quick adjustment, her hand shot forward and closed around his throat.

With a series of wet crunches, cartilage gave way. The whites of the Apostate's eyes expanded as they bulged in shock. His arms lost purpose as his mouth opened, trying to pull air through a collapsed windpipe.

Fury continued to hold him by the neck, supporting him as his legs threatened to give out. She held her enemy long enough to watch his expression lose its arrogance.

This was the enemy's chosen? This was their elite? How many humans and Altered had he killed and maimed?

She opened her hand, and he crumpled to the floor. He tried to get up and made it onto one knee. Then both. He looked up as she reached for his face once more.

But a streak whistled by.

A dagger's hilt sprouted from the Apostate's temple. The cesspool of his eyes went blank, and he folded back with a clatter.

Fury waited. For *something*. Annoyance. Anger. Satisfaction. Accomplishment. Anything.

She felt nothing.

When a throat cleared, Fury turned to the four others who had joined them. Their armor was similar, not only in design but also by the amount of blood splattered across it.

"Glad we're enjoying ourselves," X-Ray said, stepping forward. His silver eyes glimmered as they settled on Fury.

His large teammate, Chapel, crouched to retrieve the dagger from the first Apostate's forehead, pulling swiftly on its handle. The head thunked onto the stone floor.

"Took you long enough," Alphabet called out from his chair.

X-Ray moved around the fallen Apostates, past Fury, and toward the rest of the group. His two squadmates came behind him. The nearer one gave Fury a brief nod, while the other offered nothing, their skullhelm sealed tight. Probably one of the new human recruits, still skittish about radiation. Regardless, they were on the same side. Even if Fury had forgotten both of their names.

"Their infighting did most of the work," Vengeance said.

"Unlucky," X-Ray replied.

Another head thumped unceremoniously as Chapel retrieved the second dagger. He flicked the small blades in the air, ridding them of blood, before he passed both to Fury.

The others continued to speak normally, lacking any care that their voices traveled up and around the vaulted space. Of the eight now gathered, New Guy 1 and Chapel's attention darted to the stairs and half level above. The alarms from outside blared, but enemy reinforcements were nonexistent.

It was disappointing. Fury had expected more. Returning to the group, she unhooked her skullhelm and placed the square over her ear, the tip of her finger just touching her embed. Her helmet folded out until the light material encompassed her crown, leaving the mandible open.

X-Ray sighed as if this were all an inconvenience. "It confirms the factions breaking apart." He looked around. "We're sure there's no other way out?"

Alphabet motioned toward the tall windows. "Not unless he decides to…" He whistled and traced a downward curve with his fingers.

Boy Scout hummed. "I hope he is still alive."

"Sky-Eye had a signature before comms went out. Heat means not dead. Not yet."

"Alone?" X-Ray asked.

"We'll find out in a few seconds." Alphabet jumped up and tossed Fury her carbine. "Shall we?"

They positioned themselves back into two loose columns, boots over dust and old stains. The main stairwell curled upward like a reverse Fibonacci spiral, a reminder of the extravagance of a previous life on Earth when this building's interior was full of opulence. The wail of the dead city's alarms ebbed as they climbed. Each ledge they scanned was clear. There was no final ambush. If any remaining Apostates hadn't attacked during the squad's leisurely wait downstairs, there would be none coming now.

The fireteam cleared floor to floor until they reached the seventh level. It was dark, the building's lights off from the previous floor and up. Fury's HUD was unresponsive, rippling with interference. She didn't need it anyway. Green eyes glowed in front of and around her, but these were her teammates'.

They moved into the largest hallway, splitting as the path forked in two, four fanning left, four right, to encircle the central room. Fury's skin prickled as the whispers started. A name, over and over, bubbling like water over river rocks, a dilapidated song and chorus of languages.

"Kartik…"

"我們來殺你了…"

"Your time has come…"

"Kartik…"

She didn't join in, but the others continued to sing like wraiths through the fissures in the door. The sound skimmed above the hard floor and slithered hauntingly into the walls.

In front, Vengeance sniffed the air and in that moment, Fury envied her squadmate's genetic engineering and heightened senses. Could she smell him? Could she smell his fear? Fury hoped he was afraid. She wanted him to be afraid.

Like a candle flame extinguished with a single blow, the voices ceased. The silence ground into Fury's ears.

Vengeance stopped at the doorway. Touched it. Prodded it. Rusty hinges groaned. Everything about this place was broken, suspended in a time when the generations before had ruined the planet. As the door opened wider, it creaked with the old world's age and wounds.

Inside: darkness.

Fury struck a flare against her wrist and tossed it ahead. Orange flame danced across the room, casting long shadows.

They swept in, four abreast.

In the back, a chair. A figure.

A small twitch of motion and a single shot cracked.

Restrained.

Something clattered to the ground. A blade.

Then came the drip. And drip.

Torches illuminated around Fury, and she blinked, her vision adjusting. The shape in the chair slumped lower, one arm dangling, sliced open from elbow to wrist. Beneath fingertips, blood had already puddled.

Another drip.

Kartik Finlay sat before them, conscious. Frail shoulders rose shallowly then faltered. The single hole above his breast gleefully stained out across his collared shirt. Alive.

X-Ray stepped forward, grabbed the Apostate's white hair, and tilted his face up. Green, brown, and blue multicolored eyes, once sharp and calculating, were now dull and wet.

Kartik blinked one time.

Again.

Then no more. The strategist, the leader of the Altered terrorist uprising, died without a word.

Someone flipped on the main room light. A single bulb flickered above like a dying star. The copper tang of blood reached Fury's nostrils, a scent layered over bleach and mold. She looked around. Bare shelves and broken furniture.

A hovel. A hiding place.

Her upper lip curled. Weak. Almost pitiful.

Fury's scowl deepened. What a fucking disappointment.

Vengeance stepped forward, disengaged her shield, and reattached the rod to her back. "Bag him."

As if he were leftovers.

Fury stared at the body, waiting for something to spark.

Pride. Joy. Closure.

But nothing.

The edge of the stimulant waned in her blood. She felt the headache as it tugged at her consciousness, her high coming to an end. Every kick was too fleeting, too short now. She could feel the pain in her joints from the drop and landing; the sprint and surge were catching up to her. Aside from the physical discomfort, she could also feel the looming behemoth of darkness as it prodded at her.

"This is the great Kartik Finlay? The general, the puppet master of the coup and war?" Alphabet spat on the corpse. "Coulda killed yourself years ago, saved us all the trouble."

Vengeance ignored him. "Names, dossiers, drives. Five minutes," she ordered.

And Fury fell in with the rest, into their usual routine as they searched drawers, toppled shelves, and peeled tech from walls. No one spoke.

Boy Scout nudged her then pointed in the corner at a battered data console buried under ruined office furniture. He paused and frowned. "You are hurt."

Fury followed his sightline to her side, where a small knife jutted, piercing the gap in her armor. She hadn't felt it during the fight with the Apostate. Still didn't fully feel it.

"Chapel," Boy Scout called out.

She waved him off. It could wait. The stims hadn't fully worn off yet. When they did, it would hurt. The ache and crash would come. She'd already burned through a calmer before, then stimmed contrary to usual guidance. But guidance didn't understand her environment.

When the airships arrived at their hasty LZ outside, the team loaded Kartik's body and clambered aboard. Fury slouched into a seat and hovered her thumb over the secure compartment on her kit. Then she dropped her hand. Not yet.

The first aircraft peeled away, and hers followed low and fast over the ruins, through and out of the irradiated zone. Fury peered down at the bag in the single aisle between her and the others, glaring at its silent presence.

They had killed Kartik Finlay. Or they had found him, assisted and witnessed him on his own cowardly journey out.

The mastermind. The strategist. The hidden face behind years of blood and ash. It was done. Over.

She had promised her brother, and she had kept that promise. So why did she feel nothing? Where was the release? All she felt was emptiness, and it reverberated from her gut into her bones. She stared at the black bag, but it didn't answer.

As the ship passed over ruined farmland and craters, Fury let her eyes unfocus out the open doors, past her HUD as it blipped to life. A throb blossomed in her side, her knees, and her lower back. This pain she welcomed and wanted. But with it came something else edging at her mind and thoughts.

Fury's thumb pressed down on the scratched compartment, and it opened. A small cylindrical capsule slid out, and she snapped it between her fingertips then held it up to her nose. An inhale in, and the sting hit instantly. For a few seconds, she felt the shadows grip her; she could feel everything, everywhere, on every millimeter of her skin. Even her metal arm. Coolness spread through her capillaries and bloodstream, and her heart slammed once, hard, then settled. Familiar but strange faces, blond hair, gray eyes, brown hair, light brown eyes, all surged in her mind. Then blinked out. The sedative was faster this time.

And below, the world continued. Little specks and shapes moved, unaware and unafraid. Or were they aware? Were they afraid? Fury watched them shrink beneath the haze, and she exhaled slowly as the outlines slipped away. There were no more concerns, no more care.

The bag in front of her remained closed and motionless.

But there was no end to violence.

Even in death.

RETURN ORDER

[PROTECTED]

ORIGIN NODE: UMF CENTRAL
TO: RYAN, SAM
SUBJECT: RETURN ORDER

YOU ARE HEREBY ORDERED TO REPORT TO UMF
    CENTRAL COMMAND - STATION CITY FOR
    ADMINISTRATIVE PROCESSING AS SOON AS
    POSSIBLE. THIS IS YOUR THIRD AND FINAL
    NOTICE. NONCOMPLIANCE WILL INITIATE
    ESCALATION PROCEDURES UNDER UMF CODE
    §12.8.b.

CONFIRM RECEIPT WITHIN 24 HOURS.

[PROTECTED]

3

———————

THE SERAPH

HOT BREATH SCRAPED Fury's left shoulder, irritating puffs bouncing into her ear. She waited another second, letting it grate, then pushed off the slick counter warm from her own body. As she straightened, skin met skin. Hot and sweaty.

She recoiled.

He leaned into her as if a single brush meant permission. Her lip curled, and she peeled herself away, out from under his body, shedding the touch like dead skin.

The sex had been exactly what it needed to be: motion. A method. Something to bleed out the last dregs of accelerant despite the previous sedative. The effects hadn't lasted as long this time—a few hours, maybe less—but the mixture had made her restless in a way she hated.

The ache was returning to her legs now. And between them. A familiar hollowness closed in, like the world had stepped away from her, weightless in a bad way.

She tugged up her pants and crossed the small space to the only standing row of lockers where clothes spilled out of the open door, clinging to the single shelf inside. She dug through the mess with impatient fingers, scratching her neck before forcing her hand back to the task. Until she found it. A narrow tin.

"What are you doing?" Heathen mumbled, voice buried in his arms as he slumped over. His skin glistened with sweat and the remnants of his previous shower.

She ignored him, shaking the container next to her ear in two brisk motions. There were several rattles and plinks before they settled.

"Should've known."

It was a familiar tone. Not exactly disappointment, not exactly concern.

Fury could already feel the ache drilling deeper, could feel the stitch in her side where the Apostate had stabbed her the day before. She had run out of calmers earlier and had since turned to stims, but they were now bleeding out of her system. She wasn't about to sit around waiting for the flood of hurt. Physical, emotional, all of it.

The mild dismay was fleeting as she opened the tin and considered the little white pills with the double triangles etched into them, still in their factory form. Fury plucked one out and dry-swallowed. It was better than nothing.

"You mixing again?" he asked. "You're not supposed to do that, you know."

She didn't answer, just fished a pouch from her pocket and dumped the tin's contents into it. Little tablets cascaded like hail. Two weeks' worth for a normal human. It'd hold her for a few days.

"All of it?"

"You don't use them," Fury muttered as she tucked the pouch away. She picked up her sleeveless top from the ground.

"Never liked the things." Heathen pushed himself up, one hand to his groin, and tossed the contraceptive aside. "Fucks with everything down here." He swept over his genitals before he reached for his towel nearby. "You should really lay off those."

Fury's cheek twitched, but the movement was hidden as she weaved her arms through her clothes. She tossed the empty tin back into the locker, where it clanked before falling into the folds of a black shirt. "Didn't ask for advice," she said.

"Yeah, well, I'm looking out for you."

"I didn't ask—"

"Yeah, yeah." He winced as he stood, then arched backward, stretching his spine, arms, then wrists. Scars scored his chest and ink covered his left arm in an elaborate sleeve of wings and eyes, all tangled and watching.

"Can you put on some clothes?"

Heathen straightened, then muttered, "I was showering. You're the one who jumped me." He stepped toward her.

Fury moved to the side, out of reach.

"Wasn't expecting you so soon," he said.

She thumbed the pouch in her pocket, then maneuvered it open with a flick. She popped a second calmer into her mouth, and it scraped on the way down. Fury willed it to work faster, willed it to tell her she wasn't ashamed, even though she knew this arrangement had been more frequent than usual.

"What now? Killing Kartik wasn't enough?" Heathen asked as he dried the back of his head then draped the towel over the open locker door. He grabbed a shirt from the pile. "We got the big one, but there's always more to hunt down."

Fury said nothing.

"You know, I don't mind being your downer fuck buddy— not complaining, just…maybe one day we can try a cot? Shit, an actual bed." He slung his shirt over his shoulder. "I don't remember the last time I slept in one. My back would love it. Shit, I sound fucking old." He laughed. "Shit. I *am* old."

"Heath."

"Yeah?" He turned to her, one hand on his hip. Still naked.

"You're chatty after a fuck."

He chuffed. "Should've shagged the quiet one on your team. Brute, was it? Or whatever his callsign is."

Fury didn't bother correcting him. Brute had been KIA two years prior. SRAF squads rotated too fast to keep up with. The only constant was turnover. They didn't socialize or mix much with others, not unless they were in the same region and sharing a camp. Like now. She scowled. "I don't fuck teammates."

Heathen waited for more, but she didn't oblige. "Lucky me." He huffed once more, then scratched himself. "So what's got you all in a tizzy? Antsy about less Apostates to kill? Don't worry, they're out there—just making us work for it now. Speaking of which, we're heading out again—another lead on Beric. Sky-Eye's tracking movement. Could be fun? Tell Vengeance to settle it with Sky and join. If you want to work out some emotions…"

Fury shot him a look. "UMF wants me to report back."

He snorted, but his expression flattened. "Oh, you're serious. How'd they find you?"

She shook her head. "Sky-Eye."

"Figures." He stepped one foot through a pants leg. "They want Val—"

Fury's eyes flashed, and the callsign died in his mouth.

"Easy, killer." He threaded his other leg through, tugged up his pants, then raised one palm. "You at the end of your contract?"

She grunted. It was about that time, but the idea of an end felt fake. Did contracts actually end? They just changed shape, and she'd keep doing the same shit until she was dead.

"Unbelievable. They can't handle it on their own without dragging you back in?" Heathen fanned out his shirt and yanked it over his head. "Didn't bat an eye when my contract ran up. Passed my discharge through Sky-Eye, and that's it. Ghosted. All those years through the grinder, and all I get is a fuck-off packet."

Fury kneaded metal fingers into her temple. The calmers were starting to wash at her periphery, but she wished they'd hurry. The space between sober and numb was where the memories liked to wriggle in.

"Guess I'm not too bothered. We're Seraphim. Can't shove us back into stuffy rules and regulations now. We're spoiled masochists."

The blanket of nothingness pulled over.

"They'll run you through the full eval gauntlet."

Fury tried to return a long stare, but the effects had kicked into high gear. She wasn't sure if Heathen had said it as a statement or a question, but she was used to tests and medical evaluations. Since Fury was five, she'd been the experiment, welcomed onto an active United Military Federation outpost. At six, she'd fired her first gun. At twelve, she'd enlisted. A test subject from the start, a weapon in no time. It was what she'd been trained for. There had never been a version of her that wasn't an instrument. That wasn't used.

"So when are you heading out?" Heathen asked.

"Soon."

"And?"

"And what?"

"Are you going to extend your contract?"

Fury hadn't considered it in the last years, hadn't really thought about UMF. Until now.

"Nah," the man said. "You're like me; we don't settle. Can't. Can you imagine? What would we do? Work a boring job, get married, pop out some wee lookalikes, build a home, then retire and farm?" He laughed. "That's not for people like us. We don't get happy endings. This is the best we've got. A team on your side, assholes on the other, and enough ammo and blunt objects for therapy."

Heathen really talked too much, but he always had a stash of unused, issued calmers. And he had familiar scars, a similar past. It worked. For now.

He continued, but Fury had stopped listening. She let herself fall into the double dose, and she sat before she swayed.

Then, someone cleared their throat.

"Vengeance," Heathen said, turning to the only entrance and exit.

In the doorway, the Altered woman nodded, stiff and clipped. Her nostrils flared and her cheek twitched. A flicker of judgment passed over her face, visible in mismatched green and blue eyes. She'd changed since Fury first met her in the South, and not just in name. Now she showed emotion. Barely, but it was there.

"The others are waiting," Vengeance said.

Fury hummed and pulled herself up.

"You all heading back to Station?" Heathen asked. "Some rest and relaxation?"

"This *is* rest and relaxation," Vengeance responded.

He chuckled. "Lucky us."

"Aegis says your team is moving on Beric."

Heathen shrugged. "A couple leads came in on him and other ascension potentials. How about you guys?"

"Sky-Eye cracked some tech we found with Kartik. She thinks they're coordinates for training sites and wants us to verify."

"So much for downtime." He gestured toward Fury. "Bummer for you, doing UMF admin bullshit while the others are out playing."

"It won't take long," Fury snapped.

"Sure. That's what everyone thinks."

She started for the door.

"Oh, Fury."

She stopped and turned.

"Pick up extras while you're back there, yeah?" He closed his fist and tapped his neck.

"Thought you already got a fresh batch of jabbers," Fury replied.

He shrugged.

"Will you be here if I bring some back?"

"Probably not, but pass it along. It'll make its way to me somehow."

Still at the door, Vengeance made a face.

"What? You've never been tempted to try?" Heathen asked.

"No."

The man propped against the locker and drummed his fingers along his bicep. "Easy for you to say when you're designed that way. Us mere mortals, we've got to cheat to keep up with you freaks."

"Questionable," Vengeance said.

"Tell that to the ones who didn't make it." Heathen ran a finger across his throat. "Or not."

He had a point. Most humans who joined SRAF and didn't stim didn't last.

"So this is goodbye?"

Fury arched an eyebrow at him. Every mission was a reshuffle, every parting a goodbye. Her *own* team could be different by the time she returned. She hadn't bothered to get to know the new members on X-Ray's squad.

But Heathen stepped forward and clasped Vengeance's arm. He did the same to Fury, his hand cupping her elbow, the warmth and pressure of his grip delayed on her prosthetic. "It's been a delightful couple of fucks," he whispered, leaning in.

She returned the squeeze. Harder.

He yelped and pulled away, laughing as he shook out his limb. "You're a fucking hoot. When this is all over—if we're alive—you're welcome at mine. Of course, if it's still standing."

She didn't answer, didn't want to. That offer, a soft half-joke, was more future than she deserved.

"You too, Vengeance."

The Altered woman forced her lips together, an attempt at a thin smile. "I'll let Alphabet know."

Heathen made a face. "Fuck no. He can stay on a leash outside."

♟

"Any last words for this piece of shit?"

No one in the aircraft answered.

The black bag lay between them, restrapped and resealed. Inside was Kartik Finlay. Or what was left after the souvenir vultures were done with him. A former target and enemy had been reduced to mass and nothing else. No glory, no final speech, no cinematic ending. Just a body stripped of meaning.

In the open doorway of the airship, Fury braced herself opposite Boy Scout. Together, they hauled the bag forward, Vengeance and Alphabet guiding from behind.

The aircraft hovered low, and wind gusts hit its sides like invisible fists. Beneath them, the blackness of the ocean yawned at them, unfeeling.

Fury watched the bag slide over. It flipped once, half again, then hit the water with an inconsequential blip. No splash. No wake. Just a hole devouring it whole. And that was it.

She didn't blink, didn't breathe. Just stared. She waited for something. Some part of her expected the Altered figure, the Apostate leader, to surge back to the surface, finger pointed upward, condemning her and her inferior genetics with words she couldn't hear.

Instead, the waves pulled the bag under. One. Then another. Gone.

Fury stayed there, upper body leaned out in the open air, bracing against the turbulence. Her free hand drifted to the pocket on her kit, fingers searching, trying to trace the chain necklace she knew was nested inside. She tried to summon the memory of its silver links on her skin, but she wasn't sure what that felt like anymore. She hadn't opened that compartment in ages.

Abandoned.

How could it be abandoned if it was still there? *She* was still there. But somehow not. Anchored to nothing.

Fury studied the ocean, but it offered no answers. She let her pinky slip off the handhold. Then her ring finger. Held on by two. She could fall now.

Just...

Fall.

Let the darkness take her. Would it hurt?

With stims, she had felt waning rage, even disappointment. With calmers, she was a passenger behind glass. But she held nonetheless.

The airship jolted, a sudden lurch underfoot.

"Au revoir, asshole," Alphabet yelled as he stuck his head out beside her. He added in a mumble only she could hear, "Good fucking riddance."

Fury didn't look over, didn't respond, only pulled herself in. When her teammate followed shortly after, the door sealed with a hydraulic hiss, muting the outside world. She moved past Vengeance and the others, some seated, some chatting near the cockpit of the large craft. They were all phantoms with borrowed names.

Alphabet tagged along. "Ya ready?"

She gave him a look over her shoulder, then dropped into a half sit, half sprawl across the long bench along the cabin's side, leaving a space between herself and Boy Scout, who had only sat just before. The Altered man gave her a nod, then gave Alphabet a dirty look. He shut his eyes, his head resting back.

"How long's this ad-mi-ni-stra-tive bullshit gonna take?" Alphabet asked, voice too loud for the quiet.

Fury didn't answer. If it took longer than a week, she'd find a way back.

Her teammate slouched into the seat across from her. "Gonna say hello to family?"

The calmer blunted the question before it could cut.

"Are you *ever* quiet?" Boy Scout asked, one green eye cracking open.

"Ah, fuck off. This is a joyous time, and we're off to do more cleanup work. Fury's leavin' me with all y'all freaks."

Boy Scout closed his eye again.

"I didn't choose this," Fury said.

"Yeah, yeah. Have to report back to the mothership." Alphabet pulled one leg up, plucked his serrated knife from a concealed sheath, and picked at the treads of his boots. "Don't stay out too long. They'll replace ya with another one of these freaks. I don't even know that one's name." He poked the tip of his blade toward the front of the aircraft.

Boy Scout sighed, eyes still shut. "Her name is—"

"Doesn't matter. I can't be the only original."

"You have Vengeance."

"Vengey-poo doesn't count. She ain't human."

Boy Scout's eyes flew wide.

"Ya know what I mean." Alphabet smirked. "Team's getting lopsided."

"You are starting to sound like—"

"A Charonite? They're not too bad." Mischief gleamed in Alphabet's teeth.

"But you are with us."

"Am I? *I* don't like any of you. Vengey-poo is an exception. But you? I'd give you up in a heartbeat."

Boy Scout's eyes grew wider. His mouth opened, but—

"Do not feed the goblin," Vengeance said as she joined them.

Alphabet blew a kiss to the Altered woman. "Too fuckin' easy."

She promptly ignored him.

"Where next, my love? Station City? Hu-man central?"

"No. Your North, Ursus, to drop you off." Vengeance gestured her chin at Fury. "You will hitch a ride back to Station from there. And while you sort whatever you need to do, we will move on to the next coordinates in the region."

"Joy," Alphabet said, throwing his hands behind his head. "Back to the ol' stompin' grounds."

"With Kartik gone and the others on Beric, we will move on the training grounds, help chisel what we can to assist the push into Nakuan—"

"And Arshangol after that," Alphabet recited.

Fury closed her eyes. For her, Ursus was full of ghosts. So was Station City.

She slipped her fingers into her pocket, the motion automatic like muscle memory, a ritual etched in nerves, and the pouch yielded without resistance. She kissed the small tablet to her lips and folded it into her mouth, pocketing the savior and quiet curse in her cheek. It didn't taste of anything. Just another inch of nothing. And she'd need more soon, but that was a problem for later.

Fury rolled her salvation on her tongue and against her teeth before she swallowed.

Waited.

And let the world dull.

PART 1

ACTION

4

____

STASIS

SUNLIGHT PUSHED half-heartedly through the single window, reluctant to enter the annex space. The front office was a tad larger than a people-sized shoebox, a narrow room divided unequally, one part for visitors and three parts hidden away behind the counter and its partial door.

Miriam didn't care for this place. She disliked everything it signified. She impatiently tapped her fingers against the counter, then winced, realizing the rudeness of her action. Instead, her hand drifted to the diamond tab affixed to her collar and worried its jagged trim. Her gray-and-black UMF uniform fit, but the life inside it had grown tight. She was tired, but stubbornness had a long shelf life.

Finally, the waist-high partition slid open with a soft click, and a small-framed marine appeared shortly after.

"Oh! You're back." He bounced up onto the high stool, already spinning toward the terminal. "Lists are updating now."

She knew. That's why she was there.

The clerk bent around the opaque screen and sucked his teeth. "You know the list is on the network, right? You don't have to come in every week."

It wasn't every week—not anymore—but Miriam didn't correct him. She had started falling off in consistency in the past year. First one week, then two between visits. The old teller had transferred out to some company rotating north, looking for action. She'd liked him; he hadn't asked questions. The new one standing in front of her didn't seem to remember that this terminal, and only this terminal, carried a particular list that wasn't on any unencrypted line. And she wasn't going to explain it again.

The marine made a pleased noise and tapped the display. The once-opaque screen facing her blipped and revealed a presentation mirror of his view. He then leaned into his hand, gaze drifting to the small office window behind her, watching the base and world beyond.

Miriam was already scanning the holoscreen as names populated, line after line rolling down. She jumped to her usual section, fingers ready, heart not.

She looked for the name. She always looked for that name. She checked the next section, too, in case someone had flipped the order, surname first. It was unlikely; UMF rarely made those mistakes. Nevertheless, she checked.

There were new names, fresh ones, marked by tiny glowing symbols. But not Sam. Not Ryan. Not "Valkyrie." Not reported, at least.

Miriam wasn't certain if UMF still tracked the individuals who'd transferred to SRAF. The last marine who'd gone over, she'd seen his name on the list, but that had been ages ago. No one really knew much about the joint human-Altered strike teams. Even the acronym varied in retellings. SRAF, Special Requirements Allied Force—or was it Special Response Assault Force? Surveillance, Reconnaissance, Assault, and Fire Support? Everyone had a theory; no one knew the truth.

What mattered was the name the field had given them: Seraphim. Their operators: Seraphs.

Myth layered over myth. Unapologetic brutality disguised as

tactical mandate and tools wielded by strategic necessity. SRAF operators were weapons pretending to be people. Or people pretending to still be people.

The clerk exhaled loudly. "Done?"

Miriam nodded faintly, hand flicking upward in an automatic motion.

He jabbed a finger into his screen, and the exterior display blinked out. "Kinda morbid, isn't it? That they're just names after a while? Every now and then I see one—maybe I knew their brother or sister. I don't know. It's just lines and characters on a screen."

She didn't reply, only gave him a glance.

"Find what you want?"

No, but that was good news. Miriam offered a neutral hum. Noncommittal. Safe. A sound that meant nothing and everything, depending on context.

Sam was still alive. Or she wasn't registered as dead. Yet. It could be a delay or it could be worse. Sam "Valkyrie" Ryan could be buried in a file that would never reach the list on this terminal. The woman was a ghost that haunted her.

Sometimes, Miriam's anger returned fresh, and sometimes heartbreak as well, as if the loss had happened the day before, not years ago. Like the wound had never clotted properly. But she knew time had carved new distance, had sanded the emotions down with it. She had learned to carry them or been forced to learn.

Miriam raised her fingers, not exactly a farewell, but close, and turned to go.

"See you next week!" the marine called behind her.

"Sure," she murmured.

She hoped not.

The guilt came like an aftershock. There'd be closure, at least, if Sam's name ever did show up. It'd be a finality she could hold, a line drawn beneath the ache.

The thought made her stomach churn. That wasn't what she meant. Not really.

Ahead, the buildings of the city reared up, and she walked toward them, the heaviness in her receding with every step.

"Tan!"

The familiar voice pulled her from the weight of her thoughts, and Miriam turned as a shape jogged toward her, a crooked grin on his face.

She smiled, warmth creeping in despite herself. "Hey, boss."

Vallen Krill embraced her, arms firm but careful, then stepped back. "Not your boss anymore."

"No, just everyone's now. Should I call you 'sir' instead?"

He made a strangled sound.

She winked and tipped her head. "Haven't seen you in a bit. Command treating you well?"

"Eh, it's only been a couple weeks—"

"Been a month since you transferred."

"I didn't transfer—"

"No, just promoted. Again. Mr. Big Shot…"

He gave her a pained look. "You're heading out?"

She nodded. The team briefs were done, and she had requisitioned and packed what she needed for the mission.

"I'll walk you," he said.

"Not busy enough?"

"Just stretching my legs." He looked back at the office she'd come from, close to Command's main buildings, but if he had questions, he didn't ask.

As they fell into step along the compound streets, Miriam flexed her fingers then rubbed her arm absently. "I'm giving you shit. I meant what I said before. You earned it. First Elly, and now fast-tracked into the big contract with the heavyweights? I'm happy for you."

"Thanks…I guess." He paused. "Are you renewing?"

She raised an eyebrow, then remembered they'd enlisted at the same time and shared similar contract schedules. "Not sure yet," she replied, though she already knew the actual answer. "We don't all have our lives figured out."

Krill gave a noncommittal shrug. "It's only been a couple weeks—"

"Month."

"—but I miss team life."

She scoffed. "Right."

He shot her a look.

Miriam blinked. "Oh. You're serious."

"It was easier. People were more direct."

"You really miss being interrupted by the same five degenerates every briefing?"

"At least you all told it straight. Now I'm decoding politeness like it's encrypted intel. Is a 'no' actually a 'yes' or is it a 'no' with some darn caveat?" He rubbed his throat. "And the ass-kissing..."

"Are you the ass or the one doing the kissing?"

He groaned. "Both, probably."

"Well, you wanted to be the adult in the room."

He puffed out a laugh. "I hear Echo's heading north?"

Miriam's throat caught slightly with the change of topic. She inhaled, held the air in her lungs, and let it out slow. "Yeah. You're following that?"

"Of course. With Kartik gone, the wunbies fragmenting... and now, missing marines?"

"What were they doing?" she asked. "I thought we stopped sending Division companies over there."

"I know I'm relatively new, but it's all still a little fuzzy to me. Turns out Command is no better when it comes to sharing information. Everyone's in their own bubbles and lanes." His voice lowered. "I know not everything is connected, but... Just be careful. That region, it isn't..."

"Yeah, Krill. We know."

He rubbed his forehead, eyes darting toward the skyline as if the answers might live somewhere above it. "It's been like drinking from a firehose. I can't keep up. One week it's Charonites, the next it's back to the wunbies, and BigInt, well, they're not sure which faction. Every time I read a report, the environment and boundaries shift. I don't know how anything in the area has survived the fighting there. If we ever get it back..." He paused. "How do you rebuild that?

"We don't," Miriam said. "Not really."

He frowned. "Is Ursus helping? Any Titan teams supporting?"

She shrugged.

"It's been a mess ever since Kartik." He sighed. "You'd think with him dead, there'd be some resolution. At least a ceasefire."

Miriam exhaled slowly. Killing a leader, a symbol, didn't stop the movement or the reasons behind it. It actually made things worse. The wunbies, Apostates, Promised, or whatever the Altered terrorists and supremacists wanted to call themselves—different names for the same evil—they didn't disband; they only splintered apart, and every different group had their own agenda.

"Command and BigInt are monitoring, but I have a feeling it's going to get messier." He gave a humorless chuckle. "Hard to believe anything could be more dangerous, although dangerous might not be the word. Just...less logical? Kartik at least had a strategy that made sense."

And now there were offshoots of Apostates, boundless in their rage, decentralized, and driven by a singular purpose: to eradicate humanity and claim supremacy.

"We're going to need good minds, good leadership," Krill said. "More so now."

"Isn't that why they promoted you?"

He gave Miriam another look.

She sighed. "You're worried."

"It's Echo. I'm always worried about Echo."

In name, only. Miriam was the only remaining team

member from their original roster before the Apostates' coup, before the fall of Arshangol. Before the mission in the South. Before Sam.

"You can chat with Gumede, you know," she said.

"No." He waved a hand. "No, it's fine."

"Hino, then."

"She's solid. A good second."

They walked.

"Remember when things used to be simple?" Miriam asked after a while, her voice low. "We used to complain about protection and tedious ops."

He dipped his head. "Times have changed."

They had *all* changed.

"Have you heard from the others? Greggo? Nas?"

Miriam sighed. Krill was tactful enough not to press, especially when it came to Yuri Gregov, their former teammate and her former best friend. Whatever'd happened between her and Yuri hadn't ended with a fight, but the distance spoke for itself. In the last months on Echo together, they had remained cordial, albeit more aloof, until he took an early retirement from his contract. They would've been on the same schedule, the three of them, if he and Krill hadn't bailed early. Miriam was confident it wasn't fully because of her; Yuri hadn't transferred to another Special Operations Group unit, like their other teammate, Benjamin Fox, had. Strangely, she should've still seen Yuri around, ever since he'd taken a position at Station General, the city's main medical center—and her parents' business—but she never spent more time there than she needed to.

"Last I heard from Nas was a year ago," she said.

And that had been a short message back with general platitudes, opinions on new eateries, and one-sided biotech updates.

"I ran into him here, actually," Krill said.

"On base?" The last time she'd seen Nas in person, he'd

been in recovery with his spine half-ruined, legs braced, and body hunched. She hadn't imagined he'd ever be back in a UMF uniform.

Krill raised his hands at her expression. "Not like that. He was with a biotech company. Civilian-side. Advising Command. I think he's landed on his feet—er, found a decent gig at least. He looked good. Still Nas."

"That's good," Miriam replied quietly.

They reached the gate in silence, in their own reflections of an old Echo. Frankly, the team had never really recovered since Kai and Nas were hospitalized. Miriam had been badly injured, too, but not to the extent they had. The scar on her abdomen had faded under a meticulous ointment schedule, but she could feel its lasting reminders in certain weather. And even if the scar was gone, the wound didn't always go away.

As they passed through the exit, Miriam surveyed her old team lead with mock suspicion, trying to lighten the mood. "You gonna walk me home, too?"

Krill tipped his head toward the street corner. "Nah, I wanted to say hi to your ride." He strode forward.

A woman with shoulder-length dark brown hair stood waiting in neat civilian clothes. Her backpack bulged slightly, and Miriam knew it was the white research coat she had folded and stuffed away. Brown eyes crinkled with a grin.

"Emma Dubois," Krill greeted as he embraced her.

The woman replied with a warm laugh. "Hi, Vallen."

Miriam smiled despite herself.

"We can set you up with visitor access, you know. You can meet Tan inside," Krill said, as he pulled away. He gave Miriam a pointed look. "Or is she intentionally keeping you out?"

Emma tilted her head and looked at Miriam with gentle amusement. "I like my boundaries, but thank you."

Miriam leaned in and gave her a light kiss. *Hi*, she mouthed.

Krill watched them both with exaggerated disbelief. "I know you've been together for a while now, but I can't get over this."

He wagged a finger between the two of them. "If you knew the woman she used to be—"

"Please don't." Miriam rolled her eyes.

Emma smirked. "Oh, I've heard the stories."

"Hell, Em. You're supposed to be on my side."

"What? I've lived in the city my whole life. It's actually not as big as you think. People talk. I have—*had* a social life, you know."

Krill burst into laughter.

Miriam rolled her eyes again and nudged the man toward the gate. "Don't you have somewhere to be? What happened to first impressions?"

He resisted. "I've been in a month. We're past first impressions."

Emma clicked her tongue. "Don't push away your only friend."

"He's not my only friend."

"Oh? So where are all these friends then? Hiding for a whole year?" The woman crossed her arms, wearing a smug look. Then her face softened as she turned toward Krill. "I'm only teasing, but I *have* been nagging her about keeping better tabs on you all." Emma grinned as Miriam shook her head. "It's nice to see you, Vallen."

"Yeah, goodbye *sir*," Miriam added.

"Ah, that's my cue then." Krill raised his hands in surrender and moved toward the gates with a small grin. "Okay. I'll catch you later, Tan. Good luck up north. Nice to see you too, Emma!"

The woman waved back at the same time Miriam raised a middle finger.

"So you finally have a departure time?" Emma asked as they crossed the wide city avenue into the grid of streets, the buildings rising around them like concrete sentries.

Miriam hummed an acknowledgment.

"How long do I have you for?"

"Minus shuttles and prep..." Miriam checked her commcuff. "Thirteen, fourteen hours."

"Alright. Dinner and breakfast, then."

"And dessert?" Miriam's finger poked mischievously into the woman's pack.

Emma returned an exasperated but playful look, and Miriam smirked.

"Breakfast? I thought your conference starts early tomorrow."

"It does." Emma shrugged, unbothered. "They won't miss me."

Miriam's lips curved. "They won't miss their lead scientist?"

"Not at all. Plus, I delegate well. Keely's got most of it covered." Emma snorted softly. "I'm forcing her to, at least. She's terrified, but she'll be fine. Vertex collects high-potentials and geniuses, but half of them don't know how to talk to a room."

"Oh, and you do?"

"Better than them!" She paused, already anticipating Miriam's reaction. "Minutely better is still better. They'll have to get it sorted without me soon, anyway. Not everyone can be the smooth-talking charmer Miriam Tanner."

"You like me."

"Maybe." Emma's mouth curled in sly amusement. "Maybe a bit more."

"Oh?"

"Yeah. I like you a lot."

"Oh." Miriam cast a sideways grin. "Good to know. Considering I love you..."

That earned a quiet laugh. Not the teasing kind, but one that slipped through naturally, soft and real. The two walked in sync, their bodies angling closer as the city massed around them. The perpetual warble of pedestrians, vehicles, and machinery wasn't loud, but it was present. A low, ambient rhythm. A reminder that life went on.

And Miriam let herself drift. Not aimlessly, but intentionally. She was good at that now, letting her thoughts wander far enough to mute the sharper fringes of memory.

Krill, Yuri, Nas, Fox, and Kai. Even Sam and Scott. The old Echo squad scattered by time and conflict. They felt distant, traces of who they'd been. And yet here Miriam was, still carrying the team's name, still moving forward in the same direction, even if the faces beside her had changed, even if her former self would no longer recognize her own.

But that was okay.

She peeked at the woman next to her, her girlfriend with warm brown eyes and loose strands of dark hair twining beneath her ears. Emma was someone grounded, someone who didn't need answers to love what remained. The ache that pressed behind Miriam's ribs eased. Not entirely, but enough.

Together, they crossed into their residential district, where the scent of ionized pavement and roasted food from open-air restaurants crept in with the summer breeze.

Emma gently bumped into Miriam's shoulder. "What's going on in that brain of yours?"

"Nothing," Miriam said.

Emma inclined her chin. "That kind of nothing, huh?"

Miriam gave a faint smile. "The best kind."

They kept moving. And for now, that was enough.

___

INFLECTION

BEFORE THE WAR, there had never been a reason to travel to Ursus Outpost. Station City, the North, the South, and the little population centers between were all self-sufficient, separated by thousands of kilometers of dead land and water, tethered loosely by their UMF affiliations. In the North, Ursus had mostly been in its own orbit, the second-largest military post, with its own dedicated Special Operations Group, the Titans, while Station had its Spartan and Razor teams.

But now the distinctions blurred. SOG teams and UMF companies moved freely between posts, and the only marks of difference were the different shades of gray in their regional uniforms and the subtle insignias on sleeves and collars. It wasn't only the marines either. More aid, research, and tech organizations also streamed between the once-divides.

Perhaps that was the silver lining. War had at last forced some semblance of unity.

Nowadays, Miriam couldn't count how often she'd been to the North. UMF's operations were consistent enough that a routine cycle of transports shuttled between Station City and Ursus. Fresh bodies filtered in, and tired ones were spat out like parts on a conveyor belt, indistinguishable beneath uniforms and armor. She and Echo would be moving up soon, part of the new routine.

She settled against the outer wall of the gray SOG building, watching the base's flow of traffic. To the rest of the Station City compound, it was another day of relative quiet and numbing efficiency. For Razor-Echo, it was the calm before their flight and mission. Miriam had kissed Emma before they separated, had squeezed her hand as an unsaid promise that she'd be back in a few days. At the memory, a smile crept onto Miriam's face.

It fell, however, as a hand caught her attention from across the way. She lifted her own in a flick of acknowledgment. Two fingers from her temple to the air.

Nimo Talwar was the newest addition to Echo, and he was still shiny with youth. It was his second contract with UMF but his first with SOG. He was twenty-two years old. Nearly a decade older, Miriam felt the wear on her body, but she didn't feel older in spirit, just that the new marines looked younger and younger.

Talwar waited for a pair of white-uniformed legionnaires to walk by, shifting slightly, a scowl on his face. But then it passed. He jogged over, posture stiff, trying to look more confident than he probably felt.

"Makes my skin crawl," he muttered.

Miriam wanted to press, force her teammate to verbalize his phobia, but frankly, she didn't have the energy to engage. Instead, she leveled a flat stare his way.

"Have you seen Goom?" he asked.

She let him steep in awkwardness before she answered. "He's probably at the TOC for last briefs. With Hino."

"Oh." Talwar tapped his thumb to his collarbone. He leaned on the wall beside her, then thought better of it and straightened. "I checked the rigs and gear again. I've got Hush Detcord, discs…anything else I need to run through? Get from LOGS?"

"If it's not already in your pack or on the way to the airfield, you're too late." She gave a small shrug.

"Oh. And now?"

"Stand by to stand by."

He looked mildly crushed.

This was the job. Most people didn't understand. They only saw the "run-and-gun" part—what recruitment shills touted to lure more fodder into the military machine. Most of UMF work was standing around for hours, conducting training after training until something snapped into motion. At least that was how it used to be. Now, with the war against the Apostates, the ratio had been thrown off. But waiting in uniform was still true, especially now, when they had a set launch time.

Miriam tugged at the collar of her black shirt. A younger version of herself would've hated that she had stuck around UMF this long, and maybe Miriam still hated it, deep down. But it'd been a necessity.

Her commcuff buzzed, and she glanced at the reminder about her contract renewal. She dismissed it with a shake of her wrist. Was UMF a necessity for her now?

At her side, Talwar fidgeted once more, but his impatience was cut short, saved by the arrival of two others.

Celestine Hino, Echo's second, nodded to Miriam. Beside her was another former teammate, puffing lazily on his nicosynth device, attention flickering between the marines and their surroundings.

"Tan," he said.

"Jace," Miriam replied. "The brief's over? Goom?"

"Leads had a stay-behind."

Miriam's brow raised. "And you didn't stay?" Intelligence, especially an officer from Command, usually did.

Iniko Jace only shrugged. "Admin shit. Shouldn't take long. They've probably already broken up."

"I'll go find him," Talwar offered quickly. He jogged off in the direction they'd come.

Jace watched him go.

"New engineer," Miriam said preemptively.

"What happened to the last one?"

"Washed out."

"Not everyone's cut out for this." He sighed. "This one's got a lot of new-guy energy."

"Talwar," Hino said, glancing back to make sure their teammate was gone. "He's nervous. He'll manage. It's his first big mission, but he follows orders, gets along with the team." She looked over at Miriam, who nodded in mild agreement.

"Too many new names; it's hard to keep up," Jace muttered. He flicked the device in his fingers. "We're heading to the Pit. Want to join?"

Miriam brushed a piece of lint from her sleeve. "Sure."

She pushed herself off the wall, and the three proceeded toward the outer ring of the compound. They passed a small Ursus company heading the opposite direction—probably to the DFAC for breakfast, judging by the time. Miriam's eyes drifted over the line of marines, most stripped down to T-shirts in the summer heat and their gear slung loosely over shoulders and secured in the crooks of their arms. Her gaze snagged on flashes of dark ink along a couple of exposed forearms and biceps.

She frowned.

Jace caught her expression.

"That was—"

"Yeah." He sucked on his device.

"Are we not doing background checks anymore? Ursus is allowing Charonites in?"

"Don't say it so loud."

Miriam scowled. "Why? Are we scared of them now? We're UMF. SOG. Since when have we allowed the bad guys in?"

Hino scratched her jaw and looked away. "Desperate times."

"We can't be *that* desperate. Are we recruiting straight from their disciple pool?"

"Those looked like second contracts," Jace muttered. "Converted, probably."

"Hell."

Neither added anything more.

"Is this happening in Station, too?" Miriam pressed. Charonites. If there were Altered supremacists, the Children of Charon—COC—wore the same face, although on the opposite end of the radical spectrum. These were human supremacists and just as foul, albeit in a more homegrown way. Before the Apostates surged, UMF saw the domestic terrorists as an annoyance, sometimes an enemy and threat. But now the military was allowing this riffraff and rhetoric in.

The Echo second looked toward the intelligence officer, whose lack of response was an answer itself.

Miriam's stomach twisted. She scanned the area again, this time with more intent. The UMF compound was busy as usual, although there were fewer white legionnaire uniforms than she remembered.

"And Legion?" she asked.

"The Altered are still around, but they *have* been moving most of their operations out to the airfield. Ursus has a handful of liaisons, and SOG Titan has their attached unit like us and Spartan," Hino said. "I saw one earlier. Probably here to sync up."

"But?"

Jace sighed. "What do you want us to say?"

"That we're not aligning with people we were fighting a year ago. That we haven't reversed course on our alliances. Is that why Hadeon's team isn't joining us?"

"That's not why Legion isn't joining your mission. It's a delicate situation, okay? Between the COC and—" Jace sighed. "Look. Overall, we haven't. We're not reversing anything with the Royals or Legion. But between Kartik's death, COC expansions, and SRAF ops, everything's stabilizing out. The Royals are redirecting their focus in general; they're moving assets to look at long-term Arshangol strategy. And it's been a lot longer than a year, Tan."

He stopped at the sidewalk splitting toward another nondescript gray structure. Miriam looked up at the squat, windowless building nestled in a row of other windowless annex buildings. This was the Pit. She'd only visited once years before, briefly. Echo had dropped off a handful of captured Apostates at the door. Most SOG marines knew about this place but hadn't been inside. Herself included.

"You were Spartan-3," Miriam said to her teammate. "Your entire mission set was *against* those bastards."

The muscles along Hino's neck tensed. "I know."

How gradual had this change in UMF's enlistment and personnel suitability been? Miriam considered herself quite aware, more so than the average marine, but now she felt like she'd missed something massive and in plain sight.

After another deep inhale from his nicosynth device, Jace walked the short distance and opened the door. Miriam followed Hino hesitantly.

Inside, the fluorescent light was harsh, flattening the color from the room. A stout marine at the counter stiffened as they approached, but Jace waved his cuff, murmured something, and a partition slid aside. They deposited their commcuffs into individual lockboxes near the wall, then proceeded forward. Miriam half expected to be stopped—she wasn't in the intelligence specialty like the other two—but the marine didn't give her another glance. She passed through into a short corridor lined with reinforced cells.

Each door was closed, the narrow food slots at the bottom shut as well. There was no sound, no shouting, no rattling. Just dense silence.

Miriam followed the others into a control room that spread like a spoke to four observation pods. Through the one-way windows, she could see that three of the rooms were occupied. The individuals inside had shaved heads, bowed with faces blank. Their uniforms were the color of emergency beacons—bright orange and hard to miss—as if their multicolored eyes wouldn't give them away first.

Apostate prisoners. They looked empty. Not only quiet, but resigned. Their defeat had sunk deeper than skin. It would be close to pitiful if Miriam hadn't known the brutality and violence they sowed.

"What are we doing here?" she whispered to herself. She was certain the Altered couldn't hear her through the windows and walls, despite their genetically enhanced senses, but this place demanded a solemn and dreadful stillness.

No one answered, but she hadn't expected them to. This wasn't for her. Miriam didn't have the clearance for interrogation oversight—not officially—but Jace did. He was wrapping up last-minute information before SOG's operation, and she and Hino were simply passengers and witnesses.

"SRAF got Kartik," the intelligence officer said quietly after a moment. "That mattered. It cut momentum from the Apostates, took their knees out from under them."

"But?" Miriam prodded.

"Before Kartik's death, the Apostate movement was already slowing—or, really, getting complicated. We suspected they were fighting for control in their ranks, already arguing about strategy and methodology. There were reports, but frankly, we didn't know for certain. There's more going on, but it's stuff we're still trying to untangle."

Of course. Nothing was simple anymore. Or it had never been and Miriam was remembering some false narrative that everyone disillusioned themselves with.

"Infighting," she said. "You think there's a power vacuum? Someone vying for his spot?"

"History's seen it before... Remember how we thought the Apostates were lone-wolf actors? We thought it was bad when Kartik united the factions. Shit, he and Beric conditioned the

Altered population enough that they didn't lift a finger to help the Royals in the coup. Now that he's gone, the instability…"

"This mission…" Miriam whispered. "I thought it's a search-and-rescue. Is it something more?"

Jace gave her and Hino a look—neither confirmation nor denial—and knocked on one of the observation room doors. It opened, and a uniformed marine stepped outside, joining them in the central space.

"Any updates on location?" Jace asked.

"Not precise coordinates," the marine replied. "But we've got a general zone north of Woodchik."

Hino straightened. "That's at least five towns. Who has control of the area now?"

"Well, depends on the weather and the week… But *this* week? If everything falls in line?" Jace tapped his device on the module station. "Our *friends*."

The Charonites.

"Lucky day," Hino muttered. "Lucky us."

Miriam frowned. "If they let us through."

"They will," Jace said. "We dropped a whole caravan of aid on them."

"Command's sure it wasn't the Charonites who did it?"

Maybe the missing marines her team was being sent to find in the North *weren't* missing. Maybe the Charonites had kidnapped or killed them. Or the marines had gone and joined the human supremacists. She didn't understand the appeal, but they all knew UMF and Legion's fight against the Apostates was systematic and limited to rules of engagement. The Children of Charon weren't bound by the same uniform, scope, and guidelines. Arguably, they *were* better positioned to fight the Apostates in the region.

Understanding rippled through the room, but no one gave her an answer.

Jace shrugged. "Anything else from this batch?"

The marine spun his finger in a small circle. "We'll keep working these ones until a new group comes in."

"Alright, thanks." Jace turned. "Need anything before y'all head out?"

Echo's second shook her head. "That was the last bit I was looking for. Anything more precise is appreciated, so pass it along, preferably before we hit the jamming zone. But we can work with this." She looked at Miriam. "I assume you've hit the clinic already. Did you receive confirmation from Titan-2?"

Miriam nodded. "Liu's available. He's solid. Used to be with Razor-Charlie. Between the two of us, we're as good as we can get, short of lugging a MedJet." She directed her next question to the intelligence officer. Though it had already been asked in their team brief, she wanted to hear it directly from him. "We're sure the four marines... They're alive?"

"We're hopeful," he replied after a short pause. "The company lost contact, but the liaisons say they've been receiving pings. Not regularly, but enough. The signal's probably bouncing through jammer gaps. One of these..." Jace jerked a thumb to the cells, "implied as much. Best-case scenario? Our marines are scuffed up but dug in, and now they're waiting for Echo to get them out."

"And worst?"

"It's a trap."

Miriam didn't flinch. She'd known.

"We'll get enough information so you *don't* step into a bad situation. Or at least enough to prep for the worst-case scenario." Jace tapped the console.

"And we don't have much choice," Hino added. "We don't leave marines behind."

Miriam and Jace exchanged a glance. That wasn't entirely true. How many people and assets had UMF left when the Apostates razed southern human settlements and attacked the outpost there? How many had they left in the last years of war and confusion?

Miriam tried to remember the missing marines' names from the brief. Goyer, Johnson, LaRussa, and Patterson...or was it Pinkerton? They were names she hoped wouldn't end up as another four lines on a list, just additional numbers to UMF's records.

"No, we don't," Jace agreed flatly. "We especially don't leave the son of a City Center politician behind."

And there it was.

"SOG is tip of the spear," he recited.

Sure. A spear that didn't care who held it.

Miriam scoffed, too tired for spoken sarcasm to land with any real bite.

"Find them and get out," Jace added. "If there're any Apostates, bring them back as well. Dead or alive."

"Dead?" Miriam muttered.

"Part of the brief." He shrugged. "Explicit instructions. It'll be extra weight if so, but Foxtrot's got your back. It'll be fine."

Miriam had heard *that* a few times before. She pressed a hand to her wrist, a familiar gesture—part habit, part reflex—but her commcuff was outside the space in its lined box. Even without the device, the substance of it and its unaddressed reminders of her contract lingered on her skin and bones. She'd already renewed twice before. Most recently, after Sam...

Miriam had stayed with Echo out of habit. Or hope. She had told herself it was for the team, for continuity, but it had been for Sam. Somewhere, beneath all the posture and practicality, she'd held on to the quiet belief that if the woman ever returned to UMF, if the wandering orbit of SRAF ever curved back to Station City, Miriam would still be in the same place.

Waiting.

With Emma, she hadn't said it aloud in so many words, but she hadn't needed to. It had been there, looming. It was less so now, but still present. Because it wasn't all about forgiveness or unfinished business. At least that's what Miriam told herself.

She had stayed.

But now, maybe it was time to let go. Her contract renewal was that opening and opportunity. Maybe Miriam would finally do what her parents wanted and pick up the management reins at the medical center. Maybe she was done with all of this, and maybe it *was* time to leave.

And though her feet automatically followed Jace and Hino down the short corridor, out the drab building, and onward to UMF's airfield in the outskirts of Station City, Miriam wasn't sure if she had actually moved at all.

6

———

GENESIS

"THEY SURE MAKE it easy to tell who's who," Miriam mumbled.

She caught the tattoos of unmistakable box lamps as she and the rest of Echo walked, sandwiched between their Charonite escorts. But was UMF any different? Miriam looked down at her gray-and-black uniform underneath her armor and rig. At least SOG didn't need to abide by UMF regulation haircuts and company insignias. Although they *did* like their plain black diamond tab. The military loved order and labels, whether it be by flags, decals, or ink, identity carved into skin and clothing for like to find like.

Miriam tugged at her collar. It did make the job easier, especially when quick judgment was survival in another form. Especially when it notified who her enemies were. And in this case, the Charonites. Their new *friends*.

"It's belonging. Everyone wants to fit in," Hino whispered at her side, thumb hooked into a shoulder strap.

Miriam glanced at Bart Gumede, Echo's lead, as he strode ahead, then to the rest of her team, where Talwar, Elmalik, Durmaz, and Liu—Titan-2's medic—trailed behind. Other than their lead and the new engineer, none of the SOG marines looked thrilled.

She didn't blame them; she felt the same. It wasn't their first time this far up in the region, but the constantly changing territories and the Charonites themselves were a crapshoot. On top of it all, the heat was excruciating. The summer sun had climbed high in the cloudless sky despite the late hour, and sweat slid profusely down Miriam's back. The day felt eternal, stretched thin like nervewire, but at least it wasn't the North's dark season. *That* was a blessing. With their sight limitations in darkness, humans were at least on a somewhat level playing ground with the perpetual daylight.

Miriam's concentration returned to the front as they approached a hastily erected checkpoint, a partially collapsed shack flanked by two prowlers cobbled together from scavenged parts. It looked postapocalyptic, but everything around Woodchik did. The Apostates' Blightbringers had poisoned and ravaged patches of terrain, and everything was run-down, more so than the first time she had been in the North.

A Charonite exited the shack, a large radio slung across his scrawny frame. Although his face and body were right on the cusp of adolescence and adulthood, his dark eyes were much older, betraying his age. In the middle of the broken road, three boys stood like short bollards denying access to the pocked and destroyed land beyond. They clutched rifles in their spindly arms, the weapons massive in comparison to their underdeveloped frames. If it weren't for the live rounds of ammunition, Miriam could've mistaken them for children playing pretend.

One boy scratched his head, lifting his dirty cap enough that a tuft of blond hair sprang out. The color was a contrast with everyone's around him, and the sight snagged her, memory surfacing. Her stomach knotted as her gaze dropped to his face, his eyes, and then the red scratches along his neck. She'd seen similar marks on the other Charonites surrounding them. She was actually quite used to it now, but it was still a shock to see the raw lines on the boy. On the children next to him as well.

Stims. These Charonites were junkies, and they started the dependence and addiction young. This was who UMF was allying with.

Miriam frowned. Perhaps it *was* a good thing Hadeon and her legionnaire squad hadn't been included in this mission. She could imagine twitchy Charonite fingers and piss-poor judgment derailing the entire mission before it even started.

The Charonite at the shack barked something she couldn't make out, and the three children moved to the side, their tattered shoes kicking up dust. Miriam's attention followed the blond boy, whose eyes never looked up to meet hers. Were they blue as well?

"Are we good then?" Gumede called out.

The Charonite swiped a grimy forearm across his mouth and nodded.

Behind Miriam, Liu adjusted the portable litter on his shoulder. No one had mentioned the rolls of black body bags strapped to the Titan-2 medic's pack, but Echo knew why they were there.

Just in case.

"And our colleagues as well?" Hino asked. "They're behind us. They'll arrive shortly."

SOG Razor-Foxtrot. Echo's contingency. Their shadow.

Also a just-in-case.

The marines had no air or heavy armor support, only their SOG mindset, skills, and whatever they could carry in a daypack. It was a short job with no logistical backing and little margin for error. Given the environment, UMF didn't want to risk larger numbers. There was a reason why the military had stopped trying to hold the area—why the Charonites held it instead. But here SOG was, the teams called upon for higher-risk missions.

Tip of the spear.

"Do we *all* have safe passage?" Hino said, ignoring the flare of irritation across Gumede's face.

The Charonite turned and shrugged as if his tolerance for their presence was a coin toss.

Miriam scoffed. *Safe.* With them in the middle—Charonites on one side and Apostates on the other—what was safe? Her stare swept over empty eyes, some blown wide, others statue-still and unblinking. *Were* they on the same side? She shuddered at the thought.

The Charonite only fluttered his hand forward.

"Let's move," Gumede said.

And they did. Elmalik—or King, as the rest of the team called him—hoisted the second litter onto his back. As they passed through the broken checkpoint, his light machine gun swung up. The air felt thinner as Miriam followed, walking past the boys and last dregs of *civilization*, every step dragging counter to her instincts.

She moved her focus to their next threat: the dead land around them that served as a cushion between the Charonites and Apostates. There were no perimeter markers to define where it began and ended, just a highway of sorts, with the carcasses of buildings scattered every several meters.

Though she saw no movement, Miriam couldn't shake the feeling they were being watched and studied from all sides. She glanced at the dwindling specks behind them. The Charonites didn't follow, but she disliked having her back to them. She couldn't stop imagining how little pressure it would take for one of those skinny fingers to pull a trigger by accident.

The landscape stretched on, an endless trudge as Echo tried to stay within the meager shadows of spalled walls and strewn debris. It wasn't much cover from the angry sun, but it provided enough concealment from the direction they were headed. By the time a couple hours had passed, Miriam's undershirt clung damp to her skin, and the straps of her kit had carved grooves into her shoulders. Still no resistance, no figures moving against them, but the silence smothered as hard as any ambush. Every ruin felt watched. Heat shimmered and made the distance lose definition until she couldn't tell rubble from potential watching eyes. The absence of contact felt like bait, strung out to fray their nerves.

A click came over her visor, and Miriam tapped back a response. Echo's comms to the outpost were dead on arrival to the area, but their internal links held. At least UMF's new tech wasn't all bluster. Collaboration with the Altered in Station City had significantly advanced many of their gadgets and gear.

Olivia Durmaz, their communication specialist, frequently checked her cuff, scanning for the missing marines' pings. It wasn't until they neared the margin of the next town with its condensed destruction and burned vehicles that she perked up, then gestured diagonally. The team followed without question, each individual watching their respective sector, keeping their heads on a swivel. The brittle silence made every bootfall sound too loud. Every now and then, something minute wavered at the brink of Miriam's vision, but she wasn't sure if it was her paranoia, overaware and overstimulated.

When they slowed, Miriam was skeptical. The structure appeared like a wound with its pocked walls and its ruin of a second floor, possibly once a warehouse or storage space. It stood out only in that it stood at all.

Gumede gestured, and the team fanned out in a perimeter while Hino and Durmaz moved quickly, shifting aside loose debris to unblock a door.

Durmaz nodded. This was the place.

Talwar hurried forward and applied Hush Detcord to the hinges and seams. The fuse hissed in the heat, and with a quiet pop, the door gave. Miriam scanned the area around them, hoping the sound hadn't attracted anyone.

Nothing.

Hino nudged the door open, and Echo swept in. There was no need to check the top floor, considering most of it was gone. Miriam followed the second deeper to another door, closed and intact. She held behind Hino, both holding their rifles on it. There was a coolness that seeped into her ankles and an odor she couldn't quite place. The others finished clearing the space, and they reconvened and reshuffled seamlessly into a new line order with King on point. Talwar stepped forward, a hand in his kit, but Hino stopped his progression with a flat hand. She shook her head and nudged the door herself.

Unlocked. It slid open a crack.

Now fifth in line, Miriam peeked around her teammates to see the top of a stairwell leading down into a dark basement. Hino signaled for the two medics and Talwar to stay, and without another word, she pushed the door fully open. King moved down, his rifle and visor scanning, and Hino, Durmaz, and Gumede followed.

Still upstairs, Miriam thought it was a good sign that there were no shots fired or shrill exclamations. But as she moved closer, her nose wrinkled. The subterranean air hit thick and sour, as if it had been holding it in, waiting for a release.

"Oh, fuck," Durmaz said from below.

The hairs on Miriam's neck raised.

"Tanner!" Hino called.

Miriam blinked away the scent and descended the single staircase. Her visor engaged, artifacting in its wide network ability, but its low-light vision worked. Off the last step, her boots stuck slightly to the grime on the floor. Someone gagged, and she followed the line of the others' rifles.

She froze.

There, on the far side of the room, lay four bodies, stomach down and necks exposed. Torchlight bounced off glints of exposed bone. Above them, the severed heads were stacked, their eyes and mouths grotesquely open, one atop each torso. Dark stains spidered outward in wide brown halos around recognizable uniforms.

King gagged again. His rifle dropped to his side, and he pushed past Miriam, retching near the stairwell.

Miriam resisted the urge to back up. "We're sure they're ours?"

Hino, who was closest to the bodies, dropped into a crouch, the back of her hand braced against her nose. She shined her light on the heads one by one then glanced at her cuff. "Yeah," she finally answered.

Fucking hell.

Talwar's voice came down the stairs. "Sitrep? What's going on down there?"

"We're going to need the bags," Hino replied without inflection. She stood and glanced at the weapons specialist as he wiped his mouth with the back of his gloved hand. "King, go."

He bolted back up the stairs, his boots thudding as he took them two at a time. As he reached the top, a sudden *click* punctuated the air.

Dread pierced Miriam in the millisecond between the noise and the door sliding shut.

"Fuck!" King shouted, nearly catching his hand in the closing gap.

The sound had been small but powerful, like it'd been a detonation. Miriam's heart stuttered, and her breath turned ragged in her ears. She forced herself to count it out, as though cadence could keep the panic from closing in. She had already instinctively raised her rifle in the sudden and engulfing darkness. But now, with her other hand, she reached for her torch and shone it up.

"King?" she asked. "What was that?"

Above, her teammate didn't answer immediately, gloves scraping the jamb. He muttered another expletive before he said louder, "Oh, that's not good."

But Miriam didn't have time to register it as her attention split. A second shock lit up the room, blinding her for a split second. A display that she hadn't noticed next to the bodies flickered on. She stood transfixed with the others.

On the screen, four marines appeared on their knees, hands bound. Alive. Miriam recognized their faces from the brief: Johnson, Goyer, Patterson, and LaRussa. They gawked nervously at the recording device, their regulation haircuts dipping in slight tremors.

Back on the stairs, King cursed once more, before he raised his voice, as if trying to talk through the door. "Talwar, stay back. Don't breach. I say again, do not breach." His voice became clearer as he turned back. "Guys? There's something here. Hino?"

The second moved closer to the stairs, her eyes still on the display. "Talk to me."

"I've got wires." He gulped. "All over. I think we triggered something."

Hino reached for her visor, but her hand stopped short. "Explosives?"

"I don't know yet. I'm looking."

Hino's hand dropped. Miriam understood. The second didn't want to risk any frequency triggering whatever their weapons specialist had found in their now sealed cell.

"King, tell them to sit tight." Hino raised her wrist, the commcuff illuminating with the motion, and her lips pursed together. "Foxtrot should be on their way. Mark our position."

While King relayed the second's instructions through the door, Miriam refocused on the display. In the recording, someone offscreen called out. Two words. *Too full?* She realized it was a different language as a man stepped into view behind the kneeling marines, masked and wearing all black.

But his vividly colored eyes gave him away. Bright and orange. Unnatural.

Altered.

Miriam recognized the familiar pale mark on his neck, a triangle with a circle around its top point. An Apostate. But a specific faction. She had seen and fought them in the South, some in the North over the years as well. There was something off about the brand, another scarred line through the circle above the triangle. Intentional?

The Apostate spoke, his voice clear but words foreign. The old Altered language.

Durmaz prodded a console she had found closer to the screen. The communications specialist called out to Gumede, but the lead was frozen, unmoving. His attention was fixed on the decapitated bodies.

"I think this is going out live…a delayed trigger?" Durmaz said. "It's broadcasting."

"Can you stop it?" Hino asked. Her face had paled, but her expression remained set.

"I'll keep looking."

The second nodded.

"Hino." Miriam spoke, her voice low. "What is he saying?"

The team second and intelligence specialist's throat bobbed once before she translated. "'This is a message to the filth and dredges of humanity. You are responsible for the degradation of this world. We pay the price for your selfish decisions.'"

On the recording, the masked man took the first marine's forehead—Johnson's—and pulled back. The long knife in his hand glinted on the screen.

"'This will not end until every last pest and every traitor who feeds you is dead. And to the family who flaunts their pure-design, your evil alliance with these vermin will only accelerate your destruction.'"

Hino stopped, a gurgle in her throat as the blade pierced Johnson's neck, then sawed. Miriam averted her sight, but she couldn't silence the horrifying sounds.

When she looked back, the marine had crumpled. The masked man held the head by its hair and ear before setting it down on its owner. Beside him, the other kneeling marines shook and cried. The third one, Patterson, the politician's son, tried to move to his feet, but his limbs were bound. He fell instead. The Apostate made no attempt to retrieve the marine as he wriggled and inched away.

Meanwhile, Johnson's blood pooled out.

Someone offscreen said the same two words once more. "屠夫."

Not *too full,* but *Túfū.*

A name. Or a callsign.

Miriam glanced down at the bodies in front of her. She couldn't watch the feed anymore; she already knew its result. The cruelty was right there.

"Guys? Still here," King shouted from atop the stairs. "I need help."

Miriam's stomach clenched.

"I've got a countdown now."

"To what?" Miriam said, pulling herself out of her silence. She needed something to do. There was nothing she *could* do for the missing-now-found marines.

"Do we want to guess?" King responded.

Miriam looked around the dimly lit space, at the bodies and the display. Like it was a stage. The setup was too careful, too *theatrical.*

"King!" Hino shouted up. "Get Talwar on a sitrep. Do they have eyes on Foxtrot?"

The masked man had moved on to Goyer, who called out for his mother. Another masked figure had dragged the crawling Patterson back to the killing line. Miriam glimpsed the same triangle circle brand with the additional line on the other Altered's neck. She turned her head as the cutting and gurgling sounds started again.

"He says no!" King exclaimed. "Hino, I think we tripped something when we came down."

A sensor? Had it been timed?

Everything felt choreographed. A calculated performance.

"Can he open the door from outside?" Hino offered.

"No," King replied. "Tan, I need you!"

Miriam adjusted her rifle and took the steps carefully until she was behind her teammate sprawled out on the top of the slatted staircase.

"Come here," he grunted, shuffling his body to the side. "You've got smaller hands."

Miriam unslung her weapon, propped it against the wall, then cautiously flattened next to King. Now closer to the door, she could hear Talwar's voice on the other side.

"Describe it again."

"It's a connection to some black box. Size of my palm." King lifted one hand out of the way so Miriam could see.

"Anything around it?"

Miriam illuminated the space underneath the top step with her handheld torch. King had already opened a panel, and a complicated motherboard sat inside. Miriam fixed on the dim display of a small console, its digits pulsing as they descended one by one. She bent back as she followed the connections branching out and stifled a gasp. The network of wires stretched out around the doorframe and into the basement walls. Echo hadn't noticed it in their rapid descent. Her stomach dropped with every second, like a hammer blow reminding her that time was running out.

"Other than the scary fucking countdown? No. Is this the power source or not?" King said roughly.

Talwar's end went quiet. And then a faint voice came back. "Yes."

The confidence was reassuring.

None of them knew what they were dealing with, and they didn't know how extensive this system was, whether it was explosives or something worse. King handed Miriam his multitool, its clippers out, then pointed at a specific junction of conduits inside the panel.

"Update?" Hino shouted from below.

Miriam glanced at the display. The descending seconds seemed to speed up.

"Tan, right there. Cut it."

"That's it?"

It was too simple. Too comically simple.

"That's what he described. You can do this."

"Talk to me." Hino called anew.

The marine eased to his side. "We're working on it."

Miriam shook out her right hand and peeled off her glove with her teeth; it tasted like earth and metal. She took a deep breath, then carefully threaded her bare hand into the cramped space. She held the clipper exactly where her teammate had indicated, lines pressing her knuckles. One wrong twitch and she imagined the whole system reacting. Not with a spark but with an end. The seconds on the display flashed in her periphery, faster now, or maybe it was her pulse making them judder.

"Tan," he urged.

"Talwar, are you absolutely sure?" Miriam said loudly through her teeth and glove.

The engineer was quiet, but his tone was infused with a minuscule amount of confidence. "Yes."

Shit. Okay.

Miriam held her breath. Then squeezed.

She felt King flinch at the tactile release of the wire. The countdown blinked once, twice, then went dark.

"We're positive I didn't just turn off the display?" Miriam whispered, not moving.

King nodded once, collected himself, then nodded more confidently again.

When nothing happened after a few seconds, Miriam exhaled in relief. Next to her, King's forehead bowed into the step, and when he lifted it, a smudge of sweat remained. He patted her on the back before he extricated himself from his prone position and tried the door.

It didn't budge.

"King?"

"We're good," he called down to Hino. "Locked in, but good."

"Hey," came Talwar's muffled voice on the other side. "Back up, I'm gonna try something."

"No det," King said, "we don't know what—"

"I know."

Something scratched the door, then stopped. It was followed by a shuffle of commotion.

"Talwar?" Miriam said. "Liu?"

And then something thudded hard against the door.

"Shit," Miriam exclaimed, pulling herself up. "King, get back."

"Fuck, new guy. More heads-up would've been nice," he murmured.

She moved down the staircase with King close behind her.

Another thud came. For a moment, no sound followed.

Just as Miriam was about to call out, the door dented in with a crash. A second hit broke the darkness with fissures of light around the seams, and a consecutive one warped the edge. Another pushed the entire door out of its frame.

Miriam and King jumped away as it slid and crashed at the bottom of the stairs.

At the top, a large figure was silhouetted in the space.

Miriam recognized his build immediately, despite the shadows across his face. Her relief and recognition were snuffed out as Benjamin Fox stepped aside and SOG Razor-Foxtrot's lead walked past and carefully down the steps. He stopped short in the middle and acknowledged Miriam and King. If the smell bothered him, he showed no sign of it. The lead's attention settled around the basement, taking it in.

"Ho, Young."

"Hino," the Foxtrot lead gruffly responded with another

glance at Gumede, still frozen. "We've got the perimeter, but we should probably get a move on."

"I'll get the stuff," Miriam offered. She didn't wait for a response, already skirting up past Young, grateful for the brief respite from the stench and situation. She touched Fox's arm as she passed. A silent greeting. They'd catch up later.

"We need the bags," she said to Liu.

The other combat medic didn't look surprised. He quickly passed two to her, and they both descended into the basement. This time, though she expected it, the stench was worse, choking and noxious. Miriam willed her stomach not to turn.

At the bottom, Hino and Young were in soft discussion. The display next to the bodies had turned off, and Miriam sighed shallowly.

Hino looked up at their arrival. "Durm, King, scrub the place," she said to the others. "Talwar! Get down here and help." She turned back to the medics. "Let's bring them home."

Miriam moved toward the bodies with Liu.

Behind them, Young called up the stairs, "Foxtrot, give me one."

Talwar's steps were loud as he clambered downstairs, first eagerly, then slowly. She heard another set of boots descend, but she didn't have to see who had come down to assist. Despite the years, Miriam recognized Fox's lumbering steps.

The medics worked quietly, spreading black bags over the bloodstains. Miriam straightened, then paused at the bodies; she wasn't sure of the etiquette or proper way to respect their remains. Someone moved behind her, a hand outstretched, but before it landed, Miriam moved forward. She crouched and reached for the first marine's head before she realized she had never put her glove back on. It was too late, and her fingers touched the too-soft yet slightly rubbery cold skin. She took it gingerly between one gloved and one ungloved hand, unsure of what to do next. In the end, she placed it on the ground, an apology she kept to herself.

Then, with Fox's help, she moved the body into a bag. As he adjusted the flaps and straps, Miriam scanned around, looking for her glove. She had either left it on the steps or it had fallen somewhere in the rush. An amateur mistake.

She swallowed. It didn't matter. She went back for the set-aside head and disassociated, letting her muscles react automatically. Clinically. It wasn't a marine or a human anymore, but a cadaver. Parts. Miriam tucked the cranium in with the body and secured it as best she could before she sealed the bag.

As Liu and Talwar worked on the second one, Miriam moved on to the next, repeating the same steps, but this time with mental distance. Before she knew it, the last bag was closed. She inhaled, moving forward to transport it up the stairs, but a hand settled on her forearm.

Hino.

"I'm fine," Miriam muttered.

"I know, but let me."

Between the two Foxtrot marines and Echo, they had enough people. Miriam lingered back as they moved swiftly, bags strapped onto mobile litters then secured on her teammates' shoulders and backs. Fox gave a nod, shifted his load, then turned up the stairs with Liu, Talwar, King, Young, then Durmaz in tow with a small sack of whatever she had exploited in her sweep. The rhythm of their boots marked the team's exit.

Other than Hino and Miriam, only one person remained.

"Gumede," Miriam said.

The Echo lead stood in the same spot he'd been in last. He hadn't moved throughout the entire ordeal, his rifle slack in his hands, eyes now fixed on the blank screen where the broadcast had ended minutes before.

"Gumede."

The stench of blood, rot, and something chemical clung to

the concrete. Dust speckled and flew in the light of their torches. The only thing that didn't move was the lead.

Someone called from above. The team needed leadership.

"Go," Miriam said to Hino.

The second briefly hesitated, casting a last look around the room before she left.

Miriam stepped forward, scanning Gumede. He didn't blink, but she could see the small twitches, the tension coiled in his shoulders, and the feathering muscles along his jaw. She had seen this paralysis before, and she shouldn't have been surprised. She wasn't. This was an incapacitation born not from trauma but from someone promoted for the wrong reasons, someone who hadn't fought to get there, who'd only benefited when someone else made room.

Gumede had never been ready to be a leader—still wasn't— but like the marine with the right connections, the Echo lead's extended family also had the right amount of pull. That had been enough.

Miriam didn't pity him, but she couldn't leave her teammate either. She had been wrong before. She did have a job here. And though it wasn't a physical injury, this was something she had to step in and address before it infected the others. Careful not to startle, Miriam took another step, stopping beside Gumede.

"Bart," she said.

The man blinked like he'd been pulled from sleep.

"We're done here. Let's go, Bart."

That broke through. He cleared his throat and without acknowledging her, turned toward the stairs.

Miriam let him pass, then trailed a short distance behind, her movements mechanical. The stench of blood and death still hung, cloying. However, it had strangely lost some of its suffocating power. A chilling thought settled over her. Had she already grown accustomed to it?

7

DECOMPENSATION

"WHAT THE FUCK WAS THAT?"

"Goom," Hino warned. "Keep your voice down."

"No, seriously. What the fuck was—no, this is bad. This is really, really—"

Hino stood. "Gumede." Her tone carried a firm steadiness, no louder than before but honed at the edges.

Echo's lead was unraveling, shoulders tight, jaw working as he paced the short span of the wall behind them. He stopped abruptly, bracing both hands on the table. The cups jostled under his weight, one nearly toppling. Across the table, King's lips pressed thin. Durmaz avoided eye contact altogether, her attention fixed on the condensation sliding down her cup.

Gumede's eyes flitted around the outpost bar like it was closing in on him. "It should've been over," he muttered, loud enough to draw glances from the barkeep and a nearby group of patrons. "Kartik's gone. That should've been it. That was supposed to be it."

"Let's step out for a second. Get some air," Hino said, tapping the lead's nicosynth device on the tabletop. She was offering him an excuse to remove himself. A graceful retreat.

Gumede grasped it like a drowning man to a buoy.

"Yeah. Okay, yeah." He shuffled toward the door, hunched.

Hino followed, her side-eye to Miriam restrained but telling. Gumede was a nice guy, but as a leader... The thought of what Echo had witnessed was daunting, but he was cracking—*had* cracked—like glass under pressure.

When the two were gone, the silence around the table thickened. Durmaz ran her fingers through her damp, just-showered hair and gave Miriam a brief, searching look before returning to her drink. King lowered his eyes and tapped an erratic rhythm on the tabletop, restless, while Talwar rubbed his temple with the heel of his palm as if trying to drive the memory of human remains out.

They had all seen the same thing. It was one of the *worst* things Miriam had seen. But their lead's behavior and reaction only confirmed that it was all too real. The fear hovered around them, palpable and contagious.

Durmaz was right. The feed had been broadcast to the wide network, a clip of the execution forced out before the major media hubs had shut it down. The Charonites in Woodchik had also been buzzing about it, eyes prying at the black bags as Echo and Foxtrot passed through on their return. Despite Ursus's attempt to maintain a low profile with the SOG teams' arrival, the compound's atmosphere was full of whispers. For now, it was fear. Except Miriam considered everyone else more fortunate than Echo, who had physically been in the room. She thumbed the condensation on her cup but didn't take a sip.

"Have you ever seen anything like that?"

Miriam blinked. She realized Talwar was talking to her. The question was earnest. Her teammate was trying to square what he'd just faced with how the world was supposed to work. What they'd encountered was evil beyond imagination.

She shook her head. No, she hadn't seen anything like it, though she'd seen the same branded Apostates before. They were relentless, and they'd been known for their heavy use of their own stimulants. Violent, but never this cruel.

Miriam squared her shoulders and looked around at her teammates. She was the senior member on this team now, the one with the most missions under her belt. Even Hino, as experienced as she was, had started an SOG contract a year after. Miriam knew she had to address the situation, but she wasn't sure how.

What solace could she offer? What words of comfort existed for that brutality? She had thought the atrocities in the South were bad; she still woke up from nightmares on random nights. It'd been months since the last one, more than a year since they'd stopped being as regular, but now, this felt like another summons.

Miriam searched for something to say, but she felt like she had been in a similar situation before. Not that exact moment, but where her mind couldn't still enough, couldn't string together what she knew she needed to do. The words slipped past her.

"I thought the wunbies were done," Talwar said.

"We don't know what they did to them," King muttered.

The words hung there, unfinished.

"What?" Talwar asked.

"The four marines," King clarified. His fingers drummed once, hard. "I'm just saying. What the wunbies did…we don't know what else happened before the recording started."

Miriam endured the silence that followed.

"Fucking rats," Talwar said. "I thought…the wunbies were supposed to break up. They were supposed to be weakened…"

"They're desperate," a new voice added, low and worn.

The group startled, Miriam included.

Benjamin Fox planted his hands on the table, and his hazel eyes swept over the group before settling on Talwar. "When someone's back's to the wall, when they've got nothin' to lose…they're at their most dangerous. To everyone, includin' themselves." He exhaled like the words had cost him.

"What we saw," Miriam started. Her former teammate had been the jump start she needed. "It's going to stick with you."

It'd stick with her. The image floated behind her eyelids: severed heads stacked like trophies.

"It's fucked-up," she continued. "No one's denying that. But we'll get through it together—"

"Welcome to the war, Talwar," King interrupted. He folded his arms, hands diving into his armpits. "We're SOG. Suck it up."

Miriam's eyes narrowed, a pointed retort ready, but Fox beat her to it.

"That works." He scoffed quietly. "Until it doesn't."

King met the large marine's eyes, but whatever he saw there made him look away.

"First mission?" Fox turned to Talwar. "I've lost count of how many I've done, but take it from an old geezer. You can't hide from it. Don't drown yourself in this." He tapped the new engineer's untouched drink. "And don't pretend it didn't happen."

Talwar gave a tentative nod.

Fox straightened, then clapped the marine's shoulder. "You've got a team around you. Talk to them. Shit, come find me if nothin' sticks. But like Tan said, we'll get through this together. One day at a time." He looked around, letting his words sink in. He squeezed Talwar, then waved his hand, signaling across the bar. A few of his Razor-Foxtrot teammates wandered over, casual and loud. "For tonight, though? Boys, help me welcome…"

"Talwar," the engineer offered meekly.

"Talwar here popped his SOG cherry."

A small round of exclamations went around, and the Foxtrot marines thumped the engineer on the back and head.

The mood had already turned, easing as crass jokes flew around, a warmth in the roughness. Another table and several chairs scraped across the floor as they connected. Survival shaped like camaraderie.

Talwar tried to hide his grin, and Miriam found herself smirking as well.

"Next round's on me," Fox exclaimed over the reprieve.

The others hooted as he left for the bar. As lighter conversation started up afresh and her Echo teammates drew in, Miriam excused herself quietly. When she arrived at the counter, Fox was already settled, a cup in his hand. She eyed it.

"Relax, it's water," he said without turning.

Her eyebrow rose.

"Three months and three days," he added. "Would've been longer, but..." He gave a lopsided wince. "Slipped once. Wasn't a full bender, but Young's been supportive."

"I'm—" Miriam tried to find her words. She leaned into the bartop and let herself anchor to the one thing in the room that could give her relief, even if only momentary. "I'm proud of you, Fox. I really am." She rested her hand on his arm. Warm. And alive. Unlike the marine's skin she'd touched. "Back there, what you said to Talwar..."

"It was nothin'."

The man was so different from the one she had known when he was still with Echo.

"No. It wasn't nothing." She pulled back her hand. "I didn't know what to say, and that—that was really good."

He snorted. "Is that a compliment? From you?"

Her mouth tugged to the side. "I mean it."

He didn't answer. In the pause, Miriam glanced back at her teammates and sighed.

"You alright?"

She dragged a finger across the line of the counter. Miriam was okay with her team, this version of Echo, but there was something that didn't fit quite right. And now with Fox's presence, she felt more at ease. Perhaps it was the reminder of the closer-knit Echo she'd loved and known, the team she knew *this* version would never be.

"I missed you," Miriam said.

Fox scoffed. "Just saw you the other day."

"In passing. Doesn't count."

"Sure."

She huffed.

"Team's shaken up. Your lead okay?"

Miriam hesitated.

He tilted his head. "If you're tired, if it's not workin'… Gotta take care of yourself, too. Maybe not the best timin' right now, but have you thought about transferrin'?"

She shook her head immediately. It'd never been a thought. "I can't."

It was Fox's turn to raise a heavy brow.

"I don't know. It's fine." Miriam sighed. "Gumede's… Gumede. Ever since Krill left after Yuri—shit, after *you*… It's not the same."

"Missin' the old crew."

"Every day." She drew another finger along the bar's lip, then pointed lazily at him. "I miss our chats."

He laughed heartily. "Well, now I *know* you're just sayin' that."

Miriam scoffed. "I'm not."

Fox took a long drink, then studied his cup. "You still holdin' a grudge?"

"Which one? You have to be more specific. The grudge against you being an asshole or the grudge against you transferring, abandoning us?" She chuckled. "I guess they're both somewhat the same."

He laughed again. "You know I wasn't—" His voice softened. "It didn't feel right. I let down the team. If I had my shit together, Kai, you…"

Miriam's fingers curled. It wasn't his fault half of Echo had been hospitalized years ago after the big offensive attack in the North, but all the what-ifs had their own gravity. What if Fox hadn't gotten in a fight with Nas? Would he somehow have stopped them from walking into an explosive trap that severely injured half the team? Would anything have been different?

What if Miriam hadn't gotten hurt? Would her infidelity have been revealed the way it had? Would she actually have told Sam? What if Miriam had said those three words she needed to, wanted to, when she should've? What if, what if, what if. The postulating was endless, but Miriam knew she was the only one at fault for what she *had* and *hadn't* done.

Suddenly, a drink splashed beside them; a small droplet danced on her skin. The acute scent of heavy alcohol followed, cutting through the air. Down the bar, the patron motioned apologetically, but Miriam ignored them. She watched Fox, his eyes on the liquid as it pooled.

"Want to get out of here?" Miriam asked.

A finger of spilled liquor reached out toward them.

Fox's throat bobbed. "Your team won't miss you?"

She shot a glance back. Talwar was laughing now, surrounded by the others. "Nah. You did a good job; they've got other things on their mind now. Plus, you'll always be my team, Fox."

More than that. He was a friend. He was family.

Fox broke his focus from the counter. "Sappy." But he nodded.

Miriam led the way outside, and when they pushed past the door, she looked around for Hino and Gumede, but they were gone. She was relieved that the heat of the day had broken, replaced by a cooling twilight. She wasn't sure if she was projecting, but even the outpost breathed in a slower rhythm.

The calm was interrupted by the low buzz of her cuff. Miriam checked the notification, hoping for a message from

Emma. It had been a long day, and though she was with Fox, she wanted more. That feeling of home.

It wasn't Emma.

> N. NGUYEN: Fuck. Did you see those marines?

Miriam palmed her wrist, and the display darkened.
Her cuff buzzed again.

> N. NGUYEN: I miss your face and we need to drown that shit out. Bring back the old times when things were better? Old times for me, of course. I don't dare cross Ems.

Air puffed out Miriam's nose, and she rolled her eyes. She dismissed the message once more.

Fox dipped his head, his eyebrow arched.

"Settle down," she said. "It's a friend."

His brow remained in its high position.

"Hell," Miriam muttered. She wasn't that person anymore; she hadn't been in a long time. "Actually." She chuckled as a memory came together. "*You're* the one who slept with her. Remember my friend Talya?"

He shrugged. Of course he didn't. It'd been years before, after another terrible mission, when he'd found solace at the bottom of a cup.

"Forget it." Miriam rolled her eyes again, then moved on. "You're getting along well with Foxtrot."

He grunted.

"I'm serious. Back there, they listen to you."

"Huh. They're scared of me."

She laughed. "There's the Fox I know." Miriam leaned into the wall. "*My* team listened to you."

"I'm no Krill, although he's not so much the uptight boy scout anymore, even with his big-boy raise," Fox said. "Plus, your crew's pretty new. New lead, new teammate. It's a lot of change, and now they're shaken up. They just need reassurance."

Miriam quieted as Fox's words seeped into her. He hadn't said it, but she felt the same consideration from before. She was Echo's senior member, the one that Talwar and the others would look to for non-operational direction. Especially with their team second taking care of their shaky lead.

"I have a feelin' it's gonna get worse," Fox said. "That was meant to be a spectacle. Shock and awe."

Miriam's stomach pinched, and she turned away. "If it's okay, I'd rather not think about it right now."

"Sure." He inclined his head. "Remember. When it rains, it pours. There'll be a flash flood soon."

She huffed. "Such a way with words."

But if she let herself dwell on it, she knew how it would play out. Every action would create a reaction. Each escalation only set the pendulum to swing wider, gathering speed until neither side could stop it.

He rested against the wall, close enough that his arm brushed her shoulder. One boot kicked up behind him as he folded his arms. "Sleepin' any better?"

Fox asked that every time their conversations went beyond surface greetings. Honestly, this was the longest they'd been alone together in a year. She wasn't sure when so much time had slipped away.

"I was, yeah. But after today? I...I don't know."

"It's good Echo's headin' back soon, then. Tomorrow, right?"

She gestured her finger in a curve. "Command's pushing it a day."

Their mission had blown up into a much larger problem. The outpost leadership wanted them to debrief again, which felt redundant, especially considering they'd probably have to do it once, if not multiple times more when they got back to Station. And now with the four recovered marines the way they were, the processing would take more time. The mission had accounted for the possibility of dead marines, but it hadn't considered *this* grisly display of death. Especially broadcast.

"Rough," Fox said. They fell into silence before he spoke up once more. "It hits me randomly. Jun, New Zapala, everything that happened. But the noggin's weird like that."

Miriam didn't reply. There wasn't anything to add. They both knew what it meant to carry memories that never lessened, only sank deeper. Time had helped, but she still woke up when she least expected it, sweating, a nightmare returned. She felt silly when she reflected on it. What had sparked it before, everything that had happened in the South, in Matam, in Temunco, was nothing compared with what had followed, what she had lived and experienced in the last years.

Today, however, was another level of violence. She was shaken, but there was something else to it. Fatigue. And somehow, the farther she was from that basement, those stains, and that smell, the more there was a numbness to it. Miriam couldn't comprehend the feeling that her mind had somehow steeled itself. Had she adjusted to the war's atrocities?

"She good to you?"

Miriam looked up at Fox, whose gaze raised above the horizon as the sky darkened. Across the outpost, lights flickered on.

"Emma?" she asked.

"Who else?"

"Yeah," Miriam said with a chuckle. "She's *too* good to me. I'm happy."

"But?"

"What. Does there have to be a 'but'?"

Fox shrugged. The motion nudged her slightly, but Miriam didn't mind.

"How about you?" she asked. "Something good back home to balance all the shit in the world?"

He scoffed, but then his attention diverted. "Check it out." Fox nudged his chin down the road.

Miriam followed the direction until she saw a mishmash of tall silhouettes crowded outside a small building. She squinted. They were in the shadows, but in the dim light she could tell their uniforms were different. Not UMF or Legion.

"Seraphim," Fox confirmed.

"SRAF," she corrected. Miriam didn't care for the name others had given the group.

A caravan of prowlers and rhino vans rumbled by.

"Whatever," Fox said louder. "Still don't know what the hell those letters mean."

No one did.

Between one of the passing vehicles and their headlights, one figure turned. Miriam stiffened.

Even with the distance, she could make out the person and the glint of green night-eyes. They had fought on the same side together before. A former legionnaire. A woman. Her short hair had grown longer than Legion's regulation style, and a large pale scar sliced down her left cheek, but it was her. The last time Miriam saw the woman, Sam had still been in UMF. Still been *with* Miriam.

A passing van obscured her view, and Miriam pushed away from the wall. She stifled the urge to crane her neck to get a better look.

From the glimpse she had seen, even this Altered had changed. Other than the cosmetics, there was something else about the woman. She looked leaner and more angular. Meaner. The Altered woman was also scarred in ways the genetically engineered race wasn't supposed to be. Miriam wasn't sure if that was commentary about the level of fighting and violence SRAF was part of.

"What?" Fox's attention darted to the group. "Got a thing for alties now?"

She glared at him. "They're not all—no, that's that legionnaire."

"That's no legionnaire. Seraph, now."

Miriam remembered. "Varya. Her name's Varya."

Fox shrugged, then kicked off the wall. "Want me to call her?"

Miriam opened her mouth, then closed it. She wasn't sure. Was Sam in that group? Her chest locked, and terror washed through her. Maybe Miriam didn't want to know. After more than three years of nothing, maybe she was finally letting herself move on.

Before she could decide, Fox cupped his hands around his mouth. "Varya!"

His voice surely couldn't travel that distance over the noise of the moving caravan, but the woman down the street turned, her eyes glinting as they latched onto Miriam and Fox.

Miriam raised her hand. Barely.

But then the woman turned away. By the time the last vehicle passed by, her back was to them as she engaged with the rest of her group. Miriam squinted, trying to make the others out, but she knew from their frames that she probably wouldn't recognize anyone else. They weren't the right size, the right person.

"Saw us, I think." Fox grunted. "But I guess the Seraphim have better shit to do. Think they're here 'cause of those marines?" He nudged Miriam with an elbow when she didn't respond. "Hey. You okay?"

She shook her head, deflated.

Fox waited.

Miriam rubbed her fingers into her eyes. "I thought..." She trailed off, internally batting away the what-ifs and reminders.

When she didn't continue, Fox muttered a soft expletive. He hesitantly curved one arm around her shoulders, but when he pulled her closer, the motion was certain. Miriam leaned into the warmth of his companionship and tethered herself to it. She took a deep breath, gathering all the fear, the hurt, the regret, the remaining memories and looming nightmares. She exhaled, trying to cleanse it out.

She inhaled again, but the feeling remained like tar in her lungs. It was the feeling that Fox was probably, most certainly right. That things were going to somehow get worse, much worse, before they got better. Miriam didn't want them to get worse. Things were already better.

And she had to let go.

She knew she had to let go.

8

DISPLACEMENT

"HEY, TAN."

Miriam paused, her fingers rested against the seam of her kit inside her locker. She looked up as Echo's second entered the team room, stopping at her own locker, her boot nudging the kit that had sat untouched since they got back from the North.

"Hino," Miriam replied.

The team had returned from Ursus a week before. Like a silence that came after too little sleep, the shuttle ride from the airfield and every administrative process after had been quiet and numb. Things had been uneventful and had settled in strange ways. Echo completed their debriefings, turned in their after-action reports, and answered the same questions phrased a dozen different ways. And then nothing. The team withdrew and returned to their routines of in-between work: fitness, maintenance, and training. And off work hours, off compound, Miriam and her teammates had drifted to their own corners of the city, trying to pretend that mission hadn't left them caged in its aftermath.

On this particular day, Miriam had stayed on base longer than intended. It wasn't that she hadn't wanted to go back to the apartment, but with Emma busy with work, Miriam didn't know what to do with herself once she got there. So, she found productivity in assisting with the final death reports for Goyer, Patterson, Johnson, and LaRussa. She hadn't known the Division marines personally, but it was a way to keep moving. She added their names to the other set in her mind: Junpei, Artem, Porevit, and more.

Meanwhile, Hino still hadn't opened her locker. The woman's arms were crossed too tightly, mouth pinched with some unresolved thought. She'd been more reserved since the mission, especially after Gumede's small outburst then denial in their last Station brief. Whatever had passed between her and the lead in private had left a mark. Still, it was as if Hino wanted to say something or was waiting to be asked something she didn't want to say out loud. The woman's mouth twitched downward.

"Everything okay?" Miriam offered.

A sound escaped Hino's lips, nearly a laugh but without the humor. She shook her head, stopped herself, and sighed. "Are *you* doing okay?"

"For the most part."

Surprisingly, it was true. Miriam had expected the nightmares to dig their claws in, but they never came. Perhaps they'd come another night, eventually, but so far? Nothing. The anticipation was worse. She had stopped trying to make sense of it.

"You?" Miriam tried again.

Hino hummed, still unmoving, not quite meeting her eyes.

"How's Goom?" Miriam prodded.

The question landed like a stone in still water.

Hino didn't answer right away. "I need a favor," she said finally. "The others. I know you're already doing it, but can you check on them? Talwar, especially. Says he's fine, but I think it's all surface. I don't mean to catch you like this, but...can you give him some extra attention?"

Miriam inclined her head. "Sure. Of course."

"I talked to him before," Hino continued. "He's going to be with family for the weekend, which should help, but—"

"I'll check in." Miriam knew it was part of her job. If there weren't actual physical injuries, the team medic checked in on the team's morale and mental wellbeing, something she'd been failing at recently. Plus, beyond her unofficial duty, she had the years and the experience. It was the curse of survivorship. Everyone assumed she knew how to hold the others up because she was still around.

Miriam shook the bitterness out of her head and closed her locker, turning fully to the team second. "And *you?*"

Hino dropped onto the nearby bench. Her face sank into an open palm. "Honestly? Not great, but the work doesn't stop, right?" She didn't continue.

"And Goom?" Miriam added.

The second peeked at her through the slit of her fingers, her mouth contorted underneath. "Let me deal with him."

Miriam didn't push further. "Any more chatter from Command or BigInt about the Apostates and marines?"

"Nothing concrete right now. At least the frenzy's slowed, although the media shitshow isn't helping. UMF's briefing City Center about it, supposedly, but a lot's still speculation."

Miriam huffed. "Think they actually remember the marines' names now?"

Hino grimaced, understanding and response within the expression. "The whole thing's definitely blown up. But I'll keep an ear to the ground. If I do hear anything, I'll let you know first. Try not to worry about it, okay?" She scoffed and combed her hand through her dark hair. "Fuck. I know it's just words, but take a breather while you can. I know we can't pretend this shit didn't happen, but we're some distance away now. Might as well revel in it." She dipped her chin. "Get out of here. Say hi to Emma for me."

Miriam didn't protest. However, when she reached the door, she stopped. "Hino?"

The second looked up. She hadn't moved from her seat.

"You're doing a good job," Miriam said.

That got a twitch of a smile.

With a wave, Miriam left the room and SOG building. Out in the afternoon sun, the weather was too warm, and the city buzzed in the distance. She nodded absently at two marines as she hurried toward the main gate, as if a slower pace would somehow imprison her in the uniform for eternity. Without breaking a stride, Miriam placed a call on her commcuff. It took several seconds before it connected.

"You're on your way back?" Emma's voice floated up.

"Yeah."

"Damn. I'm still at work."

"That's okay. Just wanted to hear your voice."

"I'll recite some poetry if you'd like. I can't promise it'll be any good."

Miriam chuckled.

There was a slight pause on the other end. "Do you—"

"No," Miriam cut in. "Not right now, if that's okay."

"Okay," Emma responded. Her tone lightened. "Oh. Guess who I ran into?"

"Do I really want to guess?" Miriam asked. It could've been anyone. A one-night stand or arrangement from her past. Station City was a big place, but apparently not big enough.

"Your old buddy from uni? *Nat and Tan?*" Emma held a second of silence before she laughed. "Is that really something you said back then?"

Miriam groaned. "Hell. Talya. I'm sorry you had to deal with that."

"She says you haven't answered any of her messages."

"True."

"She said something about a night out?"

"Oh." Miriam slowed to a stop. "Shit. You didn't..."

The line went quiet.

"Em."

"Right. Well, I guess we're going to Buzz tonight."

"Em!"

"Sorry! She's very persuasive!"

Though it was a voice-only call, Miriam knew Emma's face had contorted in a mix of annoyance and amusement.

"We didn't have any plans, anyway. Right?" Emma said. "And it's been a while. I thought we both could use a night out, some drinks, some music, I don't know. Especially after…" She trailed off. "We can leave early, babe, but it could be fun!"

Miriam didn't answer right away. A weight had lodged behind her eyes. She was tired, but not in the physical sense. More like her thoughts had recently been clinging to everything too tightly. A distraction *wasn't* the worst thing.

"Okay," she whispered.

Emma had been talking, but she paused now.

"Fine," Miriam said, louder.

The line broke out in a light chuckle. "Really? I don't want to force you."

"No. You're right. It's fine. Let's do it," she added, trying to stress some casualness into her words.

"Your enthusiasm is music to my ears." Emma laughed once more.

Miriam huffed, but her mood had lightened.

"Alright," Emma said. "I'll see you in a bit."

Miriam ended the call with a quick farewell and a sigh. Her feet picked up, starting for the main gate again, but this time with less motivation.

Until a glint of white caught her eye. A tall figure moved with purpose along an intersecting path. Miriam jogged to catch up and fell into step behind the senior legionnaire.

"Tanner," the large Altered woman said without turning.

"Hadeon," Miriam replied, quickening her stride to match the woman's long legs.

The senior didn't slow, nor did she speed up. It was in line with her personality: impassive, always moving forward, and always measured. Miriam had served long enough beside legionnaires to know that silence did not equate to coldness. Especially not the silence from Hadeon. This kind was restraint, control, and precision.

"You're by yourself?" Miriam asked.

"Should I not be?"

Legionnaires typically moved in pairs, if not with their fireteam, even off-duty, but Miriam didn't push further. She switched tack. "You're heading out for the day?"

Hadeon only angled to her, a flat expression on her face. She'd never engaged in pleasantries or small talk well. The two exited the compound, past the sentries and access points, and stopped at the corner of the wide avenue, waiting for the flow of traffic to halt.

"You heard what happened?" Miriam asked.

"Yes. And we should have been there."

Miriam would've liked for Hadeon's team to have been there as well, but she wasn't the one pulling the strings or making the decisions.

The senior legionnaire made a low, rough sound. "Your leaders were afraid our presence would complicate things with your northern group."

The Charonites.

"They're not our—" Miriam winced. "You know they don't represent all of us."

"They represent enough," Hadeon said simply.

They crossed the busy intersection, and Miriam hung behind the tall legionnaire, using her as a shield, like a plow blade through the small pedestrian crowd. Although there were a couple lingering glances, no one paid them any serious mind.

"I saw your teammate in Ursus," Miriam tried.

Hadeon continued walking.

"Varya."

Hadeon glanced to the side. "Alive, then?"

Miriam nodded.

"That's good."

"You don't stay in contact?"

"You are surprised."

Miriam frowned. "You two served together. With what happened in the South, and then after…"

"She is no longer Legion," Hadeon said, like it was an easy matter of fact.

"I thought…"

The senior glanced over again. "Varya chose to leave. SRAF is not Legion. It is the same for UMF, no? We have our own objectives."

That was it, direct and final, like the words had been sealed in concrete. There was no anger, not even annoyance. Just a resolute fact.

Miriam let the response and ensuing thought sit. She had hoped, foolishly, that the legionnaires had an inner network with the rest of their genetically engineered comrades. *Despite* what uniform they wore. They were on the same side, weren't they? Miriam was disappointed, but how could she be when she herself couldn't stay in contact with her friends and former teammates on a regular basis?

She continued by Hadeon's side until the streets thickened ahead. The colorful sector of cafés and small shops buzzed with chatter. Miriam used to love this part of the city, but now there were too many faces, too many unknowns she didn't particularly care for. And she wasn't sure when, but she'd started pulling closer to the edges. Perhaps it was a part of aging—that disinterest in things she'd once thought meant more.

"Are you accompanying me back to my sector?" Hadeon asked.

"What?" Miriam blinked. She had been in her own head, mindlessly following, and she had missed the turn for her apartment. For a second, she thought to head back, but then remembered she'd have to be at a bar and dance club later. Knowing Talya, Miriam would probably need enzyme nanocapsules for the inevitable hangover the next morning. She nearly palmed her face; she should've picked some up from the clinic on base, but now she didn't feel like going back.

"No, if you don't mind, I'm actually—well, I'm headed to General, and it's on the way." The medical center wasn't, really. Miriam didn't want to go there either, but it was better than doubling back to UMF. She'd drag her feet less in the other direction.

Hadeon grunted, and Miriam took it as acceptance.

She trudged along, steeling herself for the last-minute change and detour, for the possibility of running into her parents. As they passed a shop, Miriam glanced at her reflection in the front display. It had been days since Echo was in that basement, but she somehow still looked battered and spent.

"I saw the full recording of your comrades," Hadeon said, as if she'd sensed her thoughts.

Miriam was grateful when they passed a windowless wall and her reflection disappeared. "Apostates. I saw the brand mark on their necks."

If Legion had been included in their mission, would the Altered have helped find the marines earlier? Miriam shook the idea out of her head. UMF and their Altered counterparts had learned from their past mistakes. Information was shared more freely. Miriam also reminded herself of the dark and worn stains on the ground. Even if Hadeon and her squad had been with Echo, they had been too late.

"Have you heard anything more?" Miriam asked.

"There have been rumblings since Kartik's death, but we are waiting for confirmation," the Altered woman replied. "Their *general* united the factions before, but without him, they fragmented."

Instability. Just like Jace had said in the Pit.

In one sense, the breakup of Apostates worked in humanity's favor. The Royals, too. The Altered terrorist group —now *groups*—were vulnerable. They'd be easier to strike down while their structure collapsed. But disarray came with its own danger. Without order, there was nothing to hold the players in check. No leash or boundaries. And if that execution had been any sign of what came next, chaos was already knocking.

A passerby came too close to Miriam, and she veered, stepping closer to Hadeon, triggering an odd feeling. She avoided the city's civilians and most UMF marines now. A few years ago, the idea of proximity to an Altered—no less a legionnaire—would've made her nervous, but battle changed things. She had fought side by side with Hadeon, and though the woman was still as closed-off and frigid as an unsympathetic refrigerator, Miriam trusted the genetically engineered soldier more than most people. There was something to be said about sharing sweat and blood in close-quarter combat.

Miriam observed the surrounding street. Frankly, most of Station seemed accustomed to the Altered. Most. In certain outlying sectors, there were displays in store windows with exclusive language. But this sector that she and Hadeon were currently transiting was integrated.

People of different sizes bustled about the sidewalks, and strange eye colors mixed with the browns of humans at restaurants and cafés. Of course there were cliques, and she rarely saw a group or pairing of Altered and humans, but this day was like any other day.

Miriam kept from scoffing. She and Hadeon weren't close, per se, but *they* were walking together. A human and an Altered. *She* was one of the rare sightings.

"Progress," she murmured.

"Is it?" Hadeon asked.

Miriam shook her head. She was about to clarify how her

thoughts had deviated from their brief conversation when the senior legionnaire's hand twitched out.

In an instant, Miriam froze. The instinct was muscle-deep, honed over all their missions together. She held her position, keeping the legionnaire in the corner of her eye, and scanned their surroundings. Other than the easy chatter from the patio nearby, the clink of plates, and the clatter of cutlery, nothing stood out.

"Hadeon?" Miriam whispered.

A beat passed, and then Hadeon bolted, fast and without warning. Miriam didn't hesitate, just pushed off the curb and followed the woman down the street.

Hadeon rounded the corner of a narrow side street, her boots hammering the pavement in clipped bursts. Miriam gave chase, her lungs catching the sudden rush, her body falling into rhythm as muscle memory took over. The world constricted into the churn of movement, a clean precision of pursuit. But pursuit of what?

Then Miriam heard the scream. It was high and ragged as it split the air and cracked something inside her. It hurled her backward, not in body but in memory, back to the basement, to the marines' cries echoing through a screen.

She dashed into a broad street smeared with sun and shadow. In front of a small restaurant, under an awning, a boy, maybe twelve, writhed on the ground, his small hands clamped over his face. An older adolescent stood over the boy, his expression twisted beneath the fold of a black cap. His fingers curled around a small, cylindrical canister.

Miriam barely had time to process it all before the door of the adjacent shop sprang open. A woman in light-colored clothing barreled out, her face contorted in panic. Just outside, a second figure emerged next to her, his own black cap low over dark brows. His arm came up fast, and the back of his hand struck the woman across her jaw. She staggered but didn't fall. Another black-capped accomplice joined, this one armed with a bat. He swung hard into the side of the woman's head.

The thwack of it echoed, pointed like gunfire.

She collapsed like a rag cut loose from a line.

Miriam shouted, but it didn't matter. The two attackers were already moving, towing the youngest with them.

Already farther ahead, Hadeon surged in a snap of movement. The legionnaire's hand clamped down on the adolescent, and he squeaked as she wrenched him back. The man with the bat reacted, a wild swing at Hadeon, barely missing his own colleague. He swung again, this time the tip hitting the back of Hadeon's hand as she stepped in, parrying it. In her abrupt movement, the adolescent slipped free.

However, in his freedom, items fell to the ground with small clanks, followed by the sound of something rolling and rolling. The adolescent dropped, his hands scraping along the pavement in a frantic scramble, chasing whatever metal he had lost. Unfortunately for him, they had fallen in the legionnaire's direction.

"Stay back, freak!" The man jabbed his bat forward, trying to make space. Hadeon didn't falter. She only stood watching, waiting.

"What are you doing? Let's go," the other man yapped at the two.

Not needing further encouragement, the adolescent obeyed, scrambling to his feet and breaking into a sprint without a glance back. The two adults joined, their feet pounding down the street.

Making sure they wouldn't turn back, Miriam watched them leave. She frowned as she caught the lamp tattoos blazed on the adult's exposed arms before she turned back to the storefront where the younger boy's screaming had subsided into cries. She closed the distance quickly, first checking the status of the woman on the ground. She was alive, although black hair was thick and clumping, already matted down with blood. Miriam's hand automatically went to her waist, but she didn't have her medkit, her sling, or her pack.

"Hadeon, I need your help!" Miriam called out. She looked back to where the legionnaire was crouched, a hand to the ground. Miriam turned back to the downed woman, then locked eyes with a server standing frozen inside the restaurant door. "Call SecTeam! Now!"

He made no movement.

Miriam thrust her hand out at another patron staring from behind the window. "You! Get an ambulance here!"

Still nothing. Why did people freeze when it mattered?

Thankfully, another customer farther back nodded. Miriam saw the lift of a handheld device, and she figured it was enough. She turned back to where Hadeon was now beside the boy. However, when Miriam strode over, she stopped short with a gasp.

The child's hands had stopped moving, held out and above him as if his limbs had lost all strength. His face and neck were powdered white, already speckled with red. The skin had blotched and mottled. A faint, acrid odor clung to the air around him, something chemical-like but mixed with a hint of garlic, an earthy musk, and rotting seafood. It clung at the back of Miriam's throat.

Hadeon reached out.

"No! Don't touch it!" Miriam snatched a cloth from a nearby table and tossed it at the legionnaire. She then threw her mouth and nose into the crook of her arm, speaking into her skin. "Brush it off. Keep it away from his mouth and eyes, but don't touch it, and *don't* breathe it in."

The boy whimpered, then coughed. The air shimmered with residual powder.

Hadeon's hands moved quickly, and as she worked, Miriam glanced at the blood that had welled in a slender line down the back of one, likely from the scrape before. But even as Miriam noticed it, the red was already drying.

Legionnaires. Fast healing in their biology and design.

Miriam looked for another cloth to assist, and another reminder was on the tip of her tongue when something shifted in the awning's shadow. A tiny hand shot out, snatching something from the sidewalk nearby, then withdrew beneath a table booth.

While Hadeon continued behind her, Miriam dropped low. Her knees scuffed the ground and she bent, straining to see. She could make out a figure: another child, this one significantly younger by the size of his curled limbs. A toddler from the looks of it, huddled in the dark.

Miriam's voice softened. "Hey…it's okay. I'm here to help, but I need you to come out, okay? It's safe now."

No reply.

"Okay," she murmured as she inched closer. "Okay."

The table didn't budge when she pushed it.

Bolted down.

"Shit."

Miriam dropped to her stomach and wormed forward, her arm stretching out. Her fingers found soft-worn fabric, and beneath it, trembling warm skin.

"Buddy, I'm going to pull you toward me, okay?"

She tugged gently, careful not to startle. The child pulled away.

"Whoa, hey. It's okay. I'm not going to hurt you, I promise. I just need to get you out and make sure you're okay." She reached farther, this time catching a wrist, a skinny arm. They struggled, but she held fast, coaxing them forward until she could slip her other arm under their torso. She pulled the child into her arms.

They immediately latched onto her hand, burying their face into the crook of her shoulder. Another tremor moved through the child's body, but no sound accompanied it.

"Okay," Miriam whispered. "That's okay. You can hold on. Are you hurt? I've got you."

She swept a hand along the child's back. No blood and no powder. The kid had also made no sounds or indicators that they were hurt. That was good, at least, but she'd feel better if she could get a better look.

"Hadeon. Sitrep?" she said, careful not to scare the child.

The boy's whimpers were weaker now, replaced by soft groans and moans. His chest fluttered. He was slipping.

"Where is the fu—where is the ambulance?" Miriam muttered. She tried to raise her cuff, but the child was covering it.

They didn't have time for this.

"Hadeon." Miriam's head swiveled as she oriented herself. "The hospital's five, six blocks away. We can cut through Main, get there faster." She glanced down at the boy, then the sprawled woman.

Still breathing.

"Can you move him?"

The legionnaire was already a step ahead. She lifted the boy easily. Most of the powder had been swept off, but there were wet traces around his closed eyes and mouth. The boy's head lolled forward, chest rising fast and uneven.

As for Miriam's own package, the toddler clung to her, face pressed into her shirt. "Okay, buddy," she said to him. "I need you to let go." She looked to the crowd of bystanders who had gathered in a scattered formation. She tried to find a parent, a guardian, or a competent restaurant worker, anyone she could leave the child with.

"I can't—I need you to stay here, alright?"

The grip on her fastened. Surprisingly strong.

Miriam sighed. They really didn't have time for this. "Shit. Guess you're coming with us. We can get you checked out, too. But you better tell your parents I didn't kidnap you, okay?"

She rose with one fluid motion, balancing the child in her arms. Her eyes found the same frozen server inside the restaurant door. "You. Keep people away from that powder.

And keep that woman on her side. Do *not* leave her alone, you hear me? Wait until SecTeam and help gets here."

He opened his mouth, but Miriam was already moving. "Hadeon! Follow me."

The legionnaire fell in beside her, pace controlled and careful with the delicate boy in her arms. Miriam's heart thundered, legs pushing as they tore through the street, past open stalls and startled civilians scattering out of their path. They continued on until the medical center loomed ahead, sterile, white, and blessedly close.

Hadeon shoved through the emergency room doors, where a receptionist shot up in alarm. Recognition flickered across her face as Miriam passed, but there was no time for protocol. They flew past.

"Hey, you can't just—" a nurse started as she stepped away from the wing's command node. When she saw the boy in Hadeon's arms, the challenge died in her throat.

"Charonite attack," Miriam said. "Some powder substance. Was responsive before."

The nurse barked out instructions, and Hadeon lowered the boy to a gurney with quiet efficiency. A few other medical staff closed in, already swarming with diagnostic words and instructions.

Miriam tried to listen in, but she ultimately moved to the side, unable to be of actual help with a toddler in her arms. Something poked into her skin, and she looked down. A small tin box poked out of a small meaty hand.

"Hey, bud," Miriam said. "I need to set you down."

She needed her hands, but the child only clung harder. The corner of the box dug into her forearm.

And then the other child screamed, a sudden and keening cry. His shut eyes clenched together, lines creasing across his face. One hand twitched like it was trying to shoot up to his face, to paw at it.

"Hold him down!" a nurse shouted.

Hadeon delicately pinned the boy's arms to the gurney while another staff member darted in with a flush pack and saline. Miriam watched, helpless as they worked, bracing the boy, forcing solution into his eyes. The shrieks peaked, then quieted into whimpers again. Small hands shuddered underneath Hadeon's, but his body was like a lead weight, no longer fighting.

Something had worked.

In the quiet that followed, Miriam heard the abrupt inhale from the lead nurse.

"Contact the embassy," the woman said, her voice piercing the open space. She turned to another colleague. "Contact the Royals. *Now*."

Miriam's attention whipped to Hadeon's blue and green eyes. For what felt like minutes but was actually not even a second, neither spoke.

"He is one of them," the legionnaire said at last.

Miriam's stomach dropped. What was a Royal child doing out and about without protection? Station City was safe, but for a Royal without the usual escort? Then Miriam remembered the woman who'd been hit, who they'd left on the sidewalk outside of the restaurant. Had she been his chaperone? His guardian?

Miriam looked down at the child in her arms. Her attention drew down to the sweat-matted hair, a light brown chestnut color. And at that moment, the toddler, a little boy, peeked one eye up at the same time.

Miriam's breath caught.

Royal gold.

But it wasn't the gold that surprised her; it was the gray-blue flecks that accompanied it.

9

___

DESIGN

THE ROYAL STRODE in like conviction given form. She entered without a word, yet the hush that followed her arrival, the presence of a tall, slim guardian clothed all in black, was louder than any announcement. The Royal's steps were deliberate, as though the path and outcome were already known. Hospital staff bent instinctively out of her way, then shrank farther from the long shadow behind her.

Kuan-Lin's gold eyes swept the room, pausing only when they found the boy clinging to Miriam. At the sight of the woman, the child's grip broke. Miriam barely caught him as he wriggled free, his limbs slipping and pushing. The tin he'd held clattered to the floor, spinning once before it settled. Little legs carried him across the smooth tile, and the Royal scooped him up, folding around him like armor.

Miriam squatted, reaching for the forgotten metal box, but her attention never left the woman and child.

Kuan-Lin cradled him, her cheek flush with his before she smoothed a tuft of light hair out of the boy's face and withdrew a spectacle-like wrap out of her pocket. She carefully secured it around his head, covering his eyes. He didn't squirm, as if this were something he was accustomed to. The Royal's brow lowered to his, and her lips moved, just barely, too soft to be heard. When she straightened, whatever gentleness had touched her expression was gone.

"My nephew," she said, her voice a commanding song. "Longwei. Where is he?"

Miriam stepped aside from the door into the private room, and Kuan-Lin passed with a curt nod. Her shadow of a guardian followed. Miriam waited until both settled inside to draw a breath.

As she moved down the corridor, she absentmindedly turned the tin over in her palm. She had already done the math, but the Royal's presence had only confirmed it. The ache in her chest grew.

"You alright?"

The voice came tentatively from behind. It had been some time since Miriam heard it without a wall of distance between them. She turned as her old friend approached. She hadn't seen Yuri Gregov in a while, and less frequently since he'd left his UMF contract early. The timing had been right for him, and, of course, they'd exchange platitudes in passing, but it'd been a long time since it was just the two of them.

She knew much of it was her own doing.

Her cheek lifted with a faint smile. "Come down from your office suite?"

In her head, the words sounded lighter, but out loud, they landed as a barb. Miriam saw it in the way his mouth quirked, in the pause before Yuri answered.

"Well," he said, "when the prodigal daughter makes a return..."

She huffed.

He offered a half smile in return, his eyes flicking toward the private room. "We don't usually get alties in Station General, especially not Royals. So when someone says we do, I show up." He glanced at Miriam. "Is that who I think it is?"

Sam's Royal.

"Yeah," she breathed.

Miriam lowered herself onto the hall bench, her legs folding slowly, every movement a reminder of how long the week had been. When her back touched the wall, she allowed herself to sink into it.

Yuri remained standing, his posture easy. "Didn't know she had kids."

"No—yes. I don't know." Miriam tapped two fingers to her temple, then twirled them, the tin tucked in her palm. "Her nephew, I think." She was pretty sure; Sam had mentioned it before. "I don't know why they didn't have more protection. You'd think—"

She stopped as something caught her eye. A small pink bloom mottled the back of her hand, and nestled in its center was a dusting of the same white powder that the boy had been attacked with.

"Shit." Miriam winced. It stung with heat and pinpricks now that she was paying attention. And this was only on her hand in a minuscule portion. The Royal kid's screams suddenly felt painfully understated.

"Oh. Shit," Yuri echoed as he leaned in for a closer look. He raised his head, about to signal for assistance.

But Miriam held up her other hand. "Give me one of those containers. And a cloth," she instructed, nodding toward a rolling cart down the hall.

When he came back, she carefully skimmed the remaining powder into the sterile container. The trace was tiny, inconsequential, but she sealed it tight anyway.

"Here." She handed it to Yuri. "Just in case you don't have enough from them."

He took it wordlessly, the set of his jaw tightening.

"Mr. Gregov?" a staff member called out from the other side of the corridor.

Yuri glanced their way, then back at Miriam. "I'll call someone over."

She shook her head, eyeing the same cart. There had to be general medicated bandages or responsive gel that could take care of chemical burns.

"Okay," he said hesitantly. "Give me a sec. I'll be right back."

He hurried off, drawn back into his responsibilities as one of the medical center's managers, the prize child her parents had wanted but never had with their only offspring, Miriam. Now alone, she pulled herself upright and rifled through supplies until she found what she needed. She cleaned off the irritated skin, applied a strip, and ignored the scathing glance from a passing nurse.

When she was done, Miriam returned to her seat, and her eyes fixed on her now bandaged hand. It was a strange and cruel method of attack. Why target the Royal child? She confidently assumed the black caps were Charonites and that they knew their mark or marks were Altered, but the method felt random and reckless. She and Hadeon had arrived at the scene right after, and the main perpetrator had been an adolescent, only a little older than the Royal he'd attacked. Miriam remembered the two Charon lamp tattoos on the adults, but she couldn't recall seeing any ink on the youngest member. Perhaps this was a disturbing rite of initiation, a savage test she couldn't yet understand.

Miriam shook her head and swept her gaze around the hospital wing. Staff had returned to their routine. With the Altered now sequestered out of view in a private space, the novelty of the rush and moment was gone.

The last time Miriam had spent longer than a passing errand in Station General had been during her medical evacuation from the North alongside her other two Echo teammates, Kai Wester and Saif "Nas" Nasiri. Miriam watched Yuri as he conversed. Other than his smart civilian attire, he looked the same. The stress lines that had been etched into his face from his SOG time were gone, replaced by early signs of wrinkles around the corners of his eyes. When was the last time they hung out, laughed together like they had in their childhood? She averted her eyes as he glanced back. She was a terrible friend.

Miriam's attention was drawn lazily back to the surrounding space. At least she wasn't in the same wing as when she'd been hospitalized. She wasn't anywhere near the atrium where Sam had sat on those steps, where they had unraveled. That part of the medical center was still there, no doubt with the same sterile walls and rooms, but she was grateful not to be there now.

And her previous visit to Station General had been to her parents—separately, of course. They never were in the same room unless the recording devices were present or the press narrative required it. Miriam had played her part, smiled when directed to, and then left quickly afterward.

Across the wing, Yuri laughed.

Miriam's mouth tugged at its corners. Her old friend's laugh was so natural. The former Echo second had always known how to be around people, exuding a warmth and smile that set others at ease; Miriam's parents must've loved that for public engagements. Yuri was their perfect substitute child, the one who stuck around and did everything right. Miriam wasn't jealous, nor did she resent him. It was an objective fact. Her parents' situation had been a marriage and partnership of business. They'd wanted her to stick around Station City and take the reins with them, but she'd wanted to leave. Perhaps it was the way she'd been nurtured—or *hadn't been*. Perhaps it was why she was the way she was.

With a weary pause, Miriam pulled herself from her roving thoughts and composed a quick message to Emma, an apology that she'd be a tad late, assuming this didn't turn into a much longer affair.

Reflections and her task done, Miriam's eyes dropped to the

tin in her hand, the one the boy had picked up at the restaurant. She hesitated, thumb resting on its lid, before flicking it open. She shut it just as quickly with a glimpse of its contents.

Tablets. Pale and square. It was the kind too common now to be mistaken for anything else. Stimulants.

"Sorry 'bout that," Yuri said as he returned, brushing a hand across his breast as though wiping away the interruption.

Miriam's fingers firmed around the metal container. "Don't be sorry. It's busy."

"Are you waiting for them?"

She nodded mildly. "Them and SecTeam, I guess, if they bother sending anyone. I imagine some reports will be processed, but if SecTeam isn't coming, I should probably self-report." She rubbed her knee.

"Whatcha got there?" Yuri nodded at Miriam's hand.

She held the tin up, and he took it, then opened it.

Yuri gave a low whistle. "Tell me these aren't yours."

"They're not."

"Well, that's a relief. There's been an influx of users, and the cases have been piling up here. This street stuff is nasty. Cut and diluted, I imagine, but really unsafe."

Miriam nodded absently. "Saw it up north, too," she murmured. She waved a hand as he tried to hand the tin back to her. It was better for him to destroy it.

"Charonites?"

"Mostly." She didn't elaborate. It wasn't like SOG missions had them traveling through thriving towns and cities. The parts they frequented had long been evacuated of normal civilian activity. Only UMF, mercenaries, and Charonites transited through there now.

Yuri studied Miriam a moment longer, his eyes narrowing. "So how'd you get pulled into this?" He threw a finger back at the room.

"I'm a shit magnet." She offered a bitter smile. "First that mess up north, and now this."

His expression sobered. "The executions. That whole situation is—" He let the sentence hang. "You were there for that?"

"I've showered and scrubbed so many times since, Yuri. I don't think I'll ever get the smell out of my head."

"You *are* a shit magnet."

Miriam's hand moved up to her chin, and for a split second she thought to raise a finger at him, but she didn't. "Thanks," she said instead.

"You said it first."

"Yeah, but when you say it like that, now it's really out there." She meant it lightly, but the silence that followed pressed in. Whatever closeness had once held them together had slackened over the years, most of all after their mission in Sunali and what had come out in the days that followed.

"I'm sorr—" Miriam began.

"Want to talk—" Yuri said at the same time.

They both stopped. The awkwardness lasted only a second before Miriam gave a quiet chuckle and shook her head. "It's strange seeing you in civvies."

"Well, I *am* a civvy."

Miriam's attention broke as a nurse grazed past them in haste, muttering something to himself.

"Who's the new lead?" Yuri asked.

Miriam shrugged. "Goom. Gumede. He's..." She didn't finish, but Yuri understood.

"At least you have Hino," he said. "Hino's good people."

"She's not you."

"No." He gave a lopsided smile. "She's better."

"Hush."

Farther down the hall, someone hollered for a doctor. A door hissed open and shut.

"I don't—I don't know," Miriam said. "This shit with the marines, the Apostates, the Charonites, the kid—"

"Junkies in the street," her friend continued. "Missing alties—"

"It was a kid, Yuri. The Charonite. And why did he have—" Miriam's hands fluttered up. "—whatever the hell that stuff was?" She sighed. "These Charon assholes are in UMF, all over the North, the city now. It's too much."

Yuri folded his arms. "When everything smells like shit, even the new shit stops standing out."

She played with the bandage on the back of her hand. The sting was lessened now with the medication gel.

"I'm glad you're out."

He gave her a look.

"That's not what I meant. I'm not glad you're gone, I just —" She let the words fall away.

"I know. I miss you, too."

Miriam closed her eyes and braced her head against the wall behind her. She and Yuri had grown apart, but talking like this now, it was like nothing had happened. With him, it was *that* easy to fall back into rhythm. They had known each other too long.

"We should grab a coffee soon," she said.

"Yeah?" He tilted his head. "I'd love that."

He smiled warmly before a voice rose from the central station, strained and uncertain. "Ma'am? You can't just take him. He—"

Miriam stood as the Royal's bodyguard emerged from the treatment room, ducking his head underneath the doorframe. Kuan-Lin's nephew was cradled effortlessly in his arms. Pale medicated bandages traced lines down the boy's face and along his limbs. Behind him came Kuan-Lin with the toddler resting into her shoulder. Hadeon followed like the second half of the Royal's shield.

"Thank you for this," Kuan-Lin said, her voice composed.

Just inside the room, a hospital doctor held a syringe as if he had been interrupted pre–blood draw.

"Longwei *is* stable, correct?"

The man gave a stiff nod.

"Thank you. We can care for him now," the Royal continued, not unkindly. "Your work is appreciated, but our physicians are better suited to our…biology. He will receive the appropriate treatment under their care."

Outside the room, the nurse stepped forward again, clearly torn between protest and deference. Her words came haltingly, then stopped altogether when her eyes caught on Yuri.

Miriam's friend straightened. "You're welcome to stay here, ma'am. This is the best medical center in the city, hell, the best on this side of the world. We're here to help however we can."

The nurse's mouth curled into a smug smile.

"But we won't stop you if you prefer to move him closer to home," Yuri added.

The smile faded, and the nurse blinked in disbelief. "But Mr. Gregov, the specialists have already been called. They said to keep the alt—the *guests* here. They're on their way. Ver—"

"I appreciate you, Holly," he said, gesturing briefly. "But we're a human hospital. Not saying that to be exclusive, of course," he added quickly, "just the truth of it. We're working on advancing our capabilities to accommodate your kind, but if you believe he'll have better care elsewhere, I trust your judgment."

Kuan-Lin dipped her chin.

"Mr. Gregov," Holly said.

Yuri ignored her and bowed his head to the Royal. He turned toward the console, beckoning the nurse aside.

While their voices fell into subdued tones, Kuan-Lin approached Miriam, pausing just out of arm's reach. "Thank you," she said. "To both of you." Her glance moved between Miriam and Hadeon.

"We've met before," the Royal continued. "But we've never been formally introduced."

It was true. The last time Miriam had seen the woman was after Scott "Mute" Reckert's funeral. Sam's older half-brother. And before that, a different day altogether when Sam had told the Royal off, severing her ties.

The golden-eyed woman adjusted the little boy in her arms and extended a hand. "I'm Kuan-Lin."

She nodded toward the man to her side. Dark spectacles obscured his eyes, but Miriam knew there was shocking red color underneath.

"This is Dmitri. And you helped my nephew, Longwei."

Miriam gave a shallow nod. She recalled Sam mentioning the other Altered, but they weren't the introduction she was waiting for.

"And this is Ren," Kuan-Lin said, her eyes steady on Miriam. "My son."

There it was.

The words settled over Miriam. She swallowed, the formality catching in her throat. "Miriam Tanner."

"Yes. I've heard of you."

Miriam offered no response. She wasn't sure what answer or reaction the moment called for.

The Royal said nothing more, but her scrutiny lingered. There was a question behind it, something unspoken yet plainly shaped. Miriam braced herself.

"You don't think this is fate," Kuan-Lin said. "*You* being the one to help my son and nephew?"

Miriam squared her shoulders. "I don't believe in fate."

The Royal's expression did not change, but a note passed through her voice as she replied, "Wise."

"Excuse the interruption," Hadeon said quietly, "but we should go, *diànxià*."

Miriam glanced at the senior legionnaire then drew in a

short breath. The skin along Hadeon's forearms, where she had carried the child, was irritated and red.

"You need to get that looked at," Miriam said. She raised a hand toward the doctor idle inside the room.

"I will be fine," Hadeon answered. She turned to Kuan-Lin and dipped her head.

Miriam frowned, unsettled. She had served beside the senior legionnaire long enough to read her caution, even unspoken. Something had stirred the woman's instincts. Miriam's eyes cut toward the bodyguard, but Dmitri's shaded eyewear and expression gave nothing away.

"Come with us, legionnaire," Kuan-Lin said. "We'll have that seen to."

She adjusted Ren in her arms and moved toward the exit. Angled to the front, Dmitri led the way, the other boy in his arms, as Hadeon flanked.

For a beat, Miriam stood motionless, but then she stepped forward, drawn by something she couldn't quite name. She caught up to the Altered as they reached the bay doors.

"Kuan-Lin."

The Royal turned. She glanced at the others before she retraced her steps back toward Miriam.

"Is he…" Miriam began. Her voice faltered. "Is Ren…"

Kuan-Lin only watched her.

Miriam already knew the answer. She hesitated, then spoke a little above a whisper. "Does she know?"

Golden eyes flashed and for a moment something between them shifted. The Royal's mouth twitched before she blinked slowly. When she spoke, her words were measured.

"Thank you for your assistance, Miriam."

The lack of an answer was an answer in itself.

Miriam stood in the corridor and watched the Altered go. She couldn't explain how her day had been derailed so far from what it had been, could only feel that something *had* changed.

She made her way back slowly across the ward, searching

for Yuri. The ordeal had ended, at least for now, and it seemed only right to say goodbye. She saw him on the other side, back where they'd all been, leaning on the central counter, a tablet balanced on his fingertips.

"We'll make sure they're found and brought in. You have my word, Ms. Wester."

At the voice and name, Miriam turned. In another branching corridor a few paces off, she saw a man with gray hair, his back to her. Something was off about him, but Miriam's attention was short-lived. A woman stood in front of the gray-haired man, her own contrasting dark hair cropped shorter than it had once been. It covered the faint scar and metal plates beneath, only noticeable to those who knew where to look. Like Yuri, Kai looked nearly the same, if not for the cut of her suit and the stiffness in her shoulders. It was strange seeing the woman like this. For years, the only remnants of Echo in Miriam's life had been Krill and Fox, and even those meetings were fleeting. Now another stood before her. All within a single week.

As the gray-haired man excused himself, he gave a nod to another individual in his departure around the corner. Miriam locked in place. There had been a saying Fox used to throw around. Something about rain, or when it stormed, it... something.

The individual's dark hair had grown out in curly waves, wound around his ears. Heavy but manicured brows sat over brown eyes full of mischief, and farther down, though the braces around his legs were minimal, they were made obvious by his gait.

Krill and Fox a week before. And today, Yuri, Kai, and...

Nas.

All Miriam was missing was Sam.

Neither of her two former teammates had noticed her yet, caught up in conversation with a different man who had hurried to join them—an aide, if the suit and weary face were any measure. Miriam thought about approaching, but the discussion looked too involved. She angled toward Yuri instead, casting a few backward glances as she went.

"Did you call City Center?" She gestured behind her.

Yuri lifted his head, craning his neck. "Oh, wow." He set down his device and leveled a glare at the nurse who had objected earlier. "No, not me. Word spreads fast, I guess." He sighed, rubbing his forehead. "Why do I feel like I'll get chewed out for letting the Royal walk out of here?"

Miriam narrowed her eyes.

Yuri muttered incoherently before he lifted a hand high above his head. "Baby Echoes!"

Kai, Nas, and the aide looked up. Kai murmured to the other man, who departed shortly after. The two former teammates walked over, and Yuri met them with a large stride, wrapping them in an embrace, one after the other.

"It's a mini reunion!" he exclaimed, releasing Nas.

Miriam stepped forward to hug the former intelligence specialist next. Nas squeezed her back. When she embraced Kai, the contact was brief and the woman's posture remained rigid. It irked Miriam; it was vastly unlike the Kai she knew, but Miriam tried to remind herself of the situation. The surgeons at Station General had done excellent work, but they could only do so much. The excitable engineer from their former Echo days was gone. What remained was much cooler.

"Shit, it's good to see you two," Nas said. "What are you doing here?"

"What are *you* doing here?" Miriam replied.

"I was just meeting Kai for lunch when she got word to come by." He shrugged. "Tagged along."

Of course he did. Kai and Nas had been inseparable on the team. It wasn't any different post-injuries and UMF discharge.

Kai observed Miriam and Yuri with a neutral expression, though a heartbeat later, her mouth curved upward. Miriam had seen the same transformation and semblance of a smile on her parents during public events.

"Hello, Yuri. Tanner."

Miriam frowned but tried to pull it back up. "Hey. Haven't seen you in a while. Both of you."

She really hadn't done a good job of keeping in touch.

"Ah, it's probably my fault," Nas said, leaning onto Kai's shoulder. "Work's been crazy. I don't want to speak for both of us, but things have been picking up." He looked around. "Tech advancement doesn't stop for anyone."

Kai shrugged him off, but the man didn't seem to care. His focus, and his feet, had already moved past the group, looking for the next exciting...something. He'd been known for his curiosity. It was no different now.

Miriam turned to Kai. "And you? How's City Center treating you?"

"It's busy," Kai replied, voice level. "A headache at times, but a lot is happening, especially now with these Heretics. We were already dealing with water filtration and factory issues. Add on the Royals complaining about missing Altered, and this circus—" She gestured at the same aide who had returned, followed by a couple of others carrying recording devices. A hospital staff member trailed after them in dissent.

"Wait." Miriam looked back at Kai. "Heretics?"

"I'm sure you've seen the broadcast executions."

Miriam only nodded. She didn't know the Apostates were called Heretics now. For a second, part of her wanted to say something, relay her own involvement, but she bit it back. She and Echo had been of no help to those marines.

"I was told some Royals were admitted," Kai said to Yuri.

"Not really admitted," he replied. "But you just missed them."

Kai gave a distant note of frustration. "That's irritating." She made a motion to the others, and they slunk back.

"Everything alright?" Yuri asked.

Kai hesitated before her shoulders squared. "It would've

been nice if they'd stayed. I thought I might speak with them. Outside of the embassy and Center."

"For a press junket?" Miriam asked dryly. She glimpsed the recording devices disappearing as the hospital staff member herded them away. She hadn't expected Kai to fall in line with City Center's affection for the media.

Kai's brown eyes swung back, the contour of annoyance quick to rise, but a second later, it passed.

"Is Center everything you wanted?" Miriam tried, softer this time.

"If it's not posturing, it's politics or strategic imagery," Kai said flippantly. "Nothing is said plainly, and every word hides a different intention. It's all manipulation and influence."

One of the hospital employees stood from the central station. "Mr. Gregov, your meeting. They're here."

Yuri groaned. "Ah, shit. Time to go do some damage control." He clapped the two women lightly on their shoulders, smoothed out his shirt, then hastened down the corridor, his pace easing as he spotted the approaching party.

Kai watched after him, her eyes narrowing slightly before she looked around, presumably searching for Nas, who had somehow disappeared in the ward.

"You know who they are," Miriam said, somewhere between a question and statement.

The woman nodded. "Representatives. From Vertex. I was recently at their headquarters."

Miriam straightened and eyed the neatly dressed individuals across from Yuri. She couldn't tell if they were management or scientists—they all looked the same in white coats. Vertex was the parent organization that had bought out Emma's employer, the one she worked for—*had* worked for. The same company Nas was with as well.

"I didn't know they had business with Station General."

As she watched from afar, Miriam then caught motion through the window of a corner room. The same man with wavy gray hair from before stood on the other side, one hand in his pants pocket and the other holding a white stick-like thing.

Miriam squinted until recognition stuck. An unlit cigarette. No one used those anymore, just the various types of nicosynth devices. But she'd seen it before, outside of old records and images. The item tugged at a long-buried memory.

And then it came like a battering ram. The cloying scent of tobacco penetrated her like a potent specter. Miriam's heart lurched. It was the Charonite council member, the same one Echo had met in Matam, in the South. They had been underground then, and he was without his henchwoman now, but Miriam was positive it was him.

She grabbed Kai's elbow and pulled the woman into an open treatment room. Miriam closed the door to a slit. The patient inside was asleep, undisturbed.

"What?" Kai's reply came brusque, more irritation than confusion.

Miriam peeked out. "That man. He's one of them. A Charonite. Remember in—" She stopped. Kai hadn't been with them. She'd stayed at the inn in Matam as backup while the other half of Echo had tried to find the Children of Charon council. But she had also been talking to him in the hall just before.

The woman blinked, then adjusted her jacket with a measured tug before moving toward the window. "Oh, Chalo."

Miriam's grip on Kai's elbow strengthened. "What?"

"This asshole's been working with Center. Advising." Her voice was flat, not defensive. All matter-of-fact. "And lobbying."

"You mean he's your contact?" Miriam sputtered.

"It's not like that."

"Kai, I just watched Charonites attack children. That man is a leader, a council member."

At least he had been, years before in the South. She remembered the barefoot man making his speech advocating for the decentralization of terrorism. What one hand did, the other not knowing... It was all bullshit.

To her surprise, Kai only sighed like she was exasperated Miriam didn't understand. "The Children of Charon aren't going away. We can't destroy an ideology by burning down every movement and cell. It only generates more contention, and we need to be realistic about that. We need them."

Miriam stepped back. "We *need* them? Hell, Kai, do you hear yourself? Did you not hear me? Charonites attacked Altered children."

"If we had concentrated on curbing recruitment, pushed for structure over disorder, perhaps we could have shaped them." Kai's awareness flicked toward the door. "We can still shape what comes next; it's not too late. We, City Center, should be addressing root causes, not swinging a hammer at shadows."

Miriam shook her head. She wasn't sure what stunned her more, the words or the way that Kai's voice carried no heat, no remorse—only strategy. She believed it. Maybe it was the time apart; maybe it was the surgeries. Medical technology had advanced, especially since the Altered had joined them, but human brains were delicate things. Or maybe it was the political company Kai kept now. Miriam didn't know this person in front of her.

"You don't actually think this, do you?"

"Tanner."

"It's Tan."

Kai gave a slow nod but said nothing more as she left the room. Miriam followed into the hallway and watched the woman stride toward the Charonite, like she hadn't been speaking of terrorists and sympathizers in the language of diplomacy. Miriam bristled as Kai extended a hand and disappeared around the corner.

By the time Yuri returned, Miriam had folded into herself on the same bench she'd sat at before, her jaw cramping.

"That was quick," she muttered.

He followed her line of sight to the end of the corridor, but no one was there. "You don't look happy."

Miriam scoffed.

"Where'd the babies go? Kai?" Yuri said, looking around.

"I don't know, and I don't know what the fuck just happened."

Yuri grimaced. "We've all changed."

"I don't recognize her anymore."

He sighed. "We're either dead or broken. That's what war does, right?"

10

INEVITABILITY

"MIRIAM?"

Emma's voice floated from within the apartment.

"Yeah," she called back, the door shutting behind her. Miriam shed her boots with a kick and stripped her shirt, tossing it into the hamper on her way through the bedroom to the adjoining bathroom. Emma stood there, fixing her hair.

In the mirror, Emma's smile widened, then faltered as she turned, her eyes running over Miriam. The footage was already gone from the public feeds, buried beneath the latest headlines, but Miriam knew it had unsettled Emma. It had unsettled nearly anyone paying attention.

"Are you okay?"

Miriam opened her mouth, but the words stuck. She hadn't told Emma it was Echo who found the marines, though Emma clearly knew something had happened. Officially, it was SOG protocol, OpSec, but truthfully, she preferred not having to talk about UMF with her. She liked that her girlfriend wasn't part of it, that their relationship didn't revolve around war and deployment.

And how could she explain what had happened? The

screaming, the blood, the stink that still clung to the inside of her nose and throat.

Emma cradled Miriam's hand. "What happened?" Her fingers stroked tenderly over the bandage.

"Oh." Miriam blinked, surprised. She'd forgotten about the chemical burn. Somehow, this was the injury she had come home with. Nothing visible from the North or the mission, but this from Station City.

She could talk about that, at least. The Charonites, the attack, the Royal child. All of that was fair game. But trying to explain her connection to Kuan-Lin felt like pulling a stitch that hadn't quite closed.

"I'm okay," Miriam said, pulling her hand back and drawing Emma into an embrace. When arms returned around her, Miriam leaned in and let the tension slip from her spine and muscles.

"Really. I'm okay. Just… Charonites."

Emma pulled back. "In Ursus? Did they—"

"No." Miriam braced herself against the doorframe. "Here. But not me. They attacked…kids. Altered kids. Can you believe that?"

"Hell. That's awful." Emma hesitated. "Kids now? Wasn't there a report a few weeks ago as well?" She shook her head. "But that's beside the point. Why would they do that? Was it near the base?"

"No, I was walking back with Hadeon. Never mind. We intervened, and I got stuck at General." Miriam's fingers rubbed small, slow circles into her brow. "If it's not one thing, it's another. You'd think the Charonites would lay off with everything happening."

Or maybe it was the opportune time for them.

"Well, it's Station."

Emma was right. The city was privileged in its insulation.

"I'm not asking for people to be scared out of their minds," Miriam said, voice low. "But something. Some acknowledgment." Irritation spiked in her words. Perhaps this was the downside of Emma not being a marine. She and the other Station civilians didn't understand.

Emma slipped an arm around Miriam's waist. "People are exhausted. *You're* exhausted."

In the mirror, Miriam saw them both: Emma close, her head resting on Miriam's shoulder, and herself staring back like a stranger. She had expected the images from the North to haunt her, yet sleep had come easily. Too easily. It wasn't the bodies or the execution that loitered, but the smell and the sounds. The nightmares would come, she was sure of it. What frightened her more was not that she couldn't sleep, but that she could.

She'd kept company with violence too long. The mind adjusted, protected itself in strange ways. A week ago, she was holding marines' severed heads with an ungloved hand. Now she was in her apartment, changing into more comfortable loungewear.

"Are they okay?" Emma asked.

"Who?"

"The Altered kids."

"It was really just one. And the woman—"

Shit. She hadn't followed up on the other victim.

"Miriam?"

She shook her head. SecTeam and the hospitals would handle it. If the woman was Altered, her people would see to her.

"I ran into some old faces," Miriam said instead.

"Oh?"

"It's been a strange day." She glanced at the bathroom counter cluttered with makeup and tools. Signs of preparation. "What's going on here? Are you going out?"

"Well, speaking of old friends..."

Miriam narrowed her eyes.

"Buzz Hallow?" Emma offered.

Miriam groaned.

"You forgot."

She had.

"Can we still say no?" Miriam asked.

Emma pouted playfully, but her expression softened. "We can, if you want."

Miriam sighed.

"With everything...something different wouldn't be the worst thing. A change of scenery? You haven't seen Talya in a while. Or anyone, really." Emma gave her a squeeze. "I love having you all to myself..."

"But?"

Emma smirked.

"I'm getting on your nerves." Miriam rolled her eyes.

"I never said such a thing." Emma laughed. "But if we're being honest, I could do with a night out, too."

"And you picked Buzz? I know I haven't been in the scene for a while, but there are classier dives than that joint." Miriam paused. "Talya's trying to rope in another vapid mark, isn't she?"

"Well, she chose Buzz. I just said yes," Emma said breezily. "And 'mark'? Wow."

"Not inaccurate, though."

Emma grinned. "Actually, she said she met someone. At work."

"Oh, hell. From the base? That's worse. You're not supposed to shit where you eat, or whatever Fox would've said." Miriam winced. "Talya's going to showboat the entire time. I really don't want to see that."

"Be nice."

"I *am* nice."

Emma kissed her cheek. "I know. We'll stay a couple hours, and then we'll make up an excuse and duck out. I've got a site visit in the morning, anyway. It's been crazy at the labs with all the transfer and exit stuff."

Miriam moved out of the bathroom and toward her closet. "You're still feeling good about leaving, though," she said over her shoulder. Not a question.

Emma picked up her comb, then offered a small smile that didn't quite reach her eyes. "Yeah. I just…don't love the direction things are going, and ever since the stim wave…" She took a breath. "This is right for me. The new org might actually let me right a few wrongs."

She didn't elaborate, and Miriam didn't press; the distance from each other's work and field went both ways. So Miriam continued sifting through her clothes. She hadn't gone out in a while, and everything she had available felt outdated.

"So, tomorrow morning's a site visit?" she said. "Is it early?"

"Are you trying to talk me out of going tonight?"

Miriam's hand rested on a stack of old pants. "Is it working?"

"No." Emma chuckled. "And if I told you about it, would you understand?"

"Probably not."

"It's a last favor to GenTech," Emma said, twisting a strand of hair behind her ear. "Before the merger. Behind the scenes, of course. We don't get to mingle with the influence or the money."

Miriam finally fished out a simple shirt. "Because you'd scare them off with all your math and molecules?"

"You really have no clue what I do."

Emma's laugh filled the bathroom, and Miriam turned toward it, a smile tugging at the corner of her mouth.

"The people in power never want to know the 'how'," Emma added after a beat. "If we tried to explain, they'd fall asleep. All they care about is the result, what they can see. But the boring parts matter."

Miriam flinched just slightly. A hairline crack under the surface. That word stirred something buried, and whereas she would've once bristled, it only filled her with a heaviness now.

But Emma didn't notice. "Boring gets the job done. Boring works. Hell, most of what actually matters happens because it's so mind-numbingly procedural." She threw a finger Miriam's way. "Not all of us are gun-toting grunts."

"Is that all I am to you?" Miriam asked, mock-offended. "Do *you* know what *I* do?"

Emma grinned. "You're lucky I broke my no-UMF-dating rule."

Miriam only hummed as she plucked a plain pair of pants and threw them onto the bed.

"Oh? Fine. I'll just go to my other girlfriend, then."

Miriam arched her brow. "I *knew* there was someone else living here."

"She's very discreet."

Emma dissolved into giggles, and Miriam drew her close. Arms looped around her neck, Miriam kissed her slowly, then pulled back to brush a thumb along her girlfriend's chin.

"I'm lucky," Miriam whispered.

"Damn right you are."

♟

Miriam took a deep breath and followed Emma into the club. She'd been a few times before, enough to recognize the renovations. Priorities, of course. Some called it resilience, others a coping mechanism. The city and its inhabitants had done it multiple times before. Paint over the trauma, upgrade the lights, add new cocktails to the menu, and pretend the attacks, the destruction, and the death never happened. What a bit of polish could do for a place built on forgetting.

Or avoiding.

Miriam glanced around at the crowd, wondering how many had seen coverage of the executions or cared that the North was still caught between two terrorist factions. How many of these city folk had simply carried on? Like herself, apparently.

"Tan!"

Miriam turned to see her old friend waving both arms. To the side, Emma mouthed *be nice* before nudging her. "I'll grab a table," she added out loud, humor clinging to her voice.

"Order?" Miriam called after her.

"You know what I want!"

Miriam braced her shoulders, stretching her upper back, and started toward the bar. She made it five steps before she was smothered in an embrace.

"I'm shocked you came! I'll have to go through Emma to get to you from now on."

Miriam rolled her eyes. "Hi, Talya."

"Nat and Tan, back together again!"

Miriam's eyes practically ached from how much they were rolling. She took another deep breath. "Em said you met someone. Are you finally settling down?"

"Fuck, no. Are you kidding? With you off the market, the city's been ripe for my taking."

"Are there even that many people? You haven't had any repeats yet?"

Talya grinned. "Who knows? I could start fucking the alties! How's boring life?" she added with a teasing shove.

Miriam scoffed. "Boring is nice. Boring's a luxury these days."

She should've chosen *boring* a long time ago. Some lessons only sank in after the damage was dealt.

"One day I'll believe you maybe, but you're lucky. Not everyone has an Emma," Talya said. "I like her. A lot."

"You trying to poach?"

"I'd consider it, but nah, she's not my type." Talya laughed and took a sip from her cup. "Too sane."

Miriam smirked. "So, where are you assigned now?"

"BigMED, if you can believe it."

"Fuck."

Talya laughed again. "It's not too bad, actually. Did you hear UMF's running trials on a new aid?"

"Aid?"

"Yeah, the partner recently published numbers on some new sympathomimetic compound. An upper, basically."

Miriam narrowed her eyes. "Stims? Sanctioned?"

"Apparently. It's not addictive, or so the experts say."

"What experts?"

"UMF partnered with a big research group," Talya said with a shrug. "It's legit. Some hospitals and clinics are in on it, too."

Miriam's jaw worked. She'd have to ask Yuri if Station General was involved. The medical center was the city's best for a reason: its collaborations and constant push for new breakthroughs.

Talya shrugged once more. "Look, it's their job to test and sign off. It doesn't just happen. City Center has to approve it. Which means it's paperwork *I* don't have to push, thank fuck."

The woman's awareness wavered, and Miriam traced her sightline to a group that had just walked in, attractive and flashy, dressed to catch the eye.

Talya leaned in with a grin. "Anyway, Tan—shit, I like Emma, but you're missing out. Don't you want it again? This life's got its perks."

Miriam let the comment hang. That life had been empty, nothing but motion to keep her from facing the void. She was glad she'd left it behind, even if she'd done it too late.

She didn't have to answer as Talya's cuff chimed, and the woman gasped. "Shit. Order us drinks, yeah? Be right back!"

She hurried off toward the entrance, and Miriam gathered herself before signaling the bartender. It took her two tries. Once, she wouldn't have had to wait. Perks, as Talya said.

With the order placed, Miriam craned her neck toward the booths along the wall and found Emma already settled, moving to the beat with that familiar ease. The soft curve of her mouth was private, untouched by the buzz around her. It shone through the haze. Miriam smiled, something close to peace stirring in her, the closest she'd felt all week.

Then Talya's excited chatter carried from behind her, quick and giddy. Miriam inhaled, bracing for the inevitable whirlwind. She turned—

And the air left her lungs.

Sam.

Over three years of silence, of nothing, and there she was. Her hair was longer now, pulled back with the sides shaved down. And the scars. Her lower lip was split by a pale line that carved to her jaw.

But it was Sam. Her irises, that shocking blue. The color was right, yet something felt off. She didn't seem to fully see Miriam.

They locked eyes. A second. An hour. Three and a half years, stretched thin and wordless between them.

Miriam didn't speak. Couldn't. But that had been her failing, hadn't it? Her throat bobbed, and when her voice came, it was nearly inaudible. A name breathed more than spoken.

If she hadn't been transfixed, she might've missed the jump in Sam's lip. A smirk? A sneer?

Meanwhile, Talya kept talking, oblivious. "—but everyone calls her Tan. And *this* is Fury."

Miriam blinked.

Fury?

The word landed wrong like static out of place. It wasn't just the name; it was the wrong version of the woman, like a distorted copy. Miriam took Sam in, searching for recognition. The metal arm was there, barely concealed beneath the short sleeve. The lines of her body were leaner now, carved down to sinew and edge. Even her face was hollower, more angular, like something essential had been stripped away.

Sam.

Not Sam.

"Fury," Miriam echoed, slow and disbelieving. The callsign tasted unnatural in her mouth. Wrong.

The woman—Sam, Fury, both and neither—looked at her once, impassive, then let her concentration slide past Miriam's shoulder as if she weren't there.

Still Sam. But not.

Talya grinned. "She's with the Seraphim team. You know, the joint—"

"Yeah. No, I know," Miriam cut in, eyes fixed on Sam's face. She knew the blonde woman in front of her recognized her, yet the pointed absence of acknowledgment unsettled more than it stung.

Behind her, containers clinked as the bartender set drinks down.

Sam's eyes tracked something or someone behind Miriam. "I'll be back," she said.

Even her voice was alien, cold and empty. She turned and stole into the crowd. As she slipped away, her fingers dragged once across the side of her neck, an unconscious abrasion that left the skin pink.

Miriam watched her go. Dark ink climbed the side of the woman's neck, black lines spreading down beneath the hem of her shirt. The way she moved carried echoes Miriam knew too well, and yet every step felt foreign.

"What the fuck was that? Did you scare off my plus one?" Talya folded her arms, squinting. "Wait. Do you two know each other?"

Miriam tried to force her diaphragm to relax.

Talya groaned. "Dammit! Sloppy seconds? Fuck." She paused, then shrugged. "Oh well. Wouldn't be the first time."

She kept rambling, words spilling one after another, but Miriam wasn't listening. Her pulse thundered in her ears, drowning out the bass of the club. Three and a half years, and then Sam. Simply there.

Sam, but not Sam.

"Yoo-hoo, Tan." Talya waved a hand in front of her face.

Miriam blinked, fingers gripping the side of her cup. "Sorry, what?"

"I said, are you going to behave yourself?"

"What?"

"Are you—" Talya clicked her tongue. "Never mind. Get the drinks and get back to your woman. I'll wait here. We'll be over in a sec."

Miriam nodded mechanically as if her body moved on borrowed will. She gathered the drinks and carried them to the booth, heartbeat still erratic in her chest. She set Emma's cup down with care as though its weight alone might unbalance her.

"Thanks, babe."

Miriam slid in beside her, hand locked around her own drink.

"Saw Talya come in. I'm guessing the blonde's her date? Love the hair. That dye job's incredible. You never see that shade anymore." Emma giggled.

"It's natural," Miriam murmured.

Emma nudged her. "It was a joke." She chuckled. "Nat really knows how to find them, doesn't she? She sure goes after the rough and tough ones."

Miriam didn't answer.

"You okay?"

She lifted her head. Concern shadowed Emma's face.

And then Talya swept in, laughter spilling over as she steered Sam toward the booth. They sat across from Miriam and Emma, the club's heat and humidity closing in like a cage. Sam's expression flickered before settling into something practiced, a mask smoother than the one she'd worn at the bar. Her blue eyes skimmed over Miriam and Emma, glazed, distant, and disconnected.

As Talya launched into introductions, Miriam stayed quiet, her attention trained on the woman across from her. Sam didn't speak either, though her features adjusted at the right cues, subtle changes that felt rehearsed, as if she were mimicking responses without meaning them. As if the script were there but the lines never reached her.

Miriam felt a soft elbow at her side.

As Talya kept talking at Sam, Emma leaned close. "It's her, isn't it?" she whispered.

Miriam gave the smallest nod.

Emma's hand slipped into hers beneath the table. "Do you want to leave—"

"Lovebirds, keep it in the bedroom," Talya interrupted with a grin, dragging on her nicosynth device. She wagged a finger between Sam and Miriam. "So, how exactly do you two know each other?"

Miriam stiffened. Sam didn't so much as blink.

Then, unexpectedly, Sam spoke. "We worked an assignment, had a brief arrange—"

"No." Miriam's voice cut more jagged than she intended.

Was that really what Sam had told herself? After all these years?

The others turned toward her. Miriam released her jaw and forced the words out. "We were together." And then quieter: "I didn't... I..."

Sam watched her, unflinching.

"I cheated."

It'd been a onetime mistake. A panic and knee-jerk reaction when Sam had told her three words she hadn't been prepared for. But the mistake had compounded into something much worse when Miriam never had the chance—the right time—to explain it. And things like that never aged well, especially in the conditions at the time.

The table went still. The thrum of music and voices swelled around them.

Talya's grin vanished. "What? Fury's a Seraph. She hasn't been back to Station in years..."

Beneath the table, Emma's fingers closed softly around Miriam's.

Miriam cleared her throat. "Sorry, it's just, good to see you. I didn't know you'd be back."

"UMF admin," Sam said, clipped and flat.

Miriam ran the numbers in her head, then gave a slow nod. "Renewal." She had known Sam was still loosely tied to UMF, but she hadn't realized that returning to UMF and renewing was an option. "Are you?" she asked.

"No."

The shortness of the response startled her. The Sam she remembered had wrapped her identity around the military organization; now this version, *Fury*, dismissed it without a flicker.

Silence pooled between them again, heavy and strange.

Mercifully, Talya shifted. "Emma, how's life at the labs?" Her eyes slid toward Miriam, exasperated.

"Oh, I'm not in the labs anymore," Emma said with a smile. "Well, a couple more weeks and then I'm out. I'm moving into remediation work."

Talya blinked. "Huh."

Emma laughed. "We live in such different worlds. I'd only bore you high-speed operators."

Her fingers squeezed Miriam's again, but Miriam stayed taut, too aware of Sam across from her, trying not to fixate. She was failing.

Talya blew out a puff of air. "So, how's the pay? Anything over there for washed-up medics without a cushy hospital gig waiting? For those of us not born into Station General royalty?"

"I'm not—" Miriam began.

"I don't think so." Emma hesitated, then offered an apologetic smile. "Not unless you're into the regulatory field."

"How about a test subject? Right price, and I'll let them poke and prod."

Emma chuckled.

Talya turned to the woman at her side. "Fury, what about you? Any big plans now that you're not renewing? Or are you sticking with the Seraphim?"

"It's day by day," Sam answered flatly.

Silence returned.

Talya drained her glass and pushed to her feet. "Um, guess we're running low. Want to grab another round with me?"

But Sam, already rising, had other plans. "I'm getting some air." She didn't look back as she cut across the floor toward the back, the crowd parting for her.

Miriam half stood, then sank down. Emma's brown eyes found hers, lips forming a single word. An instruction and encouragement. *Go.*

Hell, she didn't deserve this woman.

"Should I—well, fuck, this isn't awkward," Talya muttered behind her as Miriam moved.

She eased out the bar's back exit into a narrow alley, a forgotten crease between buildings. The door shut behind her, muffling the music, and the night air kissed her skin.

Sam stood against the wall, head tipped toward the sky. She rolled her neck slowly from side to side but didn't turn.

"Sam?" Miriam said, tentative.

"Don't call me that."

The voice was harsher than it'd been inside. Not dispassionate, but void, like something had been excised of everything that once filled it. Whatever tone Sam had performed for the others, this was the real thing. Reserved for her. Directed at her.

Miriam stepped closer. She hadn't expected warmth if their paths crossed again. In truth, she hadn't expected to see her at all; she had long assumed Sam's name would surface one day on the death register.

And she had no delusions about the anger. It was warranted. Sam had survived an attack on her home outpost, returned maimed, endured months of administrative purgatory to claw her way back into active status. And then the Apostates had taken what little remained—her only family, her half-brother, lost in the Station City attack.

But this rage in her now was something else. It wasn't grief or even hatred. It was bordering on indifference. Apathy. And that was worse.

Sam's observation traveled behind her, and Miriam turned. At the alley's mouth, a half dozen figures loitered, black caps pulled low. Were they the same Charonite group from earlier? No, these were older, late teens, early twenties at least. They didn't bother concealing the small tins that passed between their hands before vanishing back into pockets; two scratched at their skin between trades, irritated and jumpy.

Drugs. Stims, more likely.

But why here?

Miriam scanned the group, but aside from the black caps she found no insignias, no tattoos. Beyond them, the city's foot traffic drifted past. Were they going to target more Altered? She couldn't pick out a clear mark in the crowd anymore. She wasn't sure if that was good or worse.

Her mind snapped like an elastic band.

Ren.

She turned back, but Sam was already moving, sleeves shoved up.

Miriam reached instinctively, fingers grazing the prosthetic arm. "No, they're stim—"

Sam's eyes flared, and Miriam recoiled at the venom there. The hatred wasn't subtle. It was raw and absolute. And the color. Before, they had been an irregular blue, but now they were near black, pupils blown wide.

Without hesitation, Sam strode forward, her approach unhidden. One of the black caps tapped their ringleader, and the group turned. A few smirked, raking their eyes over her with the greasy confidence of boys who thought themselves dangerous. Others frowned, squinting as they measured her up.

"Heads up, Mitchell. I think she wants your number."

"Hi, sweetheart," another said. "Why don't you smile for me?"

One of the boys in the back squirmed, hand snapping up to cover his face. At least one had a shred of sense and dignity.

"Stop," the ringleader, Mitchell, said, stepping forward.

To Miriam's surprise, Sam did. She halted no more than two meters away.

The same boy in the back pointed, eyes riveted to the ink snaking from Sam's neckline. "Wait. That's a Seraph."

The group fell quiet.

"No Seraphim in Station," Mitchell muttered.

"I'm telling you, that's one of them."

"Fucking filth. Working with the rats."

Sam fixed her stare on the Charonite, and his mouth clamped shut. The others eased back a step, instinct taking over and leaving the man exposed. Miriam caught the betraying swell in his throat. A hard, nervous gulp.

Sam lifted her metal hand, studying it as if the rest didn't exist. "The other day," she said, voice mild. "I almost crushed an Apostate's skull with just this." Her fingers slowly flexed and curled. She rotated her wrist, palm open to him. "I wonder…"

Her gaze rose from her hand to his face.

"How brittle is yours?"

His chin quivered before he locked his jaw.

And then Miriam wasn't sure if she had blinked, but Sam had already closed the gap. She hadn't lunged, hadn't sprinted. She'd simply *shifted*, like a ghost between frames. Now she stood within reach.

Her left hand snapped forward, clutching Mitchell's collar and hauling him close. The fabric bunched between her fingers, and her prosthetic hovered near his face, fingers splayed like the jaws of a trap.

"What are you scheming, Charonite?" Her voice was calm,

verging on conversational, as if she were remarking on the weather.

"Sa—" Miriam started, then bit it back, hissing instead, "Stop!"

But the woman didn't react. Either she hadn't heard or she simply didn't care.

Behind them, the door cracked open, spilling music into the alley. Emma stepped out and froze. Whatever she had expected, it hadn't been this. Miriam lifted her hand, palm spread behind her in warning, keeping Emma back.

Sam didn't blink.

In her grip, the man writhed, pawing at her left arm in panic. His eyes locked wide on the unmoving metal hand hovering before his face. His shirt stretched, fabric biting into his throat, but she didn't let go.

"Fucking freak," someone spat.

Miriam exhaled hard. *Why?* Why did people throw fuel on fires they didn't understand?

Sam's prosthetic hand shifted, fingers splaying as they climbed the man's throat. Her thumb nested beneath his jaw with a strange delicacy. Once, that touch had been tender with Miriam. Now the same intimacy had become calculated violence.

Meanwhile, Sam's eyes didn't rest on Mitchell at all. She looked past him, at the others.

"Some people say we're scalpels," she said clinically. "Cutting away tumors, rotten flesh." Her thumb traced idly along the young man's skin. "There are larger crises elsewhere, but there's a cancer here, too." Her fingers pressed deeper, leaving small hollows in his cheeks. "What are you scheming?"

"Why must everything be scheming?" a new voice asked.

A woman stepped from the alley's other corner. She had short hair and a hard-boned face. The memory struck Miriam faster this time, more acute for all the reunions of the past days.

"You," she whispered.

First the gray-haired Children of Charon councilman at Station General. And now here, the same revolver-bearing shadow who had stood at his side in Matam.

"You Seraphim are all so paranoid," the woman said. "You say 'scalpel,' but you're nothing more than a saw. My peers think otherwise, but I disagree. You *are* doing useful work eradicating that rat scum in their nests. But don't get too cozy. Your rat comrades will turn on you the moment they can."

Miriam leaned toward Emma, her eyes locked on the Charonite woman. "Call SecTeam," she said.

The woman didn't so much as blink. "Is that meant to frighten me?" Her lips curved in a faint, joyless smile. "Go on. Call them. We'll see whose odds are better."

Miriam cursed. She hated that the woman might not be wrong, that Charonite rhetoric had seeped into Station's SecTeam ranks, and, frankly, into UMF, too. Too many wore the uniform now with loyalties bent elsewhere. Whom they would protect was no longer certain.

"Are you finished?" the woman asked Sam, unruffled. "Intimidating boys who were doing nothing at all?"

Sam let go.

The man staggered back, both hands flying to his throat. A red mark already bloomed along his jaw, darkening toward a bruise, though Sam's grip had seemed effortless.

The woman tilted her head. "I remember you. The hair. Although *that* is new." She gestured loosely toward Sam's right arm. "You abandoned the South, but that was expected."

A breeze cut through the alley, lifting the hem of her shirt. A revolver glinted in the waistband before the fabric fell back into place.

"There was a brother, wasn't there?"

Sam gave no reply, but a muscle flickered at her jaw.

Behind them, the door opened again. Miriam caught Talya's voice. "Whoa, hey."

The Charonite woman's smile tightened. "Stay in your lane, and we'll stay in ours."

Emma's hand slipped into Miriam's.

A gob of spit hit the pavement at Sam's feet as the group backed off, middle fingers raised, taunts exclaimed, retreating like bullies who had tested their luck and found its limit.

"Fuckin' alty-lovers!"

The alley fell into a strained lull, as quiet as the city and club behind them ever allowed.

Talya blinked at the retreating caps, then at the women before her. "Yikes. I missed something." She paused, glancing at Sam rooted in place. "But that was...fucking exciting."

Miriam couldn't summon a reaction. Her pulse hadn't settled. Sam hadn't moved either, shoulders squared, chin tucked, her posture wound as if the fight hadn't ended or even begun. She was here, among them, but unspooling in silence. Alone.

Alone.

Miriam wasn't sure if it was instinct, or guilt, or a desperate hope that something might be repaired, but the words flowed before she could stop them. "Sa—"

The woman whipped around, her dark eyes tunneling into Miriam's.

"Have you seen—have you spoken to the Royal?"

Sam's nose wrinkled.

"It's about Scott."

Sam's focus cut deeper, honed enough to flay muscle and tendon from bone. Like Miriam had no right to speak her brother's name.

She stepped back. She couldn't be the one to say it—not here, not like this—that Scott had left behind a son, that Sam had a nephew. Half-Altered. Half-human. Hybrid.

"I don't know how long you're here," Miriam said, "but you should talk to Kuan-Lin."

Sam's lips parted, and Miriam braced herself. But the woman only sneered before turning away.

"Shit, did you scare her off? Again?" Talya asked, already in motion.

Miriam doubted anything she did could scare this Sam.

Talya stopped short, her shoulders hitching high. "I'm still going to…"

Miriam said nothing.

Her friend shrugged. "I mean, if it bothers you, I'll reconsider. But we've already—shit, Tan, she's a fucking madwoman with those digits—"

Miriam cut her off with a barbed look. "I'm with Emma."

"Yep. So…"

Another look.

"Excellent." Talya jabbed a finger at her, then winked. "Forever surprising me, Tan. You really know how to spice things up. We should do this again soon. Who knows, maybe I'll have another sloppy second lined up for you to piss off."

"Talya," Miriam snapped then hesitated, the words bitter in her mouth. She couldn't believe she was saying them. "Be careful."

Unstable wasn't the right word for what she'd witnessed. What she'd seen in Sam hadn't been frenzy or madness, but something colder. Aloof, brutal, and terrifying.

"I always am. Well, mostly." Talya flashed a grin. "I'll be fine. I've fucked crazier."

Miriam winced as she watched the woman run off into the throng of pedestrians.

"That was…something," Emma murmured beside her. When Miriam didn't answer, she wrapped her hand lightly around her arm. "You alright?"

Miriam shook her head. "No, yeah. I don't—" The words faltered. With Sam gone, everything processed anew. "I didn't know—I wasn't—" She closed her mouth and tried again. "She's so different."

Hardened. On edge, despite the facade.

"I've only heard of the infamous Seraphim before, but if they're anything like her, hell. She was intense."

Miriam's lips cracked open, but she only managed a nod.

Emma hummed. "Was she using when you two…were together?"

"No. She detests—she detested junkies. Her father—" Miriam stopped herself, her pulse tightening. "Why are you asking? What do you mean?"

Emma's eyebrow arched. "Her pupils were constricted before. I'm pretty sure she's on depressants. At a pretty heavy dose, if I had to guess. The tremor—in her left hand, at least—you don't see that in most people. I don't know how she's upright. And then just now, dilated. Unless I'm wrong, did she stack it with a stimulant?"

"What?"

"Did you see her take something else? Mixing." Emma exhaled. "I can't say for certain, but that's one of the worst cases I've seen, Miriam. You *don't* mix the two. Well, you don't take them at all, but that's beside the point, isn't it?"

The muscles in Miriam's neck rippled. She had felt something was off, but she hadn't wanted to face it. A part of her had already known, but denial had been easier. Easier than admitting that what she'd done back then had helped lead Sam into this. Her breath escaped raggedly.

"I see why you don't hang out with Nat anymore."

Miriam huffed, something caught between a choke and a laugh. She didn't believe in coincidence, but there was no ignoring the magnitude of seeing Sam again, and nearly all her former teammates, in the span of a week.

"When it rains," she murmured.

"Sorry, did you say something?" Emma asked.

Miriam shook her head.

She'd spoken too soon about fate.

11
____

REMINISCENCE

SLEEP HADN'T COME. It clung to the corners of her body and mind but never landed, hovering just out of reach. It wasn't from the nightmares she'd expected—and which still hadn't come—but from everything else swirling inside her head. The last mission, the executions, Kuan-Lin and Scott's child, and Sam.

Fury.

Sam. After all these years.

She hadn't known what to expect, but it hadn't been that.

Miriam eased from the bed with care, unwilling to rouse the woman asleep beside her. The floor met her feet like ice, unforgiving in the stillness of night. In the kitchen, shadows stretched long across the walls, bent by the wash of a small nightlight. Her hands worked automatically as she filled a cup with water, but her thoughts tangled.

What had Sam been through? Miriam hadn't asked. She hadn't known *what* to ask. How long had Sam been in the city? How much longer would she stay?

She closed her eyes and drew in a measured breath, pressing against the knot in her chest. The scars had been one thing, the callousness another, but the drugs? The stimulants and the depressants, that was something else entirely.

How could she make any of it right? Did Sam even want her to try? That look of disdain, the contempt etched on her face, Miriam couldn't scrub it from her memory.

The bedroom door shifted.

"Everything okay?"

Emma's voice anchored her, pulling her out of the spiraling past. A yawn slipped into the end of her question.

"Em. Sorry, did I wake you? You should go back to bed."

But Emma padded across the floor and curled into the chair beside her. Knees tucked up, chin resting on her arms, she studied Miriam through the dim light. "Nightmare?"

Miriam shook her head, then hesitated. It wasn't the kind of nightmare that chased her from sleep. This was the other kind, the one that came when her eyes were open.

Emma reached out and caressed her cheek, and Miriam gave herself to the touch as if she could hide inside the gentleness. How had she ended up here, after all the years of self-punishment since Sam left? To have this, Emma, gentle and patient, loving in ways she didn't deserve. Not after everything, not with how much she had broken. Sam hadn't been the one who shattered it. *She* had.

"I can feel your mind racing," Emma murmured. "Want to talk about it?"

Miriam let out a slow exhale.

"Is it about her?"

Of course it was. There was so much going on, but it still came back to Sam. Always Sam. But to admit that aloud felt childish, shameful, when the world itself was destabilizing.

"Talk to me. We said we'd be honest with each other."

"She wasn't like that—at all, Em. I—it's my fault."

"Miriam..."

She looked away, unable to hold the softness in Emma's eyes.

"It's not your fault. She's an adult. She made those choices."

"But I pushed her toward it. *I* was the tipping point."

"You don't know that."

"I—"

"She's responsible for herself."

Miriam pressed air out through her lungs, frustrated. "I need to—I want to help her."

The words hung between them. It wasn't only want. It was compulsion, an ache she couldn't quiet. She needed to fix things.

"Does she want help? Miriam, she's volatile. I heard the Seraphim were using concentrated doses, and I believe it after that spectacle. That's really hard stuff. She could hurt you."

Miriam shook her head. The Sam she knew was fiercely protective, and she'd never hurt the people around her. But that was a different Sam. If this version wanted to hurt her, maybe Miriam deserved it.

"Some people don't want to be helped."

"I don't—" Miriam's brows pulled tight. "I don't want to talk about this anymore."

Emma settled back. "Okay. I'll give you space. If you want to talk, I'll be in bed, alright? I'll probably scroll until I fall back asleep." She stood and kissed the crown of Miriam's head, her hands lingering on Miriam's face. "I'm here. I love you."

"I know. I love you, too."

Miriam had loved Sam once, though she had never managed to tell her, a realization that had come far too late, regret compounding everything else that had slipped past her reach. Always too late.

She sighed again. "Em?"

Emma paused and looked back.

"Thank you." Miriam hesitated, words tugging loose. "Is this...too much? I'm sorry."

"I can't say it's my favorite thing to talk about," Emma

admitted, "but you've been up-front since the start." She gave a small shrug. "I guess I should've known it would come up sooner or later."

"I wouldn't..." Miriam rubbed at her temple. "I wouldn't cheat on you. If you're worried. I'm not..." She swallowed the rest. She wasn't that person anymore.

Emma waited a moment. When Miriam didn't continue, she smiled softly. "Never crossed my mind."

And then she was gone. Miriam listened to the creak of the mattress as Emma settled back into bed, the sound fading into the hush of the apartment.

Miriam sat in the dim light a while longer, restless hands moving before her mind caught up. Her commcuff glowed to life, and she sorted through threads she rarely visited anymore until she reached it: an archived channel, silent for years, its last message like a scar.

> M. TANNER: I love you.

> M. TANNER: I should've told you earlier. I should've told you all of this before. I'm so sorry, I know I messed up.

> M. TANNER: I love you.

> M. TANNER: Please talk to me.

She hadn't opened this channel in ages.

Miriam remembered the lasting ache when the account had gone dark, the moment she first believed Sam might be dead. Later, when she learned that the names of the marines who had gone to SRAF appeared one by one in the death registry, the wound cut deeper. Sam's name never surfaced there, and yet she had vanished. And now, standing in front of Miriam again, it felt no different. The woman she had known was gone. Whoever bore her face, her voice, her skin—this Fury wasn't her.

Miriam exited the channel. Her finger hovered over the delete option. Sam wasn't her responsibility.

"Miriam?"

She looked up. "Em? What's wrong?" Miriam crossed to the bedroom, where Emma sat upright in bed, her holodisplay casting pale light up into her face. One hand was cupped over her mouth.

Miriam peered over Emma's shoulder. The screen showed a town reduced to ruin. The buildings were unfamiliar, but a mutilated sign scrawled in foreign characters marked it as deep in Altered territory. Her eyes flicked to the network source, one of the smaller Altered-aligned channels. Why was this being shown? The thought was bleak, but how was this any different from the endless carnage they'd already lived through and witnessed?

"I don't understand. What is this?"

Emma said nothing.

Then Miriam's commcuff trilled, and her gut squeezed. She rubbed Emma's back once before connecting the call.

"Hino?"

"Sorry. It's late," Echo's second answered, her voice cutting through the bedroom.

"I was already up," Miriam murmured, lowering the volume. It didn't surprise her that Hino was the one to reach out; the two had grown closer in the past year, bound by workforce trauma and shared duties. But the tremor in Hino's voice, the way it frayed at the edges, sent a jolt through her.

"What's happening?"

"Have you seen the broadcast? The story hasn't made it to the big network yet, but it's out there."

Miriam glanced at Emma's holodisplay. "Another attack?"

"They're not showing the full footage, thank fuck. At least they had tact."

"Hino." Miriam's forehead furrowed. An attack in Altered

territory wasn't unusual, not enough for her second to call in the middle of the night.

"They're saying this recent attack—"

"Why—" Miriam said at the same time. What made this different? UMF and humans weren't stationed that deep. "Wait, hold on." She muted her cuff.

Miriam reached over and palmed Emma's device, the feed cutting out with a flicker. "Em, don't watch this. I'll be back, okay? Let me finish this call." She held her touch on Emma until the woman gave a small nod. Miriam stepped back, mouthing, *I'll be right back.*

"Okay," Emma whispered.

Miriam closed the bedroom door, then moved to the kitchen where she found her earpiece, fitted it in place, and reconnected.

"Hino, it's in Altered territory."

"Children," Hino replied. "Legion confirmed it. Their sources saw what happened. They sent a partial—shit, Tan, it's bad. They were kids. You could see the det harnesses. One was still intact. They used children, Tan."

Miriam's chest clenched. "Who?" She already knew, but she needed to hear it.

"The New Apostates."

Her stomach knotted.

"First the marines, and now they're strapping bombs to Altered kids. What are we dealing with?"

The question felt both rhetorical and not.

"Heretics," Miriam whispered.

It's what Kai had called them.

Miriam shut her eyes. "Are we being deployed?"

"BigInt's been scrambling to confirm these tactics, this new group. We're waiting for Command to decide next steps." Hino held for a moment. "It's all theater. Fear. City Center's leaning on UMF to respond."

"Respond? We don't go into Altered territory. SRAF?"

Sam. Not Sam. Fury.

Would she already be moving on this?

Hino huffed. "No one controls SRAF, but I imagine they're already tracking. There've been sightings of them in the North. BigInt says SRAF's been hitting training camps, looking for the Apostates' mouthpiece, Beric." She paused. "Center, Command... We have to do something. Even Legion knows it. If we don't, the fear, it's going to keep growing. It's what they want."

If Sam was departing Station City soon, should she reach out, try to make things right? Now that Miriam knew she was alive, she couldn't leave it be. She had to fix it.

"UMF will probably want a show of force," Hino said.

Miriam shook her head, willing herself to focus, but the words slid past her.

"These children the New Apostates are using, they're from Altered territories. They're changing the landscape and lateral limits. What if they move these tactics into the North? What if they start abducting human children? Pressure's coming down from the top."

Miriam leaned into the counter, palms flat to the chill surface as though it might center her while the implications settled.

"So SOG's being sent back."

"There've been no official orders yet," Hino said. "But yeah. Show of force. I imagine we'll be pulled into a brief tomorrow."

Miriam bent forward until her forehead touched the countertop. "Hino."

"Yeah."

"Goom's going to volunteer us, isn't he?"

Of course he would. And Command wouldn't argue. There were always more marines to spend.

"I shouldn't have said anything," Hino muttered.

"No, I'm glad you did." It wasn't the distraction Miriam wanted, and it wasn't good news, but it was honest. The heaviness of everything threatened to overwhelm her, and she forced air deep into her lungs. "What can I do? You don't have to deal with Goom alone. What he does affects all of us."

"I'm the second. I should be handling this."

"No, Command should."

Miriam heard a low curse on the other end, then silence.

"Sorry, Tan," Hino said at last. "I shouldn't have called. I shouldn't have dumped this on you."

"No, I needed to hear it." Miriam straightened, though her thoughts snagged in every direction. "Look, I can talk with Krill."

"No, don't. He's got more important things going on." Hino sighed. "I was spiraling, but this helped. Thank you. I'll see you tomorrow?"

"Yeah. Try to rest, if you can."

Miriam disconnected the call and stood in place, the impact of it all pressing down like a vise. It was too much and all at once. Her nerves stuttered, but she grounded herself in the counter's coolness, the low whir of the kitchen's machinery, the sight of the floor underneath her toes.

"Miriam?"

She drew in a steadier breath. "Yeah," she replied. "I'll be there in a sec."

Dragging her hands down her face, Miriam pushed off the counter and returned to the bedroom where Emma sat, device dark in her hands, still waiting. Miriam climbed into bed and pulled her close.

"Is everything going to be okay?" Emma whispered.

Miriam held her tighter but didn't answer. Emma wanted comfort, and Miriam wanted to give it. Miriam wanted to believe it herself. But she couldn't.

12

DESOLATION

"IT FREAKED OUT EMMA."

"I'd be worried if it didn't," Hino said. "It'd freak out any normal person."

Miriam huffed. "So you're saying we're not normal."

"We're SOG. I think we've long passed what the average person should acclimate to. And for the record, I don't think anyone *should* acclimate to this."

Miriam checked her commcuff then scanned the team room where oil and weapon solvent clung to the air. King and Durmaz were by the lockers in their own conversation, their posture tight. At the table, Talwar's leg bounced, fingers drumming on his knee.

"How is he? The others?" Hino asked.

"Talwar? Better," Miriam said, though her eyes lingered on the engineer's restless movements. She shook away the sudden memory of Sam and her own nervous tics, tiny habits she used to memorize. "Or he and the others have buried it better. I made sure they checked into psych for their base evals. And Goom?"

Hino quieted her as the door opened. Gumede strode in,

brisk and confident, like he'd rehearsed his leadership in a mirror.

"Oh, good. Everyone's here," he said, heading for the chair at the front. "Hino, mind briefing the team?"

Before taking her usual seat, Miriam patted Hino's shoulder.

The second waited for the others to settle then walked to the end of the table, opposite Gumede. "Command picked up a feed on the latest attack in Altered territory. Across the strait," she began.

"Wasn't on the network this morning," King said.

Talwar's eyes fixed on the table.

"No, it hasn't made it to the major network yet, but I imagine it will. It started on one of the smaller channels."

Miriam grimaced. The lack of network time for the event wasn't surprising, considering the attack *was* in the Altered territories. She probably wouldn't have known about it without Hino's call. Or Emma staying up and scrolling through the channels that most Station City civilians ignored. And though the media hadn't fully latched onto the news yet, Miriam fully expected they would once fear could be spun into something more marketable.

"But this attack's different," Hino continued. "Not bigger. Just uglier."

"Evil," Durmaz muttered.

"Agreed. The Royals and Legion don't know if the children were kidnapped, missing, or worse, volunteers."

Miriam folded her arms.

"These New Apostates, or Heretics as the Altered are calling them, they're escalating. And this method doesn't seem to be isolated. Legion's been providing multiple verified reports."

"Are they sure the kids weren't caught in the cross fire?" Durmaz asked.

"No, but their intel's been spot-on. Legion sources confirmed charge signatures consistent with detbelts—child-sized. BigInt's reviewed the partial footage. *They* were the weapons."

"If so, that's not volunteering," King snapped. "That's brainwashing. Grooming."

Hino nodded. "Well, there's precedent. The Ursus attack years ago was possibly a hybrid suicide bomb run, and Ursus SOG logged suicide bombers years ago. Those ones, we chalked it up to isolated lone wolves, but reports said the last one was a young adolescent. It might be the same faction that started it all in the South."

The Apostates with the triangle-and-circle brands.

"These are the same ones who—" Talwar started.

"Yeah," Hino confirmed. "The same ones behind our missing marines."

The silence fell like ash, heavy and suffocating. Talwar stared forward, his fingers flexing. Miriam saw it. So did Hino.

"I know it's heartless," Durmaz said, "but why are the attacks over there our problem?"

"Tactics migrate."

Durmaz gave a low whistle. "Okay. That's…something."

Miriam uncrossed her arms and planted her palms onto the table. She'd been turning this over in her head since Hino's call in the dead of the night. "So what's the plan?" she asked, her tone steadier than she felt.

"Echo's not doing anything, not yet," Hino said. "We're waiting for a clearer picture. There are other moving parts, but we've been told to prepare. UMF was already pulling ground ops out. Well, until that last company. That was an exception."

Miriam *still* wasn't sure why those marines were out there in the first place.

"Territories are changing faster than Command can model. Charonites are pushing one way, Apostates another, and now these Heretics are splitting the line. The corridor keeps flipping. Supply and logistics are a nightmare for UMF." Hino sighed. "And on that note, we've been volunteered—"

"It was the right call," Gumede cut in. "Echo's ready."

Miriam pursed her lips together. Across from her, King's head angled toward Durmaz, and the curl of her mouth wasn't agreement but disbelief.

"Other teams, the Titans especially, have more time in region. They're embedded," Hino said pointedly.

"But Echo's tip of the spear. We're not green," Gumede shot back.

They were, though, as a team.

Across the table, Talwar and Durmaz fidgeted in their seats. Echo's second had been keeping her frustrations with the lead separate and private, but now they were seeing the growing friction in leadership.

"We've seen the terrain firsthand and most recently of all the teams. It's our chance to make up for the last mission, to stick it to these motherfuckers. It's our time to shine, show that we don't stand for this shit."

The lead wanted it. Too much.

Hino let the silence stretch, then spoke, "We'll wait for more information, but if we do go, we're going to have to move in with COC. UMF just doesn't have the support infrastructure there."

"Shit," Durmaz muttered.

"Pretty much. I don't like it either, but they're the ones who are on the ground daily. Unfortunately, *they* know the environment best." Hino rubbed a knuckle into the table. "It's messy, but whichever teams do go up, Legion's been requested to go with."

Talwar looked up with a frown.

Miriam's brows furrowed. "Requested? Why now?"

Echo and Foxtrot hadn't run with Hadeon's squad in the previous mission, and from what the senior legionnaire had said, they were explicitly *not* requested then. Miriam didn't care for the reason, but she understood it: Legion were Altered soldiers, and Children of Charon didn't interact well with Altered. Their ideology wasn't exactly subtle.

Hino shrugged. "It's messy."

Miriam felt the old flicker of tension behind her eyes. Hazy details and vague missions. And now, Gumede volunteering Echo before anything was concrete, probably because he had been embarrassed of his slipup before. She focused on her respirations and said nothing.

"Gumede, anything else?"

The team turned to the lead.

"Goom," Hino repeated.

The lead blinked, jolted from his thoughts, and shook his head.

"When?" Miriam asked. "Do we have a timeline?"

"Stand by to stand by," Hino replied. "In the meantime, fill up on what you need, and get those requisitions in. We'll hopefully know more soon." She gestured a hand at Talwar. "Make sure you talk with LOGS for additional det. Deconflict with the other Razor teams on supply."

"Already done," the engineer said. "I can—"

"If you've got time, help Tan."

Miriam met Hino's eyes before a soft sigh slipped from her nose. "Let's go, Talwar."

"How're you holding up?" Miriam asked as she and her teammate made their way to the MED depot. She kept the pace brisk, her mind split between the briefing and how to mend things with Sam.

Not Fury. Sam.

"Fine," Talwar muttered.

"Nervous about returning north?"

"What? No."

"What we saw wasn't normal," Miriam said. "And whatever you're feeling, it's okay. I want you to know that."

"Yeah. I told you I'm fine, Tan. Really."

She slowed enough to study his face. His voice was flat, his response too quick. Something else was brewing.

"Spit it out."

For a moment, he hesitated, then, "You're not worried the alties might turn on us?"

Miriam stopped short of their destination, turning to face him fully. "Who?" Her eyes narrowed. "Hadeon and her team?"

He cast his eyes downward.

"What do you mean?"

His voice dropped lower. "Can they be fully trusted?"

Miriam fought the urge to scoff. "You're new," she said. "This is your first op working with them, but I'm telling you right now. Hadeon, her squad? They've bled beside us and *for* us. They've dragged our asses out of fire more times than I can count. They're on our side."

Talwar's gaze skated across the ground as if hunting for an exit from the conversation. "I heard they leave you behind if you can't keep up."

"So keep up." Her tone sharpened. "Hell, Talwar, who's feeding you that shit?"

"Forget it," he mumbled, pushing inside before she could press.

Miriam's jaw set, but she followed. She wasn't sure what bothered her more, his comment or the way he hadn't tried to hide it.

Inside, the depot air was stale but cooler. Crates lined the walls and scanners crooned. The assistant at the main desk didn't bother to look up as they anticipated the newcomer's next move and spun the display around.

Miriam extended her wrist, her commcuff transferring the requisition. Jaw still clenched, she tapped through. A few items were out of stock, but she adjusted her list and confirmed the rest. Once done, she leaned her elbows on the counter and tapped her fingers, and behind her, Talwar sagged into a chair, not relaxed but tired. Guilt, or discomfort.

Miriam wasn't in the best mood, and perhaps she'd been too harsh. She didn't look back, but her voice eased. "This part? The waiting? It's the job. Everyone thinks SOG and UMF are all go-go-go, but the training, requisitions, admin shit? That's the majority of the job."

"Sure," he muttered.

Miriam kept her eyes forward.

"Tan?"

She turned just as a woman barreled toward her like she'd won something.

"Twice in twenty-four hours? What is this? My birthday?"

"Talya."

"Let me sit." The woman dropped into the seat beside Talwar, unbothered by his blank look. "I can't walk straight. I don't know how you kept up with that one." Talya flexed her right arm. "Fuck, I think you riled her up. Rough. Different. I liked it, but damn."

Miriam pinched the bridge of her nose, shutting her eyes and trying to maintain her composure. Talya's account of her night with Sam was the last thing she wanted.

Talya reclined, legs stretched.

Miriam's eyes snapped open. "Where is she now?"

The woman shrugged, face contorting. "How would I know? I'm not her keeper. Unencumbered, remember?" Her grin widened. "Although I'd consider leashing that one. Why? Jealous? Looking for another ride?"

"No. Hell." Miriam shook her head. "Didn't you say she was leaving soon?"

For a moment, everything else faded. Miriam knew she was juggling too much; she was on the precipice of being utterly overwhelmed. Why did everything have to happen at the same time? But Sam had always been a priority. Except for the one time she hadn't.

"Do you have her contact?"

"She's a Seraph." Talya snorted. "She barely responds. But too bad, you just missed her. Saw her a bit ago."

Shit.

"Do you know where she's going?"

"Who do you think I am? Her bitch?" She chuckled. "But actually… She did say something about the alty sector."

Talwar's lip twitched, but Miriam ignored him.

"Or the embassy? Said she had things to do, people to see." Talya tilted her head. "Shit, if you do see her, tell her I didn't mean she could take *all* my stims. Well, not mine, but the trial's. Fucking saw her take a hit right before she left!"

Miriam froze. "What?"

"I guess I can get more." The woman laughed. "I asked her if she was looking for a fight. Of course, she *is* a Seraph—"

Miriam's pulse kicked. "Talya."

"They always look like they're out for a fight. If I didn't have to come in, fucking do this report on how my Seraph one-night stand stole my shit, I would've loved to see whoever she's about to crush. It's hot when she gets—"

"Dammit, Talya!"

"What?" The woman blinked twice. "You think I'm going to stop her? She's a Seraph."

Being a Seraph wasn't an excuse.

Miriam glared. "Was it the embassy or the housing sector? Which one?"

"I don't know. Does it matter?"

But Miriam was already thumbing her commcuff, swiping channels she'd never used. No line to Kuan-Lin, no embassy contacts. How did one warn a Royal? Was there a hotline for incoming threats?

"Shit." She started for the exit.

"Hey!" Talwar called after her. "What about—"

"Bring my order back!" Miriam shouted. "Tell Hino I had to run. I'll message her."

Or she would if she had time.

First she had to warn someone. And pray she wasn't already too late.

13

BLUDGEON

MIRIAM JUMPED off the people-mover before it fully stopped, ignoring the thorny reprimand from the driver. She kept moving, eyes fixed on the Altered Sector ahead. Familiar, yet foreign.

Over the years, the place had changed. Old Town and its streets were cleaner, the rough edges smoothed by a planned gentrification. Though there were pop-up markings of Charon lamps, there were noticeably fewer. She and Emma had ventured out to try different cuisines in the area, and she had to admit the Altered food was quite tasty, but she never came for any other reason.

The physical fences were gone, a gesture meant to foster unity and accessibility between humans and Altered, but the invisible ones remained. Human-run businesses lined the border, hybrid shops appeared now and then, but true integration seemed out of reach. And those same open streets meant an enraged and stimmed-up human, specifically a blonde Seraph, could also walk right in.

Miriam didn't have to venture far. The crowd led her, clustering in ripples around a clearing off the plaza, near a playground. The tension in the air pulled tight in her gut as she pushed through the perimeter.

In the center, she spotted the shock of blonde hair.

Sam.

The pit in Miriam's stomach deepened as she took in the rest. Sam was squared up, energy taut and simmering. On the other side, the Royal stood firm, one hand resting protectively on the child behind her. The boy peeked out, the wrap around his eyes too large for his face. Other children loitered nearby, some bending around their guardians to watch. Most adults, both human and Altered, kept to the outer margin of the gathering, uncertain whether to intervene or observe.

At first, Miriam felt relief. Sam hadn't done anything yet. But then she took in the stillness, the lack of movement or shouting, and her relief turned to dread. Sam was a burning fuse.

Among the onlookers, black caps dawdled at the back, devices already recording. Of course this had to be in the public view, and of course Sam would irrationally choose here and now to unhinge. Miriam exhaled in a short burst, frustration prickling.

"Don't bite the hand that feeds you." Kuan-Lin's normally elegant voice pierced like ice.

"You think you're holding the leash?" Sam snarled. "You're not."

The crowd murmured but stayed rooted.

"Is that him?" Sam demanded.

Kuan-Lin said nothing, only tucked Ren's head behind her. The Royal didn't look like a fighter, but what did Miriam know about the Altered? Perhaps Royals had hidden talents designed into them as well, or perhaps motherhood had shifted something.

Miriam skirted around, angling behind Kuan-Lin. The Royal didn't turn, but her ear tilted in her direction, a subtle flick of awareness.

"Sam," Miriam called out, palms open.

If the woman heard, she gave no sign.

Where was SecTeam? Legion? The Royal's bodyguard?

"Show him to me," Sam said with a sneer.

"I'd prefer not. You're frightening him."

"Who's the father, Kuan-Lin?"

The question came with a bite.

The Royal ignored her, though Miriam caught the twitch underneath her eye. Sam's stare stayed locked on the boy, and Miriam's gut churned. This was her fault; she somehow had to fix it.

She stepped forward. "People are watching, Sam. That's enough."

No response.

"Is this another play, another piece in your game?" Sam's tone flattened, callous.

"Sam," Miriam tried again.

The woman whipped toward her, pupils wide and glassy. "I *told* you not to fucking call me that."

The words were venom.

"It's your name," Kuan-Lin said without missing a beat. "Scott gave it to you."

Miriam's stomach bottomed.

"You don't get to say his name," Sam hissed, her attention back on the other woman.

Kuan-Lin didn't flinch, her expression hardening. "*Scott* would've hated to see you like this. You've lost sight of yourself. Do you even know who you are anymore?"

Sam's face darkened. "Don't you fucking say his name." She stepped forward.

Kuan-Lin pressed her son back toward Miriam, who kneeled and scooped him up without hesitation. She had only lifted him when he burrowed his face into her neck, his breathing fast and shallow.

Sam paused. Her eyes widened, then contorted. It was

betrayal, but something more than that. Hatred. Miriam recoiled, clutching Ren, no plan beyond instinct. She hadn't thought about what came next; she didn't know what she was supposed to do or where she could go. Where did Kuan-Lin live? Could she get back to the embassy? Would Sam follow?

Around them, the crowd went still.

Sam's voice dropped into a growl. "Was that your plan? To use him to get what you wanted?"

"You don't know what you're saying," Kuan-Lin answered, eyes flashing.

The hair on the back of Miriam's neck stood on end. Without her son next to her, the Royal's back and shoulders had rounded out. Miriam had never known the Royals to fight. Was that next?

Sam advanced. "Did you make him believe he mattered?"

Another step.

"Did you lie to him the same way you lied to me?"

Despite the woman now directly in front of her, Kuan-Lin remained unmoving. Sam hooked her fingers into the Royal's blouse, and a collective gasp passed through the crowd.

"*He* shouldn't be yours."

"No." Kuan-Lin grasped Sam's wrist. The grip wasn't violent, but there was no mistaking the authority clasped within it. And if it hurt Sam, the woman didn't show it. "Is this your way now? Your brother would be ashamed."

Sam's eyes blazed. "My brother would be alive if not for you."

"Is that what you tell yourself?" Kuan-Lin's voice was calm steel. "These drugs have addled your mind. Unhand me. This isn't you, *Sam.*"

The woman threw her face closer and bared her teeth. "I told you—"

A dark shape streaked by.

In the blink of an eye, Sam staggered backward, her grip wrenched free.

And between them, Dmitri now stood, tall and unreadable.

Sam clutched her chest. Miriam couldn't quite tell how the Altered man had done it; whatever grip or hold he'd used had been too quick to see.

Sam's eyes flicked upward, then down to Dmitri's hands. "Your dog," she spat, straightening slowly, rolling her neck.

Unfazed, Kuan-Lin smoothed her blouse.

With a terrible glint in her dark eyes, Sam feinted, but Dmitri blocked her path with ease. She lunged forward, but he didn't budge. Her left arm sliced the air with sudden speed, faster than Miriam expected. She was stimmed—no question. The strike missed, Dmitri shifting just enough to let it pass.

"No," Miriam gasped.

Another punch followed, then a jab, heavier than the last. Sam surged forward again, and Dmitri slipped past her, redirecting her toward the plaza's center, toward the large abstract sculpture as its monument, her movements herded without contact. Sam tried to pivot back toward Kuan-Lin, but Dmitri was there, cutting her off and angling her away.

She growled and lunged. This time, metal collided. Stone split with a thunderclap and fragments sprayed out.

Miriam froze. She had seen Sam defensive, angry, and even desperate, but this was different. Years of combat, or whatever the SRAF had shaped her into, were now layered with whatever stims were coursing through her system. It wasn't defensive or angry anymore; it was something terrifying, dangerous, and worse. It was something that didn't care who was watching or who was on the other end.

Meanwhile, Kuan-Lin walked toward Miriam. She extended her arms, and Miriam hesitated only a moment before guiding Ren into them, her attention fluttering back to the activity behind. Without a word, Kuan-Lin turned, the crowd parting.

"Wait," Miriam whispered.

The Royal paused.

Behind them, Sam swung again, but Dmitri intercepted it

with a motion so smooth, it looked like nothing more than a whisper of air. His hand met hers and steered it harmlessly aside.

"Fight me, you fucking coward!" Sam snarled.

She kicked out then followed with another jab, but Dmitri remained elusive. A flick of his wrist sent her strike wide. His open palm smacked across her cheek with a fierce clap.

Miriam held her breath.

Sam spat to the side and looked up, her lips curled back. Blood was speckled across her teeth.

"Dima," Kuan-Lin said softly. She adjusted her grip on her child, drawing him closer, one hand shielding his head, the other trying to cover his ears.

Dmitri turned toward her. Behind him, Sam struck again, but he slipped out of reach effortlessly, without a glance back.

"Kuan-Lin! Don't you fucking leave. You coward!"

The Royal lifted one hand, making a subtle and coded motion. Miriam didn't understand the signal, but the praetorian did, responding with a small nod. Kuan-Lin met Miriam's eyes briefly, then continued walking a short distance away. Miriam didn't have time to process any of it, her breath catching.

With her hands flung out, Sam lunged. Dmitri redirected her limbs downward, and Sam staggered forward, catching herself in time to rip a vicious elbow back.

It connected. With his face.

Mid-step, Kuan-Lin paused, her expression flickering with surprise as she looked back.

Dmitri lifted his head, and Miriam nearly groaned. His shaded glasses sat crooked, askew on his face. A drop of blood formed and then traced a line from his top lip.

Sam laughed and spat to the side, a spray of pink within it. "The dog bleeds."

Without a sound, Dmitri removed his glasses. He folded them neatly, then slid them into a pocket.

And Sam didn't wait any longer. She lunged again, shoulder low.

"No." Miriam's chest constricted.

They collided. Sam wrapped her arms around Dmitri's waist, but the grip didn't hold. The man broke free, and she came up swinging, an uppercut that missed by centimeters. Their limbs overlapped as they exchanged blows in a quick, brutal rhythm.

At first, Sam kept pace. And barely. But Dmitri was faster, cleaner. An open palm struck Sam across the face again, and her knee crunched into the ground. She shot back up, grasping for his leg, but he wheeled around, and her fingers closed around his shirt. She pulled to destabilize him, rising in the same motion, but he hammered a fist down hard between her shoulder blades. Sam dropped again, this time to both knees.

Stay down, Miriam wanted to shout, but no sound came.

A low gurgle spilled from Sam's throat before it flowed into a laugh. She rolled her head up and spat again at Dmitri. This time, he gave the slightest of flinches, but it was enough as she launched upward, her prosthetic clipping his chin.

Dmitri answered with a crushing fist across her face.

Sam crumpled.

"No. Stop," Miriam whispered.

But Sam stirred and tried to rise.

Dmitri kicked her shoulder, pitching her sideways, and she lay there, limbs splaying across the plaza pavement. For a moment she stayed down, chest heaving.

Then she slowly pushed herself up to her elbows. Her head lolled back as she wobbled upright onto her knees. Sam laughed, her teeth stained with blood.

"Do it."

It was a challenge. A dare.

Self-destruction.

"Kuan-Lin!" Miriam called out, voice cracking. "Call him off. He'll kill her."

The Royal turned her back.

"She's Scott's blood. She's your *son's* blood!"

That halted her. A warm breeze lifted and swirled in the open square.

"Dima."

"No." Sam's face fell. Her hand reached out, dragging toward the praetorian's shoe, but he stepped back.

"We're done here," Kuan-Lin said, her eyes leveled at Sam.

And then the Royal departed, her son, Sam's nephew, in her arms. The crowd split like water around stone. She didn't rush, nor did she look back.

"Alright, that's enough gawkin'!" A burly SecGuard's gravelly bark broke the billowing silence. "Clear the area! Christine, get those people movin'. Y'all got better things to do." He shoved through the rows of bodies, forcing the hesitant crowd to scatter.

Miriam advanced with caution, closer to Sam and Dmitri still standing over her.

"Come on now, we all have better things to do," the SecGuard snapped at the lingering black caps. "I said, scram!"

One thumbed his nose, unimpressed, but eventually turned to go. As he did, Miriam glimpsed ink on the underside of his forearm. She glared after the Charonites.

"Fuckin' junkies tryin' to pick fights with alties again?" the SecGuard muttered. "When do y'all ever learn?" Then he looked up at Dmitri, whose red eyes fixed him in place.

The SecGuard froze, his throat bobbing with a heavy gulp.

Dmitri said nothing, turned, and strode after Kuan-Lin with his long legs.

The SecGuard blinked, then looked down at the battered woman on the ground. His eyes hovered over her metal arm and the dark tattoo up her neck. "Why the—what the shit happened here?"

Miriam slowly approached. "Are you going to arrest her?"

His eyes bugged. "You're a fuckin' hoot. Am I goin' to arrest a Seraph who picked a fight with a fuckin' red-eyed alty?" He backed up and jerked his chin at Sam. "Do I need to call an ambo?"

Miriam watched Sam stir, and she scowled. "No," she muttered. "She's got a hard head. She'll live."

The guard scratched the back of his neck and took another step back. "Never seen one before. A Seraph, I mean. Heard stories." As Sam pushed herself to her hands and knees, he backed farther away. He made a show looking around for his partner, who had meandered off. "Seems like y'all got this handled."

Miriam ignored him as he hurried off. Despite her instincts, she hesitantly offered a hand out. "You should go to the hospital."

Sam eyed her, then stepped off one knee. "Hits like a fucking pussy."

Miriam didn't bother to respond. She had a feeling the praetorian hadn't fought with half his capabilities. She knew Sam knew it, too.

"What are you doing here?" Sam snapped.

"You and your fucking scuffles," Miriam replied, her own fear now souring into irritation. "Someone had to make sure you didn't get yourself killed."

"My fucking hero." Sam spat blood to the side. "I liked you better when you weren't trying to save me." She rose, slow but steadier this time. "Actually, no. I think I liked you better when you were lying to me. I don't need your fucking help."

She turned and walked off, her steps uneven.

Miriam scowled again at her retreating back.

When Sam's legs buckled and gave out a few meters later, Miriam huffed before she closed the distance. She called out to the SecGuard, who hadn't gotten far.

They'd need the ambulance after all.

14

CONFLAGRATION

"IT'S good seeing you again, and so soon, but hell, you *are* a shit magnet."

Miriam grimaced as Yuri joined her outside the treatment room.

"She looks like three prowlers hit her," he added. "Back-to-back."

Miriam huffed, glancing through the window. Sam had always looked younger and peaceful when asleep—unconscious, in this case. Despite the beating and stim crash, she didn't look as bad as Miriam expected. There were welts, bruises, but nothing catastrophic. And this was Yuri's first time seeing her in years; she wasn't sure if he meant the damage or her overall demeanor.

"It was a praetorian," Miriam said.

"What?" His brows shot up. "She tried to fight a praetorian?"

"She *fought* one. Made him bleed."

Yuri let out a low huff, caught between disbelief and awe. "Where the hell did she come from? It's been...forever. Are we sure it's her? I mean—besides the hair, the eyes, the arm, and the fact that it's her."

Miriam exhaled through her nose. "She's on stims."

"Yeah, no shit. And calmers. But this isn't street trash, Tan." He tapped the pouch in his pocket, the one the nurse had taken off Sam. "This is refined, concentrated. And how many did she take? Anyone else would be on a slab, not a stretcher."

Miriam sank into the same bench she'd sat on a day earlier. It felt colder now.

Yuri dropped beside her, shaking his head. "How long's she been on this?"

"How would I know?" she snapped, then looked away.

But part of her did.

She leaned forward, elbows on her knees, face buried in her hands. This situation—Sam, their meeting the previous night, the fallout—had detonated in her lap. She'd been teetering already, and now this was one more impossible weight added to the pile.

"We're running blood work," Yuri said quietly.

Miriam tilted her head. Her frustration hadn't been meant for him, but it never landed where it should. That was another fault of hers—she aimed it at the people she loved. Her voice softened. "She let you?"

"Came in by ambulance. Hospital precautions. She didn't get a say. Being unconscious helped."

Miriam sighed, tucking her hands under her arms in an embrace. "Can you help her?"

Yuri's eyes softened. "Does she want help?"

She turned away.

"I'm surprised you're out here," he said gently. "You don't want to be in there?"

She scoffed. "She can't stand me. Trust me, you don't want me in there when she wakes up."

Yuri let out a slow sigh. "That bad?"

Miriam rubbed her face. The walls threatened to hem her in and crush her from all sides.

"So why are you here?"

"I couldn't just leave her," she murmured. "Talya said she's leaving, going back to SRAF."

And soon, she and Echo would be gone, too. There were so many things left unsaid. Things Miriam needed to say while she had the chance.

Her commcuff buzzed. A new message flashed on the team channel, asking where she was. She silenced it without reading further.

"Tan." Yuri's stare weighed on her. "Do you still—"

"I'm with Emma."

"I know. But—"

A crash from inside cut him off. Miriam flinched, but Yuri was already moving. They reached the door as Sam shoved the nurse's hands away. Still in bed, her movements were nimble but disoriented, jaw locked and eyes wild. She tore through her pockets frantically, hands trembling.

"Where is it?" she hissed. "Where the fuck is it?"

The nurse faltered, and Yuri stepped forward between them, shielding her.

"You're not cleared yet—" the nurse began.

Sam's eyes snapped to the doorway, to Miriam. Her voice slashed like a blade. "*You.* You took it, I know you did. Where is it?"

Yuri's hand lifted.

"Don't play with me," Sam snarled, starting out of the bed.

Carefully, Yuri drew the pouch from his pocket. "Valk. I've got it. Hey—look at me."

Sam tore her glare from Miriam just long enough to snatch it. Miriam's stomach knotted as she ripped it open, pulled out a tab, and brought it to her mouth with a shaking hand. Her throat worked once, twice. And although Miriam doubted it had taken effect so fast, a long exhale followed, as if its introduction into her system, the ritual alone, gave the woman relief.

"Valk," Yuri said again, quieter.

Miriam pressed a hand toward him. *Wait.*

Sam straightened, voice low and rough. "Yuri."

He stepped closer, then stopped when she lifted her eyes. Something in them held him back.

Sam's gaze darted back to Miriam and the room's only exit. "Are you trying to keep me here?"

"Look. The staff hasn't cleared you yet," Yuri said carefully.

"I'm fine." She brushed past him.

And Yuri gave way. "Whoa, easy."

When he shot a look at the nurse, she stammered, "Bad concussion. Maybe a fracture. It could take a day or more in the MedJet."

Sam whipped around.

The nurse wilted. "Some of the bruising *is* deep."

With the woman momentarily distracted, Miriam's eyes tracked the ugly welt on Sam's cheek. It wasn't as bad as it should have been given the strength of the blow. Especially not from a praetorian, even if he was holding back.

She flinched when Sam's eyes returned, boring into hers. It was the same intense hatred she had felt before. Miriam's instincts told her to move, but her body didn't obey.

"It'd be safer if you stayed," Yuri tried. "To get a full check."

Blue eyes cooled, still groggy but coherent. "I'll be fine." Even her voice was steadier now.

Behind Sam, Yuri shook his head, and hesitantly, Miriam stepped aside.

"I don't need your permission," Sam muttered as she trudged past.

The words were meant for Miriam.

Her breath hitched, and she started after Sam.

"Wait. Tan." Yuri's voice followed her.

She angled back.

"You going to be okay?"

"Yeah. I'll talk with you later?"

"You know where to find me."

Miriam picked up her pace, chasing after Sam, who only scoffed without slowing.

"What do you want?" she demanded.

"Please. Can we just talk?"

Unexpectedly, Sam stopped short, and Miriam nearly barreled into her back.

"You want to talk?" Sam spun, anger radiating. "Okay."

Miriam faltered, instinctively stepping back.

"You knew."

"I—"

"You didn't tell me."

What did Sam mean? Was this still about Kuan-Lin and Ren? Or had they already slipped backward, careening toward the conversation they'd never had? The one that never got the air it needed after everything came out, after Miriam's mistake, after the truth was laid bare and Sam—mostly accurately, but not entirely—jumped to her conclusions.

Miriam had been at fault. Of course she had. But Sam hadn't made it easy either. And yes, Miriam should have said something, should have said *everything*, before they got to that point.

But Sam had *left*. She'd shut the door.

Now, standing there, that storm of unresolved emotion surged up from deep inside Miriam. All that hate and pain in Sam's eyes wasn't just rage or withdrawal. It was that narrow window between hits, between stims and calmers, when Sam was *Sam*. Not Fury. She was vulnerable and lucid.

It was the most *Sam* Miriam had seen from her since their first reunion. And Sam didn't get the monopoly on hurt. Miriam had years of silence piled up, too.

Her hand dropped forcibly to her side. "How? How could I have told you?" she shot back. Even if she hadn't found out the day before, she wouldn't have had any way to talk to Sam. Hell, they were only here now because she *did* tell Sam when she could. "You shut me out. You shut *everyone* out."

"You—"

"I hurt you, I know. But we could've found a way, Sam."

"Don't call me—"

"You *are* Sam. You're hiding behind whatever the fuck this all is, and I know I played a part in it. It kills me. I didn't tell you when I needed to, I know I fucked up, but I *loved* you, Sam."

The woman's upper lip twitched.

"It's easier, isn't it?" Miriam went on. "To believe I didn't."

Sam's eyes narrowed, but she didn't move. Her words distilled to their sharpest point. "What's the purpose of this?"

"I don't know. What's the purpose of anything?" Miriam's voice cracked out. "I—I can't watch you do this to yourself."

"Then *don't*. You're not responsible for me."

Emma had said the same. But Miriam *did* feel responsible.

"I can't."

In front of her, Sam's shoulders slowly sagged. Her eyelids hooded briefly before they came back up. Her irises were vividly blue again, her pupils pinched tight. Calmers. Depressants. The woman was balancing on a razor's edge.

"I'm not having this conversation with you," Sam said, her voice already slowing.

Miriam scoffed. "Oh, good. Because that's what we did. Neither of us talked about what really mattered."

A flicker of fire burned in Sam's eyes.

Miriam held firm. "What? Are you going to hit me, too? That's how you solve all your problems now, isn't it?"

Sam's left hand flexed at her side. Her cheek quivered, but no words came. Miriam didn't truly think she'd strike her, but after their two encounters, that lagging doubt gnawed at her. She fought to push away the crushing thought that this wasn't the Sam she had known.

Fury. Miriam shook her head. The woman before her was a shadow, a misaligned reflection, but she was still Sam somewhere, buried deep beneath the drugs and violence. She refused to believe what Emma had said. Sam had to still be there.

And this was her best chance. After all the years, she had the opportunity to say what needed to be said, especially before the woman returned to her unit, back to the battlefield against their ruthless enemies, before Sam was lost forever.

Or maybe she already was. She was present, flesh and blood, right there in front of her, but perhaps she had never truly been hers. This wasn't the woman she'd loved. This was what SRAF had forged, what grief and anger had corrupted, what Miriam herself had helped create.

Sam spun on her heel, about to walk away.

"I loved you," Miriam blurted, words tumbling out raw and desperate.

Sam whirled, teeth bared. "It wasn't love. It was infatuation at most. A silly crush."

Miriam felt the serrated blade slip in, but it didn't twist, not yet. It sat there, hurtful, cold, and cruel. Her lip curled in a bitter scoff. "You told me you loved me."

"Did I?" Blue eyes narrowed into slits. "It was a mistake."

There it was. The twist.

"A mistake," Miriam echoed, voice low, steady despite the ache flooding her core. She stepped forward. "I loved you, Sam. I was *in love* with you."

The woman's jaw worked. "So what?"

"I—"

"Did you say this so you can feel better? Fine. You said it. Good for you. Are you done now? Because whatever you say, I don't care. None of this matters." Sam turned, her back square to Miriam. "We barely knew each other."

And then she was gone.

Again.

PART 2

DECISION

15

IMPERATIVE

"SO A DIVISION COMPANY was out there helping scientists evacuate?" Miriam's voice cut into the quiet of the SOG Tactical Operations Center. "Is that why the marines were caught?"

The four: Goyer, Johnson, LaRussa, and Patterson. She hadn't been with them when they died, she didn't even know their first names, but she'd remember what she could.

Her gaze fixed on Jace. The question wasn't rhetorical, not entirely. She studied the intelligence officer's expression. Had he known? Had he stood in the Pit and lied to her face when she asked if there was more to that so-called search-and-rescue mission? She flicked a look to Hino, but Echo's second gave nothing away. If this was new to her, she hid it well.

"Tan," Gumede warned beside her.

Miriam didn't look at him. Her mood had been pent and sour for days, one long unbroken cord stretched tighter since Sam's departure. "What were these scientists doing out there in the first place? They didn't see the war happening around them, that the area's crawling with Apostates? Heretics? They couldn't have pulled out sooner?"

The questions hung.

They'd only just learned their next mission and that their

last was interlinked with it. Some idiotic research facility and its arrogant staff who'd stayed long past sense. Three and a half years ago, the rest of the North had evacuated. That had been time enough.

But arrogance was a stubborn thing. They'd puttered around until they needed rescuing. UMF had sent a company of marines to pull them out, and four never returned. And they still weren't done. The thought turned Miriam's stomach.

Somewhere to her left, Durmaz gave a quiet nod.

Miriam's eyes slid to the holodisplay. The map was familiar, the same one they'd been shown on the last mission. The imagery hadn't been updated. Buildings stood in the top-down view, untouched in the render, though the ongoing conflict had gutted them. The marked target zone had rotated, tucked deeper in the region, a town northwest of where they'd found the basement and missing marines.

"And why the secrecy? Why are we only hearing this now?"

Jace's fingers dug into his hips. His exhale was the only other sign of strain. "Because it wasn't relevant."

"It *feels* relevant. We're being stovepiped."

"Tan, are you done?" Gumede's voice carried across the room.

She didn't answer. Not in words. Miriam crossed her arms instead and forced herself not to glare. The edge of her temper felt worn and frayed, too spent to be useful. She was still angry with the lead for throwing them into this blind with so little context, and at Jace for whatever else he wasn't saying.

Krill made a small sound at the podium, lips popping before he grimaced and looked away.

But Jace met her eyes. "You're not being stovepiped."

The denial was too neat. The word was wrong, but the outcome was the same.

"The mercs and COC control that area now. It's not UMF's priority. Our supply lines can't support the region until the passage is in more stable hands, but our focus *is* on Bonford and the coast. We can't hold it, but the Charonites can."

His statement fell flat. They didn't answer the questions that mattered.

"I get it," Jace said, resigned. "We're being sent in to clean up someone else's mess."

Bitterness flared. It wasn't what he'd said; it was the way he'd said it. As if they were all heading out together. As if Echo, Charlie, and Legion weren't the ones going past enemy lines while the others stayed back. Miriam doubted Herrera had volunteered Charlie; the way his team sat now, subdued and shoulders set, said otherwise.

Herrera raised a hand, his eyes flicking toward Miriam before he spoke. "How did they keep this facility hidden with a whole war on top of their heads? Is this lab a bunker?"

"I'm not sure," came the reply. "Trust us, we asked for details, but they didn't offer much more."

Herrera leaned back, unsatisfied. "So they expect us to bail them out but won't cooperate. Why not send in their mercs? Or pay the Charonites?"

Gumede answered quickly. "Have you seen those guys? They probably want professionals."

Krill pumped his hands. "You're not wrong. SOG is the best of the best. And with this set of legionnaires, it should be manageable. No one's happy about being kept in the dark, but whatever Vertex left behind, we can't let it fall into enemy hands. Command's clear on this—whatever this is, it's tied to Vertex's contingency program with Center. Prototype or schematics, doesn't matter, but if the enemy gets it, it tips the balance. Get in, secure if possible, or destroy if not. Their lack of planning shouldn't have become our problem or emergency, but it is now."

"It's been empty for weeks now, right? Evacuated scientists and all," Charlie's second, Bretner, piped up. "What changed? Did they forget to lock the place up?"

Miriam's questions had cracked something open. Now the others, especially the seasoned ones, were speaking up, voices weaving in a growing unease. Or irritation.

"They're saying they lost signal to their detection and notification system," Jace replied. "We've got a Vertex advisor in the outer annexes feeding us what they can."

"Countermeasures," Durmaz muttered. "We could barely get the long-range working up there."

Jace didn't disagree. "That apparently wasn't an issue for them before. But now they're saying they can't tell if someone breaches the facility. And yes, it's everyone's issue now. They left behind some weapon they were working on."

Grumbles and curses rolled through the room.

"You're fucking kidding me," muttered Miriam, her voice stacking with the others.

Krill knocked the podium until it quieted. "It's a recovery if possible. Destroy if not."

Hadeon's voice rose from the back where the legionnaires sat. "Does our leadership know of this?"

Krill grimaced. "Yes."

"What kind of weapon?"

"What kind of lab?" another marine from Charlie asked next.

Miriam squeezed her eyes shut as the murmurs built again, flaring like sparks. It was all absurd. Scientists playing their games while the rest of the world burned. Human recklessness was astounding. And stupid. Their lack of foresight was embarrassing, just arrogance dressed as innovation.

"Tech," Jace said. "Vertex has assured us it's not the actual weapon; they say it's a prototype or schematics. But it's enough to be sensitive. Catastrophic if it falls into Apostate or Heretic hands."

It was definitely a major screw-up.

"Command and Vertex are highly confident that they don't

have the capability to detect the lab," he continued. "Most of the top scientists in the Altered community left Arshangol early on and have been here in Station City, but it's not far out there to assume that some stayed. Maybe they've been forced, or worse, they're sympathetic and share the same Apostate ideology. But it's all unverified."

"So, what's the play?" Gumede asked, leaning back in his seat.

Miriam drew a breath, slow and deep. At this point, she didn't care if it was noticeable.

Krill tapped the trim of the podium with his index finger. "You'll be linking up with the parties in Woodchik—"

Her chest contracted. Charonites. Just because UMF had taken to calling them something else didn't *make* them something else. Terrorists by any other title still carried blood on their hands.

"They'll help move you into the target zone," Krill went on. "You have the site location, but they have better ground knowledge. Their people know the terrain, the movement patterns. It's fluid out there. Safe routes change by the hour."

In the back, Hadeon lifted her chin, assessing, and Miriam watched the band of legionnaires seated near the support staff. This mission was already different. Legion hadn't been included in the earlier ones, mostly because of longstanding tensions between the Altered and Charonites. It was less policy, more raw animosity.

"Two SOG teams and a Legion squad," Krill said. "One team takes point with Hadeon and crew. The other will move with the locals, holding perimeter."

"We've got it. Echo will take point," Gumede interjected.

Miriam's stomach sank. SOG bravado was outweighing tactical prudence. If *she* were in charge, Charlie would take point. The other team had more leadership and experience, more time in the field. But she wasn't surprised.

Hino's mouth thinned to a line.

Krill refolded his arms. "You sure?" He looked to Herrera, Charlie's lead.

"Yeah," Gumede said with a nod. "We're good. We've got it."

And Herrera gave a noncommittal shrug. "Sure. We can hold secondary."

"Okay. I wish I could say this is simple and clean-cut, but I'm not going to lie to you," Krill said, eyes sweeping the three teams. "Take care of each other out there. Mission window's tight—couple hours, tops. This isn't a dig-in op. Get in, secure or burn, and extract. I'll buy the first round when you get back."

"I'm holding you to that," Gumede said with a grin.

"Team leads will send out essentials lists," Krill continued. "Durmaz, Kuo—make sure you stock up on demo. Just in case."

"Won't need them if we do it right."

Krill ignored Echo's lead again. "That's all we've got. Anything more and you'll get it on your cuffs or through your leads."

With that, the room shuffled and broke up. Chairs scraped back and boots scuffed. The deployment anticipation moved like a wintry draft through the room. Miriam stayed seated as her team filed out without comment. She didn't look back until the last of them passed. She inclined her head to Krill, who leaned into the podium.

"You doing okay?" he asked.

"Yeah. Great." She didn't bother hiding the sarcasm.

"You're not usually—"

"What? The one who speaks up?" Her edge was more pointed than she meant, and silence gathered close until she exhaled. "I'm off," she added, softer. It wasn't an apology, but it was close enough for one.

"Not exactly what I want to hear from my favorite medic before a mission."

She cracked the barest smile. The weight behind her eyes didn't lift, but the pressure shifted. Miriam knew this wasn't the right headspace, knew it as she sat in it.

Krill glanced at the nearly empty room. "Thought I'd be done giving briefs."

"You're the one chasing promotions. Can't dodge responsibility when you choose it, boss of my boss."

He rolled his eyes, the tiredness plain.

To the side of the room, Jace finished his exchange with Herrera and Bretner, then joined her and Krill. The room settled into the low drone of the servers and consoles. The only other person left, the watch officer Price, remained in the back, head bent over his display, disinterested or wisely detached.

"I know you're not happy, Tan," Jace said. "But we weren't given much."

"Did you know?" she asked. "Before?"

He shook his head. "Barely. We knew Division marines were up there, but Vertex didn't exactly mention what for. Not until they must've realized they couldn't hide it anymore." He sighed. "I'll be heading up behind y'all, working another angle and running some leads on that Butcher."

"In the field?"

"Shit, say it like that and I'm wondering if I should be offended." He tried a smile, but it didn't stick.

"I don't know how you can do it. Break bread and drink with them. The Charonites."

"They're just like us."

She stared. "And how do you come to that?"

"We're all fighting to survive."

"Jace," Miriam said, leaning forward. "They terrorize the Altered. The other day, they attacked children. Here. In the city. You can't seriously tell me you think they're right."

"Right. Wrong." He shrugged. "Does that matter when we're all trying to burn out the real threat? The Apostates, the Heretics, are maiming, broadcasting torture, executions, and they just started strapping bombs to kids. The Charonites are bad, but these monsters are pure evil."

"The Charonites would kill Hadeon and the others if we weren't watching."

Jace scoffed, though there was something brittle in it. "If they tried, they'd die. We know who the real enemy is, Tan. And right now, we can't give them more fire to throw back at us." He flicked his chin to Krill and plucked his nicosynth device out of his pocket, already checking out. "I'll be outside."

Miriam shook her head as he left.

"Tan," Krill said.

"I'm tired."

"You're having a bad day. He's got his own shit, too. You're not the only one dealing with this."

"It's been years of bad days, Krill, and I've never defended Charonites. That's a *really* bad day when you start sympathizing with them."

"They've helped the North. They're holding ground UMF can't. I'm not defending them, but ease up on Jace. He isn't sympathizing. It's his job to get close and gather intel. That's how it works."

"Didn't get us much here, did it?"

He gave her a stern look, and something tightened in his spine. Though he was facing her, he wasn't really looking at her anymore.

"Did *you* know?" she asked.

His pupils snapped to her. "I'm not holding anything back, I promise. We don't know how this facility's still standing. I really don't know. I'm sorry." He looked away. "I thought about asking Nas."

"Does he have something to do with this?"

Krill gave a helpless shrug. "He's with Vertex now. I actually thought he might've been one of the advisors to UMF, but guess not. Either way, he's been helpful before. He might've heard something."

She said nothing. She'd last seen Nas at Station General with Kai. Perhaps Emma was right—she knew Emma was right—she should have kept in better contact with them, the younger Echo teammates, the Baby Echoes. But time did its own thing. People drifted. Grew apart.

"Would Emma know? Didn't GenTech get bought out by Vertex?"

Miriam nodded absently. "Yeah, but I doubt it. Even if Em wasn't in her last week there, we can't ask her about it; she's not UMF."

He sighed. "Has she started the new job?"

"Not yet, but it'll be a change. She thinks they'll offer her a few options, which she'll love. She does love a challenge." Miriam smirked dryly. "She's with me, isn't she?"

Krill's answering smile was small but real.

"You can ask her yourself," Miriam added. "We could do another double date. You, Elly, me and Emma. We haven't done one since you moved up."

In the back of the room, Price cleared his throat. Miriam looked over.

"Yeah, we should." Krill stepped from around the podium. "You know it's weird, being on this side, watching Echo go out."

Miriam stood. "You're welcome to come back. Take the reins."

He didn't answer, not verbally, but he understood. The two started for the TOC door.

"Goom's going to get someone killed," Miriam said quietly.

Krill rubbed his eyes. They'd had an opportunity to move their conversation beyond work, but while they were in uniform, inside the operations center, it'd gravitate back.

Miriam nodded at Price as they passed and stepped into the empty corridor.

"You have to be able to do something. You're Command."

"That's the thing. You'd think a promotion gives you power,

maybe choices and options, but it doesn't. It just shackles you tighter." He took his commcuff from the shielded lockboxes and clasped it around his wrist. "I can't pick my office color, let alone fix what's broken."

"Then what's the point? What's the point if you can't protect the ones who need it?"

"I know you're frustrated."

Miriam huffed. "You're telling me the system's built so that even good intentions fail."

"It doesn't fail. It just works out another way—"

"Or gets buried. Nothing changes."

"Hell, Tan." Krill gave her a look. "You're running hot and cold. I'm not your enemy."

"No shit."

He leaned into the wall. "What's going on? *Really* going on?"

Miriam was too deep in it. Too old for this shit. When she'd extended her contract, it'd been chasing a ghost or waiting for that ghost to come back. But after everything that had happened, after that last encounter, renewing again seemed impossible. If she made it that long. She shook the thought off. It really wasn't the right mindset before a mission.

She paused in front of the lockboxes. "Just don't forget we're people down here."

Krill's face screwed up. "What do you mean?"

"Command forgets. We're numbers and warm bodies until we're not. And then we're just names on another list."

He looked away, then back, guilt in his eyes. "Look, I didn't want to say it until we hit the official point, but..." He drew his thumb along the wall. "I took the Command job when we first found out Elly was, well, she's pregnant."

Miriam froze, hand over her device. "Shit. You're really going to be a dad?" She cleared her throat. "I mean, congratulations. Seriously."

Krill smiled. "I can't keep running ops with a little one on the way. I didn't want to leave you and Greg, but with him out... I didn't abandon you, Tan."

"I know."

"This—having some work-life balance—is important, I know it is, but I don't know."

Miriam placed her commcuff on her wrist. "There's more to life than running and gunning."

He squinted. "Not if the Heretics get their way, but... we've been fighting for so long. Do you think I'm being selfish?"

"For taking care of yourself? Your own? No." She rubbed her eyes. How had she become so tired again? She was sleeping at night. Mostly.

Her cuff pinged, and she glanced down.

Paused.

Miriam wasn't sure if it was real at first—it could be a scam, or someone playing a joke on her—but it looked legitimate. An invitation from the Royal to an unfamiliar address. Not the embassy.

Krill straightened. "Everything alright?"

"Yeah, just...someone I wasn't expecting." Miriam looked up. "I think I'm being summoned."

"Do I want to know?"

"It's probably better you don't. I'm not sure how I landed into this one." She stepped back.

"You're going?"

"Might as well," Miriam said, moving for the door. "I'll see you later, Krill."

"Yeah. We'll do that double date."

She had one hand on the exit when he called after her. She turned.

"You'll never just be a body and number to me, Tan."

Miriam gave a dry snort. "If it came from anyone else, I'd be skeptical. But you don't have a sense of humor, so thanks, I guess."

Krill narrowed his eyes, muttering something she couldn't quite catch.

She grinned as the door slid shut behind her. "You're gonna have to work on those dad jokes."

16

———

SOLACE

MIRIAM WAS glad she had changed out of her uniform as she moved toward a residential block of Altered Sector apartments. She wasn't sure if she was more grateful it wasn't the embassy with its curated formality and legionnaires at the gate. Between the midday rush and the early drift into afternoon, the city had settled into that strange lull, the streets not quite empty, but no longer busy either. She considered sending a message to Emma, composing it in her mind before deciding against it. This side errand was close enough to feel routine, brief enough to seem irrelevant, and yet the guilt lingered all the same. Not deception, but omission.

There was something about this meeting, about the Royal's invitation and the child involved—Sam's nephew, no less—that pressed on the part of her still unsettled. That part remained bruised, not ready to be seen or discussed. She had spoken of Sam to Emma before, given her enough pieces to understand, or at least to try, but this felt different. This wasn't a memory or story. This was presence, a tether that held despite Sam's rejection, her wrath, her departure. Miriam wasn't ready to explain why that mattered. She wasn't sure why it mattered herself.

As she moved through the weave of buildings, she caught glimpses of other humans, some passing through the sector as a shortcut, others moseying to speak with neighbors or vendors, their interactions casual. It struck her then, without ceremony, that Sam had probably walked this same route many times on her way to visit Kuan-Lin, albeit with much more animosity and many more barriers—physical and otherwise. Those markers weren't gone, only submerged, still in the undercurrents.

As soon as Miriam stepped out of the apartment lift, she had already picked out which door must be Kuan-Lin's, though she wasn't sure how she knew. The hallway warped as she walked it, stretching long enough to let unease settle in her bones, then shortening as if forcing her onward before she could reconsider. She'd never set foot in Altered residential spaces before. Over the years, her fear of the Altered had diminished, but being the minority here carried its own edge, a reminder that she was out of place despite being born and raised in the city itself.

Before she could knock, the door opened. Ren peeked through the tiny slit, his gray-blue and gold eyes lighting up. He smiled with bashful delight that loosened something inside her, and the anxiety rolled back. He ducked behind the line of the door as if gladness itself were something he wasn't supposed to show.

"Hey, kiddo."

Ren then flung the door open and stood back. He smirked, and the expression caught her off guard. The angle of his mouth, the spark of mischief beneath the surface, reminded her so vividly of Sam. Of Sam's brother, too, now that she was looking at his child. Scott had died before Ren was born. Sam hadn't known he existed, and yet the resemblance was there. How could a child imitate nuanced gestures and behaviors from family he had never met? What was instinct, what was learned, what was memory passed through other people's stories?

Miriam peered down at him, and he reached out a small hand. Without thinking, she took it, and he pulled her gently over the threshold. The door sealed behind them with a quiet sense of ease. Arrival, not separation.

The flat was larger than she'd imagined, spacious but cluttered. Toys in bright primary colors were scattered across the floor like a painted garden amidst the cool, architected design of the furniture. What had once been sleek and intentional was now layered with warmth, transformed, not diminished, by the presence of a child and all that came with him. Life had moved in and stayed.

"Miriam."

The name landed without warning, and Miriam absorbed it. She wasn't used to hearing it from the Royal's mouth. It came stripped of title or deference, carrying familiarity without warmth. Gold eyes darted to her civilian clothes then softened, as if pleased she hadn't come in uniform.

"Is something wrong?" Miriam asked.

Something that couldn't be said over devices?

"No, not at all." The Royal touched the top of a covered chaise. "It was Ren, actually, who wanted to see you."

"Oh." Miriam glanced at the boy still holding her fingers. He tugged her toward the hallway past the kitchen, and she looked back at the Royal, who seemed moderately amused. This wasn't the same woman she had seen after Scott's funeral, or the one who had stood head-to-head with Sam a week ago.

Miriam let herself be led, caught between the strangeness of being inside the Royal's private space and the natural ease of following the boy deeper in. The formality of the visit had been undercut by the informality of Ren's quiet claim. Behind her, Kuan-Lin followed at a measured pace, neither intruding nor withdrawing, as if she, too, were unsure of what this would become.

Ren pulled her into the first open door along a hallway lined with five others. Miriam slowed as she stepped inside, taking in the brightness of sun-filtered walls and color. The space was scattered with the marks of a child's personality, toys in and out of bins, drawings tacked without symmetry, and corners where imagination had taken up residence.

She sat on the edge of the small bed while he rummaged, and when he returned, he laid a 3D puzzle on the ground with the gravity of ritual. Miriam slid down beside him, cross-legged and waiting. It was quickly clear he didn't want help so much as an audience. He worked with concentration, occasionally handing her a piece with no instruction and less expectation.

Miriam glanced up to where Kuan-Lin stood in the doorway, eyes fixed on her son. The unspoken answer to Miriam's question resurfaced: this meeting hadn't been Kuan-Lin's idea.

"I'm surprised you caved," Miriam said, turning a puzzle piece in her hand.

A breath escaped the Royal's nose, a sound between a sigh and a laugh. Her eyes shut briefly, then opened. "Me, too." And then a pause. "I've forgotten my manners," Kuan-Lin said, straightening. "Would you like anything? Tea?"

Miriam nodded. "Sure. Yes. That'd be great."

"Yes." Kuan-Lin idled a moment longer, as if uncertain whether to leave her child with Miriam, then turned away, her bare feet quiet on the floor.

While she tinkered in the kitchen, Ren leaned into Miriam's thigh, then somehow splayed over, absorbed in his task. Miriam pulled her legs in, and he settled in the well of her limbs.

When Kuan-Lin returned, she carried two cups and an inscrutable expression. Miriam started to rise, but the Royal motioned for her to stay and crossed the room, carefully handing her a cup.

"Forgive my welcome," she said, retreating again to the doorway. "It's been a while since we've had company, and after…"

Miriam tilted her head.

"We don't—well, it feels silly now that we've seen you twice —but we don't often leave the sector." Kuan-Lin's fingers rested lightly around her cup. "Of course, the one time I let Longwei and Juané watch Ren so I could handle some business… And then the other day…" Her chin lifted.

She was avoiding talking about Sam. And for now, Miriam indulged her. There was a certain grace in not forcing it, in allowing the silence to stand where it was still too heavy. For her as well.

As she took in the flat and the people in it, Miriam sensed a loneliness that was no longer acute but had quietly settled into the furniture, into the pauses between their sparse conversation. Once, Kuan-Lin might have stood at the center of something far larger, had carried purpose and urgency, had dared to reach across the divide between humans and Altered, even if only unofficially, by accident, through one unlikely connection with a UMF SOG recon specialist. And yet now what remained? The woman here did not hold that same weight, at least not in the way Miriam had seen her last. Whatever title she bore did not live in this space. It had been shed somewhere along the way, left with the speeches and the summit halls, replaced by something smaller, more personal.

"How's your nephew?" Miriam asked.

The Royal lifted her cup before speaking, her words measured. "Bitter, in moments. In others, still very much himself." Her eyes didn't meet Miriam's. "There will be scars, of course. The acid on top of the paralytic agent was particularly cruel, but it's not the skin I worry about. Some wounds don't knit. Not quickly. Especially at his age." She paused. "And despite his sister's care and my own, there's his mother's voice in all of this. Things between our people and yours have improved, but rhetoric lingers. It always does, no matter how far we think we've come."

Miriam nodded slowly, though she wasn't sure what she was agreeing to—understanding, acknowledgment, or simply that nothing else needed saying. The Royal went on, now speaking of the woman who'd been with Longwei. A friend? A guardian? Miriam tried to listen—something about how the Altered woman had never come by to check on Longwei—but her thoughts swirled. She still wasn't sure how she'd ended up inside a Royal's apartment. Alone. Why she had heeded the invite at all. Maybe it was the fragile strand of connection, still tied to Sam, attenuated by absence yet unbroken.

"I'm afraid I'm babbling; I'm out of practice. Are you staying around?"

Miriam looked up.

"The city," Kuan-Lin clarified. "Although, I apologize—did I take you from your work?"

Miriam waved a hand.

"Ah. Well, thank you for coming. I imagine UMF is busy? You'll be heading up, I assume, with our legionnaires accompanying."

Miriam pressed her lips together, neither confirmation nor denial. She and the Royal had broken some barrier, but she wasn't about to discuss her team's operations.

"Those Heretics are such ghastly business," Kuan-Lin went on. "I've heard from Xiaoling and others that it's not just your North. They've been terrorizing our towns as well. They're apparently dissatisfied with others' attitudes and methods—not extreme enough? Not that I'd give them advice or they'd take it from the likes of me, but they're treading a precarious line. Brutally antagonizing their own over the smallest differences, and with children no less. The people will turn on them if they continue down this path. Not that we are the same, but my family made the same mistake in its own way. We didn't gauge the sentiment or listen to the people enough, and look how they turned on us."

"The conflict never ends," Miriam said. She gave a small nod, unsure what else to offer. "Hadeon and her squad won't say it, but I know they aren't thrilled about the mission either. Especially not with the Charonites in the area."

She held her tongue about the rest. Although the human terrorists in the North lived the daily violence of Apostates and Heretics, those in Station City did not. They wrapped themselves in ideology and used it as license to inflict cruelty on Altered, including the Royal's nephew. How different was that from the Altered terrorists?

"You don't like them. The Children of Charon."

Miriam scowled. "How can I?"

Her expression softened when Ren completed the last puzzle piece and looked up, pride small but bright. Miriam returned the smile, and he dove back into a bin, already hunting something new, as if the tension in the room was nothing more than background noise.

"We fought them," Miriam said. "And now we're helping them."

She heard it as she said it, what it implied. Not about the Charonites, but the same argument about the Altered, about the very woman opposite her now.

The corner of Kuan-Lin's mouth shifted.

Miriam thought back to Station General, to Kai and the way she had spoken about the Charonite man. An *advisor*. Was the leader trying to actually legitimize the Charon movement through the city government and administration? How many lines had blurred without her noticing?

"Has that been an issue with Center?" Miriam asked. "The Charonites or their rhetoric?"

Ren returned and sat on her foot. The contact grounded her more than she expected. He handed her a cube puzzle, translucent and glowing, and looked at her expectantly. She turned it over, uncertain.

"You have to twist it," Kuan-Lin said. "Change it up so he can solve it."

Miriam rotated the puzzle until its shape reconfigured, then passed it back. He accepted it solemnly, already studying the new pattern.

"There's been activity, yes, and shifting attitudes, but I'm not in the main circles anymore," Kuan-Lin said. "I haven't been involved much. Not since…" She gestured toward Ren.

"How have they taken to—"

"*Xiǎo bǎo*, I'm going to speak with Miriam *Āyí* outside, okay?"

The boy didn't look pleased, but he conceded.

Miriam rose and followed Kuan-Lin to the kitchen, the warmth of her tea permeating the cup in her hand.

The woman rounded the counter and pulled out a chair but didn't sit, her gaze fixed on Ren's room. "Children. They understand more than you think," she said. "I'd rather not talk about certain things around him."

Miriam nodded, then glanced at the fine lines near Kuan-Lin's eyes. Subtle, but there, a quiet erosion. "You're not at the embassy anymore?"

"It's complicated. His existence is still…radical to many, not just my family. The reality of him is more than they care to handle." She offered a smile that didn't reach her eyes. "Not quite a pariah, but close."

Family. The Royals weren't Ren's only family.

"I'm not excusing what she did—" Miriam inhaled. "But is it fair to keep Sam from her own blood?"

The Royal's fingers spread across the countertop. "Blood does not equate to family. You, as a marine, know this."

Miriam stayed quiet.

"Of course, I wanted to tell her. I reached out once, but she made it very clear she wanted no contact. Especially not from me."

Miriam frowned. "You reached out? How? I didn't know SRAF could be—"

Kuan-Lin sighed.

Miriam's eyes narrowed. Sam had once mentioned Kuan-

Lin's reach ran wide, that the peace summit between the Altered and humans had been her design before it collapsed.

"Did you sanction the SRAF?"

Golden eyes flashed before dropping. "A select few members and advisors from the family, yes. But it was a joint effort."

It took a moment to click. SRAF wasn't just Altered operators; there were humans as well. Sam among them.

"City Center," Miriam whispered.

Kuan-Lin's lips pinched. "There is no direct oversight anymore."

What was it? Plausible deniability? A separation for future political necessities? Miriam didn't know the details and processes of the political and government world, but she could see the shape of it.

"They're independent," Kuan-Lin went on, though both of them knew independence didn't mean much without support. "It's since evolved on its own. SRAF was just about the only efficient thing our two sides have ever truly done together. Although thanks to you, there's perhaps one more we can add. Station General and my kin are sharing research, building a bridge in health and medicine. Your friend has been keen to push it, and I admit, it's good to feel part of something meaningful again. Of course, an upside of a terrible event."

She let that hang, then added, softer, "But with SRAF...it's like giving a beast a scent and hoping it hunts where you intend." Her voice faltered. "And after what happened recently, with Sam..." Kuan-Lin looked down, buried in her own stinging memories. She shook her head sadly before her golden eyes lifted. "Thank you. Again."

The gratitude caught Miriam mid-sip.

"With Dmitri. I wasn't—" Kuan-Lin faltered. "I've made things worse. I wasn't expecting him to be there. He hasn't, well, he wasn't supposed to be escorting me anymore, but we fall into habits, old loyalties—"

The Royal was flustered. A rare vulnerability.

"With Ren, it's delicate."

Delicate didn't begin to cover it. Ren wasn't just a child of human and Altered lineage—he was Royal-born, carrying a status neither people knew what to do with. Miriam didn't know if the silence around this home was a wall Kuan-Lin had built or the result of her being edged out. Maybe both. And over it all, the shadow of Sam persisted, a drug-dependent ghost spiraling into something unreachable.

"Ren likes you. He's not easily won over. I've made him cautious, I suppose." Kuan-Lin traced a slow circle around her cup. "Earlier, you said you were surprised I caved, but I'm surprised you actually came."

Miriam lowered her eyes to her tea, aware of the woman's scrutiny. She had claimed she was out of practice, that she saw little company, but the Royal's presence carried a gravity difficult to ignore. More intuition than analysis, her attention cut through Miriam.

"You still care for her."

It wasn't phrased as a question, and Miriam didn't argue. The answer came haltingly, but it was there. It had always been.

"You're surprised," Miriam said, after.

"It's strange," Kuan-Lin replied. "I've been here in Station City for years now. I've seen enough of your world to stop being surprised, and yet—yes, I suppose I am."

"Do you not still care for Scott?"

Golden eyes flicked upward, and Miriam thought she saw the slightest muscle tense in the woman's cheek.

"It was too brief." And then the Royal said nothing more.

Silence settled between them, softened by the distant shuffle of blocks. Miriam's thoughts turned inward. Her time with Sam had been brief, too. Compressed into something she still couldn't describe. It had been half as long, perhaps less, than her time with Emma, and yet it had never left her. How could it? Emma brought calm, a level rhythm Miriam hadn't known she needed until she had it. But what if she hadn't ruined things with Sam? What if that safety had been possible there, too, if the timing and circumstances had been different?

Movement drew her attention: a small hand curled around the corner. Little specks of green glowed in the shadows before they came into the light. Gray-blue eyes with gold flecks.

"Hey, kiddo." Miriam leaned on the counter, cupping her tea like it might anchor her. "We've been a while, huh? Go grab that last puzzle and bring it here. Show me how you solved it."

He grinned, whispered, "Okay," and padded down the hall, his footsteps soft.

When Miriam looked back, Kuan-Lin hadn't moved. She stood as if suspended mid-thought, her eyes distant, her grip on the present looser than before. Miriam let the silence breathe. Two women, wholly different in posture and purpose, tethered by the same pair of golden-haired siblings and what they'd left behind.

17

———

CONCESSION

WHEN SHE RETURNED to the base for final checks, Miriam begrudgingly returned to her uniform. She wasn't on her last mission, not yet. A couple of months remained before her contract lapsed and the expulsion into a different life became final. But even with the end in sight, fastening the diamond tab to her collar and smoothing the uniform's seams made her feel smaller and contained, like the fabric didn't just cover her skin and make her like the others, but folded her into its hierarchy, its rituals, and its constant demand for more. She knew she had to endure it. That was the deal. Yet every wear now felt like donning a costume, something that still fit but no longer suited her.

And what would wait for her when she folded the uniform for the last time? Station General? She no longer felt guilt about leaving the war if she took on a different title, but the idea of trading into a business suit carried no spark either.

By the time she returned to the apartment, she had peeled herself out of her UMF role. A soft shirt, worn lounge pants, and she was at the kitchen counter, cuff open, words swimming uselessly before her eyes. Her thoughts drifted instead to the window, to the distant ocean caught between two buildings, a restless strip of dark water in constant motion.

She'd had a week to sort through the thicket of thoughts, or at least to stack them into smaller, compartmentalized piles she could ignore. But back on the verge of deployment, they loomed again, overwhelming. The Apostates had splintered, but the Heretics were holding lines with their fear-inducing cruelty, new executions filmed with the same grim reverence, this time staged with Charonite presence. On the network broadcasts, it didn't matter who they represented; they were humans, and that's all humans saw. Reports of suicide bombings came with names of towns she didn't know but could imagine by ruin. Charonite recruitment surged, their influence woven deeper into the cycle of violence. And UMF was complicit.

Most of her peers leaned into the new mission with fervor, eager to return to the North, their zeal stoked by the Heretic's cruelty and this new figure, the Butcher, whose orange eyes haunted every execution feed. Miriam, however, only felt drag. Sam haunted her on top of everything, and the war inside her chest felt worse than any bullet or shard.

So when Emma's hand touched her arm, Miriam flinched before she registered her presence. Concern blazed in Emma's eyes. Had she said Miriam's name?

The moment reset. They slipped into routine—*how was your day, anything new*—the rhythm of familiarity that didn't slip into anything impactful or deep. When Emma paused, her head tipped and expression careful, Miriam braced.

"Krill messaged," she said, casual but not quite.

"Double date?"

Emma wrinkled her nose. "Hm? No. He seemed worried."

The urge to roll her eyes nearly won, but Miriam held it back.

"You have people and friends, Miriam. And you really haven't been yourself."

There was truth in it, and Miriam didn't argue. She folded her arms against the counter, grounding herself in its pressure.

Unease flickered in Emma's face. "How long do I have you for?"

Miriam's throat compressed. "No change. We're leaving in the morning."

Emma nodded. "And what's in that head of yours?"

"Nothing."

The woman waited.

"Everything," Miriam admitted at last. She pressed into the counter's edge, its bite welcome. "I'm tired."

It was the truth. Harmless on the surface, weighted underneath. She didn't want to go, didn't want another round of orders and objectives, didn't want to pretend she knew what it was all for. She also knew it was the worst mindset to take into the field. Krill knew. And now Emma did too, her gaze unflinching.

"Do you still love her?"

The question landed like a blow. Not because it hadn't lingered, but because hearing it out loud made it much worse.

Did you ever love me?

Miriam blinked. "What?"

Emma didn't repeat herself. She looked down, fingers tapping once against the counter before falling still.

"Em," Miriam said.

Silence.

We barely knew each other.

"I loved her. But that was a long time ago."

Miriam stepped around the counter and Emma's shoulders tensed, bracing, but not pulling away. Miriam wasn't doing this again; she'd been here before. She wouldn't repeat the same mistakes, and she wouldn't lose someone she loved again. Especially not for a revenant.

She lifted Emma's chin. "Em, I love you." She said it again when brown eyes locked onto hers.

And Emma's voice broke. "I know. I'm sorry." She tried to look away, but Miriam cradled her cheek. Emma sighed. "This is poor timing."

"Where's this coming from?"

"You're not over her."

"It was over years ago. She—I made sure of that. She left. She's gone. I said what I had to say."

"But was it enough?" Emma asked.

Miriam cupped her face more firmly. "Closure isn't always satisfying. But I'm here. You're here. I'm not leaving." She kissed Emma's cheeks, one at a time. "I'm sorry. How can I make this right?"

Emma exhaled shakily, air against Miriam's ear. "Just keep talking to me, okay? We're both stressed, and you—I don't want you going out like this. I don't know how to help."

"It's just another mission."

Emma gave her a look.

"I'll be back in time for another shitty bar run with Talya and her next conquest. Hopefully one that doesn't land anyone in the hospital."

Emma huffed, unconvinced. "Speaking of that..." She reached for a small case on the counter and opened it, revealing a silver-gray banded device. "Yuri dropped this off. Said it's from the Altered—the Royals, I think? I quote *his* quote, 'a gift given in the spirit of goodwill.' He also mentioned something about you helping General open that door." She tilted her head, studying Miriam. "Apparently whatever you did with the Altered kids there made an impression. Enough to start talks, at least."

Miriam arched a brow.

"I guess he's been meeting with the Altered medical community, doing some legwork for a partnership or collaboration." Emma gave a dry smile and nudged the case closer. "I think he thought this might help in the field. Do you know what it is?"

Miriam frowned and shook her head. "Something medical, if they gave it to Yuri, and if he regifted it to me…" She turned it over in her hands. She'd have to search for instructions—if there were any—but it looked nothing like a MedPort. It was more compact and sleek, a wide and soft band underneath, like a mouth at its center. Possibly a mix between a tourniquet, stabilizer, and a blood-loss cell saver. Altered design.

"I hope you don't need it," Emma said softly. She gave a small smile. "I'd *like* for you to come back."

With a chuff, Miriam set it down and rested her forehead against Emma's shoulder, anchoring herself in warmth. It was undeniable and real. "If I don't come back," she murmured, "you have my blessing to date that hot server at Liv's."

Emma's body shook with an incredulous laugh. "Oh, good. Cause I've been waiting for that."

Miriam smiled into Emma's shirt. For a moment longer, they stayed that way. Miriam let the woman laugh longer before kissing her again, clinging to the closest thing she had to home.

♟

Their stay at Ursus Outpost was brief. The legionnaires had arrived before them, five white-armored monoliths among the sprawl of UMF gray. Their stark contrast only underscored how little Legion remained in the North.

"Get your radioactive ass away from me," one of the Razor-Charlie marines teased behind Miriam.

The legionnaire next to him started to respond, but the marine waved him off. "It was a joke. Shit, Perun, I saw you in Station. Relax."

Talwar's eyes tracked the exchange, nervousness stiffening his scowl.

"At least we're not spending the night," the same marine said. "Food up here's shit."

"You try hauling supplies this far," his teammate shot back

from his seated position, a few meters away. He and another sat with King and Durmaz, cards in hand, boredom and anticipation passing between them in quiet laps.

Meanwhile, Miriam kept herself apart, orbiting without anchoring. She hovered near Hino, Herrera, Bretner, and Hadeon—close enough to listen but not enough to be counted in.

"We'll have air support?" Herrera asked.

"Only if it goes to hell," Hino replied, eyes skimming her cuff. "Countermeasures are a concern, and we don't know the full extent of what they've got." Her focus shifted briefly to the senior legionnaire.

"Legion will provide exfiltration," Hadeon said evenly, "But their response time will not be immediate."

Because the airships couldn't station closer. Because of the Charonites.

Charlie's lead and the two team seconds checked their buzzing cuffs.

"Well, that's that," Herrera muttered. "Green light. Where the hell's Goom?"

"He'll be here," Hino said, though the flicker in her eyes betrayed her doubt. Empty reassurance.

Herrera glanced at Bretner, who signaled the others in.

When the group gathered, he cleared this throat. "Everyone knows the plan."

Nods and murmurs followed.

"We move as one. If they stop us, I'll do the talking. Stay in your vehicles. Echo pulls rear."

It was partly for formation, partly for optics. Legion didn't need babysitting, but the last thing they all needed was a Charonite taking a potshot at Altered armor before the actual work began.

"Two minutes and we roll."

And Miriam returned to the third prowler in the five-vehicle caravan, the rhino van lumbering second to last in the line. She tossed her med pack into the back and slid her sling behind the driver's seat. The new device Yuri had given her jutted awkwardly from inside her bag, its impression unfamiliar.

Hino took the passenger seat and Talwar climbed behind the wheel without a word. Nerves. It *was* only his second mission, and after the first, she understood where it was coming from. The vehicle rocked as Hadeon pulled herself in, her armored mass dragging the suspension taut. The rest of her squad fell into place around them.

Then Gumede appeared, strolling as though on a morning walk, chewing a nutrient bar, weapon slung lazily over one shoulder. Without looking, he pitched the wrapper over his shoulder.

"Cutting it close," Herrera called from the second prowler.

"Nah." Gumede grinned, wiping his hands on his pants. "Keeping everyone on their toes. We ready?"

Miriam felt her expression twitch, smoothing it before anyone could notice.

Gumede cuffed Talwar on the arm with a breezy, "Let's do this," then swung into the last vehicle.

And Miriam took her own seat. As the convoy rolled forward, she watched the outpost walls recede into the distance, the summer heat already dampening her temples. She closed her eyes briefly and concentrated on the vibration of the engine and road travel up through her boots.

Just another mission.

Just one more.

Debris crunched beneath Miriam's boots as she trailed behind Hadeon through the decimated town, indistinguishable from the one they'd passed a month before. Any of Gumede's previous arguments that Echo knew the terrain better than the other SOG teams was pure drivel. And now, this time, the legionnaires stood out against the amoeba of Charlie and Echo grays, popping out like white thumbs, a jarring presence on friendly ground. Not that this place was friendly. Not even close.

Ahead, Charonites clustered in knots, hard looks simmering in the noonday heat. This thing between UMF and Charonites wasn't an alliance, it was convenience. A temporary deal with too many devils.

The checkpoint just behind the crowd looked nearly identical to the last: scavenged panels, a makeshift roof, a crude shack perched on a slab of broken concrete. This brink of town now marked what the Apostates and Heretics had claimed, and where the Charonites had been pushed back. The next town beyond was a fresh cushion zone, a new no-man's-land.

Miriam knew the mission brief—retrieve or destroy whatever Vertex had left behind in its lab, but the deeper question hung in her gut. What the hell were they doing there?

"That's our party," Hino said over Echo's private channel.

Herrera and Bretner moved to meet the checkpoint. A wiry young man stepped down from the shack, face half-buried in a flimsy hood, his body tall and bony. He and Herrera traded words too low to catch.

Behind the marines and legionnaires, more Charonites appeared, fanning out but keeping distance. Dirt-streaked clothes, sun-browned skin, and hard expressions served as their uniform. Miriam spotted red blotches along necks and arms. Junkies here, as well. Their jeers stayed silent, but their stares drove into the Altered among Echo and Charlie.

"They bring the goods?" the Charonite called over his shoulder. Blue eyes blazed from the shadows, then vanished again beneath the hood.

A voice from behind answered in the affirmative.

"Everything agreed upon is in the rhino," Herrera assured.

The young man scratched at his neck, eyes flicking over the five armored legionnaires. "Fine. Deal's a deal." Dirty fingers lifted toward his mouth, but he hesitated. "You've got a short window," he continued, speaking out the side of his mouth. "We're pulling out soon. This town doesn't hold long. Them rats been poking again, probing lines. We're expecting a push."

Then he folded his lips around his fingers and let out a shrill whistle. A dozen more figures emerged from the broken structures. Echo and Charlie's supplemental "force."

Miriam's heart sank. "You've got to be kidding me," she muttered.

These weren't soldiers. They weren't even adults. She clocked them instantly by their posture, their uneven gaits, the too-large rifles that dragged at their shoulders. One might've been in his early twenties, but the others were anywhere from ten to eighteen, the ones closest to her had wisps of facial hair patching their skin as if they were trying to will manhood into being, but their biology hadn't caught up. Miriam was more than twice their age.

"How old are they?" a Charlie marine asked.

"Old enough."

"For what? A fucking carnival ride?"

A scrappy teen stepped forward, squaring his shoulders, and spat onto the cracked pavement between them.

"They're trained. If you're worried," a man behind the line said, older than the rest.

Miriam's cheek twitched. That wasn't the concern.

Not the real one.

"Tan," Hino warned quietly.

But Miriam's words were already out. "How are you any better than the Heretics?"

The same man stepped forward, peeling away from the others. Early thirties, a little younger than Miriam, muscle filling his shirt but not the kind that came from frontline fighting. The way the others shifted around him made his rank and authority obvious.

"You comparin' us to head-chopping psychos who strap bombs to kids?"

Miriam met his glare. *"They're* kids."

"They're adults. UMF's done the same for decades and you're on a soapbox judgin' *us?*"

Her jaw flexed as her attention caught on the youngest in the group, a boy with scruffy light-brown hair falling into his eyes. Was this what Sam had once been? A scrawny twelve-year-old issued a rifle and told to kill for humankind? What made this different? Charonite, Heretic, Apostate, UMF. They all had different rhetorics and missions, but when it all boiled down, the method was the same. Wrap it in duty, honor, loyalty, and dress it in survival. The justification was war, but it opened the door to so much worse.

One of the smaller boys clambered onto a broken ledge and leaned close to Perun's helm. The legionnaire didn't move, his closed visor blank and sealed, but Miriam had spent enough time with Hadeon's squad to imagine the invisible scowl—blue and green eyes burning beneath the armor.

And could Legion judge them? These soldiers had been designed, bred, and ordered for combat from birth. The Altered were no better. Each tier divided into Royal, praetorian, research and science, administration, and the countless "black-market" offshoots that filled the gaps; each caste created for its use.

"What? Training's barbaric only when it's not sanctioned by City Center or UMF?" one of the Charonites challenged.

"There's structure—" Durmaz began.

The man raised a brow.

"You're sending them to their deaths," Miriam said.

"We're resilient," one boy shot back, puffing out. "Born warriors."

This wasn't nature. It was nurture. Would they all end up like Sam? Shaped too early by the craving to belong. By fear, by adrenaline mistaken for courage, and by the wrong kind of praise? The Charonites were already dosing them, feeding them stims and supplements. It was dependency masquerading as resilience. They parroted lines and false pride, repeating what they'd been told. Plasticity was mistaken for willpower, as if raw youth could stand against the enemies waiting on the far side of no-man's-land.

"Brave warriors," the man crowed, rallying the others with a grin that curdled Miriam's stomach.

"Tan." Hino's voice, warning.

Miriam didn't turn. Her jaw locked, her lips pressed into a hard line. There was nothing more she could say that would change this moment, nothing that would take the rifles out of those children's hands. The cards were already dealt.

"We're burning daylight and wasting breath," the Charonite said, his tone flat with finality. "They volunteered. They're ready."

And Miriam's eyes lingered on the youngest faces. She could already see them in her dreams, could feel the familiar weight pressing at the edges of her mind. Nightmares she thought had dulled over years of service, threatened to return in vivid focus. She knew every mind carried its scars differently, but disgust rose hot and sour in her throat all the same.

Her expression hardened, but she felt the ache behind it. She was too tired, too old for this shit. Just a mission, she reminded herself, though the words landed hollow. Just a couple more months.

"Do we want to keep standing around?" the hooded Charonite snapped, impatient. "Job's not getting done any faster."

"Just tell them to keep their fucking guns out of my face," one of the Charlie marines growled, forcing his way forward.

Then the formation shifted forward, each unit peeling back into its own orbit—Charlie at the front, Hadeon and her armored squad following, then Echo closing the gap. As Miriam moved, Hino's hand brushed her shoulder, a subtle anchor. Miriam jerked free, her pace unbroken.

"Fucking cowards," she muttered, the words more exhale than speech.

She tracked the Charonite adolescents as they fanned out clumsily, rifles too long for their arms, forming a perimeter around the UMF caravan. It was bordering on comical, if it weren't so sickening. Children sent to guard marines and Altered soldiers. Children sent to do the dirty work.

Miriam's stomach tightened, and her jaw clamped until her teeth ached. She understood the desperation—resources stretched thin, wars demanding more than anyone could give— but that knowledge didn't diminish the disgust simmering within her.

This wasn't necessity.

It was failure.

It was humanity digging into a new low, one deeper than she'd thought they could reach.

18

THRESHOLD

"HEADS ON A SWIVEL," Hino muttered over the visor as they crossed what must've been the invisible territorial line out of no-man's-land and into Heretic ground. The transition was uneventful, but the landscape told its own story. Craters gouged the earth in every direction, deeper than Miriam remembered. Or perhaps she had forgotten how bad it truly was.

The scars went beyond shellfire. Whole swaths of terrain lay pale and dead, leeched of color and life where the Blightbringers had passed. The air held a metallic tang and the taste of soil gone sour. Nothing green dared take root in this ground. Wrongness clung, rising through the soles of Miriam's boots until it settled like cement in her chest.

As Echo advanced in staggered formation, the legionnaires pushed ahead, their hulking white forms stark against soot-stained ruin. Up front, Perun, his ax attached to his back, stepped over a collapsed wall as if it were a pebble. The scale difference between him and the adolescent Charonites trailing nearby bordered on absurd. Miriam nearly believed he could punt one of the kids clean across the disputed land without breaking stride.

She adjusted her stance automatically, shoulders low and tight, fingers wrapping her rifle grip. There was no movement beyond their group, and they weren't prioritizing stealth, but her body remembered how to move in Apostate territory.

On her wrist, her commcuff flickered. Network degradation was expected, especially considering the constant transference of regional ownership. Countermeasures stacked over counter-countermeasures until the whole system buckled. Communication would be patchy the rest of the way, but as long as the team stayed in proximity, their channels would continue to work. Miriam glanced at Durmaz's pack and the long-range unit strapped there. They'd need it to work for any air support.

Ahead, Hadeon raised her hand. Legionnaires and marines froze, then crouched in unison, sweeping into cover. Out of the corner of her eye, Miriam caught the Charonite youths throwing themselves flat in the dirt where they stood. At least they had the sense to stay quiet.

"Tangos?" Gumede whispered.

Hadeon's helmet dipped. A silent no.

"So, is that it?" Gumede pressed.

The answer came without words. One by one, the five legionnaires shifted from cover, weaving between the skeleton of a downed structure and the rusted husk of what might have been a prowler. Their movements were precise, unspoken, and long-practiced. Miriam raised her rifle and scanned her sector, the weight steadying her as her stomach remained taut.

Across the way, Charlie's lead leaned into the oldest of the Charonites. A few quiet words passed, then he looked back to his team and Echo. "These guys confirmed it's past this block," Herrera said. "Hold for Hadeon's signal."

"Can't believe we're taking instructions from alties and kids," Talwar muttered at Miriam's side.

She kept her eyes forward, jaw tight. It wasn't worth answering.

And the silence stretched, broken only by the faint buzz of their comms. Then, a soft squelch hissed over the visor channel, but no visual followed. No flash of white armor.

Miriam's brows drew down. That was odd. She wasn't the only one who noticed. Shifts of unease passed through Echo's line.

"Charlie-1, any visual?" Gumede asked.

Herrera turned and shook his head once. Negative.

"Alright, well," Gumede said. "Have a couple of the kids push out, just in case."

"Use them as canaries?" Hino responded, her hand over her visor. "No. Wait for Hadeon's signal. You can't send them out first."

Gumede shrugged, lips twisting. "That's what they're there for, right?"

"Fuck, Goom. That's someone's child."

"*I'm* someone's child." He rolled his eyes. "They want to play grown-up soldier? I'm giving them the chance. We've all got a job. They've got theirs, and right now it means going to see if it's safe."

Miriam's tongue pushed against her teeth. She kept her rifle high, but her eyes cut toward Gumede, disbelief hardening her face. However, another sound squawked over the comms, followed by the faintest shift of white—one of Hadeon's legionnaires edging around the jagged corner of a collapsed wall.

Miriam adjusted her gear, already anticipating the next movement. Every nerve itched at the waiting, standing still when threats were unknown. With the Apostates, the Heretics, it was never a question of *if* they would come. It was *when*.

Charlie's lead cut a glance toward Echo, a wordless prompt.

"Let's go, team," Gumede grumbled. He slapped King's kit in passing and announced over the visor, "Moving."

Echo broke cover in staggered pairs, boots crunching across debris-strewn pavement. Miriam moved with them, her weapon raised, eyes sweeping the empty windows and frames of buildings. They passed a legionnaire posted at the street's lip, who didn't so much as flick an eye toward them, helmet fixed ahead, angle locked. The others held their stations with equal discipline, white armor stark and unwavering against the ruin.

At the block's far end stood what might once have been a hardware store, though the splintered sign was the only trace left of its old identity. Looted, gutted, and burned. And waiting before it, posture stiff, was Hadeon.

It didn't look like a lab. But Miriam didn't dwell on it long. She fell in with Echo, sliding into position, filling the gaps behind two legionnaires already forming a loose circle of defense. Miriam caught a glimpse of Perun's broad silhouette vanishing through the store's wrecked doorway, another legionnaire shadowing him on the flank. Charlie's marines and the Charonites spread wider, forming a second ring.

"This is it?" Gumede asked.

Hino checked her cuff, then gave a nod.

"Inside," Hadeon confirmed, helm drawn back.

"Already cleared?"

Her mismatched green and blue eyes burned before she stepped over the threshold. "Come."

Echo filed in after her, reluctant but obedient. Inside, the ruin looked as if a dozen disc grenades had gone off at once, but the walls had held. Reinforced? That explained why it hadn't collapsed outright. Would they ever have noticed this place in passing? Miriam doubted anyone would have recognized it without coordinates directing them straight there.

They moved toward the back, boots crunching glass and plaster, each step raising a fresh stir of dust. Miriam's throat contracted against the urge to cough as they climbed over beams and collapsed shelving to where the wreckage ended in a narrow corridor half-caved in. Beyond the choke point outside, she glimpsed Perun and the other legionnaire, motionless sentinels, holding the area.

Within seconds the back room felt crowded with Echo crammed shoulder to shoulder and Hadeon filling the space with her silent bulk. Gumede opened his mouth, confusion plain on his face, but Hino cut him short with a raised hand. She gestured crisply, directing Miriam, Talwar, Durmaz, and King back.

Just outside, Miriam watched the team second and intelligence specialist move around Gumede along the back wall, fingers skimming every dent, systematic and searching. Understanding dawned. Hino was looking for a trigger, a seam, some hidden or visual cue. Miriam bit back a curse. Vertex and Command had sent them in blind with no schematics and no details.

"Why the back room?" Miriam whispered, moving closer to Hadeon, who'd stepped out of the room as well. The coordinates had led them to this store, but why had the senior taken them past the main floor?

"There is a...smell," Hadeon said. "Very faint, but stronger. Here."

Hino froze mid-search, head lifting. A soft click answered. Subtle and delicate. A panel shifting?

"Talwar," Hino called.

The engineer hurried forward.

Miriam's stomach squeezed. "Smell?" She glanced out toward the storefront, toward the restless perimeter outside. "Chemicals?"

Hadeon tilted her helm. "Clean. But not. I cannot explain it."

Miriam met her mismatched gaze. What the hell was this place? Neither of them liked what they didn't understand.

Gumede's voice cut through again. "Hino? What's the holdup?" Too loud.

Miriam clenched her jaw. As much as she wished he'd lower his voice, she did agree with him. They were moving too slow, staying too long. Every extra second here stretched the risk.

Hino bent closer to the wall. "It's old," she murmured. "No, it's mechanical. Do we have a code?"

Gumede's face blanked. Then recognition flooded. He fumbled through his kit until he plucked out a small, blocky device and tossed it to Talwar. Miriam caught a glimpse as the engineer steadied it in his palms. A small analog display, an old-generation device that felt all too familiar. She had seen one before, but the memory slipped before she could place it.

A glare sparked across Hino's face. The second hadn't known about this either. So much for open communication and transparency. So much for contingencies. They were being strung along. Set up to stumble, if not fail outright.

Device in hand, Talwar crouched, following the scrawl on its narrow display as he worked the wall panel. He manipulated a sequence of different combinations and manual switches inside. It didn't take long before he was done and took a step back.

At first, nothing moved. Then a hiss, like breath released after being held too long. Miriam felt it more than she heard it, a draft across her skin. For a heartbeat, she wondered if she smelled what Hadeon had mentioned. Surrounded by the musk of destruction, it was a specter of nothingness but also sour at the edges. Wrong.

Hadeon was right. She couldn't explain it.

"I've got a door," Hino said. "Stairs."

"Let's get this moving." Gumede shouldered past.

"Wait—" Hino started, but he was already inside the small room.

Hadeon followed, and Miriam fell in behind. But they didn't get far. Gumede had stopped short, already backpedaling, bumping into the others. In front of him, a hatch gaped in the floor, metal stairs leading down into blackness. All of Gumede's confidence had bottomed out.

Rifle angled low, Miriam held. The last time Echo had taken stairs down, it hadn't ended well. And though it was midday, the back room seemed darker with the maw open, whatever shadow below pitching out.

"Torch," Hino whispered.

Gumede didn't move.

"Goom."

He looked back, throat working. "Hadeon? Maybe one of yours takes lead?"

Hadeon didn't call for her legionnaires. She moved forward, clipped her rifle to her back, and drew a short rod. With a flick, it expanded into a doubled-edged blade, her close-quarters weapon of choice. Her eyes glowed green as she stepped down into the dark.

Under Talwar's wide-eyed stare, Hino followed. Miriam took a deep breath, maneuvered around Gumede, and descended a few steps. Below, Hadeon had already stopped in a medium-sized chamber. The beam of Hino's torch caught her tapetum, the reflection burning in the gloom.

"There is another door here," Hadeon said.

"Breached?" Gumede asked from above.

"No. Talwar?" Hino's voice carried up.

The engineer slipped past the lead and Miriam, moving quickly but cautiously, and joined the others at the bottom. Hadeon shifted back to give him space in front of the heavy door set into the far wall.

"Goom, check in with Charlie and the others?" Hino offered while Talwar worked at the large door.

"Right," the lead muttered, already retreating.

Miriam glanced back at the narrow stairwell. So far, everything Vertex and Command had given them had panned out—barring the glaring pieces they *hadn't* bothered to mention. And despite the relative quiet, she didn't relax.

"Bingo," Talwar whispered.

Miriam leaned toward the hatch, peering into the now lit space below where Hino had aimed her torch upward into a corner.

The door cracked open. From where Miriam stood, it was like a vault; she could see the material's thickness. There was no chance someone could have forced it easily. Not even legionnaires or someone with heavy tools. Miriam realized something else. Nothing about the space looked disturbed. There was no dust, like the rest of the store, no footprints or tracks.

Something was off.

If the mission was to destroy, Talwar and Charlie's engineer didn't carry enough det to breach that kind of door, let alone erase whatever Vertex was guarding. How large was this facility? And how far did it run underneath? The entire storefront above was no bigger than one of UMF Station's annexes, yet the hidden construction below suggested something far more sprawling.

Hino stepped in to help Talwar brace the door, and it swung heavily until it locked into a recessed groove in the adjoining wall. Miriam shifted to get a better look, but her vantage was poor. She couldn't see inside. At the threshold, her teammates and Hadeon waited. No one crossed.

"What is that?" Talwar asked, voice low.

"I don't know. A wall? A window?" Hino adjusted her torch. The beam caught and reflected sparsely off whatever lay beyond the doorway. Glass or something close to it.

Talwar raised the old-generation device. "I don't see another console."

"Is it pressure-sensitive? Do we just...walk in? Push?"

Hadeon stepped back up the stairwell, and Miriam caught the subtle change in her posture. The Altered woman's nose twitched. The scent. Whatever Hadeon had sensed before, it must've been stronger now.

"What's going on?" Gumede barked. His head popped through the backroom entrance.

Miriam flinched.

"Some barrier," Hino answered without looking up.

"Okay, but it's open, right? Let's get a move on. Talwar."

But their teammate didn't move. None of them did.

Because the gunfire came first. A single burst split the air outside. The sound sliced through them like a wire drawn tight.

Everyone froze.

Miriam's pulse spiked, a hot stab behind her eyes. For a heartbeat, the world held still. She couldn't see beyond the main floor, but Durmaz and King had crept forward, rifles high, bodies rigid, waiting for a target that hadn't yet shown itself.

"Sitrep!" Hino demanded over the visor channel.

"One of the kids!" Herrera's voice came back, strained with disbelief. "What was he shooting at—" His words cut out mid-sentence, the question clearly meant for his own team.

Accidental? Perhaps someone's nerves had given out and with that, a negligent squeeze of the trigger.

King glanced back. "There's nothing out there."

Kids on the line were dangerous enough, but firing into nothing? No enemy, no movement in the wreckage. None of it made sense.

And then another volley clapped, louder this time. Shouts rose behind it, confusion tangled within.

"What the fuck is he doing?" King muttered.

Whatever the Charonite had set off, it was drawing attention like blood in the water.

Then Miriam's gut twisted. A new sound ripped through the clamor: an electric murmuration followed by the hard snap of legionnaire weapons. The charge-up was unmistakable. It didn't belong to the Charonites or SOG rifles. Miriam felt the air pull from her lungs.

Hadeon surged forward, armor brushing past as she moved into the main space without hesitation. If she was speaking to her team, Miriam couldn't make it out.

"Tan! What's happening?" Hino shouted, halfway up the stairs.

But there was no space for explanation. A heavier fusillade

erupted, layered with deeper concussions and the zipping burn of Altered weapons. Not the legionnaires' this time. It was the Apostates', or worse, the Heretics'.

At the lip of the mangled storefront, Durmaz and King dropped into cover. They held position but didn't fire; they had no visual on what the Charonites and legionnaires were shooting at. Only noise and disorder. Miriam slid in beside Hadeon, bracing against a toppled shelf, straining to catch sight.

Across the street, Charlie held formation, their muzzles flaring behind broken walls, firing west. Dust spat up where return fire lashed back.

"How'd they find us?" Gumede yelled. "How'd your team miss them?"

Hadeon turned her head, but King interrupted any response.

"Hey! No—fuck! The kids!" He waved his left arm, but whatever attention he was trying to get failed. "They're running!"

Miriam turned in time to see them, small shapes bolting from cover, weapons clutched awkwardly, limbs uncoordinated in the way only panic could make them. The Charonites had abandoned their positions—had abandoned *them.*

Some stragglers stayed, kneeling and firing in jerks, hanging on to the small cover they had. One boy opened fire and toppled back from the recoil. A couple of others clutched their weapons, paralyzed while Charlie and the two legionnaires laid suppressive fire.

"We've got ten, maybe twelve!" Herrera's voice snapped through comms. "West side! Possible flank your way! We're holding, so get this thing done!"

"Hadeon—" Hino began, but the senior legionnaire was already a step ahead.

Two sets of armored steps thundered past as the rest of her squad pushed to reinforce.

"There are more coming," Hadeon said, evenly. She paused. "Vehicle. Something large."

"Fuck," Hino muttered. She glanced at the lead, who only mumbled out a stream of low and aimless expletives, like he'd forgotten the channel was open.

In the absence of orders, Hino toggled her visor. "Charlie-1, you copy? Possible technical. Worse." She then turned to the others while she waited for Herrera's response. "King, Durmaz —you're up! Assist Charlie! Hold them back."

But at that moment, it all stopped.

The firefight outside stuttered, then ceased.

A second passed.

Two.

"Why aren't they pushing?" Talwar whispered.

That was when Miriam heard it. A shrill, descending whistle. Her gut turned, and dread raked her skin.

"DOWN!" she yelled, hitting the floor.

19

———————

EXTRACTION

THE FIRST SHELL HIT OUTSIDE. Talwar and King dropped flat, arms over their heads. The next landed on the roof. The building groaned, beams rattling as dust sifted down in clouds. Each impact followed the same dreadful rhythm: whistle, boom, shock wave.

Miriam stayed prone, one arm shielding her head, the other braced against her rifle as she tracked the bedlam outside. Another round struck close. The wall beside her shuddered. Then nothing.

The seconds that followed weren't relief. They were loaded and fragile. Hadeon rose from her crouch and was gone, already moving into the open. Miriam pushed up after her, sweeping for her team and any ensuing injuries. There were visible cuts and scrapes, but nothing critical. Outside, white-armored legionnaires regrouped, gliding through the wreckage like wraiths.

A voice crackled through her visor. "We're good here."

Others followed. No casualties.

Then gunfire roared anew.

"Talwar! Tan! Get below and find the weapon!" Hino shouted. "You've got three minutes!"

Miriam pivoted for the hatch, Talwar behind her.

But she met resistance.

Gumede's hand clamped on her arm. "No," he said, breath ragged. "We need to retreat before they trap us in."

More whistles rode the gunfire, followed by fresh impacts that rattled the structure. Miriam ducked low, trying to wrench free, but her lead's grip tightened.

They were exposed, but they were there and close to done. The legionnaires and Charlie still held the perimeter. It wasn't the best defense point, but they'd held worse before. Miriam glanced toward the open hatch. They were right there.

Gumede reached for his visor.

Miriam's hand outstretched. "No, wait—"

"Abort!" he shouted. "Abort!"

Herrera's voice fired off in her ear. "Say again? Are we holding or bailing?"

"Retreat!"

And then Echo's lead did the dumbest thing yet.

He ran.

Straight past Hadeon, past Hino, bursting out into the street. He slammed into cover beside King and Durmaz, hugging the dead skeleton of a vehicle.

"What the—" Hino started, but Gumede had already pushed King and Durmaz toward Charlie's line.

"What the fuck—where is he going?" Talwar yelled.

Over the visor, Herrera was also baffled. "Echo-1, what are you—"

"We've got to go! We can't stay here!" Gumede's voice shook over comms.

Someone needed to shut him down. Fear and panic were contagious.

Hino pivoted back, visor catching the light. She raised a hand toward the hatch, weighing her options fast. "Tan, get down there. Lock it up. Talwar, with me."

"But the weapon? Det?" Talwar's voice broke. "We're supposed to secure the damn site! The mission—"

"Lock it up. Now."

Miriam didn't argue. She hit the stairs two at a time, boots pounding, knees jarred with each step. Darkness claimed her vision before she skidded to a halt before the vault.

Beyond the door stood a partition, a seamless frosted composite, ethereally glowing with embedded strips within its frame. Light bled through in a hazy wash, diffuse and sterile, obscuring whatever lay beyond. She pulled at the heavy door, straining until it groaned free of its groove. But the mechanism snagged and wouldn't lock fully.

"Tan!" Hino's voice cracked like a whip. "We've got to move!"

"It's not lock—"

"It's good enough!"

Miriam bolted. She nearly collided with the second at the top of the stairs. Hino hammered her palm against the mechanical panel and the hatch sealed, folding clean into the floor until it looked untouched. If Miriam hadn't come from below, she wouldn't have known it was there at all.

By the time they spilled out into the street, gunfire was everywhere. Shapes darted through the southern ruins, shadows between unsound walls. Talwar and King were already firing, rifles barking in short bursts. They were being surrounded. Their flank was gone. Gunfire rattled farther ahead in longer sprays, ragged and less controlled. The other Charonite youth who'd fled toward no-man's-land.

Then, for one long second, a scream split the ruckus. Miriam strained to hear more, but nothing. Their enemy was tightening the noose, trying to box them in.

Charlie's comms buzzed in her visor. Their specialist was already calling for air support, an evacuation. They had escalated straight to the last resort. Everything had fallen apart in less than a minute.

Miriam held her breath, wondering if the signal would make it through. The marines and legionnaires were too deep, and between the countermeasures, there was too much interference, too much motion, too much heat.

But the response came, crisp in her ears.

"Ten mikes!" Charlie's second shouted.

Others repeated it, a chorus of echoes.

Ten minutes. Could they reach no-man's-land in that time? Or at least close enough?

Hino's orders snapped them forward, and what was left of Echo collapsed toward Charlie's position. Gumede was already well ahead, barreling after the Charonite teenagers, the few still running. Miriam glimpsed their bodies scattered in the dirt like discarded gear. King trailed in the lead's wake.

It was the only choice left. Their lead had sealed it, shattering any formation, any cohesion they'd had. They couldn't stay.

"Echo's moving!" Hino called, directing Durmaz and Talwar forward.

Two clicks came in response from Charlie.

"Let's go, kid!" Durmaz hauled a Charonite teen upright by the arm as she passed. The boy stumbled but kept pace.

Then the line peeled back in staggered pairs. Cover, move. Cover, move.

Miriam hadn't seen the enemy yet, but she knew they were there. Shadows darted between collapsed walls, motion at the fringes of her sight. They were there, steering the marines, Charonites, and legionnaires, already forcing their retreat off course, causing tighter turns and cutting their angles short.

Their enemy knew the terrain better. And their Charonite escorts, the youth, though acquainted, were not suited for this stress. Miriam caught sight of one boy across the street. He was small, light, and lagging. He turned, yelled something, then opened fire.

It was too much gun for his body. The rifle kicked wildly.

She wanted to shout at him, tell him not to stop, to keep running, but he planted his feet and stood his ground.

Bravado. This was what happened when you trained fear out of children. Sometimes it worked too well, overriding what nature would've made sure to prevent. Sometimes running was the better option.

A streak sliced across the boy's breast and sparked against the wall behind him. He didn't scream, just went rigid. Miriam clenched her jaw and forced herself forward. She didn't dare move toward him. If he panicked and turned that weapon her way…

"Keep moving!" she yelled instead.

More zips and rounds fired, and she looked away. Even if they hadn't been obviously fatal, she wouldn't have been able to stop and help.

"Durmaz, update!" Hino called out.

"Too hot," came the breathless reply. "Ships can't land. Half a click out. Flat ground!"

"King!"

Two clicks answered. Miriam had lost sight of him and their lead. They'd have to trust it, make it work.

The rest of Echo advanced forward in a staggered, unsustainable run, bodies burning as they approached more level ground. Miriam risked a glance back, finding the first bobbing heads of Charlie as they followed a block behind. White armor trailed farther, holding down the rear and firing back.

Herrera's voice rasped through the channel. "Charlie, hold at the next structure. We've got perimeter with Legion. Echo, secure the LZ."

"What about the mortars?" Talwar shouted behind Miriam.

Hino shot him a hard look, sweat streaming down her face. No words were necessary. They all understood it was a tremendous risk. The heavy weaponry had stopped once they started moving, but the moment they held position to mark a landing zone, they'd be targets again. And this time with less cover. And worse, the aircraft and pilots would also be in danger.

Herrera had made the right call holding back at the buildings. The terrain gave way toward the ass-end of town, less cluttered and more exposed with structures spaced farther apart. But there was no real choice left. Echo and Charlie were slowing. They were being funneled, herded like cattle. They wouldn't outrun their enemies like this. Legion might, but the rest couldn't. And no one knew how many were out there, chasing them, stalking them. With the area lit up by gunfire and noise, Miriam knew the other side's reinforcements were on their way. And they were fast. Faster.

Hino shouted new orders, and Miriam dropped into the cover of a single home beside Talwar, one knee slamming into the ground, rifle tucked into her shoulder. Most of the fire came from the rear, but she swept her new area and sector.

Somewhere behind them, something hissed. Smoke. Miriam twisted enough to see the green plume rising. King or Durmaz had marked the landing zone with canisters. It was improvised, exposed, and uneven, but it would have to be enough.

"Durmaz?" Hino snapped.

"Five mikes!"

Five.

Miriam's pulse thudded in her throat. How had it only been five minutes? Time moved like tar and lightning at once. And the wait was excruciating. They held their positions, digging into the surrounding destruction, counting seconds that seemed to stretch into hours. Gunfire rattled again on top of its constant baseline. Miriam stayed low behind wrecked cover, eyes trained on her sector, but it was empty. Still, she scanned.

Behind her, someone cried out, but there was no call for her. Charlie's own medic was probably addressing the injury. From what she could make out, it wasn't serious. She stayed locked on her post.

Then King's light machine gun roared to life. He'd circled back—left Gumede with Durmaz near the plume. Talwar shifted beside her, rifle ready, but still hadn't fired. Neither had she. But the line behind them was holding. She kept waiting for the inevitable whine or whistle.

"Where are they? Where are they?" Gumede's voice jittered between gunfire.

Then came the sound, like a purr, nearly nonexistent. And then a low rumble rising over the storm of weapons. Airships. Relief poked through Miriam's ribs, only to be snatched away. Fear surged in. The tempo of the gunfire climbed. The aircraft were motivators now. Beacons. Targets.

"We can't stay here!" Gumede yelled. "We need another LZ!"

Miriam's jaw set, and she risked another glance back. The ships were already inbound, dipping low and avoiding the projectiles from the enemies—wide shots—but they had to be quick. The Apostates or Heretics would dial in their weapons. SOG and Legion were exposed, but the lines were holding. They had a shot. As they pivoted, Charlie's position vanished behind smoke.

"Are we crashing?" Herrera said over the visor, voice fraught with exertion. "Echo, are we good to move?"

Hino's reply was drowned out by Gumede. "Tell them to hold off!" The lead waved his arms frantically at the descending aircraft like they were insects he could scare away.

And Hino turned on him. She crossed the distance in strides, seized his armor, and ripped the visor from his head. Miriam couldn't make out her words, but the second shouted at him.

Surprisingly, Gumede didn't resist. He only nodded.

Hino jabbed a finger at Durmaz, then back to their lead, another incomprehensible command on her tongue. Then came the sound that tore Miriam's attention sideways. Gunfire, closer.

"Echo! Need—" The transmission skipped. "Need cover—"

Hino slashed her hand toward Miriam. Her mouth rounded the one-syllable word. *Go.*

Miriam was already up. She slapped Talwar's shoulder hard, then King's. "With me!"

They sprinted back, skipping the usual staggered movement. Miriam keyed her visor. "Charlie, three coming in. Friendlies, friendlies."

When they reached the next building's frame, Miriam barely stopped, smashing into it. She let the pain anchor her and snapped her rifle up. Shadows danced between cover past the other SOG team, and she sent rounds chasing them.

At an angle in front of them, Charlie's squad was pinned. Legion had repositioned, pulling fire elsewhere, but it had left Charlie exposed on one side, and the enemy had poured into the gap, exploiting it.

"Move! Move!" King bellowed, his LMG laying down fire in brutal bursts.

Charlie peeled back in pairs as Miriam squeezed her trigger. In between, she crouched and reloaded with shaky fingers. She had somehow already sped through most of her magazines.

And then the inevitable came. The zips slowed, and the whistles followed.

Miriam lost sight of the field as she drove herself into the ground, trying to minimize her presence as the impacts came around them. King was the first back up, his LMG rattling off in relentless bursts, holding the lull together with brute noise.

"Medic!"

The call came again. Urgent.

Miriam's head snapped up. A Charlie marine was dragging a limp body across the rubble.

"Go!" King shouted. Talwar fired steadily on his other side.

Miriam sprinted, crossing the open gap. She slid into the cover of a wrecked vehicle and dropped to her knees beside the downed marine. Her stomach turned.

Herrera.

The lead's pants were soaked through, blood dark and spreading. The fabric hung in tatters at his groin and hip, where thigh met torso, as if something had chewed through him.

She was already reaching for her kit. Tourniquet. Gauze. Pressure. The noise faded around her, still a thrum in her ears but compartmentalized away. She ripped fabric open, ignoring his stammering stream of half-formed pleas. The wound was gaping. His hands fluttered toward the injury, toward his groin, but Miriam batted them away.

"Hold him," she snapped at the other marine.

She packed the dressing hard into the meat of the wound, but the blood still came. Too much. She ignored the man's bucking body and his wretched screams. She shoved more gauze in, tried to wedge it like a cork, but the placement was wrong. The tourniquet slipped, failed to catch.

Herrera's screams shredded into broken gasps. His voice cracked around one desperate word: "My—my—"

The other marine shushed him, whispering comforts Miriam didn't have time for. She didn't have time to talk.

Her hand brushed the jutting case in her kit. Yuri's device. She froze for a split second. Could it help? The thing was too small; it wasn't meant for this kind of devastation.

In the end, she returned to the wound, leaning into Herrera. He screamed again, body arching. Pressure. She needed more. She substituted her knee for her hands and dug in, anchoring her weight. At last she cinched the tourniquet over the mass of gauze and pulled until it bit deep.

Hands grabbed her shoulders. Someone called her name. She ripped away from them.

"Tan."

A voice, firm and final.

Her world tilted.

"Stop. He's gone."

And finally, her body sagged. She pulled back, hands shaking, drenched in blood. It slicked her pants, sticky against her skin. She tried to wipe them on her thighs, but it smeared, an impossible stain.

And then Bretner was there, Charlie's second. She regarded Herrera's body without expression, then nodded once and issued orders. She and another marine lifted his body and hauled him away. Another set of hands lifted Miriam, yanking her upright. She stumbled, half-deaf to Talwar's shouting, her legs numb as she staggered after him toward the LZ.

The airships hovered low now, bay doors open. Miriam watched as Bretner and the others continued forward, Herrera's body between them.

One good team lead. Dead.

Gumede's pale face loomed from the other airship. One bad team lead. Alive.

Unfair didn't cover it.

"Legion?" Hino said over the visor. She motioned hard at Talwar and Miriam, still straggling.

Hadeon came back calm. "We can get out. Go."

The first airship had already lifted, its propulsion system kicking up a small dirtstorm that needled Miriam's skin and grated in her teeth. She raised an arm to shield her face, squinting as the transport veered up and away. She and Talwar pushed forward, boots skidding across the broken terrain.

Then the world rifted. A skirling, rising whine, then—

Impact.

The structure beside them exploded, not with fire but force, a concussive blast that sent rubble arcing through the air. A chunk of concrete clipped Miriam's shoulder and spun her sideways, the ground colliding up with her. She coughed, spat dust, and forced herself upright. A haze of powdered debris hung over the zone, and her ears felt like they had been torn open. She staggered toward the rising silhouette of the second airship, now surrounded in pandemonium.

Durmaz and King were tugging someone—Hino—toward the bay doors. Blood streaked her armor, one leg at an odd cant. She fought against them, yelling, trying to turn back.

Miriam broke into a run, boots slipping on the shifting rubble. Talwar was at her side, his words drowned out by the whine of engines, propulsion systems, and the staccato of gunfire. The street tore open beneath their feet. The bay doors gaped open just ahead. Close. Just close enough to make her believe they could reach them.

But then a line of shots strafed the street, and Miriam dove, rolled behind a concrete slab. When she looked up, the airship was rising.

"No—no, wait!" Talwar shouted, waving one arm high.

They couldn't hear him. Engines screamed, ascent gunned. Shapes crowded the bay doors. Their teammates, mouths moving, hands reaching, but it was already too late. The ship banked hard, spitting countermeasures in every direction. Dirt whipped up, and Miriam threw her arm across her face, squinting through grit.

When she lowered it, the sky was empty.

Gone.

Shit. Magnet.

20

RESCISSION

"THEY LEFT US." Talwar's voice broke. "They fucking left us."

Miriam didn't answer. She bent forward, palm on her knee, chest heaving. Her pulse hammered loud in her ears. Through the settling haze of dust, she found the airships' dark silhouettes, small and shrinking. Irretrievable and gone.

Talwar raised his comms, but Miriam knew it was futile. Even if countermeasures weren't in place, the aircraft weren't coming back. Not anytime soon. Not with the Altered watching.

A hard crack split the air, and the ground to her left erupted, gravel and chunks of concrete flying. Miriam lunged, yanking Talwar down with her. They dove behind the carcass of a flipped vehicle as another hail of fire came, scattered and wild. It wasn't suppressing fire, nor was it aimed. Had the Apostates seen them? Worse, were they Heretics? Did they know they were there? Left behind? The two of them held, trying to temper their respirations.

Footsteps came next, and two shapes emerged through the dust. It was close enough that Miriam could count them, close enough she could read their posture.

Miriam didn't breathe, just gestured toward another wreck

down the street. She and Talwar moved in tandem, crouched low, rifles tense in their hands, trying to keep wreckage between themselves and the advancing figures. Behind the first pair, more shadows fanned out, spreading like a net.

The two of them slipped under a fallen support beam into the shell of a collapsed building where the interior was dim but concealing. A temporary shelter.

Miriam dropped to a knee and peered through a cleft in the wall. She could make out six enemies now. At least. They advanced with the assurance of predators, confidence in a pack as they made a slow, deliberate perimeter around the marines' hasty landing zone. One kicked a UMF smoke canister aside.

Although Miriam was happy for the eternal daylight in the North, part of her missed the dark, the blanket of security, even if it was only an illusion. The enemies outside were waiting. They knew. Or she thought they did. Had they seen her and Talwar, or were they sweeping the wreckage blind?

Then a shout cut the air, cruel and mocking. Miriam flinched as another Altered strode into the scene, dragging a compact shape by the collar. A boy. A Charonite, unarmed, his face slack with shock, already past horrifying fear. Two enemies circled him, jeering as they closed in.

Miriam's stomach turned. She looked away, bile rising. In the chaos, she'd forgotten about the Charonites.

We can't stay here, she mouthed to Talwar.

His eyes widened, and he shook his head.

She understood his trepidation. This was the last place their team had seen them. Protocol said to wait, to hold for recovery if separated, but her visor was scrambled and fried, her comms intermittent at best. Talwar's blinked, but without a repeater, without a long-range, their signal couldn't punch through.

They were on their own.

Outside, something crunched. Miriam lowered herself into the ground, breath shallow. More boots.

Talwar poked her, his own mouth moving silently. *Then where?*

She sifted through options, none of them good. The gunfire that had marked and masked Legion's retreat was gone, no more volleys from their last direction. The legionnaires would already be far ahead and moving fast. Trying to chase them down would be suicide.

Miriam shaped one word with her lips. *Back.*

Talwar looked ready to argue, but his jaw worked once, and he finally gave a reluctant nod.

It was the best choice they had. The store, the Vertex site, meant shelter. The door beneath that hatch was already open. Vertex's systems might no longer detect breaches, but devices inside could be live, fixable, or usable. If they could reach it.

She and Talwar were SOG marines. They'd trained for worst-case scenarios, and this was, unfortunately, one of them. Their priority was to avoid death, evade capture. Especially with the Apostates. Especially with the Heretics. A decision had to be made. Making none was worse.

And Miriam took the lead, but not before she glanced back at the Altered and the now *two* young Charonites sprawled in the dust at their feet. She grimaced and turned away. There was nothing they could do. Not without throwing their own lives away.

And so they left. Their movement was painfully slow, every step calculated and every space cleared. Every open stretch was a leap of dumb faith. It was counterintuitive; it felt wrong, backward, to head deeper into enemy ground, away from no-man's-land, away from potential escape, but it was the smarter move. Out there, they were exposed, with no cover and nothing but a killing field around them. It was the right move.

But time dragged like sludge. Miriam cataloged everything —the turns, the open areas, the possible chokepoints. Yet with all their maneuvering, they'd barely cleared a handful of blocks.

The facility site felt no closer, and her body ached from crouching, moving, and freezing.

Then her ears perked up.

Gunfire stuttered out. Distant.

She dropped low and signaled Talwar.

A single rifle cracked, then more.

"Legion?" he whispered, edging closer.

Miriam shook her head. Hadeon and her squad hadn't gone that way, and this didn't sound like them. The cadence was wrong. Too frantic, too uneven. It could be the Charonites or it could be Apostates with stolen gear, but it wasn't celebratory. She'd been in enough firefights that she knew the difference.

Miriam tucked her rifle to her and sliced a hand forward. The direction was risky, but so was staying put. Someone was shooting at Apostates, or causing them to shoot back, and that made whoever was out there potential allies, or at least enemies-of-their-enemies adjacent.

Talwar didn't argue. They pivoted toward the noise, moving quicker now. The fight drew them like a beacon in the fog. It was a strange hope. Exactly the opposite of what they wanted, but for now, it meant a possible escape.

Or a trap. Miriam brushed that out of her mind. Either way, it beat waiting around to be discovered.

She slowed as the gunfire swelled, and at the street corner, she shouldered her pack, lifted her rifle, and pressed her side flat against the rusted wall. Ahead, the sounds of fighting rose into a full crescendo with shots, screams, and someone shouting orders.

She held up a fist, and Talwar stopped behind her. They needed a visual first. Neither wanted to walk into the wrong end of a barrel.

So Miriam peeked around the wall. She spotted armor a few blocks down, black and dark green. An individual faced the other direction, leaning too casually against a crumbling wall, watching the firefight ahead, as if detached from it.

She wasn't used to seeing the armor. It wasn't Legion or UMF. Other than the colors, it was a stripped-down version of Hadeon's plates, modified for speed and flexibility.

SRAF.

Miriam ducked back into cover, exhaling hard. Relief hit her in a wave, and she ignored Talwar's knitted eyebrows. Her mind was already racing. How could they approach? How could they announce themselves without getting shot?

She didn't care why SRAF was there, just that they were. She flashed Talwar a thumbs-up and nodded. This was good. They had a lifeline again. Miriam leaned out again, friendly identifiers in her throat—

And something snapped. The wall in front of her ruptured, and she flinched, a sting across her cheek. Talwar yanked her back. Miriam touched her face, blood smearing the tips of her glove.

"Come out!" a voice bellowed down the street.

The sound was terrifying. Whoever they were didn't care about stealth. That confidence was alien here.

Next to her, Talwar shook his head, but Miriam had already let her rifle fall to its sling.

"Blue! Friendlies!" she shouted back, her voice foreign in the open air. "UMF!" She slowly stretched her left hand out, bracing.

No shot.

"Let's see the other one now! That's right. Nice an' slow!"

Carefully, Miriam stepped out. The same individual she had seen before now had his rifle trained on her. Beside him, a larger man in similar armor stood, one hand raised to stay the shot. Had he redirected the one that clipped the wall? She swept it from her mind. It didn't matter. She was still alive.

"UMF SOG!" she called again.

The larger one answered, voice deep. "Tell the other one to step out."

Talwar's face fell, but he reluctantly moved, revealing himself. His hand hovered near his weapon.

"Come on over," the first ordered.

They obeyed. As they approached, Miriam felt the SRAF operators' eyes rake over them. The larger one lowered his hand from where a dagger hilt peeked out of his chest plate. As she took another step, the two moved, one rifle up, the other a swift movement of the wrist.

The rifle's cracking sound split the air.

She and Talwar both flinched, the proximity unnerving. But neither were hit.

Behind, back at the corner where they'd been, a body dropped in a heap. An Altered enemy, weapon in hand, now leaked blood across the pavement.

"Got 'im first," the first man said. He nonchalantly threw his rifle over his shoulder and flashed his teeth at Miriam and Talwar. "Y'all really are stragglin'."

He was human, from the look of it, stout and gruff. Scarred, pupils blown wide. Stimmed.

"Alphabet," said the relative giant beside the human. His size and bearing suggested he was a former legionnaire.

"UMF ops in the area?" the one named Alphabet asked in a thick drawl. "Woulda been nice to know."

"We didn't know SRAF was here either," Miriam answered.

"Explains the stuff ya heard earlier." He slapped his partner's armored abdomen. "What? Didn't make the bus on time?"

She shook her head.

"Tryin' to hitch a ride?"

She nodded. Behind them, the firefight had subsided.

He studied them, gaze weighing, then paused, listening to something she couldn't hear. Miriam noted the black device fused above his ear, a metal composite soldered into flesh. She'd seen the same thing on Sam in Station City. An embed.

Alphabet spat to the side. "Alright, they're finishin' up.

'Bout time. Fuckers barricaded themselves in. Come on then, my little moochin' stragglers."

The Altered giant fell in at their flank, and Miriam followed, hesitant. Talwar's knuckles whitened around his rifle, but he moved as well.

"Watch your feet," Alphabet said.

Miriam looked down in time to stutter her step around what she thought was a puddle. It wasn't. It was a corpse, pulverized. Bones, tissue, and guts were grotesquely splattered like someone had dropped a carton of food. Miriam took in the street around them, realizing the carnage they'd walked into.

Ahead, two airships waited between broken strips of buildings. They were smaller than the standard Legion craft, one a crude cargo hauler and the other barely larger than a four-seat escort. How they'd landed here at all was a mystery.

Miriam opened her mouth to ask what SRAF was doing there, to suggest that perhaps the enemies from SOG and Legion's mission would draw people over soon as well, but the words died as another group approached. Four others were in similar armor, with two of them dragging a narrow sack. One man's arm hung wrong, shoulder dislocated, while another limped, clutching his side. His plates gleamed dark with blood.

The two groups merged, heading toward the parked ships, and the others glanced at Miriam and Talwar, no urgency behind their movement. Miriam had to remind herself they were still in hostile territory, yet the SRAF operators carried themselves like it was a stroll through the park.

"Picked up strays, Alphabet?" one called.

"They love me."

"Vengeance won't be happy."

"Vengey-poo loves me."

As they came to the cargo craft, a familiar voice growled out. "I tolerate you."

A tall woman cinched down a strap inside, then leaped out, her boots pounding into the ground.

Varya. Hadeon's old teammate. Now up close. Her face was a lattice of scars, an unusual look for a legionnaire. Other than the thick, horizontal scars on their sternums, the Altered soldiers *didn't* scar. Unless they allowed it.

The woman's mouth curved down. For a human, it was subtle, but for a former legionnaire, it was a vivid expression. One blue eye, one green fixed on Miriam before sliding away, turning toward the smaller aircraft behind them.

There, a dark hand gripped the lip of its hatch, and another figure emerged from within. They dropped from the height of the airship and strode over in a familiar swagger. Miriam's stomach knotted as the helmet peeled back. A scar along the jaw and chin, blonde hair, and dark eyes. Her breath caught.

"What is she doing here?" Sam hissed.

The words impaled Miriam. She flinched, more from the pointed and accusatory tone. Miriam met Sam's glare and held it.

To the side, Varya said nothing, though her mismatched eyes cut between them. Alphabet and another jumped into the ship to lift and hoist the bag in. They dropped it unceremoniously onto the floor of the aircraft, and the bag groaned, then wriggled, before Alphabet jabbed the stock of his rifle into its mass. A whimper, then silence.

"We don't exactly have the space," said the one clutching his side, voice clipped. His orange eyes blazed at the two marines. "Leave them or not, we've gotta go. I can already hear the vermin scurrying." With a grunt, he flung his weapon into the belly of the ship. His teammate helped him up.

Varya swept her eyes over Miriam, Talwar, and the two aircraft. Two extra bodies had upset their plans and seating order.

Miriam gestured toward the bleeding SRAF member as if she needed to help convince the woman of their usefulness. "I —we can help."

Varya ignored her and scowled. "Beric is priority. You two, over there." She pointed to the smaller ship.

Miriam endured the sting. She and Talwar weren't trusted near SRAF's cargo and catch.

Varya turned again, evaluating the group as though measuring each by their worth and weight. Her lip twitched as she looked over the injuries and to the two turrets mounted on both sides of the vehicle.

"Fury and Chapel, stay. Boy Scout, Alphabet, with me on the hopper."

Alphabet patted a hand possessively against one of the turrets. "Switch. I was 'ere first. It's my turn on these beauties." He tutted at Sam, but she didn't react. Her focus hadn't moved from Miriam.

"Vengeance, you need to stay. I will go," said the other large member of the group. He didn't wait for confirmation or permission, already moving for the other ship.

"We're wasting time," the orange-eyed Altered called out, already situating himself into a seat. The only other non-injured teammate helped Alphabet secure the body bag to the floor.

Varya made one final sweep of her team, then nodded, first at Sam, then to the one Miriam figured was Boy Scout, and climbed effortlessly into the cargo ship. With that movement, Boy Scout made for the hopper. Sam lingered, her upper lip curling before she followed.

"Let's go," Miriam muttered to Talwar, quickening her pace after the others. It was best to move before SRAF reconsidered. One, in particular, did not want her there.

As they crossed toward the smaller craft, Miriam caught it, a rising echo of voices funneling down the street, hoots and chants swelling like a tide. Her skin crawled.

At the hopper, the other Altered had already taken the seat beside the pilot. Miriam climbed in, wedging herself next to Boy Scout on one of the narrow benches. Talwar settled across from her on the other, visibly uneasy. The pilot flicked switches, tapped the dashboard, then glanced back once. His helmet obscured any reaction, but he said nothing. Whatever he thought of the new roster, their departure wasn't stalling any further.

"Should we be strapped in?" Talwar shouted to Sam next to him. When she didn't answer, he fumbled, digging around the space. "I'm strapping in!"

Miriam checked both sides of her bench, searching for a harness or buckle. Nothing. Either they'd been removed or there had never been any for passengers in her spot. Sam and Boy Scout had functioning belts hanging beneath their seats, but neither bothered to clip in. There was no time to ask.

On the other side, the larger ship hummed as it lifted. Miriam stiffened as its turrets activated with a shrill whine. Tracers lit the air, and she caught sight of Alphabet, manning one gun, enraptured by its might, spewing cover and destruction. Beyond him, figures emerged from the mouths of buildings, from where SRAF had come from. Some dropped immediately, ripped to shreds. Others scattered.

Miriam ground her feet into the floor, hand bracing on a rung inside the open edge as their own ship jolted in its ascent. She tried to shrink her profile, keeping her mass low, more worried about stray gunfire through the open cabin than the climb itself.

This ship was lighter, more agile, but it didn't boast the same weapon systems. Whatever defense it had was built into the hull or operated from the cockpit. But the other ship rained fire as both craft climbed, chewing through the block below.

Bursts of gunfire cracked beside her, both Sam and Boy Scout bracing against their respective side of the frame, shooting down, alternating suppressive fire with measured shots. Their angles were practiced; none of this was new to them.

Miriam's stomach lurched then bottomed as the hopper

passed above the rooftops. Figures rushed from adjacent structures, vaulting the gaps between the four- or five-story buildings with impossible efficiency. They carried weapons between them—large ones.

One, in particular, caught the light of the sun.

"Contact left!" Miriam shouted. "Airgun!"

"Climb! Fucking climb!" Talwar yelled.

She didn't hear the discharge, but she saw the puff of dust around the two gunners, only slightly below their level.

The ship banked hard, and Miriam's fingers dug into the grip. Her whole body whipped sideways, gut driving into her throat.

However, other than the pilot's evasive maneuvering, she had felt no impact. A near miss. Too close.

She didn't have time to exhale. Small arms fire pattered against the hull while the larger craft's turret spat a storm below. Across the street, a second airgun belched, dust pluming. They weren't gaining altitude fast enough.

The hopper veered again. This time, Miriam slammed into the inner wall, then pitched forward, her right hand torn free. The cabin's edge opened in front of her, the ground twenty meters below—not too far, but the implication still terrible. She clawed for purchase, boots scrabbling, torso spilling into open air.

The pilot yanked the ship into another correction. Too violent. Momentum rammed Miriam back into the bench, her spine lighting in pain. She gripped the frame, anchoring herself by force of will.

At least they were still rising. They were still alive.

Across from her, Talwar sat rigid, strapped in, his eyes wide, skin slick with sweat. His horror mirrored her own as gunfire blared behind them, muffled by the engine.

They were getting out.

Miriam wedged her arm deeper into the frame, securing her balance instead of collapsing into the bench. She scanned the sky and took a moment to breathe. The larger airship was already higher, climbing smooth and fast.

But too smooth. Too fast.

Miriam's eyes widened. No, not the other aircraft. *Their* ship, the hopper, was lagging. Her gut clenched as a horrible grinding shriek cut through the cabin, followed by wet, metallic coughs. Over Talwar's shoulder, the dashboard flared red. The pilot's hands flew over controls, but the ship shuddered.

Then jolted.

"Wait. No." Talwar's voice broke into a mantra. "No. No. No."

The hopper dipped.

Tried to climb.

It wasn't enough.

The nose pitched forward. Slow, but inexorable. The craft careened, then spun.

And spun.

The pilot shouted, but the words dissolved in the uproar. Miriam didn't need to hear them. She already knew. She understood.

They were going down.

And despite her grip, despite bracing low with every joint locked, the centrifugal force dragged her sideways toward the gaping side hatch.

The spin picked up.

Her boot skidded on the lip of the deck, and her weight listed, trying to compensate. Her shoulder wrenched, pain ripping down her arm as it pulled straight.

"Tan!" Talwar's hand reached from his harness, straining.

But something slammed into her side—loose gear, a body, she couldn't tell. Her right hand tore free. Miriam flailed for the railing. Too late.

Her fingers scraped off cold metal. Slipped.

There was nothing beneath her but open air.

And gravity took hold.

21

INTERCESSION

SOMETHING CLAMPED around Miriam's wrist, and agony tore through her shoulder as she was pulled in two directions at once. The ship spun, warping the world into streaks of light and shadow. Wind ripped at her eyes, forcing them into a painful squint. A shape, metal and dark, whipped past her face and struck her shoulder with jarring force before it tore loose from its strap and tumbled end over end into the sky.

A rifle, Miriam realized too late.

Then another impact. Not cargo, not debris, but a body.

The weight slammed her flat against deck grating. Her cheek scored against steel, sparks bursting behind her eyes. Air punched from her lungs, and she sucked in on reflex, tasting smoke and oil.

Through the tumult, past Talwar's shouts and the engine's death rattle, she found the armored arm pinning her shoulder, the hand locking her wrist with inhuman force. Her gaze followed the prosthetic to where it dug into the plated deck.

Sam.

The hopper bucked again, and the rear of the ship sheared open with a metallic scream, scraping against something immovable—concrete, steel, or both. Light and debris sprayed in, carbon fragments and insulation biting her skin. Orientation disintegrated in a breathless instant of weightlessness when everything was too much, too fast, that it became so slow, melting together.

Then the world punched up, the impact ripping through Miriam's body like a colossal fist, shaking teeth, bones, and every fiber of her being. Her vision went white.

When it cleared, pain radiated through her hips, ribs, and spine. Her lungs burned, and she choked on acrid smoke, gagging once before coughing hard. Her mouth tasted like copper. Despite the ache flooding in, she forced her arms beneath her.

The heaviness shifted from her back, and Sam rolled aside with a grunt that sounded mechanical and human all at once, like metal grinding against bone. The woman didn't speak, only pushed herself upright in a broken movement. Miriam felt the woman's presence at her back, heavy as ever, but stayed on the deck for half a second longer. Then she gritted her teeth and pushed up to her hands and knees.

In front of her, the nose of the craft had folded like a crushed can. Miriam's concern didn't linger where the pilot had sat; he was beyond any aid she could offer. To his side, Chapel slumped forward, unmoving. What remained of the console glared with red warnings, angry light cutting through smoke.

The compact cabin was gone, and in its place yawned a shredded carcass. The entire rear had been torn away, strewn across the street in a trail of twisted metal. A warm gust slid through the breach, tugging at straps and insulation that dangled like entrails.

Miriam turned, spine flaring in protest, and found Talwar slumped, sitting in his harness. Blood streaked his temple, but when she called his name, his eyes slitted open, and he croaked an answer. Fleeting relief moved through her.

A low groan echoed. Boy Scout was no longer where he had

been, only a smear of blood marking his side of the wreck. Whether his or another's, she couldn't tell.

Behind her, there was movement. Sam stalked toward the lip of the torn-open hull without a word or backward glance, her steps patient and predatory. A moment later, Boy Scout emerged, battered but alive, and joined her at the edge. Miriam exhaled, a strained sigh. Most of them had survived.

She tried to shift awareness to what held the two operators' attention. Beyond, the sky burned with northern light, but haze was rising in the distance, a veil of dust that warned of movement drawing near.

Miriam's stomach dropped. She could hear it now, howls and high-pitched whoops, the chorus of enemies closing in. Her joints protested as she pushed herself upright, scrambling for purchase on the slick metal. The hull groaned beneath her, and she hauled herself over the ship's ledge, then slipped, hitting the ground with a grunt that knocked the air from her lungs. Pain arced down her back and slammed through her pelvis. Something warm slid along the side of her face. Blood. She didn't try to wipe it.

Miriam staggered up, legs wobbling. Her commcuff, if not finished before, was completely dead now. The rush of blood exited her head, and she leaned against sharp trim, trying to will the feeling to pass. Her heart kicked up, pounding in her esophagus. Her brain caught up as she regained herself, making the connection before she could shut it out.

This was the second time they'd been stranded.

Her mouth went dry.

Beside her, a second body hit the ground. Talwar had cut himself free, and he stood, swaying, face stiffened by shock and fear.

Miriam searched for her rifle and pack but couldn't find them. Anything not bolted down or tethered to her had been claimed by the crash, flung out in the process or lost in the wreckage. She touched her back and found her sling bag still on her. She reached lower and felt the familiar contour of her sidearm snug in its holster. She drew it, gripping hard. A sliver of relief.

Meanwhile, Talwar's rifle shook in his hands. "We should go, right?" His voice pitched too high, words tumbling fast. Blood streaked the back of his head, glistening red. He hadn't noticed. "Like right now. We should go."

Miriam opened her mouth, but stopped. Whoops bounced off the metal and pavement, swelling louder each second. Boots slapped concrete, multiplying and drawing closer from too many directions.

"They're already here," she muttered.

Talwar's curses spilled out one after another like a prayer. She fought the urge to snap at him, to shut him up, tell him to focus, because she wasn't sure she could hold it together either.

Her hands shook. The sidearm in them felt insubstantial. They didn't have enough weapons or ammunition. They'd used too much on their first mission and then on their retreat. Whatever else had been lost.

Ahead, Boy Scout moved, and Sam mirrored him. Without words, the two positioned themselves around the ruined hopper. Two SRAF operators—Seraphs—and two SOG marines against whatever was closing in.

"How many?" Sam called. She was already digging into her armor, not waiting for the answer. She pulled a small cartridge free, threw it to her mouth, and inhaled it. Blue eyes caught Miriam's as she exhaled.

Stims.

"An advance band," Boy Scout said.

Sam looked away, but Miriam saw the transformation all the same. The hardening of Sam's jaw, the rigid set of her shoulders, the consciousness fixing like a vise behind her darkening eyes.

They weren't going to outrun this. They were going to have

to make a stand. Talwar backed up a half step, his grip on his weapon bone-white. The odds weren't there. The four of them couldn't hold out against a crowd like this. Not for long.

Miriam didn't ask how many, just moved forward.

Sam stretched her neck. "Reinforcements?"

"Likely," Boy Scout answered.

Less than a block away, the first enemy clambered onto a half-collapsed balcony, jeering as if the whole thing were sport. He leaned forward, trying to gauge the wreck and its survivors, but it was a mistake. Boy Scout popped up, flung a metal shard, and it struck with clinical force. Half the man's face vanished in a mist of flesh and blood. His body dropped like a puppet cut loose.

And that was it. The moment ruptured open, and the rest came fast. Figures, at least seven, spilled into view, weaving between broken storefronts, alley mouths, and scorched vehicles, their limbs too quick, their voices rising in a feral chorus of bloodlust, ringing louder with each step. Miriam could barely make out the pale outlines of brands on necks. Heretics.

Miriam's heartbeat hammered, and her breath caught in her throat. She raised her sidearm and felt its familiar give as she pushed forward, shooting in a lane away from Sam and Boy Scout.

Beside her, Talwar's rifle snapped in bursts. The first enemy vaulted over the wreck, a lean figure whose face pinched into a rictus grin, teeth bared, gums blackened, eyes burning under the twitch of chemical fire.

Miriam fired again. Her shots struck center mass—two, then a third for certainty—but the impact didn't slow him. His momentum didn't break. Her firing pattern was a training scar, and these Heretics weren't the usual enemies marines had trained for. These enemies were stimmed to the verge of death and coaxed to keep going. Torso shots, though critical and fatal, didn't mean a thing.

Miriam's heel skidded as she staggered back. The Heretic raised his own rifle, but before he could fire, his movement froze—cut off. A massive hand clamped down over the barrel of his weapon and yanked it down.

Chapel.

Not dead.

Trapped inside the mangled cockpit, seat harness biting into his torso, half-sunk into metal, he was still alive and fighting. His other arm shot out, grabbed the rifle body, and wrenched it from the enemy. The Heretic rolled with the motion, giving it up, but smoothly drawing a long machete from behind his back. He slashed down, a diagonal sweep toward Chapel's face.

Chapel caught the blade with the stolen rifle. It bit into metal with a crunch, and the Seraph tried to counter, to surge forward, but the straps pinned him in place.

Miriam fired again, two more rounds, fast and low, aimed at the Heretic's exposed flank. The Altered turned, expression cranking with irritation rather than pain, and slid down the warped hull toward her. No hesitation or a stumble.

And lunged.

Miriam threw herself sideways, drawing him away from both Chapel and Talwar, who was already in a firefight with others. She heard his grunts and other clangs but couldn't look, couldn't break focus.

The Heretic's blade came at her again, a brutal horizontal swing that cut toward her torso. She jumped back, instinct taking over, sidearm tucking close to her body. The edge hissed past her kit and he came at her again, the blade arcing high and too close, this time slicing a pouch free.

Miriam dropped to one knee as it passed and fired two more rounds. The first struck his throat, and the second up his jaw. Blood fountained in the air as he toppled, machete clattering beside him.

She didn't have time to think. Another enemy was already vaulting over, bearing down with terrifying speed past Chapel, who had already extricated himself, busy with another. Miriam fired. She wasn't sure how much ammunition she had left—hadn't had the luxury of a tactical reload. Her weapon chattered in her hands as she let off more rounds.

But the enemy didn't slow. He zigzagged toward her, each stride too fast, a tornado of limbs and aggression aimed directly at her. She knew he was steering her, turning her back on the others; she knew, but she followed.

And then the dull click.

Jammed.

The Heretic heard it as well.

Miriam moved to immediate remediation, but his posture had changed, dropping his evasive pattern.

"Marine!"

In the corner of her eye, Boy Scout hurled something toward her: a slab of metal, rectangular, crude in its heft and shape. He shouted something else, but his voice was drowned out by the thunderclap of another weapon discharging behind him.

Miriam caught it on reflex, fumbling before her free hand locked on. It was heavier than it looked, awkward and dense, not quite a shield, not quite a weapon. The surface was smooth except for a single ribbed rim, and as she adjusted her grip—

It shifted. A section clamped down over her arm like a cuff, forming a brace from wrist to elbow. She nearly dropped it again, startled by the seamless movement, but muscle memory kicked in. There was something natural about it. She tightened her stance and braced her pistol and hand under it, shifting her feet and legs. Whatever this thing was, she now knew where the dangerous end pointed.

And the enemy was already charging. Miriam thrust her arm forward on instinct. The weapon clamped again, tighter now, and a sudden pulse surged from her shoulder through her bones. Immense pressure fired out. It nearly knocked her off her feet.

She wasn't sure what had launched—if anything did—only that force tore the air in front of her and kicked up a geyser of dust. And on the other end, the Altered staggered, momentum faltering. He hesitated.

That was all she needed. The Heretic vanished behind a half-collapsed slab and reappeared a second later, skimming in and out of cover, testing her line of sight. She tracked him as best she could with the heavy device, every nerve live-wired. In the corner of her vision, the fight surged around her, metal against metal, limbs crashing in close quarters. Talwar's rifle barked in controlled salvos.

And then pain. A crushing density hammered into her side, and the world jerking as her body was flung sideways. She struck the ground hip-first, breath punched from her diaphragm, and a feral growl ripped in her ear. A dense body bore down against her back.

The Heretic. His hands wrapped around her forearm, the one bearing the new weapon, and he twisted, forcing it perpendicular to her shoulder with brute strength. Her elbow flared in pain. He was trying to rip it off.

She couldn't overpower him, so she pivoted. She rolled into him, pinning the weapon between them with her own weight. It stopped the disarm but brought her face-to-face with her enemy. Too close.

She felt the chomp before she understood it. A lancing pain drove into her trapezius, teeth finding the gap just past her armor strap. Then a deep grind into flesh and muscle.

Miriam yelped and snapped her free arm upward, elbowing him in the throat. His hold broke instantly, followed by a hot spray of blood against her neck. The Heretic choked, reeling back, and she torqued her right arm. The weapon rotated on its own and clamped in a new position. She drove her elbow back again. Hard.

This time, there was resistance, a mechanical kickback as the weapon surged.

But something gave. The grip on her vanished.

Miriam scrambled upright, staggered, and braced herself. In front of her, the enemy was still alive. He was on one knee, but he was still moving. Blood ran from a deep gash across his thorax. One arm dangled, half-detached, connected by a ragged flap of muscle and sinew. And yet he tried to rise. His breaths came fast, shallow and wheezing. No pain showed on his face, just confusion.

The stims. The Heretic didn't know he was a dead man walking. But he was still moving. Still a threat.

Miriam raised the weapon again and tried to reposition it, but she didn't know how to recharge, didn't know if it had a third shot. She pumped her limb forward.

Nothing.

No pressure, no surge. Dead.

And the Heretic stood, shaky but upright. His lips split, showing her own blood on his teeth.

And then he lunged.

Miriam dropped low, bending out of the way as his working arm and fingers clawed past her forehead. His nails raked skin, and she fell backward hard.

But she wasn't alone. A burst of color crossed her vision, followed by a wet crack. The Heretic's body went stiff, then collapsed in a heap, face down, cranium opened like a shattered fruit. Brain and bone were splattered across the ground.

Miriam blinked, then stared. Sam stood a few meters away, her face and stance feral with one arm raised. Whatever she'd thrown had vanished into ruin.

A blur whipped by.

"Sam—"

Another Heretic leaped from the rubble and landed on Sam's back, arms around her throat. His grip found her prosthetic and cinched tight, one arm under her chin. He rode her like a wild animal, knees against her sides, trying to pull her off balance.

Dropping to her knees, Sam then curled forward. The enemy tumbled off over her shoulder but recovered fast, landing in a crouch, and immediately kicked out again. Sam swiveled, but the blow grazed her ribs. He lunged again, but this time, she caught his leg, dragging him down. They grappled in a maelstrom of limbs and snarls.

As Sam fought to regain control, pieces of her armor and kit scattered free. A section of her shoulder guard sheared with an audible snap, tumbling away. Her exposed side was matted with sweat and residue, but she didn't slow. If Sam noticed what'd happened, she gave no sign. Her hands stayed on him.

And in the scuffle, a small case was dislodged from the Heretic's body and skidded across the dirt. He spotted it and broke free. He sprinted for it, ripped it open, and a thin jabber tumbled out.

Miriam's breath hitched, and she moved, reaching for it, but he met her, a shoulder into her sternum as he pushed her back. He fumbled then closed his hands around the jabber. Sam caught his leg, but he kicked her off. His arm moved to stab it into his thigh.

Sam's arm shot out.

"No!" Miriam gasped out.

But it was too late.

Time stood still as the battle raged on around them, Miriam, Sam, and the Heretic's small bubble suspended. Miriam followed the Heretic's hand to where the jabber stuck from Sam's forearm, sunk deep.

And then Sam collapsed to the dirt.

"No." Miriam's own voice was muffled by her ears, like her head had been dunked into water.

Sam wasn't moving.

"No, no."

But then Sam's body locked up, and the convulsions began. Sam's spine arched grotesquely, knees and legs flopping. Metal fingers knocked the jabber free and hooked into her arm. Sam flipped and her forehead pounded once into the ground. Then again.

"No." Miriam couldn't breathe. "Sam."

The woman somehow pulled into a kneeling position, then folded in on herself. Her shoulders rose in ragged jerks.

Miriam moved forward, but two things happened almost simultaneously. The Heretic changed course, got up, and charged for Miriam, but at the same time, Sam moved.

The woman shot up like something reborn, her prosthetic arm rocketing up. The enemy didn't see it coming, didn't react in time, already pulled down.

A metal hand found his face.

And for a split second, bone resisted, and the Heretic uttered the start of a cry.

A sickening crunch followed, and cheekbones caved in. Eyes bulged, and Miriam couldn't look away as the man's face disappeared in an implosion of bone, skin, and blood.

22

───────

PERDITION

THERE WERE NO MORE ENEMIES, only the rasp of lungs and the groan of the hopper's broken frame. Beneath it, something thudded, a rhythm in the rubble, faint but swelling. Reinforcements.

"We have to go!" Talwar's voice broke through the haze.

But Miriam didn't move. She couldn't. Sam stood a few meters away, covered in blood and streaked with viscera that was not her own. It clung to her armor, clotted around her prosthetic fingers. Her shoulders rose and fell in ragged heaves, her jaw clenched tight, and her eyes were deep, fathomless pits. They fixed on Miriam with an unblinking stillness. Miriam swallowed hard.

"What happened?" Boy Scout asked, voice low, somewhere to her left.

She didn't look at him, couldn't break the fragile tether of eye contact. "Stims," she murmured. "Theirs."

"How much?"

Miriam gave the slightest shake of her head. She didn't know. It had looked like the entire thing. She couldn't fathom how Sam was breathing, let alone standing. Human stimulants were dangerous enough, but the Altered strain was another order of magnitude. A full dose should've burned out her nervous system, stopped her heart, should've collapsed her in the dirt.

"Fury," Boy Scout called.

He took a cautious step closer. Sam didn't flinch, didn't blink. The whites of her eyes had been overtaken by dark pupils wide as spilled ink. Boy Scout reached out, his hand contacting her shoulder—

And everything went sideways. Sam erupted into motion, a thunderclap of limbs and raw force. Her fist cracked against his forearm, her body whipping around with wild momentum. But Boy Scout was ready. He weaved and dodged, arms wrapping around her from behind, locking her tight.

She thrashed, every muscle straining, but he held on. And then they dropped together. His mass bore her into the ground, pinning her as she writhed underneath. Her breath struck the dirt in harsh bursts, clouds rising like steam from a rupture.

Sam's prosthetic tore free from his grip, and the metal fist crashed against his temple with a thud. He faltered as she twisted, rolled, and scrambled upright again, but Boy Scout shook it off, rising fast. He planted himself in front of Miriam, one foot braced back, his body a wall.

"Fury," he tried again, hard now, no softness left.

Sam gave no answer. Her whole body heaved with ragged pulls, every muscle strung tight. A vein bulged along her temple, writhing as though it would break through skin.

"Sam," Miriam whispered.

The name rendered through whatever storm held her, and Sam faltered. But her torso folded, like a spear had struck her gut. Her body reversed, back arching, face screwing into a grimace. Sam clutched her chest, knees buckling until she hit the ground, one hand catching her weight before she collapsed fully. Her whole frame shuddered in violent waves.

Miriam surged forward, but Boy Scout's thick arm barred her path.

"No. Let me go," she cried, her voice breaking.

She ducked underneath and slid hard into the ground next to Sam, knees scraping the gravel. The woman had already flipped to her side, body in violent spasms, and Miriam struggled, then pressed two fingers against Sam's neck. The pulse was frantic, shallow, wrong. It was too much. Too much for any human body and human heart.

Miriam's hand flew to her sling, but it was gone, lost in the bloodbath. "Find my kit!" Her voice broke. "Now!"

"They're coming. We have to move!"

Talwar's panic rang out, but Miriam didn't turn. She couldn't. Her world narrowed to Sam: the spasms racking her frame, muscles seizing beneath what was left of her armor. Miriam pinned her shoulders down, keeping her from smashing into loose rubble beneath them. She dug into her rig's remaining compartments and pockets until she fished out a compact field splint, shoving the padded strip between Sam's teeth before her jaw locked shut. The reinforced material flexed but held against the clamp of her bite.

And then, as suddenly as it started, everything stilled.

"No."

No, no, no.

"Talwar! My kit!" Miriam shouted, panic tearing through her throat.

"Fuck!" His boots scraped against broken stone as he turned.

Behind her, Boy Scout snarled an order to Chapel, who slipped away into the smoke. Miriam knew the enemies were closing in, knew their time was measured in heartbeats, yet her hands stayed locked on Sam. She couldn't abandon her.

A moment later, Talwar stumbled back, her sling clutched in his grip. Miriam ripped it from him, fingers diving through gauze and wrappings, past the Altered device Yuri had given her, until they closed on what she needed: a nanocapsule and a compressed respiratory container. Neither was meant for this, but there were no choices left. No plan accounted for a human taking Altered stims.

She twisted the activation collar with her thumb. The small device hissed, unfolding a flexible piece that Miriam clamped and stretched over Sam's mouth and nose. Another hiss escaped, a pale cloud filling the little seal.

Nothing.

Miriam's pulse hammered as she jammed the nanocapsule between Sam's teeth and forced the woman to swallow. Chapel's low snarl rumbled from the wreckage, a warning that enemies were near. Miriam ignored him. Her fingers pressed hard against Sam's neck, searching frantically for change, willing the pulse to slow, to stabilize, to be something she could fight for.

"It is time to go." Boy Scout crouched beside her, his arms scooping Sam's limp form like she weighed nothing. Blood smeared across his armor, but he didn't falter, his chin tilting toward the one direction that hadn't yet filled with hostile voices. He asked for no permission.

Miriam restrained the objection surging up her throat. She understood, even if she hated it. Her stomach churned as she fell into step, Talwar at her side, Chapel covering the rear. And they sprinted, every stride shaking Miriam's battered body. Her thighs screamed, lungs burned, but she kept running until the sounds behind them dimmed. They cut through alleys, darted around rubble, took corners sharp enough to tear breath from her lungs.

At last they collapsed into the shadows of what might once have been a government building, all of them panting. Even the Altered Seraphs. Miriam braced herself against a busted pillar. Her gaze found Sam whose eyes hadn't opened. Her body was slack in Boy Scout's arms, but her diaphragm rose, shallow and labored. But breathing. She was still breathing.

Of course she was. Years of chemicals had carved a tolerance into Sam's veins that no medical professional would ever sanction. Miriam loathed the thought that the very poison eroding her might be the thing that had saved her. Worse was knowing it still might not be enough.

"You can call them back," Talwar said, words coming rough.

"No," Boy Scout replied. "Beric is more important."

"The prisoner? He can't be worth—" His eyes swept the ruined street. "Five of us!"

"It is worth the cost."

Talwar's voice cracked. "But we're the cost!"

"We will have to find our own way out."

Hands cupped over his face, Talwar groaned and slid against the pillar to his haunches.

Miriam checked Sam's pulse again, her fingers pressing against hot skin at her throat. Still rapid, but steadier. Still alive. When there was no other change, she withdrew, the ache in her back worsening now that adrenaline ebbed. The air was thin, as though she were breathing in the aftermath of a fire. Blood and dust hung in every draw, heavy and metallic. Her eyes swept across Talwar, Boy Scout, Chapel, and Sam. Two SOG marines and three Seraphs. All of them had survived something they shouldn't have. Her stare lingered on Talwar. Only his second mission, and already he had been baptized in the worst kind of fire.

"Talwar," she whispered.

"I know, I know." His reply came muffled through his palms. He sat hunched, knees drawn tight, breath laboring like he had run the length of the war. "I'm getting my shit together." When he looked up, his face was pale beneath caked salt and blood. His voice cracked again. "I'm trying."

She gave a faint nod. It was enough. For now. Miriam sagged against the pillar beside him, her body finally recognizing the deeper pains it had ignored. She lifted a hand to her shoulder, gingerly touching the crescent bite above her scapula. The torn fabric peeled back and blood clung tacky to her fingers. The flesh was broken where jaws had sunk in, not deep enough to need sealing but enough to twist her stomach. A hiss slipped from her teeth.

"Looks like it hurts," Talwar muttered.

She glanced sidelong at him. In the melee, she hadn't checked the others. "Let me see your head," she said.

He shooed her off, but she had already spotted the red streak matting his hair at the back. Another wound to keep watch over.

Despite the late hour, the light clung to the sky, but dusk pressed close, etching every ruin into harsh edges. Broken buildings rose in skeletal silhouettes, and distant cries echoed through the streets, fraying as they carried.

Miriam turned her attention to Chapel, who had not shifted from his watch. He leaned briefly into a wall, propping himself with a trembling hand. Though she couldn't see his face, she caught the lines carved into his cheek. When he noticed her watching, he straightened, spine taut with defiance. Stubborn, like all of them.

None of them were in any condition to continue, not with their wounds, not with Sam's weight, not with enemy reinforcements tracking their tail.

"We need shelter," Miriam said, quiet but firm.

Boy Scout gave a nod and adjusted, Sam still slack in his arms. The other Seraph glanced back at Miriam, a slight tip of his chin in silent agreement. But Miriam had lost her bearings. The crash and its aftermath had clobbered her sense of any map; the landmarks she thought she knew had bled together into rubble and smoke.

Talwar lifted his head, blinking hard. "We...we know a place," he said.

Her brows drew tight.

"Our mission site." His hand rubbed at the back of his neck. "But the wunbies—they might still be there."

Miriam studied him, then gave the smallest of nods.

"They should be gone by now, right? After all this." His voice caught on the last word, more hope than conviction.

"Do you remember how to get back?" she asked.

"Maybe. I'd need to get my bearings."

At that, Boy Scout flicked a look toward Chapel, who followed the silent cue. The Seraph inclined his head toward a building down the block. Half its walls had been sheared away, but its steel frame and roofline jutted higher than the rest of the street. A vantage point, if not much else.

"Fuck," Talwar muttered. He looked to Miriam, but she gave him nothing more than another nod.

Chapel moved first. Though hurt, his stride carried a fluid steadiness. At the street's curb, he stopped, ears angled, listening to sounds she couldn't hear. Then he stepped into the open, glancing back once. Talwar wavered, but only for a second, before he followed. The pair disappeared into the street like shadows chasing mirages.

And Miriam stayed where she was, her breath unsettled. She turned back to Boy Scout and Sam, the former resting motionless, the latter still unconscious. Sam's face was creased, muscles drawn tight. Even in rest, there was no peace in her body, only the look of someone enduring.

Miriam's fingers brushed her sling, her mind running through its contents. Nothing in it could help. Even Yuri's device was useless here. Sam wasn't bleeding, at least not in any way she could mend. When she looked to Boy Scout, his mismatched eyes fixed on her. His ears twitched once, but his focus never wavered.

"Miriam Tanner," she whispered. "And you're Boy Sc—"

"Yes." His answer came clipped. He turned toward the street where Chapel and Talwar had gone, and silence filled the gap. Then, without warning, he spoke again, his voice low. "You do one thing and you are branded forever."

She tipped her head, caught off guard by the unprompted response. "What did you do?"

"It is what I did *not* do."

She frowned.

"I have no markings," he said at last, his upper back flexing.

It took a moment before she understood. He had meant the SRAF wing-and-eye tattoos.

"Does it bother you?"

His look suggested she had asked an odd question. "It is a name. A tease. Some put too much worth to it."

Her gaze drifted back to Sam. A breath hitched before easing again. Exhaustion clung to her body like a second skin.

"The person remains who they are," Boy Scout said, "underneath it all."

The quiet resumed between them, broken only by the breeze curling through broken stone and the cries that tottered on the border of hearing. Miriam flinched when the muffled rattle of gunfire cut across the distance, followed by indistinct commotion too far away to name. It passed quickly, but she scanned the buildings anyway, watching for movement.

When Talwar and Chapel returned, the marine stretched his arm out in front of him, pointing as if his own body could serve as a compass. "This direction," he said, the end of his sentence rising in doubt.

It was better than nothing. It was a decision.

She placed a reassuring hand on Talwar's tricep, and he offered her a wan smile that fooled neither of them. In a staggered formation, the four of them—not counting Sam—moved, the pace cautious. Chapel took the lead, his movements calm, but Miriam caught the subtle ways his ears tilted, the split-second moment when he paused before every turn. It was different than scraping through alone with Talwar. This felt coordinated. Almost safe.

"There was a smell," Miriam murmured to Boy Scout during one of their halts. "Hadeon, our senior legionnaire—she mentioned it. Chemicals, or, I don't know, clean, like a lab."

Boy Scout inclined his head once. If he relayed it to Chapel, it wasn't out loud.

They pushed on, and the wreckage shifted into something familiar. Buildings she partially recognized emerged in the destruction. A shredded awning sagged across the street, its lettering bleached and indistinct. Then the strip of shops, less ruined than the blocks behind them.

Chapel lifted a hand. The street looked empty, yet his posture shouted with the tension of someone who sensed movement. Miriam saw nothing, heard nothing, but trusted his instincts. She didn't doubt the presence of enemies nearby, but if the Apostates or Heretics suspected SOG marines or others had returned, there was no indication. Maybe the Altered enemies couldn't catch what Hadeon had smelled, or maybe only someone who already knew what to look for would have noticed.

When they'd maneuvered across and into the hardware store, the air was still stale, undisturbed since they had last passed through. Miriam directed Talwar toward the back room, and he went straight to the wall panel. However, he hesitated when it opened.

Miriam's stomach dropped. "Do you remember the combination?" she whispered.

Talwar shook his head, staring at the switches like they might speak. Then his expression shifted. He dug into a side pouch and produced the old-generation device Gumede had foisted on him. After that, his fingers moved quickly, adjusting the switches in a calculated sequence.

Every second stretched like something wound too tight.

Then the hatch slid open.

Boy Scout drew back a step, and Chapel glanced from the front door, nose wrinkling. Miriam exhaled. Before she could speak, Talwar thrust the device toward her. He didn't want the responsibility of it; she could see it in his eyes. He was giving it up, passing the consequence to her, and she took it, reflex more than choice. It felt heavier than it should have been.

And without thinking further, she descended first.

The space was exactly as she had left it. The door at the bottom hung slightly ajar where she had failed to shut it properly. She leaned into it with her shoulder now, nearly stumbling when Boy Scout moved up beside her, Sam still in his arms. He set his shoulder against the metal and helped ease it the rest of the way, until it notched into the groove. Behind them, Talwar made his way down the stairs.

At the threshold, Miriam stood. Just beyond the door, the partition glowed, the same frosted wall she remembered, its light diffused and unrevealing. She hesitated, searching for seams, a handle, any hint of a trap or mechanism. Nothing. Her eyes flicked back to Boy Scout, Sam limp in his arms, then upward, imagining Chapel keeping watch on the street. They had no choice.

She stepped forward.

The wall stirred to her presence, panels splitting and sliding into one another until the glow collapsed into the frame. When it sealed behind her, fear surged, and she turned quickly. At her movement, the panels reopened. On the other side, Boy Scout's brows drew together.

Miriam steadied herself. She nodded, more for herself than anyone else, and moved back, allowing the partition to close once more. Inside, the space was bare, a rectangular enclosure stripped of furniture or fixtures. The walls were a uniform matte white, luminous as though light was bleeding through from within their surface. The air smelled filtered, tinged with antiseptic, and the sound of her own breath came back to her too clearly in the sealed quiet. The sterility was unsettling, more suited to a surgical prep room than a welcome chamber.

Another door waited ahead, flat and handleless, its surface indistinguishable from the wall until she neared it. Miriam approached, fingers grazing along the nearly seamless edges and the wall nearby, then retreated. There was no control panel, no manual switch, nothing at all to suggest how the barrier could be accessed.

"I don't know how to open this," she called as she turned back. "Can it be forced? Det? Talwar—"

She stopped. A muffled response came, but she couldn't make it out. Perhaps they hadn't fully heard her either. But her attention caught on two shallow triangles etched into the side wall, precise and cleanly scored. She stared at them, something tugging in the back of her mind. And then her chest constricted and she willed her legs to move back toward the partition.

Just as it split open.

"Wait—no—"

Before she could stop him, Boy Scout stepped through.

The divider sealed behind him and Sam.

"No," Miriam uttered. She pushed past him, willing the wall to open, but it remained closed. She rammed her palm against its surface. "Talwar!"

From the other side, an undertone answered. And then it was gone. The lights inside the room transitioned. Red bloomed across the ceiling and floor like warning strips. Her gut roiled.

A thud landed beside her, and she spun, heart racing.

Boy Scout had fallen to his knees. Sam's body slumped to the ground as his hands crushed against his ears, tendons rigid along his neck. Miriam dropped beside him, his face contorted, eyes screwed in pain.

She couldn't hear anything.

But he could.

His posture trembled as if trying to hold against something invasive. Miriam's hands hovered, unsure and helpless as she watched him drown in silence. Then suddenly, his hand jerked up, scrabbling at the side of his head, fingers digging just behind and above his ear. Blue-white light sparked from the embed as it shorted out. He yanked it free. It clattered to the ground and hissed before going dark.

Where she lay, Sam stirred, breath dragging through bared teeth. Miriam reached for her, finding the ridge of the embedded device in her skull. She pried it free.

Immediately, Sam's body slackened. A faint exhale escaped her lips. Miriam took her in, then the broken device in her hand.

They were cut off.

And then she heard it: a slow hiss like a leak. A sinister and invisible something.

23

FORSAKEN

MIRIAM LUNGED FOR SAM, curling over her and tucking the woman's face into the crook of her arm. She buried her own nose in a sleeve and held her breath, with no real faith it would help. Beside her, Boy Scout cinched in on himself, one forearm veiling his mouth and the other clamped hard against his opposite ear.

The room swam in red, a harsh and unrelenting wash. There were no visible vents, yet the hiss lingered. The air felt changed, fine as cobweb over the hairs of her arms, slipping under her collar, clinging to sweat.

Her lungs burned. She held it as long as she could, then drew in a meager sip of oxygen. At first it seemed empty, but then a faint tang unfurled, the taste that wasn't taste at all but a trick of the mind. Metal and a residue of savory bitterness. She all but convinced herself she had imagined it, that her mind was inventing poisons in the silence.

More time slid by—seconds or minutes, she couldn't tell— before Boy Scout pulled in a rough inhalation of his own. Some tension bled from his shoulders, and he eased one hand from his ear, then the other, blinking toward her through the red.

Miriam sat back, hands trembling though she forced them

still. Words would not form; her thoughts snarled on themselves, every question piling against the next. What had they been exposed to? The lights, the triangles, the sterility. Years ago, Echo had seen a similar underground research facility. But why was this here?

She dug into her kit for the old-generation device and presented it toward the partition, to the adjacent wall, but nothing. Not even a flicker. It might as well have been a piece of scrap in her hand. She set it aside on the floor without another thought.

She watched as Boy Scout rose and drove a shoulder into the partition, to the wall that had admitted her and then sealed the moment he entered. He crossed to the opposite door, flush with the wall, and struck that, too.

Countermeasures. For the Altered. She kept shaking her head as he hammered at the walls, because nothing was giving and nothing made sense. No further sound bled in from Talwar or Chapel on the other side. In the end, they waited and watched Sam's shallow respirations.

Then Sam stirred. Miriam flinched, reaching forward, but Boy Scout caught the strap of her rig and eased her back, arm a physical barricade.

Sam rolled to an elbow and pushed herself into a seated position. The red light made a mask of her face, erasing color from skin and eyes. She looked around, to Boy Scout then Miriam behind him, and the stare held. Her pupils had pulled back from the blown black of before. Not right, not yet, but better.

Relief pooled, though it didn't erase the weight pressing on Miriam. Sam was alive and awake, but now she was alive and awake inside whatever hell this was.

And the fixation did not break. Only when Boy Scout repeated her callsign did Sam's head turn to him, slow as if encased in glue.

On the third "Fury," understanding seemed to find her.

"How are you fee—" Miriam began.

"What is this? Where are we?" Sam asked, words dragging out like gravel.

"We're stuck."

Sam's gaze hardened. She rose, wavering, and set her feet.

"You should take it easy," Boy Scout said.

She didn't answer, just steadied herself with a low grunt and fixed on the entrance. "Have you tried the door?"

Miriam stood and felt the twinge of old irritation. It had been easier when Sam had been unconscious, rage and hate toward Miriam subdued. "Sa—"

The woman's attention snapped back.

"You need to conserve your energy," Miriam said. "You—"

Sam raised a hand to silence her, stepped to the partition, adjusted, and drove a fist into it.

For a moment, Miriam allowed herself the smallest hope.

But nothing happened.

Sam hit it again. And again. The material only rang, and rang again. Miriam started forward, ready to call her off, then paused. Maybe this was better. Every strike took something out of Sam, possibly burning off both the human and Altered stimulants still churning through her system.

"No, Miriam—" Boy Scout warned.

At her name, Sam spun, and Miriam flinched at the woman's proximity. Sam's nose twitched as the red light caught across her face. But before anything could follow, the room changed. The light cycled painfully to white, and Miriam winced, her eyes adjusting as a muffled clang echoed ahead.

The partition opened.

At the foot of the stairs, Talwar stood abruptly, relief breaking across his features. He took a step toward the doorway. "What the hell was—"

But Miriam cut him off with a raised hand. "Talwar. Stay back."

He froze.

"Get upstairs and keep your distance."

"What—"

"Talwar."

That was enough. He obeyed, backing up until he moved to the top of the steps, and then more until she couldn't even see his boots.

Miriam gave Sam one last look, then stole past her into the short run by the steps. She didn't want to be in that room any longer, and Boy Scout and Sam fell in behind. Miriam climbed, slow and careful, one palm skimming the wall for purchase. "Coming up. Stay clear," she whispered.

When she was sure Talwar was far enough away, she stepped out of the hatch and into the back room but did not stray far from its frame. Talwar had melted toward the storefront, and Chapel had pivoted to watch both the street and the interior, eyes catching light like cut glass.

"What happened?" Talwar asked, tight with worry.

"I don't know. Some kind of gas. Don't come closer."

"Gas? Are you sick?"

Miriam shook her head. The aches were the day's work; nothing else had settled in. Behind her, Boy Scout and Sam stood in silence. Neither showed signs of distress anymore—just the same rigid tension.

Outside, dusk had deepened.

Then Chapel's hand shot up.

They all went still as stone.

He pumped an open palm behind him and drew deeper into the shadow. The others matched him. Miriam glanced at Boy Scout and saw his glinting eyes narrow. She could make out a thin, dark line trailing from one ear. Whatever Chapel had heard, Boy Scout's senses no longer caught.

And they waited, long enough for Miriam's muscles to threaten to cramp. Eventually, Chapel gave another signal, and they relaxed. Miriam studied the wreckage of the store again, scanning past the canted shelves. The building was a blind, hidden in plain sight, but it was a trap, too. The narrow hallway leading to the back door led out into an open area, and the main road in front was exposed. SOG and Legion had failed their first mission through poor leadership and judgment, yes, but also because this place wasn't meant to be defended properly. Now, they were five bodies: three Seraphs and two marines, held together by grit and habit. All running on injuries and fumes.

She had glimpsed how SRAF fought and what they were capable of, but defense seemed impossible. Especially now at night. Sam was standing, but it was clear her body hadn't caught up to her mind. Boy Scout wavered, his senses clearly dulled since the vestibule. And Talwar clutched his rifle but was running low on ammunition. Even Miriam, with a half-spent sidearm, felt the pith of that imbalance.

"We can't stay here," she muttered.

They could, but the shop itself was a tactical nightmare and she didn't want to be trapped in that underground room again.

"We can backtrack," Talwar offered. "To—"

Miriam shook her head.

The Charonites had said it themselves—their front lines were collapsing. The Apostates, the Heretics, had pushed past the point of balance. No-man's-land, the strip of cushion between two warring sides, had moved. They were not only stranded but farther from relative safety.

"We need to find another site," she said. "Hold, rest, then decide."

They needed time to recover, to assess what exactly had happened past that partition. The others said nothing, a consensus of its own. Boy Scout tipped a look to Chapel, some silent communication passed between them, and Chapel moved out of the shadows. Talwar hovered, looking between the now separated halves of their group before falling in with the other Seraph.

Miriam stayed back, preparing to follow—until the shelf

beside her knocked against the wall. Sam braced herself, elbow against the metal, and Miriam reached out, but the woman straightened before a helping hand could land.

"I can walk," Sam hissed.

Hell.

Miriam bit her lip to stifle the response clawing its way out. Sam had saved her, twice in the past hours, but every glance, every interaction said she regretted it. The woman pushed past her, rigid. Stubborn as ever.

And they fell into an offset line, Chapel and Talwar at the front, then Miriam, Sam, and Boy Scout forming the rear. The night's wind picked up, slipping through the empty streets, masking their footsteps. They crossed from cover to cover, each stretch of open ground longer than the last. Aside from the Altered Seraph in front, Miriam and the others moved slowly, carefully placing their feet in the dim moonlight.

It felt like an hour before Boy Scout stopped and Sam and Miriam with him. Ahead, Chapel raised a hand. Miriam could make out his silhouette as he pointed to a squat, unremarkable structure that looked no different from the others—cracked concrete, exposed rebar like a ribcage, windows blown out.

Miriam squinted and frowned. Why that one?

Before she could ask or continue, Boy Scout's voice roughened behind her. "Something is wrong."

She turned.

"I think I need to stop."

They were still exposed. Miriam glanced toward the building—their destination only a short distance away. Talwar and Chapel had already moved on, waiting outside the lip of the entrance, watching them.

Boy Scout took a few more steps, then slowed. He peeled a seam in his armor and touched his side. Though she couldn't see well in the darkness, Miriam could see enough. The contrast of darker shades. His hand was slick with blood.

Her pulse jumped. He shouldn't have been bleeding. They

had checked for injuries earlier. There had been nothing substantial or immediately concerning.

As he faltered, Sam caught his arm, bracing under his shoulder. Boy Scout leaned into her but didn't collapse, and Miriam quickly came up on the other side.

"Inside," she whispered. "Now."

Together, they supported him, guiding him the rest of the way to the small house. Chapel had already disappeared inside, clearing the space, and Talwar kept his distance as they entered.

The interior was stripped and pocked, ceiling partly intact, three and a half walls holding. It had once been a home: torn curtains clinging to a rod, old furniture now dusty and broken. It wasn't secure, but it would do for now.

The three of them made it into the central room before Boy Scout buckled. His mass dragged them both down, and Miriam's knee hit cracked tile. Pain lanced through her thigh, but she kept hold of the large man, breaking his fall.

Now without the moonlight, Miriam adjusted her knee so she was oriented to him. With Sam's help, she lowered Boy Scout to his back. He didn't protest. Her hand found her sling, and by feel alone, she found a gel bandage, tore the seal open with her teeth, and touched his exposed side where she had seen his hand go.

"I need light," she said, words gritted out around the bandage wrapper in her mouth.

Sam's hands went to her own armor, fumbling, then frantic, but in the end, a small torch flared red between her fingers. Miriam winced at the sudden illumination, but she could see again. Her fingers found the injury, but underneath the small light, it was unimpressive, despite the blood that was pooling and flowing out. It was a gash, but shallow. Nothing into the muscle.

This wasn't the cause of whatever was draining him. She pulled gauze from her kit and wiped at the blood, then pressed the bandage down, sealing it.

"Is he going to be okay?" Talwar asked from the far side of the room.

"Stay back," Miriam answered. She tapped Boy Scout's cheek to get his attention. "Where else are you hurt?"

Green eyes glowed up at her. He shook his head then hesitated. He didn't know. That, more than anything, terrified her.

"Help me," Miriam whispered, tapping the latches on his armor.

At first, Sam fumbled with the release. She placed the torch in between her teeth and tried again. When it was open and stripped, Miriam ran her fingers over Boy Scout's undershirt—damp, but not with sweat. She found the ridge beneath his collarbone, sticky and shallow. She looked around, catching the glint of a tool in his discarded armor, grabbed it, and used it to cut his shirt away.

The only source she'd located was a scrape. Minor. This wasn't it either. Whatever was ailing Boy Scout must've been something she'd missed.

"I need to turn you," she said.

The man gave a faint sound of acknowledgment. Sam helped, and together they rolled him. While Sam inspected his limbs, Miriam's hands skimmed along his back. No gashes, no breaks. They lowered him onto his back again.

Miriam opened another bandage but then paused as she watched blood gather in the hollow of Boy Scout's throat. The abrasion just below it that she'd seen before was bleeding. Profusely and unusually so, especially for an Altered. Especially for a former legionnaire whose design was supposed to be stronger, different than the other kinds of Altered.

Miriam knew Sam was watching her, waiting, but she was trying to wrap her mind around what she was seeing. This wasn't right. Miriam had seen legionnaires heal; she had seen Hadeon heal. The Altered soldiers didn't bleed like this. Not from something so minuscule and small. Scratches. Scrapes.

Unless—

Something had happened in that vestibule.

"Infected," she whispered.

But with what? Miriam had never seen this before.

"Tan?" Talwar asked.

"Perimeter," she said. "Don't—don't come close. Either of you."

Obeying, Talwar backed into the small foyer. Chapel, who had emerged on the other side, held his ground beyond the threshold.

Miriam quickly pasted the second bandage on, but as she did, she could see the blood still slipping out from beneath the edges. She didn't know what to do. The wounds weren't fatal, not even close, but something was wrong. His body wasn't responding as it should—the opposite. It was fighting him.

Boy Scout's head lolled, and he groaned weakly, a low keening sound.

"Hang on," Sam whispered, pressing both dressings, breath rough with effort.

But Miriam's finger inched toward his wrist and found his pulse. Falling.

Yuri's device, the Altered contraption, flashed through memory. Altered MedTech. She yanked it from her sling and ripped it from its case. In the dim light, she couldn't make out its orientation but unfolded it by feel. It resembled a broad tourniquet with a small housing on one end and a soft sealing ring beneath. What was she supposed to do with this? It wouldn't fit around his torso. Or would it?

"Miriam."

Her name, hoarse and pleading, pulled her attention back. For the first time, the anger in Sam's face was gone, replaced by fear.

A wet gurgle rose out of Boy Scout's mouth.

Shit. Internal bleeding as well? Fluid in the lungs?

Miriam bent low, ear to his chest. She could hear it, the liquid rasp.

He tried to speak and choked again. "Willem," he said at last.

She met his dimming eyes.

"My name is Willem."

And then he was gone.

24

PENANCE

GONE.

Across the room, Chapel whispered three words, a benediction or a dirge, for the man, the Altered, who had once been a legionnaire, once a Seraph.

Boy Scout. Willem. He had been fine.

And then he wasn't.

Path to glory.

What glory was there in this?

Miriam sank back onto her boots, then let her legs slide out from under her, dropping fully to the floor. She hadn't known the man. Not really. Just a handful of hours, a few exchanges, but the loss still hit. It lodged somewhere between her ribs and refused to move.

The day had stretched beyond comprehension—Herrera's death, the crash, the partition, the vestibule, and now this. It was one more weight thrown onto an already compounding pile. Pressure welled behind her eyes and her chest. Her bottom lip trembled before she bit down on it hard, reining in what threatened to spill.

"What just—I don't understand," Sam said. Her voice wavered, though her face hardened in the red glow.

Miriam turned away. "I tried. I—" The words stopped. The idea of Sam's judgment hollowed her. If she thought Miriam was to blame, she wouldn't survive it.

A sound drew her eyes back. Sam fumbled at her armor, reaching for something that wasn't there. Her movements grew more frantic, and then she stood rapidly.

Unsteady.

Still.

It was subtle. A tremor of imbalance, a breath caught too long, the unfocused glaze across her eyes.

One small step back.

"Sam—" Miriam's voice thinned as the woman tipped.

She lunged and dove, her hand sliding beneath the curve of Sam's head before it struck the hard floor. Pain smashed through her bones and nerves.

Miriam rushed to her knees, cradling Sam as she examined her face in the dim light. The whites of Sam's eyes were marbled with burst vessels, dark filigree against unnatural pallor. Her skin was clammy and her eyelids flickered.

Wrong. Everything was wrong.

"What the fuck—" Talwar rasped from the doorway. "Fuck."

Miriam ignored him. Her breath stuck in her lungs as she tore at Sam's armor clasps, muttering her name over and over, pleading.

But no response.

She applied her knuckles hard into Sam's sternum, a quick, grinding rub, willing for a flicker of reaction.

Nothing.

Her urgency intensified. Fingers raked over the woman's torso, arms, flanks, searching for hidden wounds.

Again, nothing.

Miriam scrambled lower, dragging her palms down Sam's right leg, then up her thigh. Dried blood, but no tears. She repeated on the left—

And inhaled sharply.

Warm. Wet.

Her fingers hooked a seam and ripped fabric wide. In the low light, black streaked Sam's thigh, a slick trail cutting downward. Blood.

Where had this come from?

Miriam wiped at it, frantic, clearing the surface, trying to trace its source. Just inside the leg, halfway up. A shallow gash. Not wide, not deep, yet bleeding steadily. Like Willem's. It was far too much for something so slight. She clamped her hand against it, trying to stem the flow. Then she noticed something she had missed: the grazes on Sam's forehead, once clotted, now weeping in slow rivulets.

That shouldn't have been possible. These were surface wounds. They had scabbed over. Dried and stopped bleeding.

Her breathing hitched, growing fast and uneven, panic pressing into her like iron bands. She dropped her ear against Sam's chest, desperate. Listening and praying. Her lungs were clear, at least, but Miriam couldn't tell what else was failing inside her.

"Tourniquet," she muttered, reaching reflexively.

But she had none. Her main kit was gone. She had her sling and what was left in her rig, but she had lost most of what she needed. She looked at Sam's scattered armor, then Willem's, but neither had anything she could see. Her eyes caught on the dropped device she had previously unfolded. Without thinking, she snatched it up, cinched the flexible band around Sam's thigh, and sealed it against the wound. It would have to hold.

With that site addressed, Miriam made a practiced sweep for any other hidden injuries. Nothing obvious or anything critical, but she had made the same search before. It made no sense, that this tiny wound had dropped Sam. Unless there were aftereffects of the Altered stims? A collapse from mixing substances, or something Miriam had no language for.

She was out of her depth.

She unwrapped a pressure dressing and trussed it around

Sam's head, layering it securely despite the persistent seep. When she finished, Miriam didn't move, didn't sit back.

"Tan."

Miriam continued to ignore Talwar. Sam's chest moved, shallow, uneven, but it was moving. That was all she could cling to. Had she used the device in time? She thought of Willem's motionless body behind her and tried to force the thought back. They needed help, help beyond what Miriam could provide, but she wouldn't be able to move her. Not in this state, and not for long distances.

"Tan, are you—are you going to be okay?"

Her eyes lifted, catching his full of concern.

"I'm—" She faltered, fingers glancing over the shallow scrapes across her arms again. Sensitive, but dry. No sign of change. She reached across her shoulder and dabbed at the curve where the Heretic had bitten her. The fabric tacked to her skin, but the wound beneath wasn't freely bleeding. Not like Willem. Not like Sam.

She glanced at the woman again—unconscious, still breathing. The device's cuff on her thigh was holding, but the head dressing had already soaked through. Sam's face was gaunt and her skin wrong in the shifting red glow.

And yet Miriam felt fine. Lightheaded, some fog behind the eyes, but she wasn't bleeding. Her body hadn't turned on itself the way the others had.

Not yet.

Neither she nor Talwar spoke after that. Not for a long while. And Chapel kept watch by the ragged hole in the side wall. Eventually, he moved—a shape half-obscured by darkness —dragging a slab of broken drywall from another corner of the house. Miriam frowned until she understood: he was guiding it carefully into place, not to barricade but to conceal the entrance they had used. A mask, not a wall.

At some point, Talwar nodded off in the hall, slumped beside the remains of an accent table, weapon clutched to his collarbone. The consequences of the day had caught up with him.

However, Miriam didn't sleep. She stayed beside Sam and Willem's body in the room they had claimed for distance, her eyes moving between injuries that gave no answers. Her own scrapes were raw but dry. Ordinary. Whatever was happening, it wasn't happening to her.

Yet. Always the yet.

Sam stirred, once—a ragged intake of air—but didn't wake. The device cinched at her thigh worked as intended, a makeshift cell saver holding what it could, but it wasn't enough. Miriam couldn't tell if the woman was stable or merely delaying. With no one to see, she let her hand rest over Sam's, silently willing her to hold on.

Earlier, she had watched Chapel circle the house with quiet purpose. When she'd asked why this place, he'd answered simply that he could smell more earth beneath this block. She'd realized he meant a basement or a cellar—not that they had made it that far. But his movements made it clear he meant to fortify, shifting debris as though preparing for a longer stay.

He knew. He understood.

With a jerk, Talwar startled awake and blinked at the paling sky bleeding through the slats. It'd only been a couple hours, but dawn was arriving.

"You can't stay here," Miriam said, her voice low.

He rubbed a hand over his face. "We'll move soon."

She shook her head. "No. You two need to go. Get help."

"What are you—no. We're not going to leave you—"

"I can't leave her."

His eyes flicked to Sam, then back. "She's not going to make it—"

Her gaze cut him off. "I don't know what we've been exposed to. I could still be a carrier," she said, her voice breaking, then leveling. "We can't risk it."

"So we stay apart, but together. When we—they regroup, they'll come back for her—"

"Talwar," Miriam said flatly. "I'm staying."

His mouth shut. He shook his head, disbelief roughening his features.

Behind him, a quiet voice slid in. "How many rounds do you have?" Chapel stood hidden in the dark, his eyes glowing.

Miriam's hand went instinctively to her sidearm. "A few."

Talwar checked his own kit, but she shook her head. He didn't have enough, and what he carried he'd need for himself if he meant to get out.

"Save them," Chapel said. "For the end."

Talwar's head whipped up. "What?"

"One for her," Chapel said evenly. "And one for you."

Talwar's face twisted. "What the fuck is wrong with you?"

But the Altered didn't blink. "If they find you, they will take her apart, piece by piece. You know how they work. Do not let them capture either of you alive."

Miriam looked at him, then at Sam. She gave a single slow nod.

Talwar swore, jaw clenched tight. After a long moment, he rose, his hand stalling over his rifle as if he could tether himself to the decision. "Don't die, Tan."

"You, too."

He nodded, then moved toward the entrance. Chapel followed, his steps soundless. She listened to the scuff of drywall hauled back into place.

The space fell quiet.

Miriam reminded herself she wasn't entombed. There were other exits—fragile windows, broken walls, another door somewhere—but the house felt like a casket all the same. She kept her eyes from the sealed entrance, refusing to picture herself abandoned, left behind, this time by choice as much as circumstance. The urge to call them back tightened in her throat.

She swallowed it down.

♟

Miriam wiped the sweat from her brow and slumped against the wall. Dust clung to her skin and hair, but she no longer cared. She had checked and rechecked the device strapped to Sam's thigh, rewrapped the bandages after half dragging, half carrying her into the cellar. It wasn't quite a basement, only a half level down, part of the flooring unfinished, a strip of hard-packed earth yawning across one side. She had burned through nearly everything in her sling to keep Sam from bleeding out. The cell saver was the only miracle within reach, and she whispered a silent thanks to Yuri, filing away a promise to tell him later that his potential collaboration with the Altered had already worked wonders. That fragile optimism was all that kept her from spiraling.

Baby steps, she told herself. She would get Sam out. She would get them both out. But first, she had to keep her alive.

She rested the back of her hand against Sam's forehead. The woman's temperature fluctuated between cool and fevered, but at least her heart rate had stabilized. It was a little slow, but that was expected with blood loss.

The small cellar offered little light, a sliver through a narrow window partially blocked by collapsed debris. It was enough to breathe, but the lack of circulation made the air stale. She couldn't complain. It was hidden and insulated. They could hold there until the others came back.

Her thoughts wandered to the four marines who had perhaps done something similar—waited and hoped—only to be found too late. She shook her head and forced the memory away.

With one more check of the device, Miriam let herself sit back for another moment. She was slowing. The multiple adrenaline crashes and previous day's aches racked her body.

But she forced herself up and climbed the three steps, crossed the short hall, and stepped into the family room. Willem's body remained where he had fallen.

She stopped, straining to listen past the pounding in her head. No sounds. No movement. Bracing herself, she slipped her arms beneath Willem's shoulders and pulled. He barely budged. She gritted her teeth, reset her stance, dug her boots into the floor, and heaved until she managed to drag him into the next room, out of sight of any casual glance through one of the shuttered windows.

Breathless, she hovered over him and stared at the smear of blood she'd dragged with him. It'd dry soon in the heat and hopefully not catch a wandering eye. His discarded armor lay nearby. Beneath one plate, she saw the hilt of a compact dagger —the same one she'd used to cut his shirt open. Her hand hesitated before she took it, checked its sharp edge, and slid it into her belt at the small of her back.

Then she frowned. She didn't notice anything yet, but she thought about Willem's scent. Miriam wasn't sure how quickly decomposition would start with the Altered—she'd never stuck around a body long enough to know—but she wasn't willing to risk enemies catching the smell from far off. Both Willem and Chapel were former legionnaires and had more dialed-in senses than humans—and to her knowledge, more than the usual Altered—but she didn't know the capabilities of the Apostates or Heretics here. She didn't want to find out.

Quietly, she scavenged the house, gathering cloth, scraps of curtain, whatever she could find. In the bathroom, she found a plastic-like material. She layered them over Willem's form, tucking and wrapping until he was covered. It was crude, but it'd do. She promised herself she'd bring him back, though she had no idea how. There were more pressing priorities now, but she added it to the list. She had to keep her mind busy, keep believing this was temporary. That she'd get Sam out, that she'd survive.

The cabinets and drawers were empty of anything of use, stripped long ago. A ruin of a house in a ruin of a block, everything scoured by war and scavengers. Her throat burned with thirst, her fingers swollen. Sam was worse. Stabilized, but with the blood loss, she'd be close to death by dehydration alone. It was another priority, higher now than most.

Evening bled into dusk before she noticed. She stood there as it grew darker, knowing she should turn into the cellar before she couldn't see, but she lingered and tried not to panic, tried not to imagine Talwar and Chapel caught or dead. Or worse. Time moved as it wanted, cruel and careless.

When the light failed, she felt her way along the walls, careful of her step. She didn't want to make noise, didn't want to risk bumping something or alerting whoever might be near the block. As she passed Willem's shrouded form, she stopped.

A sound. A shuffle.

But not outside.

Inside.

Miriam froze, every muscle alert, adrenaline pumping tirelessly again.

Shit. Sam.

She rushed for the cellar door and slipped down the steps, heart hammering. The red glow of the small light enunciated Sam thrashing, convulsing as though electrified. Foam had already flecked her lips.

"Sam—" Miriam threw herself down, shielding the woman's head, bracing her limbs against the jerking. "Shit. Hold on. Hold on."

Her arms locked around her, muffling the worst of the movement. The cellar trapped most of the sound, but not enough. Not against genetically engineered hearing.

At last the seizure ebbed. Miriam didn't move, held position close, waiting. She had nothing for this. No sedatives, no medication, nothing. And where had this come from? Was it a side effect of whatever they'd encountered in that facility?

When she dared pull back, she dragged in a long breath. None of this made sense. She stayed with Sam through what felt like hours, sometimes reaching out to check for the rise and fall of her chest. Still alive. Barely. But alive.

At some point, Miriam startled awake, her head jerking up. Outside, light crept in. Gunfire cracked in the distance, then faded. She checked Sam's pulse. Weak, but there. The woman's skin and underclothes were drenched again with sweat, her body trembling beneath. Miriam's eyes went to the bandage and the device cinched to her thigh; the bleeding had slowed, the receptacle showing less output with each check. But Sam's body was failing for another reason.

Miriam startled as Sam jerked, gagged, then heaved. Nothing came. She caught her quickly, easing her back to the floor, whispering useless comforts. Sam stilled, but the quiet did not reassure her.

Then Miriam's spine went rigid.

The tremors. The temperature swings. The seizure.

"Fuck," she whispered, heat and panic rising in her throat.

Withdrawal.

She had been so intent on the bleeding, on the unknown agent they'd been exposed to, that she'd missed it. She scrambled back to the room where Sam's discarded armor was, rifling through every clasp and seam, but found nothing. Willem's gear yielded no better. Either Sam had burned through the last of her stim and calmer stash, or it'd been lost in the wreck, scattered in the scramble of the fight.

Another curse slipped out, this one at herself. She should have realized sooner. She dragged up every fragment of training she could recall, but all of it pointed toward overdose protocols. Not this. Withdrawal needed tapered stabilizers, intravenous lines, fluids.

Things she didn't have.

And Sam had none.

Dehydration gnawed at her.

Miriam dug her hands into her temples, head throbbing as if her skull itself might split. A human could survive three days without water in perfect conditions. These were anything but. They had already bled through more than a full day, and Sam had sweated out nearly everything she had left. The sour reek of her body had diminished, and Miriam couldn't tell if it was because the supply of sweat had run dry or because she herself had stopped noticing, her senses numbed by familiarity and exhaustion.

Her own mouth was parched, her head swimming. Wherever Talwar and Chapel were, she couldn't rely on that option. She couldn't trust they'd return in time

She needed to find water. She needed to find supplies. She needed to keep Sam alive. She needed herself alive. And the only way to do that was to face the thing she dreaded most.

She had to go out.

Alone.

25

WAGER

MIRIAM TRIED NOT to think of the what-ifs, but they came anyway. What if Talwar and Chapel had made it out, only to return while she was gone? What if they found Sam and left without her? What if Sam had another seizure while she was away—and worse, what if she made noise and the Heretics found her before she got back?

Miriam shoved the thoughts aside with effort. She had done what she could. Her hands had trembled as she cleaned Sam, then wrapped her in scraps of scavenged fabric to dampen any sound. She'd bound her arms loosely, hoping to blunt the thrashing. Sam had been unconscious then, her face pale and breath thready.

Miriam glanced back once in the direction of the house, committing the route to memory. Every street, the broken signs, the corners, the collapsed porches, every obstruction. She couldn't afford to forget.

Her chest ached. Instinct screamed to reach for a rifle or medkit, but both were long gone. The pounding in her skull had worsened, and her mouth was dry and cracked, the taste of metal and dust clinging to her swollen tongue. Every breath scraped at the inside of her throat.

She wiped sweat from her forehead before it could streak the soot smeared across her skin. She could no longer smell it, but she hoped the ash covered the reek of blood and sweat well enough.

And there were new what-ifs now. More immediate ones.

From behind the blackened husk of a kiosk, she studied the corner across the street. It was a small, unremarkable shop, perhaps once a pharmacy. After the last block's failures, it was her best hope. The building straddled the main boulevard, charred but mostly intact, and a side street torn open by a crater.

Miriam avoided the open stretch of the boulevard, measuring each step as she sidled toward the sunken road. She skirted its rim, careful not to slip into the center, her eyes catching on every detail that might guide her back.

At the shadow of a vehicle tipped on its side, she crouched and waited. The storefront sagged under its own collapse, most of its windows boarded, the front door caved in beneath the fallen second story. Along one edge, a pane had shattered, leaving a breach narrow enough to pass through.

She held, listening. No sound, no movement. She slipped forward. Through the gap she moved, shoulders scraping rusted frame and broken glass. She placed each foot with care, old muscle memory from childhood sneaks through her parents' house echoing now in grim utility.

Inside, she froze, ears straining. Shafts of light cut down through holes in the ceiling, striping the room in pale gray. Shelves leaned, some broken, some emptied. Above her, remnants of an apartment dangled, walls torn loose, hanging like skin peeled away.

She pushed forward. Spices. Scraps. Nothing useful. She needed hydration, rations, anything to replace the lost medical pack.

Then—a glint. A small cylinder tucked against a shelf. Hope

fluttered. She snatched it up, only to feel its weightless rattle. Empty.

Her breath escaped in a quiet, broken shudder.

And then, a sound. A scritch.

Her body jolted, the hairs of her neck rising.

It came again, faint but real.

She wasn't alone.

Her stomach contracted as she turned toward the noise deeper inside, but her shoulder brushed the shelf, nudging the cylinder. It tottered. She caught it fast, the metal crinkling in her grip, the sound deafening.

Shit.

Crouching lower, Miriam folded herself into shadow and went still. She counted out a long fifteen seconds before her thighs burned, a cramp threatening to force her up, but she didn't rise.

At last, she slid her pistol free, the soft rasp of metal. She kept it close. Only three rounds left—one chambered, two in the magazine. She knew what it meant. Even so, the act of holding it brought a measure of steadiness.

Movement flickered. A tuft of hair appeared at the end of the aisle, followed by a nose, then part of a face. She could barely make out the whites of the individual's eyes.

Relief flooded through her. No green shine.

Not one of them.

"Stop," she whispered.

The hair bobbed and froze.

A boy, she realized. Young.

Keeping her pistol raised, she lifted her other hand, palm out. A warning. "Friendly," she whispered again.

The boy's head turned, trying to find her. His shoulders inched into view, followed by his arms, then hands. No sling, no rifle.

She gestured slightly with her sidearm, pointed at him, then touched her sternum with two fingers.

He only stared.

"Do you have a weapon?" she asked instead.

He shook his head, voice quavering. "No."

Miriam lowered the pistol a fraction, and he stepped forward, tentative. "Stay," she ordered, palm out again. His scuffed steps had already betrayed his inexperience.

Instead, she slowly closed the distance, eyes scanning his frame. A torn rig clung loosely to him, but he was otherwise unarmed. His clothes were ripped, skin streaked with dirt.

She stopped a few meters away. He shifted again, and she snapped her hand up more firmly. Miriam didn't know what her blood carried, whether it could pass to him. She didn't want to find out.

"You're not one of them, are you?"

She frowned, shaking her head. The question was absurd, but fear bent reason. It made children foolish. It made grown marines foolish, too.

"Water?" Her voice rasped.

The boy's face brightened. He turned, motioning for her to follow, then pointed to a battered box tucked beneath a shelf. She motioned him back before she crouched to check. Inside, three water packets remained, their plastic sides cloudy with dust but intact. She tore one open, tipping it to her lips, an eye on her surroundings. The liquid was tepid and stale, but it slid down her throat like salvation.

Her chest loosened, even as her head kept pounding. She worked her throat once, then noticed him watching her, eyes too large. Miriam sealed her lips around the packet, forcing herself to hold back, and pocketed a cheekful of water.

On the boy's arm, through grime and soot, she caught the ink of a tattoo. Its lines were raised and angry. New enough to be infected.

A Charon lamp.

Of course.

He took a hesitant step, and Miriam mirrored the motion in reverse, backing away.

"Stop," she hissed. "Don't come closer."

His slender brows knit in confusion, but he obeyed.

"Is there more?" She raised the packet.

He nodded quickly and led her to another stash by the collapsed counter in the back. She waved him back before checking it. Rations. She took one, punctured it with her teeth, and sucked the contents—thick, tasteless paste. It stuck to the back of her mouth, but it was something.

"What's wrong with you?"

Her eyes cut to him. "I don't know." She softened her voice. "What's your name?"

"Ian."

She gave a single nod. "Ian, I'm Tanner. Listen. Did you see a marine and a...big guy pass through?"

He dipped his head. "No, but we were with a bunch of grunts and rats a couple days back."

Her body stiffened. So he'd been among the Charonites complementing Echo, Charlie, and Legion. She hadn't noticed him—of course not. Adolescent faces became interchangeable. Disposable. Forgettable.

"You're by yourself?"

Ian nodded, lip trembling. His eyes brimmed with tears, but he sniffed and shoved the back of his arm across his face. He sat carefully on the floor and angled away while Miriam crouched a distance away.

"Where are the others?" she asked. She wasn't sure how many had survived. There'd been two kids she'd seen rounded up by Altered enemies near their landing zone before it'd all gone to shit.

He shrugged and sniffled again, but he glanced back in the silence that followed, checking to see if she was still there.

Miriam set aside the ration and opened another water packet. "Why are you here, Ian?"

The words escaped before she knew what she'd meant to ask. Why were any of them there? For SOG and Legion, they were cleaning up someone else's mess. For the Charonites in the North, it was a grasp at regaining land. But for this boy? Was it truly his fight, or someone else's idea planted deep enough he believed it?

He hugged his knees. "My friends…"

The same friends who had either perished or been the ones to hand him a rifle and shove him into a war zone.

"And your home? Family?"

His shoulders folded tighter. Defensive. Miriam read the signs. Fragile, insecure, and isolated. The young were pliable, clay in the hands of any sculptor offering meaning and belonging. He had found it with the Charonites, found purpose, maybe, even if that purpose had been soaked in hate he likely didn't understand.

That was the trench she couldn't cross with the Charonites. The difference between indoctrination in Station City's shadow, where there was still food, still shelter, still choices, and indoctrination in the North, in fire and ruin.

Miriam felt the sting of conflict. Could she change him, help him, if she tried? Could she chip away at the poison fed to him since birth? Or since whatever catalyst that had thrust him this way? How could she save him when she couldn't save herself, when she could barely keep Sam alive, when her own blood might already be tainted? It wasn't her responsibility, but whose was it then? It surely wasn't a priority at this moment.

"Are they coming to get us?" he whispered.

Miriam hesitated. Lean on optimism? The what-ifs were too much. The truth crowded her tongue like a boulder. She opted for honesty and shook her head. The territory changed hands in weeks. Could they last weeks?

His next whisper broke. "Are we going to die?"

Miriam chose not to answer. She drank more water instead.

After a moment, her ear twitched at the crunch of gravel

outside. Her muscles coiled, though she doubted anyone could see this deep into the store, not past the boarded windows and maze of shelves. Still, she submerged herself into the shadows, breath locked in her throat, hoping that whoever was out there couldn't sense who was within.

Footsteps. Not one, but several. What if it was her teammates? UMF? SRAF?

She lifted a hand toward Ian, but he had frozen again, head dipped between his shoulders, his body shrinking into itself. Miriam eased toward the front but slowed as the sound grew louder—heavier steps this time, the cadence distinct. A procession. And then she heard the voices, indistinct but with no effort made to hide them.

Her heart sank. It wasn't UMF or SRAF. Not with that lack of noise discipline. But what if it were Charonites?

She stole closer to the break in the display wall, where part of the collapsed facade had left a narrow slit of vision. Flattening herself, she leaned and peered through.

At least four people, maybe more. The ones in the front had already passed, but this group was too close to be scouts, too disorganized to be a formal vanguard.

A clatter of chains broke the air. Miriam shifted, enough to glimpse the source. An Altered, a Heretic, held the end of a leash, its links scraping as he yanked hard. Something stumbled into view, a mass of sullied color—once pristine white, now matted with soil.

Miriam drew in a tight breath.

The legionnaire's pupils slid sideways, unerring, straight toward her hiding place.

Perun.

Miriam's pulse thundered. She dug her nails into her palms until pain anchored her silence. Had Legion returned for her and Talwar? Or worse—had they never escaped at all?

Perun's gaze raked the ruin with surgical precision, each flick of his eyes too focused, too knowing. Then the Heretic hauled the leash again, dragging him forward and out of sight.

Did he see her? Were there others?

She stayed there, rigid, until the last shuffling step receded. Only then, when silence stretched long enough to fray her nerves, did she peel herself back and slip to the boy in the rear.

"Enemies?" Ian whispered.

Miriam nodded once. He gulped.

"They have one of my teammates."

"Oh." His voice trembled. "Can he help us out of here?"

She shook her head. The odds were too steep. There were too many. And yet, if there were other legionnaires, what then?

"Did you see where they went? Should we go the other way? Unless that's where they came from, then I don't know—"

She shut him up with a sharp look. Miriam had what she needed now: limited water, a scrap of food, but it was enough to crawl back to Sam. It was enough to buy a little time. But the boy's eyes told her the truth she had already felt. He would follow. And she couldn't care for all of them.

Miriam forced herself to look at him and admit what her gut already knew: if she brought him, he would give her away with a sound or stumble or slow her enough to end them both. Sam's survival depended on her gambles being ruthless, and saving Perun—if it worked—could tilt the scales for them. She told herself she would come back for the boy, that if she made it out, she would not leave him behind. But right now, she couldn't carry both his weight and Sam's.

What if there were more legionnaires? Hadeon? If she could reach them, if she could help, maybe it would change the balance. She had counted four Heretics before, six at most. The legionnaire had fought through worse. If she freed Perun, if they struck fast, they might have a chance. Just enough of one.

The food steadied her and the water cleared her head, but it wasn't enough.

Miriam crouched, dragged her finger through the dust, and traced a crude map. "If I don't come back, I need you to find this house. Bring water. Food."

She hadn't seen the boy move until he was suddenly beside her. His hand clutched at her arm, shaking.

"Wait. You can't leave me here."

She peeled his fingers away instinctively but stopped halfway.

Their skin met. Skin to skin.

Miriam froze. Released him. Drew back as though the contact had burned her. She watched as if the effects might already show, as if his own grazes would burst open and bleed right then and there.

But Ian faced her, eyes wet and trembling. "I don't want to die."

Miriam didn't answer. She waited, but nothing came. Of course not. Willem hadn't fallen instantly. Sam's symptoms had spread in time. Had she just killed this boy? But she was still standing; she was still alive. Her head hurt.

"You can't leave me."

On this, her mind was already fixed. If she'd passed something to him, if it took an hour, or longer, it was done. There was nothing she could do.

"I have to try," she whispered, more to herself than to him. "Stay."

She rose and crossed the ruined store, silent and purposeful. Her limbs felt like iron, her brain throbbed, but her steps lengthened with intent. If she hurried, she could catch the procession, keep downwind, close enough to gauge the situation.

Hope squeezed into her thoughts, faint but undeniable.

This time, she didn't push it away.

Desperation gave it room.

26

______

OBLATION

SHE FIXED her eyes on the roof of the apartment building across from her, where a scrap of cloth dangled like a forgotten flag. It had once been a light pastel color—a shirt or curtain, perhaps—but now it hung limp and gray, stirring faintly. There was no true breeze yet. That was good.

Miriam's gaze returned to it again and again, a nervousness between the measured looks she cast down from her vantage point on the third story of the rickety structure she'd climbed. The overlook offered only a partial view of the plaza half a block away, but it was the balance she needed, close enough to see, far enough *not* to be seen.

She plastered herself down against the splintered floor beam, hidden behind the collapsed frame of a wall. Gaps in the plaster gave her just enough sightlines to the plaza. Dust coated her lips when she breathed, but she kept her chest tight. If she stayed still, the Heretics would hear only wind shifting through ruin, not the frantic pulse in her neck.

Her nerves buzzed under her skin as she observed Perun kneeling to the side of the clearing, a thick collar clamped around his throat. The chain fixed him to a stake driven into cracked pavement, but it wasn't the tether that held him, rather the four smaller sentries circling him with rifles and blades, eyes alert and pitiless. Even forced to his knees, Perun loomed large.

Beyond them, others worked with grim coordination, assembling a makeshift cage. Thick bars scavenged from wreckage had been welded and wired into shape. She squinted. There were tripods, braces, and anchor points. This was planned.

Miriam shifted for a better angle, but the floor creaked beneath her weight, and she froze. The building's bones were degraded. One wrong move and it might collapse beneath her. She retreated, readjusting herself into the stable groove she had previously held.

Below, Perun's head moved a fraction. She could make out the slight tilt of the chin, and his horizontal eyelids blinked. Did he know she was there? That she had followed?

A Heretic shouted a curt command, and the others turned toward Perun, laughing as they mocked him. One spat at him.

Miriam's hands formed fists, but she forced herself still. There were too many. She counted the possibilities: four guards, more assembling the cage. If they were stimmed, she had no chance at all. Even unenhanced, the numbers would crush her. Three rounds in her sidearm.

Only three.

She studied the plaza, hunting for distractions, for weaknesses she might exploit. If she could draw a handful away, just long enough, Perun might break free. She'd seen what legionnaires could do when unshackled. He had to have been as tired as her, but he was still strong, still a soldier without his armor. She just needed to give him the opening.

But then a voice rang out, derisive and mocking. One Heretic called to another, laughter breaking across the clearing.

Miriam stiffened. Perun wasn't the only prize here. She leaned, barely—just enough for another glimpse.

Then below, a sound broke the stillness. Something dropped on the level beneath her. The noise cracked like a detonation.

She froze. Even the Heretics stilled.

Then the order came. The leader of the four raised his hand and pointed. Two sentries peeled away toward her building.

Miriam's lungs clamped in. She flattened herself against the floor. Three stories up, her options dwindled to nothing. The stairs she'd meticulously climbed would lead her straight into them; the balcony meant a fall she might not survive. Even hidden, they'd find her. They'd hear her, smell her.

She gripped her sidearm. A single shot would give her away. She was cornered, trapped and—

A bestial roar ripped through the air.

Miriam flinched as Perun erupted upward in a single convulsion of strength. The chain shrieked, metal tearing free of earth, dust geysering outward in a plume. The Altered around him reeled back, weapons snapping toward him.

But he didn't flee.

He charged.

Chaos erupted with shouts, and weapons were raised. The two Heretics who had moved toward her building whirled back.

Perun crashed into the ones nearest him before their fingers could tighten on triggers. Even unarmored, he was ruin in motion, his body a blunt weapon. He seized the first Heretic, tore the blade from their hands and rammed it clean through their thorax. The individual shrieked once, silenced as Perun wrenched free, spinning already toward the next. He smashed into him, shoulder first, a thunderous impact, and twisted, snapping the man's neck with a sound like splitting wood.

Miriam's chest pinched, hope knifing through her. For an instant, she wanted to believe—wanted to believe he could break them all, that one legionnaire might still survive.

And Perun didn't stop. He met the returning Heretics, trading blows, before ripping one off his feet, slamming him into the cracked pavement, then driving his skull down with both hands until blood burst across the ground in a red halo.

But hope ebbed with every strike, each one pulling Miriam tighter toward despair. Perun wasn't trying to get away; he wasn't fighting for escape. He was offering himself.

The counter came swiftly before a few more individuals sprinted across the plaza as reinforcements. A rifle cracked out, bullets lancing through the legionnaire. And then a blade slid under his ribs, buried to the hilt by another Heretic. An additional weapon cracked across his jaw, snapping his head aside.

Miriam's teeth sank into her tongue, hot blood flooding her mouth as she strangled the rising cry.

Perun staggered, legs buckling. Blood poured dark across his uniform, running down in sheets that spattered the broken stone. The length of chain clinked against the pavement as though mocking him.

But he rose. One foot planted, then the other. His massive hand closed over the hilt in his side like he might rip it free through will alone. He lurched forward, arm outstretched toward his attackers.

The same Heretic who had stabbed him stepped forward and away at an angle, another blade sweeping in a merciless arc.

For a heartbeat, nothing.

Then the wet, heavy spill of entrails slapping against stone.

Perun's body shuddered. His knees gave out, sinking into the ruin of his own opened flesh. Still, his head lifted, blood running down his chin, lips shaping words Miriam didn't need to hear.

Path to glory.

The creed struck her deeper than any blade could, echoing in her bones like a curse. Her throat closed around it. This was what it meant to watch someone die, helpless and unseen. Her hands bound not by chains but by distance and fear.

The Heretic raised his blade and brought it down once more.

Miriam crushed her forehead into the floorboards until splinters pricked her skin. She shoved her knuckle into her mouth. Anything to keep from screaming. Her whole body shook, her vision fogged with tears she couldn't stop. She stayed there trembling, every breath a knife in her ribs, until a low and commanding voice cut across the plaza. Against her will, she raised her head, blinking against the sting in her eyes.

A figure all in black emerged, sauntering authoritatively across the plaza, tall and thin-shouldered, a predator at ease. Another followed, this one a bulkier silhouette, his presence brooding and oppressive. Another legionnaire? No. A traitor. A former legionnaire, perhaps, but now a Heretic, dressed in their arrogance. Both were oddly familiar.

The two sentries stiffened as their superior strode past. He gestured at Perun's butchered body, at the Heretics lying dead at his hands, and his voice carried the clipped certainty of command. With what he said, the men bowed their heads quickly, obedience without question, before moving back toward the cage and production.

There, tripods were adjusted with metallic clanks. Other individuals emerged, hefting rectangular cases that they cracked open like reliquaries. Spotlights unfolded, cables dragged through the dirt, the pieces fitted together with frightening efficiency. Broadcast equipment. An execution dressed for spectacle.

Miriam pressed herself flatter, every muscle aching from tension, her body slick and clammy with cold sweat. The breeze shifted and brought with it the fresh stench of blood and organs. It was faint, but it crept down her throat. She gagged and forced herself silent, one trembling hand smothering her mouth. She knew whose blood it was.

At the far end of the plaza, things had settled. Whatever they'd been setting up was done, and there was movement again. This time not disorder, but a march, a procession, rehearsed and choreographed like theater.

At its head, a Heretic in black strode with cruel pride, his stride exaggerated for the small crowd that had gathered there, for the broadcast to come. Behind him, two more dragged a prisoner bound at the wrists, staggering under their grip.

Miriam's diaphragm locked. Even before the figure's face was clear, she knew who it was.

Hadeon.

Her breath seized.

Even stripped of armor, the senior was unmistakable. White underclothes crusted with blood, a frame that still carried power, a posture braced with the rage of a soldier who had refused to break. The crude hack of her hair, the uneven scalp, the mockery, only made the truth louder. A senior legionnaire. A prize for the Heretics.

They shoved her toward the waiting structure. A cage. Hadeon stopped short, refusing, eyes fixed past it, past the trap itself, to where Perun's mangled body sprawled. For a second, the plaza stilled. The Heretic at her back raised a stolen blade— Hadeon's own—and tried to prod her in with its tip. She didn't flinch, only turned to face him.

Another barked an order, and the blade drove shallow into her belly, a cruel puncture meant to draw pain and submission, not death. Still, she did not yield. It took the other escort lunging in, striking with a second weapon, to knock her back. Hadeon stumbled, and in that imbalance, they shoved her fully into the cage.

Behind her, the door crashed shut with a theatrical clang, followed by the scrape of chain and the finality of a heavy bolt. The sound reverberated through the plaza and down the block of buildings like a verdict. At least a dozen Heretics gathered around, weapons in hand, posture bright with anticipation.

Miriam's fingers shook around the grip of her sidearm. Could she shoot the cage mechanism from this distance? It was too far, too risky with a sidearm. Impossible. Even if she freed Hadeon, the senior would die before crossing half the plaza. And then Miriam, shortly after. She could only watch.

The Heretic in charge raised his voice, words spilling with a cadence Miriam recognized. She couldn't hear exactly what or understand from the distance, but she'd heard the rhythm before. It was the same as the sermon before the four marines' execution.

Her gut turned as four spotlights flared at the corners of the cage. It was redundant in the daylight, but they reflected off the pan and flooring of the structure, something dark and covered in a film, a surface deliberately treated. The same viscous material trailed out in a line toward the Heretic and his behemoth enforcer behind him.

Miriam's eyes widened.

The man was finishing his speech, his hands thrown forward dramatically. And then the bulky Altered held out a small item to the man, who with a flick of his wrist, snapped it —a flare—to life. The man held it aloft, basking in the attention of his followers, his joy grotesque in its theatricality.

Miriam's heart stopped as the flare dropped in the slowest of motions. The trail caught at once, fire racing in a line like a fuse. Then the cage erupted, flames whooshing upward as though the air itself had been primed to burn. Miriam bit down on her hand until blood tinted her mouth, but she couldn't stifle the sound that escaped her throat as the blaze consumed Hadeon.

For one long second, the senior stood motionless in the inferno, her silhouette stark and terrible. Then instinct claimed her. She lunged for the bars, hands wrapping the metal, body flexing as she tried to bend and warp it. But it didn't. Her body thrashed against the walls of fire.

A scream ripped free. It tore through the clearing, through Miriam's marrow, deeper than anything she had ever heard. She was no stranger to death; she had known the cries of marines blown apart on the battlefield, the wails of enemies gurgling their last, and the screams of civilians trapped in cross fire. But never this. Never the strangling siren of someone she had fought beside, trusted, respected. This was a scream that undid her.

Blood wept through her teeth, but she kept her hand clenched between, taking the pain, as if she could take some away from the burning woman, as if she could do anything but witness.

Miriam's sidearm shook in her other hand. Three rounds. That was all she had. One could end this, if she aimed true despite the impossibility of the distance, the caliber. A mercy strike to Hadeon's head before the fire devoured her more. Or Miriam could waste it against the cage, a futile shot that would only draw every eye to her hiding place.

Her chest heaved as she weighed it. Her finger hovered over the trigger, a medic's mercy at war with a marine's cold math. Could she risk it? Could she risk failing?

She raised the barrel an inch, finger quivering. Her throat closed around a sob she couldn't voice. Her heart wrenched, tearing itself open with indecision. And in the end, she lowered the gun. She couldn't do anything.

Only watch.

Only witness.

And Hadeon's legs buckled. Her body collapsed, devoured whole. Still, the fire raged on.

27

AGON

MIRIAM WAS ALONE.

Whatever hope she'd gathered from the glimpse of legionnaire uniforms had been extinguished, gutted by what she had just witnessed. She mourned her teammates—the ones she couldn't save, the ones she'd failed, the ones who had died kneeling, screaming, burning. The ones who had once seemed invincible in her eyes. That grief settled into her bones like tar, impossible to shake.

She drifted back in a daze, her body sluggish and uncooperative, every limb a dead weight. Shock wrapped around her mind like gauze, muffling sensation, rendering her adrift, as if she stumbled through a drugged dream she couldn't wake from. And yet somehow, with all attention drawn toward the spectacle in the plaza, she made it back to the store. No one stopped her, and no one saw her. The Heretics had gathered around their theater of cruelty, and the streets between had blessed her with their emptiness.

Miriam crawled through the same breach as before, this time without the same care. Her hands raked across broken edges, skin tearing with shallow cuts, and her knees struck hard against the floor, but she hardly felt it. Her mind was still back there, locked behind constructed bars, unable to return.

She whispered a call out.

No answer.

Panic spiked and then wilted when her eyes landed on the signs. An upturned crate, her hasty map swept into nothing. The Charonite boy was gone. Maybe he had tried to follow her. Maybe he had wandered into the wrong street, gotten lost. Maybe something worse. But he was gone.

At least he had left something behind: two water packets, a couple of mashed rations. Not enough, but enough to be grateful. Barely.

She didn't know how long she sat there, but it was long enough to watch a thin line of blood dry along her thigh from where she'd cut herself clambering inside. It was long enough for the color of the day to die, shadows stretching across the floor as dusk fell and brought the quiet darkness that let terrible thoughts prowl unchecked.

She wanted to be home.

But she wasn't.

Miriam was here, and she was alone.

Eventually, she curled herself into the back corner of the shop and broke. Silent weeping racked her until her sore fist wedged against her teeth to dam the sound. The tears betrayed her—moisture she couldn't afford to lose, water her body had struggled to reclaim—and yet they fell anyway. She couldn't stop them, and she had no strength left to try.

It was too much.

She stayed like that, unmoving, unsleeping, as the images and the scents of fire and charred flesh branded deeper into her memory.

Miriam startled awake.

Her neck was stiff, her limbs numb, her body bent in a way that told her she hadn't intended to fall asleep. Daylight seeped through the slats and crevices above, indifferent, as though the world hadn't shifted, hadn't ended. She'd been out too long.

It was as if consciousness bade permission for everything to crowd in all at once. Days collapsed since Echo and Charlie had left, since the crash, the facility, the exposure, since Talwar and Chapel had separated from them. And the hours since she had watched Perun split open in front of her. Since Hadeon's scream had torn the sky apart. Every step since had been one long collapse: scavenging scraps, gambling with silence. Each failure and each death had settled onto her like anvils strapped to her body. She carried them all.

And Sam.

The name jolted her upright. Pain spiked through every joint as if her body resented her for moving at all. Her chest constricted, lungs dry, her stomach a clenched knot. She shoved it all down and forced herself to rise. She couldn't stop here. She had to get back.

She stuffed the small hoard of supplies into a sack she'd found beneath a fallen shelf. The movement was clumsy, her hands shaking, but she crimped it shut and staggered into the street. Each breath grated into her throat like sand. Each step demanded more than she had left. Hunger twisted in her belly again until it threatened to cramp her spine, but she didn't slow.

Miriam slipped from cover to cover, faster than the day before. Desperation and frustration hollowed her but kept her upright, a force greater than muscle. And the what-ifs roared back. What if she had saved Perun? What if she had shot the restraint on that cage? What if she had ended Hadeon's pain? What if, what if, what if. She tried to banish them, but they gnawed through her mind until her ears rang with them. The opposite effect.

The familiar block of residences appeared ahead, and relief

and dread tangled within her. She knew she wasn't being as careful. She just wanted to get back, away from everything. Despite the new sack digging into her back, what had been the point in going out? Doing all this?

But she was close.

The wave hit her again. What if Sam had taken a turn for the worse? What if Sam was— No. Not that. That was a what-if she couldn't bear on top of everything else.

And then—

A click.

Crisp and mechanical.

Her boot lifted before she understood.

There was a split-second tug against her foot, the metallic snap of a trigger wire jerking free. She barely registered it before instinct threw her backward, twisting toward the nearest large block of cover. The device went off waist-high, a small anti-personnel charge—more flash and concussive force than shrapnel. The low wall took most of the blast, the fragments spraying outward in the opposite direction. Miriam hit the ground, vision flashing white. Dirt sprayed her like a deluge.

When she came to, her ears whined with that high-pitched tone she hated, the sound of being alive but broken. Her limbs ached and her sides throbbed. She coughed—dry, painful heaves that pulled at something jagged inside her ribs—but even that was muffled in her head. A wave of nausea rolled through her, disorientation of a close detonation: tunnel vision, floating vertigo, the underwater thump of her heartbeat.

An ambush?

No. Stupid. Careless.

A trap.

Maybe something left behind by the Charonites. Maybe something newer. She hadn't been watching where her feet were, just focused on her destination, her next goal. It didn't matter.

She needed to get up, get away. She stretched her jaw open,

trying to clear her hearing, but nothing. Miriam patted herself and flexed her limbs. Nothing broken or serious. Tiny, hot pinpricks dotted her sleeve and shoulder—spent metal fragments that had lost their momentum by the time they ricocheted and reached her. The wall had shielded her from the worst of it.

Then her heart lurched.

The sack.

Her vision spun as she clawed across broken pavement, until she found it lying scorched but intact. She clutched it against her without checking it. There wasn't time. She needed distance, had to get to safety.

Her hearing refused to return, only the endless shrill ringing. Still, she staggered forward, one foot after another, her body moving only because her mind screamed Sam's name. The streets, walls, and alleys bent around her as though she dreamed them, but she kept moving.

When she finally reached the house, she braced against the slab of drywall Chapel had set to disguise the entrance. Her knees nearly buckled with relief, and she slipped inside through the window, pressing her back against the wall, lungs rattling as though she'd carried the whole city with her.

She hiked the sack up to her shoulder, limping through the rooms, down the dark hall toward the cellar. She stretched her jaw open and shut, again desperate to clear her ears. Still nothing but muffled echoes, an inconsistent buzz.

Miriam thought she heard something then—a whisper of movement, a breeze, behind her. Unsure, she turned back. Had she been followed? She stiffened, hand hovering over her sidearm, eyes straining against the dim light. She held her breath, the hairs on her arm bristling.

An exhale ghosted across the back of her neck. Every muscle locked and she whipped around—too late.

Hands seized her throat and slammed her against the wall. The shock snapped her skull against plaster, her teeth rattling as the air ripped from her lungs. She struggled at the grip, nails scraping. Her legs kicked out, boot striking uselessly. The mass pressing against her was too close, too strong.

Heretics. The word shot through her mind like a curse.

Her vision sparked white, each starburst colliding with the blackness that rushed in at the corners. The pressure on her throat crushed deeper until sound itself disappeared, her pulse the only roar left in her head.

She thrashed, scrabbling at the arms pinning her, her fingers tracing the ridges of muscle and scar—and then something different. Uneven. One arm warm, the other unnaturally cool, alien against her skin.

Recognition spiked through the fog.

Sam.

Miriam's throat burned raw, every nerve shrieking as the world narrowed to a single tunnel of darkness. She couldn't breathe, couldn't speak. The thought came unbidden: this was how it ended. After everything, this was her turn. Strangled in the dark by the woman she was trying to save.

Alone.

Her body slackened for half a heartbeat, resignation skimming close. Then her fingers moved, weak but stubborn, dragging down to her belt, past the sidearm she could draw but didn't, past Willem's dagger that she refused to use, until she grazed the hardness of the compact light. She fumbled and pried at it. Its hook fell out of her fingers and panic surged fresh. She groped again, this time squeezing it, engaging it.

Red light flared from below.

And suddenly, the grip loosened.

Miriam slid down the wall, gagging as her throat convulsed with dry heaves that ripped at tissue. She fought for breath as the small red light painted the hall in flat, merciless color. And though her vision was swimming, it returned enough for her to recognize Sam's boots in front of her.

The woman dropped to a knee, eyes wide. Her lips moved,

but the words reached Miriam as muted incoherence. Miriam forced a rasp of air into her lungs and heaved again. Her hearing returned by degrees, enough to make out syllables.

Too loud. They were too loud.

Noise. Stop. Sam was making too much noise.

The woman's mutters grew.

Miriam raised both hands, gesturing. QUIET.

And Sam froze.

When Miriam's breath settled, she dared a glance up. The motion dragged fire through the tendons in her neck. Sam's lips cracked open again, but Miriam gestured once more. YOU HAVE TO BE QUIET.

Sam's eyes widened more, darting between Miriam's hands, her face, and back to her hands. I THOUGHT YOU WERE— She shook her own hands out. YOU DIDN'T ANSWER.

ANSWER WHAT? Miriam tried to control another wheeze, shards of glass raking into her throat, then tapped her ear. She could already feel the swelling in her neck.

WHERE WERE YOU?

Miriam scowled, but the motion hurt. I HAD TO—

She straightened, despite her body's dissent.

The sack. The water and food.

Miriam dragged it from underneath her and opened it. The ration packets had ruptured, reduced to sludge already leaking to the ground. Water had spilled out, only half a packet intact.

Spoiled. Ruined.

Sam motioned again, but Miriam ignored her. She set aside the remaining water, threw aside the bag, and fixed on the waste, breath rasping in shallow pulls. Useless. It had all been in vain.

"I didn't know it was you," Sam whispered. "I'm sor—you weren't here, and I—I didn't—"

"What?" Miriam tried, but the word caught. She forced it out anyway. "You thought I abandoned you?"

Sam's lips shut.

Miriam's throat seized around the next breath. She set a shaking hand against the tender line where Sam's fingers had been. Speech was dangerous; she could feel the skin tightening, inflamed.

She felt Sam's hand reach out.

DON'T, Miriam motioned. The woman shouldn't even be up. She was still recovering, had to be running on fumes. JUST GO—GO BACK.

At first, Sam didn't move. Out of the corner of her eye, Miriam caught the motion—a hand, lifting slightly, uncertain. Reaching again. She couldn't tell. It might've been a reflex, or a moment of hesitation, but Miriam didn't turn to see it. She stared past the wall instead. She didn't want to know. She didn't have the clarity or the strength to make sense of it. Not now.

She stayed where she was, trying to anchor herself, bring herself back to some semblance of normal—whatever that meant. She kept her eyes on the wall where she knew beyond it lay Willem's body underneath dirty rags and plastic.

It was undignified. His death was undignified. Perun's. Hadeon's.

Miriam brushed her neck again, feeling the heat in full bloom beneath the skin. She had nearly died. Again. Sam had meant to kill her. No. Sam had thought she was an enemy. And though she hadn't killed her, perhaps she *still* thought Miriam was the enemy.

She knew she couldn't blame the woman. It had been instinct, defense, fear, possibly. Nevertheless, beneath all the reasoning, something bitter remained. Miriam wanted to blame Sam. It was a small mercy that Sam wasn't at her full strength. Miriam had seen what she could do. But she was awake now. Alive and lucid. Perhaps *that* was a blessing.

Miriam let out a scoff that dragged against her throat. The sound hurt, but not as much as the thought that followed. How was any of this a blessing?

Once she had salvaged what she could—nothing much—she forced herself upright with a groan. She paused and listened, straining for the sound of movement beyond the walls, for the echo of boots or the rattle of chains, but there was nothing but the creak of buildings around them. Whatever trap she had triggered, it hadn't brought immediate pursuit—but that didn't mean it wouldn't. They would need to be more careful now. Much more.

Under the red glow of the torchlight, Miriam shuffled into the cellar, taking each step one at a time, cautious and slow. Sam sat hunched across the space with her knees drawn tight, her arms wound over them, eyes hovering above. Her eyelids sagged, and her body was slack with exhaustion. She looked suspended between waking and collapse. She had burned through herself to fight, and Miriam had been the one to cost her that.

Miriam heard the soft intake of breath and knew Sam was about to speak. She raised her hand firmly, palm forward to stop her.

Words wouldn't conjure supplies. They wouldn't change what had happened or what was waiting for them outside. Whatever Sam wanted to say, whatever guilt or explanation she carried—it wouldn't get them home. It wouldn't undo the way they were already wilting there, two dying women in a dark, forgotten hole.

Miriam held out what little she had salvaged: a half-ruined packet of water and the remaining corner of a ration. She pushed them across the floor.

YOU NEED TO DRINK, she signed. EAT.

When Sam didn't reach for them, Miriam withdrew to the opposite wall and let herself slide down into a seated position with a painful exhale. She slumped back, head against the cool material, and didn't care about the filth that clung to it or to her. The grime was part of her now.

"I'm s—" Sam began, voice fractured.

I HAVE TO GO BACK, Miriam's fingers moved before the words could finish.

Sam's head lifted, fatigue paling beneath something sharper. Her face was gaunt, all color drained from it, cheeks sunken and shadowed beneath the bones. In the dim red light, she looked cadaverous. Her protest came, a slow shake of her head.

"I have to," Miriam tried to say, but it came out as a croak. Barely there. She wrestled the fire in her throat. I HAVE TO, she repeated in motion.

But not yet.

Her body betrayed her, and exhaustion swept over her again, a rising tide too strong to fight. The dark came quickly, shadows bleeding in behind her eyes, the lines of the cellar slipping.

And in that narrowing dark, a voice came. It whispered her name. An apology offered in a tone so familiar and distant that it made her ache. A name she hadn't heard in years. Faint, before the world disappeared.

28

SANCTUARY

MIRIAM SAT on the cellar step, tugging the strap of her sling across her chest. The pack felt wrong; it was too light, too empty—the sack taking up the most room. And the dread lodged beneath her ribs weighed heavier than any load she had ever carried.

Sam stirred with a soft moan. Her breath caught partway through a word that never came, and she tucked in tighter against the cellar wall, legs drawn up like a shell. One arm twitched, then the other. Tremors.

"I'm going now," Miriam barely whispered. The muscles around her throat were swollen and sore from Sam's hands.

The woman didn't answer. Possibly hadn't heard her.

Miriam's hands rubbed gently at her eyes, the skin around them sensitive. Each breath rattled out of her. She gave a faint shake of her head, as if the motion alone could stop her, somehow fix their situation.

"I—" Miriam stopped short of an empty promise. She didn't know how long she'd be gone, or if she'd return at all, but they needed supplies. They needed sustenance.

Sam raised a hand, but the effort split something in her. She gripped the torn fabric at her thigh instead, where the cell saver had been before. Her fingers stayed there, a futile effort to hold herself together as the tremor worsened, then passed.

Miriam sighed and crossed her open hands, palms down, across her clavicle. REST. She added in a raspy whisper, "You're no good to either of us like this."

Sam's gaze hardened, wounded. Then her eyes lowered, avoiding Miriam's. Her lashes pressed shut. "Please be careful," she whispered.

Miriam watched her without a response before she stood. "Wait."

She turned.

"You..." Sam's eyes caught hers, and her hands lifted weakly, finishing her sentence with motion. YOU LEARNED?

The question caught Miriam off guard. It was so small and trivial in the midst of everything. A sound rose in her throat, nearly a laugh, but it broke into a huff instead. She had stopped lessons a year prior—another distraction and hope she'd clung to until she didn't. She placed her left hand palm-down and moved her right in a small circle underneath it. THE BASICS.

Miriam had thought Sam would come back sooner.

And before she lost her resolve, she left the cellar.

Fury. Valkyrie. Sam. Three names. One woman.

She passed by the room where the mound of carpet and blankets hid Willem's body. Boy Scout.

My name is Willem.

Some names were armor; others were grief and rage. But beneath them, the person remained—changed, shattered, scarred, but still there. Sam might be buried beneath Fury, but she hadn't disappeared. Not completely. Some people changed names to find themselves, but Sam had changed hers to lose, to hide herself.

The person remains who they are underneath it all.

Willem's words looped in her head. He had believed them. She hoped they were true.

There hadn't been a moment to breathe, let alone reflect—

not with survival hanging in the balance, not with death so near and constant. But now, with Sam awake, at least partially lucid, something about the look she'd given her after stayed with Miriam. There'd been hesitation. A glimpse of the woman she'd once known.

Or maybe she was imagining it. Maybe this was what the mind did when it broke—when it circled the idea of dying long enough that it softened the edges. Maybe reflection was just another form of surrender.

The final stage.

She had already scoured the surrounding streets, pulled every usable scrap from the nearby buildings, and nothing. After the explosion, after the sheer visibility of it, there would be no safety in the area, or in the same routes. The Heretics were out there. And if help or assistance had been an option before, she no longer believed it. She had stopped wondering where Talwar and Chapel were or whether the others would come back. Hope itself had curdled into poison.

The person remains who they are.

The phrase echoed again, insistent.

And then a memory rose unbidden from the static.

Old echoes.

It's a test to make sure you are who you say you are.

Who else would we be?

Miriam's blood iced in her veins. The double triangles. She knew she'd seen them before. It was years before, but they were in an equally pristine lobby in the hidden underground research facility at the limit of the radioactive zone. They were under the same organization. Axiom.

Miriam hadn't considered returning to the lab. She'd avoided the thought instinctively—partly from fear of venturing that far, partly from what'd happened there. The partition, the room, the exposure. Whatever it'd been, it had killed Willem.

But it hadn't killed Sam.

The thought knotted her gut. She wasn't sure why or how,

but the aftermath—Sam's tremors, her volatility—pointed more to withdrawal than poison. And Miriam herself had no symptoms at all.

Altered. Whatever they'd pumped into the room, it had only affected Altered.

She crossed the room to the exit she'd been using, listening at the window frame. A light breeze, distant rustles, but nothing beside the minute sounds of destruction. Her hand settled briefly on the frame as she steadied herself. There was one place in this ruined town that no one had scavenged, a place most didn't know was under their feet.

Miriam watched, waited, then slipped out into the daylight, her path clear. She moved this time with purpose and a destination.

♟

The partition peered back at Miriam. Now that she was there, fear squeezed past resolve. Doubt snaked its way up her spine and curled in the back of her throat.

She glanced toward the open hatch, uncertain how to close it, but in the end she stepped forward anyway. The panels folded back in smooth, silent layers, the glow collapsing into the frame. Miriam hesitated one heartbeat more, then slipped inside. The door sealed behind her.

Past it, the room had been scrubbed to emptiness. The dust, the footprints, any sign of Miriam, Sam, or Willem—gone. Near the partition lay the old-generation device she had left behind, forgotten—exactly where she'd set it down before. Her eyes lingered on it, but her attention was drawn back to sterile light glinting off smooth white surfaces, untouched, as though the last visit had never happened at all.

A flicker of panic tickled her throat. Was someone there? She shook her head. The personnel had been evacuated, escorted by the UMF marines. The same company where the four marines had gone missing. No one could have survived in this place for so long. It had to be automated, designed to maintain itself.

Miriam crossed the vestibule with quiet steps. She approached the door opposite, the one without a handle, and paused in front of it. It didn't open. She turned slightly, glancing back over her shoulder, half expecting something—or someone—to emerge from the walls. That sense of being watched returned, impossible to shake, but the only thing staring back was the faint symbol etched into the wall surface: the double triangles, motionless.

Then the air shifted and Miriam tensed, stepping back, already moving back toward the partition, not wanting to be trapped again. She expected the lights to turn off.

Instead, the door depressed as if someone had moved the entire rectangle like a block of stone, nudging a few centimeters. She approached at an angle, cautious, every movement measured. If someone was on the other side of the door, could they see her? Would they be friendly?

Her fingers brushed the door's contour, and it retreated a few more centimeters, then split neatly down the center, folding into the walls on each side. Beyond was a small landing and a spiral staircase descending into white.

No one waited below.

No one that she could see.

Miriam stepped forward. She didn't bother to look back; she knew the door would seal behind her. She crouched on the landing and looked down, a better visual now. Below was a narrow hallway. She paused, the stillness pressing into her ears.

"Hello?" Her voice rasped, dry. She tried again, louder. The sound echoed strangely, too clean, as though the walls absorbed and then rejected it.

When no response came, she descended. The layout was odd, as if the space extended far beyond what was actually visible. Yet it only offered access to select rooms and corridors.

She tried every panel and door she passed, but nothing opened. Her fists tapped against the opaque and semi-translucent dividers. Locked and resistant. Even if she had the strength or tools, she knew she wouldn't have broken through.

But she didn't need those rooms. She'd barely questioned what lay beyond when she stepped into the one she recognized. A low groan left her lips as she crossed the threshold. Four cabinets lined the walls. She lunged toward one, flung it open, tore into a box, and yanked a packet free.

Miriam ripped the corner with her teeth and tilted it back, letting the water pour into her mouth. She drank like she'd been suffocating, the room-temperature liquid flooding her throat, spilling past her lips and soaking into her shirt. She didn't care; there were at least four boxes inside the cabinet, and she wanted to celebrate this small discovery, this small victory. Relief rippled through her. Her head still throbbed, but her stomach was no longer empty.

She thought of food next. Another cabinet, another box. She didn't care about the dirt and crud underneath her fingernails as she scooped up the clumpy contents and shoved them into her mouth. The taste didn't matter. The temperature, the texture—none of it did.

When the extremity of hunger and thirst abated, her belly full, she forced herself to stop. Reason and clarity crept back in as nourishment took hold. She couldn't afford to overeat. She'd make herself sick. And though she wanted more, Miriam sealed the containers and pushed them aside, as if that were enough to suppress her urges.

She stood in front of the cabinets, opening the two remaining ones. More food, more water. It was a treasure trove. If only they'd stayed here, they could've lived well. She was already calculating how she could move Sam—the woman was awake, and with some of these provisions, she could have enough strength to return. If help wasn't coming, they could wait it out until the Charonites regained the territory again. It felt wrong to feel this triumph, but Miriam clung to it anyway. One thing at a time.

Especially since Echo and Charlie had failed their mission. UMF and SOG would be back to finish the job; they'd come back to this location and get her and Sam out. Miriam allowed herself a tight smile.

She looked around through the cabinets again, hunting for anything else behind the boxes—first aid, a communicator, any scrap of tech that might help. The room gave her nothing but white walls and four cabinets. No buttons to push, no consoles to palm, no surveillance systems she could shout at.

She moved back out into the limited corridor and looked around for additional open doors, hesitant to leave this known room. What if she went off searching and when she came back it was closed? She couldn't afford that.

Miriam stepped back inside, surveyed her wealth and her sling that she had dropped in the corner. Despite her search, she couldn't find another bag or pack to carry these goods. The boxes were no good to carry; she'd need her hands free, just in case. It was a risk packing too much in her sling and ragged sack, but fewer trips meant fewer chances of dying. She didn't know how soon they'd get another opportunity to return. So six ration containers went into two neat stacks and a pile of hydration packets beside them. She carefully placed them in the sack, whatever else in her sling and hoisted both over her shoulder.

With another reluctant glance back, Miriam set out again into the corridor, dragging her hand along the walls, hoping something else would open. It didn't take far to feel a door give as she brushed by. She touched it, and it retracted open.

A moan escaped her lips.

A bathroom.

Two cabinets and a small shower stall.

She glanced down at herself. Her clothes were caked with muck, and dark streaks lined her arms. The filth had sunk into her skin, into the cracks of her fingers and knuckles, under her nails.

The bags of food and water were already on the floor, and Miriam stripped without thinking. If someone was watching through invisible eyes, she didn't care. She peeled off everything—shirt, boots, socks, pants—and stepped into the stall.

She moaned again when the water hit her skin, brisk and clean. She stood motionless under the stream, face tipped up, letting it wash her. Sweat, blood, dirt, all of it swirled at her feet and vanished down the drain. The sensation cut through every ache and pain like a blade.

For a moment, part of her felt guilty. Sam was lying in a dark hovel, waiting. But this? This was safety, a sanctuary carved into a war zone.

When the water shut off on its own, she didn't move. Eventually, she reached for the cabinet and pulled a folded towel from its neat and curated stack and dried herself slowly, savoring the moment. She caught her reflection in a narrow mirror, and nearly startled. Her ribs stood out more than they should have, her light brown eyes were too deep, webbed with red strands where blood vessels had burst. It gave her stare a raw, bruised edge, a reminder of the pressure that had closed around her throat. Her fingers hovered over the dark handprints marred into her skin around her neck, hard enough where she was sure if she studied it, she could make out a set of fingerprints on one side.

Sam had meant to kill her.

Not *her*, Miriam reminded herself. Sam hadn't known.

Her eyes then drifted to the pile of clothing she'd shed. The sight turned her stomach. She didn't want to put them back on.

So she took her time. She opened the other cabinet, and inside were bright white garments, much like scrubs one would wear in a hospital. Miriam laughed softly. They were clean, but wearing something so pristine outside felt absurd. Still, she rolled up a set just in case. Her sullied uniform could wait.

With the towel around her shoulders, the scrubs and her bag of provisions in hand, she nudged her dirty clothes and boots into the hall and moved back to the only other accessible room, still naked. There was no need for modesty; there was no one else there. She helped herself to another packet of food and water, and later, when she relieved herself, Miriam laughed again, even as her muscles ached. It had been so long since she'd had enough liquid for her body to function like it was supposed to. The color was wrong—too dehydrated dark—but the concern she'd normally feel wasn't there anymore.

Feeling rejuvenated, she claimed another packet of water. It wasn't just hydration; it was the security, the lack of fear and death around her. For a few minutes, no one was hunting her. No walls threatened to fall, no boots echoed in pursuit.

However, when it came time, pulling her uniform back on took more strength than she expected. The layers felt heavier now, and her boots chafed against her heels. She cinched them anyway. Miriam's mind and body fought with her as she did it, but she had to go back out. There was no question.

Sam was waiting.

29

DELIVERANCE

AT THE TOP of the spiral staircase, Miriam glanced back. She could move them both to this facility if Sam was able, but as she approached the door, unease clawed its way up her spine. What if Sam triggered the vestibule again? What if the door didn't open this time? She still wasn't sure why it had affected Sam so severely and spared her.

And then came another thought. What if she couldn't get back out? Or worse—what if she could, and the Heretics were waiting for her in the next room? She hadn't figured out how to seal the vault-like door. Too many unknowns stacked, one atop another.

She wanted to retreat, descend back down the staircase where she didn't have to deal with any of this. But Miriam took a long breath, held it until it hurt, then stepped forward.

The chamber on the other side remained unchanged. Miriam stepped through and frowned as the door shut behind her. Each step across the white space felt heavier, every inch of movement dragging her farther from safety. At the partition, she picked up the access device and slid it into her sling. She cinched it closer to her body, eliminating the slack, although there was none. The shape was awkward, jutting in points that could snag if she wasn't careful.

She exhaled. Then she moved, her feet leaden as she climbed the stairs and closed the hatch behind her. Whatever fleeting sense of security she'd felt vanished the moment she emerged from the storefront. She hadn't been gone long, probably not even a few hours, but the contrast was jarring. Miriam tried to rein in her breath. She had made it back to Sam before. She could do it again.

She advanced with more urgency, especially now that she knew what they could come back to. Every step was guided by acute awareness as the streets farther in grew too quiet. When the clustered houses came into view, she slowed. There was the blast mark to the side, where she'd tripped something before— a leftover mine or some rigged trap. Taking the other side of the street, she watched her footing more closely now.

And then she froze.

A clatter of rubble snapped her to attention. She jammed herself into deeper cover behind a vehicle, the movement painstakingly slow but quiet. Her eyes swept the street, her ears tuning to every distant creak and shift of breeze.

Whispering.

There was no doubt in the sibilant undertone of voices. Wet consonants traded low. It was close—too close.

And then the slightest of movements. A tuft of hair, an ear visible beyond a half-collapsed wall. The figure faced away from her—unaware, or pretending to be. She prayed it was a Charonite, but the desperate hope vanished as the ear twitched.

Altered. And probably not the friendly kind.

A second emerged from farther down, revealing a full head and shoulders. Miriam dropped lower, barely breathing. They were dangerously close, enough to smell her if the air turned.

Had they been tracking her all this time? Or was this pure chance, bad luck a vise closing on her ribs? Miriam clenched her jaw to keep her teeth from chattering. Her muscles strained against the tension of stillness.

She glanced behind her, but every path she'd taken now led in the wrong direction. She couldn't loiter. It was only a matter of time before a breeze shifted or they moved enough to see her in the corner of their eyes.

Miriam crouched, one hand feeling along the ground until her fingers found a rough chunk of rock, either concrete or a chipped piece of some structure nearby. She didn't look down to confirm, only closed her hand around it.

She hurled the object in the direction she'd come, the opposite direction of where she needed to go—Sam. And then she dropped back into cover. The rock or whatever crashed somewhere beyond other vehicles and kiosks.

The closest Heretic spun immediately, footsteps rustling in pursuit. Miriam peeked once. Only one had taken the bait. The other stayed rooted, interested and alert but stationary. She couldn't wait for ideal conditions.

Miriam bolted. She moved low, feet quiet but quick, her eyes fixed on her route ahead, mapping where to land, when to duck back into cover. Shouts erupted behind her. Multiple. More than the two she'd seen. She didn't pause to interpret their words. Whether they'd seen her, heard her, or were summoning others, it didn't matter.

She veered left, intentionally off course. She wouldn't lead them straight back. That would be suicide, and her detour proved wise. Up ahead, two figures stood in the lane she would've taken. They were stiff, heads scanning in staccato motion. One clutched a compact firearm. The other held a UMF-issue rifle.

She slipped into a shattered storefront, heart pounding hard. She braced the back of her hand to her mouth to quiet herself. The shouts behind her faded, but she couldn't trust that distance meant safety.

She peeked out again. The two were posted—too close to her destination. Her gaze dropped, scanning the wreckage around her, and she snatched up another stone. It had worked once.

Before she could throw it, a third figure emerged. Miriam stopped instantly. The three exchanged quiet words she couldn't catch, then dispersed into a loose formation, keeping visual contact but spreading out.

Shit.

One angled closer to her hiding spot while the others disappeared from her line of sight. She crouched lower and crept sideways, using the pocked wall for cover, the concrete in her hand.

She rolled it over the barrier, and it skittered on the far side. The Heretic jerked upright, then drifted toward the sound.

Miriam didn't hesitate. She slipped the other way, winding through gaps in the wreckage, careful to avoid broken glass and loose metal. She kept glancing for the two others but didn't see them. Last she'd checked, they'd moved in the opposite direction.

She pushed forward, avoiding the route that would've taken her back toward the store, toward the plaza and the burning cage where Hadeon had died. There were too many unknowns there. All she had to do was reach the house, the short hall, the corner of the cellar where Sam waited beneath that sliver of light. She had food, water, enough for days. They just needed to wait it out. And as she neared, relief, albeit minuscule, grew.

But as soon as she stepped carefully into the window, something was off. Though nothing had moved, something had been disturbed. The air had changed. Subtle, but wrong. She crept ahead, every instinct on edge. And when she reached the entrance of the hallway, her blood ran cold.

An individual crouched there, nose forward and working. His back faced her, but the way he leaned in told her everything. He had Sam's scent. Or he could see her in the dark.

She had failed.

The sling was already off Miriam's back, resting silently at her feet. Her hand found her sidearm before the thought finished forming. She was close enough to hear his breath, close enough to catch his whisper, words, a language she didn't understand.

"斷血者."

She set the muzzle just shy of his ear.

Squeezed.

Nothing.

The dead click echoed like thunder. Her hands moved on training before panic could flower: tap the magazine, rack the slide. He was already spinning, and she fired again before the unspent round hit the ground.

This time the shot went off. Sound tore through the confined space with explosive force. She felt the warm spray against her own exposed skin and face, but she didn't wait to confirm the kill. She shoved the body aside and sprinted, all sense of caution burned away by urgency.

Her eyes hadn't adjusted to the dark when a voice broke through the ringing in her ears.

"Mir?"

The name seared like a signal flare. She reached the steps, then stopped before the descent. Time billowed and slowed. Sam was crouched low, already halfway up. She rose slowly, her eyes illuminated by the line of light from the panel above. Blue, like Miriam remembered.

Her sides caved in. That color hit her harder than any blow. She hadn't seen it like this—clean—in years. It'd been behind glass, behind fury, veiled through blood. But here it was again, unguarded. Sam's expression flickered with concern; the set of her mouth went soft.

Miriam tightened her grip on her sidearm. It was almost weightless. Only the one round left in the chamber. How could one bullet, light as it was, be heavier than everything else combined?

Boots and shouts gathered behind her. Shadows danced in the crack above them and stretched onto the walls.

The worry in Sam's face eased into something calmer, a look that belonged to another lifetime. Miriam's throat filled with a grief so old, it felt new again. This was the woman she had known before names had hardened into armor. This was the Sam she remembered.

For one impossible moment, it was as if nothing had passed between them—not the years, not the distance, not the silence. That flicker was the Sam who had laughed with her once, the Sam she'd woken up to and wanted the future with—if not more.

Her hands shook as she raised the weapon, sights leveling between blue eyes. Miriam took a shuddering breath and forced herself to still.

Sam didn't flinch, just watched her, resigned. There was no fear, only understanding. It was the worst mercy Sam could give her. Miriam wanted resistance, an alternative, a different option. Instead, that calm acceptance left her with nothing but the truth of what she had to do.

Miriam didn't want this. Not after everything she had done to keep Sam alive. Every risk, every sacrifice, every step and ounce of pain. What had it been for, if it ended here? She didn't want to do this.

Behind her, they were already in the house. The hallway throbbed with pounding feet. They were seconds away. Less. She was out of time.

Her finger touched the metal. For a millisecond, her body rebelled, every instinct begging her to stop, to find another way. But Miriam had to do it.

Do it now.

Three words spilled out of her mouth, off her tongue, past her lips into the air, into reality. Each word enunciated, each word intended. Each making up the truth that had never changed despite the years, the anger, and pain.

She pulled the trigger.

30

RECKONING

I LOVE YOU.

31

PRIVATION

SHE DIDN'T KNOW what came first, the shot or the collision. It was simultaneous. The crack thundered through the room, slapping the walls and punching into her skull, and bodies slammed into her, bone and muscle knocking her forward. The recoil of the weapon smashed with their momentum, the motions snarled together so tightly that she couldn't know.

Miriam choked on dust as she fought to breathe, her lungs burning while the cellar floor grated her skin raw beneath her. Pain sparked across her shoulder and chest, and through it, she clamped down on the pistol. She knew there were no rounds left, but she fought for it anyway. She didn't look toward the corner where a body was slumped. She jerked against the hands dragging at her, twisting the weapon, trying to pull the barrel toward her own head. If she could angle it, if she could get her finger to obey—maybe she was wrong, maybe there was another round, maybe she could end it. She could finish what no one else would grant her.

And then a savage wrench. Something deep tore. The crack that followed ripped a scream out of her, and for an instant she saw only white. Fingers pried hers loose, one after another, until numbness won. The gun fell away and took a piece of her with it. Breath broke in ragged shards, tears cut tracks through the dust caked at her temples, but she would not lie still. Every movement was a dare, a provocation. She thrashed, kicking, scratching, teeth seeking skin. A free shoulder rammed into an assailant, sending fresh pain screaming through her ribs and broken arm. She knew the torment didn't matter. She was unarmed, outnumbered, already dead.

Let them end it.

Something struck her cheek, and the world detonated into stars—cold pricks, the memory of northern constellations. She wanted to see them once more without the battlefield, without the discomforts. She had just killed the woman she loved.

Let it end.

Hands crushed down, pinning her shoulders and hips. Rough palms tore through her pockets. They rolled her and the room lurched; her broken arm roared when she hit her back. She couldn't stop the tears now. They came hot and relentless.

Do not let them capture you alive.

She had to keep fighting. She had to make them kill her. Grant that mercy. Her body bucked once more.

A wheeze sounded nearby, followed by a torn groan.

"Mi—"

No.

She twisted toward the voice, toward the corner where Sam had fallen.

Not dead.

The thought knifed her open. She had failed. This was worse. They'd stopped her. Wasted her last round. Miriam should've killed her.

Another body dove past her, piling onto Sam. Something inside Miriam unleashed. Rage emptied the pain, and she tried to lurch up on a broken cry. "Get off her!" The words were slurred. Her face felt wrong, already swelling.

A shove sent her back into the ground. A heel mashed her shoulder violently down again.

"Don't touch h—" Sam's hoarse warning turned to a groan as they slammed her.

Miriam writhed uselessly. She had failed. The one thing she needed to do if she couldn't keep Sam alive. Survive, but if not, don't let them capture you alive. She'd failed.

A voice carried from the hall, harsh, a snarl of Altered language mixed in. "It stinks in there. 把他們帶到這裡."

The foreign words meant nothing to Miriam. Short syllables in a tongue she couldn't follow. Harsh hands yanked her upright. Her legs dragged as she was pulled up the steps, her knees scraping open, heels and toes trying to find purchase. In the hall, she found her feet, balance still off, but she kicked out, caught nothing. Behind her, a body roughly towed along the floor. Sam, hauled in the same graceless grip.

"How did you not find them this whole time? Does your 鼻子 work? Even I can smell them."

A grunt answered from above Miriam.

"Yes… Little cockroaches in the dark."

With another thrust, Miriam staggered into the main room, and her eyes adjusted to the figures in it. Two in the shadows. One wiry and one much larger. As they shifted, she caught pale puckers along their throats—burns seared in at odd angles, each the same shape in theory, but neither the same in flesh.

The smaller one, the same voice from before, clicked his tongue. "不在外面."

"为什么?" asked the one above Miriam.

She caught the end of the exchange, the rhythm of it clipped, but what struck her more was the Altered's face as he stepped toward her. His features were distorted as if something cruel and dark had surfaced before he blinked and the mask slid back into place. Orange eyes swept across her, not fully focused, like she was a detail to catalog, nothing more. His attention drifted back toward the freshly shattered window nearby.

Without warning, the Heretic behind her flung her down.

Her knees struck hard, and the pain leaped up through her broken arm and lanced at the base of her skull. She gritted her teeth, a copper tang on her tongue. Miriam shot a glare over her shoulder, but the motion lit pain through her face and neck, forcing her to squint instead.

The speaker stepped forward, clad in black, hands clasped behind him. His presence wasn't loud, but it was commanding, and Miriam felt it like pressure in the air. Without the mask, he looked much younger than Miriam had expected. The other figure loomed large behind him, his body angled outward, as if the threat wasn't from Miriam or Sam, from inside. The traitorous shell of a legionnaire. And there, scorched into the skin of his neck, the pale branded symbol. The triangle with a ring at the apex and a strike-line warped by scar tissue, the circle pulled oval where hot iron had slipped.

Her heart squeezed. Recognition hit her like a blow. These were the same ones from the plaza. The execution. Hadeon's fiery cage.

"屠夫哥," the large one murmured.

The foreign words landed like ice in her bloodstream.

No.

Miriam's breath caught in her throat. She should've known. She couldn't follow the rest of the sentence, but she knew those first two syllables.

Túfū.

Butcher.

Miriam's attention snapped to Sam behind her, hauled into view. Her hair was matted with blood and dust. A quarter of her face was slick and crimson, surrounding the wound high on her cheek where the bullet had struck. Grazed. Miriam had been too late; she'd missed when the Heretics had interfered. But her guilt and fear were mixed with relief.

Even in the poor light, Sam's eyes were unmistakably blue, wide with panic until they softened when they found Miriam, a steadiness that lasted only a millisecond before a kick sent Sam sprawling. She landed on the floor, knees then a shoulder, her hands bound behind her.

"斷血者," someone hissed.

Butcher turned at the words. His orange eyes fell on Sam and lit, like a predator savoring a tale made flesh. At the same time, another Heretic moved behind Sam menacingly as if the room had just realized the greatest threat.

"斷 血 者 ," he said, tasting the words like it pleased him. "Ender of bloodlines. Sun-Killer. What a surprise."

He took his time circling Sam, careful never to enter range, like she were a caged flame. "I'm disappointed. I expected more. What happened to the legend? The myth?" He crouched, studying her as if she were a specimen.

Behind him, the large Heretic murmured.

"好的." Butcher waved to his right-hand man. "You've made this effort worth it, Sun-Killer. And here I was wondering why the roaches were pushing so hard. Something's lit a fire underneath them...and here you are." He rose with a slow exhale. "You've made this retreat less... 苦." He then clapped his hands once, decisive. "Time to go."

Hair tore at Miriam's scalp as the Heretic behind her tugged. "這個怎麼辦?"

Butcher didn't glance back. "把他去掉," he said with a wave of his hand. "But not in here. My ears can only take so much."

Miriam's stomach dropped, a heavy plunge that left her cold. The Heretic yanked at her hair again and she yelped, moving up to her knees, instinctively trying to relieve the pain despite knowing she had to resist.

Sam jerked against the hands holding her. A strangled noise slipped through her lips.

Butcher's head tipped and studied her with unsettling stillness. Sam's eyes instantly dropped, her lashes dark with blood and residue, shoulders rising with shallow breaths. The Heretic leader watched her another moment, looked to Miriam once, then hummed and stretched a hand to pat Sam's bloodied cheek. Gentle and mocking. He studied the smear on his fingers like a sommelier.

"停止," Butcher said firmly.

The Heretic gripping Miriam froze mid-step, and Butcher rose and crossed the space. His boots thudded, and he paused before her. Up close, his orange eyes gleamed like banked coals. Fear wrapped around her spine and clawed upward, but she summoned what little resolve she had left and forced herself to hold his gaze.

Butcher said nothing at first. He simply looked her over, from her torn and filthy uniform to the blood caked into the crook of her neck. He lifted two bloodied fingers and brushed them across her forehead, intimate in a way that made her skin crawl. He then pointed to Sam with the same fingers.

"You know her."

Behind him, Sam didn't speak. She didn't look up, but the fine tremor in her shoulders betrayed her.

Butcher smiled wide. "Boys," he said to the crowded room, six Heretics at least. "We've been blessed. Good news to change the day." He spread his arms, a showman at his stage. "We have something better than just content. We have a live audience."

Snickers answered, snide and eager. The large Heretic stepped forward and muttered something low Miriam couldn't understand.

But Butcher just flicked his hand dismissively, waving the concern away. "我們有足夠的時間來做這件事. 把相機準備好."

She didn't understand, but the tone was clear. Preparations. Instructions.

The Heretic prodded Miriam the short distance back to where she'd initially been and pushed her down. One of the others who had held at the threshold of the room handed Butcher a compact dagger—Willem's, the same one that must've been taken off her. Butcher examined it, a finger along its blade before he tossed it in the air, caught it by its hilt, and spun it once more, his smile widening with the idle flourish.

"Lighting," he said. "It's all about the lighting."

With that, the others hurried in practiced movements, clearing the room of broken furniture. Whispered instructions brought a couple others—necks with burned sigils—who passed equipment into the house through the other accessible rooms. A tripod unfolded. A small recording device clicked. A panel flashed to life.

Miriam blinked at its illumination inside the space, and her breath snagged. She knew this choreography. Not again. Not here, not like this.

Not Sam.

This was worse than any nightmare she'd ever had, worse than anything her mind had dared conjure in the dark. Not even her worst fears had gone this far.

"快還是慢?" asked the Heretic guarding Miriam.

Butcher tapped the blade against his lip, pensive, and theatrical. "慢一點," he said, then gestured toward Sam. "讓這個敗類感受到一切."

"No!" Sam's voice broke like glass. She exploded up against the hands that held her. One Heretic stumbled back as Sam's shoulder smashed into him. She turned, teeth sinking into the cheek of the other. He screamed and contorted. The first Heretic struck against the back of Sam's head then yanked at her shoulders. It took a third individual to tear her away from her wriggling victim. A punch folded her at the waist, and she choked on the lack of air, shook on the floor, blood glistening at her lips.

Butcher didn't flinch. "給她戴上口套."

Before Sam could capture a breath, the muzzle came fast, snaring her head, cinched until her protests were reduced to muffled grunts and strangled sounds.

"This will be a better piece than the others," Butcher murmured, no acknowledgment to the injured Heretic as he turned. "It means something."

The large Heretic muttered again, low and urgent. He tapped his wrist.

"We have time, don't worry," Butcher said, smiling.

On the ground, Sam squirmed, terror now free in her eyes.

"Think of it, Skala. It's one less body to bring along," he said. "刀."

Butcher passed Willem's dagger to the Heretic behind Miriam, then settled between the women as if they weren't in this broken house, as if he were appraising a work of art hung in a gallery. His eyes swept between them—Miriam, frozen in helpless disbelief, and Sam, bound and bloodied, muscles in her face clenched behind the device.

"Smile for the world."

Sam spasmed forward, trying to speak, to shout, but the muzzle stole every word until only a howl hummed through it. Blue eyes flashed, desperate.

And then Miriam understood.

This setup, this execution. They were for her.

The performance was for the Sun-Killer.

Fury. Valkyrie. Sam.

Butcher moved away as the lights flared harsher. Miriam squinted and his silhouette vanished into the warped light.

Her breath quickened. Not if she could help it.

She felt the pressure of the room's attention, and before the Heretic behind her could act, Miriam surged upward from her knees and drove her shoulder hard into his groin. She ignored the pain shooting through her arm as a meaty crunch met her motion, something soft giving way. She didn't wait for the reaction. She threw herself past the large Heretic, Skala, toward the window, good hand clutching blindly for the jagged lip.

Skala's grip and regard never came, but she felt grasping fingers on her ankle by someone else. It slipped. Her momentum carried her forward, her torso pitching over the broken ledge. Miriam hit the ground outside hard, a slab of concrete gouging into her spine.

A shout came from inside, garbled and close. The sunlight stabbed her eyes. She pulled herself upright on shaking legs, arm and jaw screaming, lungs raw. There was no plan. She couldn't outrun them—not like this—but still she rose.

And then a blow slammed her ribs, and her balance was gone. She instinctively flung her right arm out to catch herself, but the moment she did, fire and lightning erupted. Her broken arm crumpled under her weight, and she collapsed with it, her face smashing against the ground. The impact stole her breath and scattered her thoughts.

A heavy body crashed down across her, hot air gusting across her cheek, and then she was yanked back inside. She yelped as her legs scraped over the window sill.

"Oh, she's a fighter. I love fighters," Butcher said with a chuckle. "It makes for a better broadcast."

As she turned her head, grit ground into Miriam's skin. Sam's eyes found hers, wild, blue, and wet. Her screams broke uselessly behind the muzzle, her bound hands straining. Her body trembled, trying to fling itself forward to reach her.

"Feisty, aren't you?" Butcher taunted. "Where were you trying to go, little roach?"

The Heretic behind her yanked Miriam up by her arm, and her scream curdled, the agony blanking everything, lancing through her entire being. He dropped her again with no grace, his boot crashing into the back of her legs. Both knees slammed into the floor, and Miriam groaned, sagging with the pulse of pain.

Butcher hissed something in words she couldn't follow, his voice rising in admonishment as he scurried forward. Then, more cordially, like a tutor to a careless student, he said, "No, no, no, no. Now we have to wait until she resets. Too much pain, too many sensations. You want her lucid for the big event.

You want her to *feel* it so the audience can feel it." He backed up. "Are we recording now? Good. Good."

Sam's muffled clamor rose.

"Shut her up," Butcher said, looking around the room. "These poor acoustics. She'll ruin the feature."

A boot cracked into Sam's side, and she buckled with a low, strangled sound, but still she tried to scream—muzzle or no— still she fought to make noise. To interrupt.

And something in Butcher snapped, his patience wavering. He closed the distance to Sam in two steps. He grabbed a fistful of her light hair and savagely yanked her head back. Her neck jolted, eyes forced upward. "All this noise, all this fight. I don't have the time, and I'm afraid you're not paying attention. I'd really, really like to have your attention."

He muttered something, and one of his lackeys came forward, a small tin presented in his palm.

Miriam's gut plummeted. "No." Her voice rasped past cracked lips.

Butcher opened the container and grinned as he lifted a slender metal pen. He rolled it between his thumb and pointer. "Would you like some elixir, Sun-Killer?"

Sam faltered, her grunts quieting.

The Heretic leader held the pen up like a relic in front of her face. "Did you know if you mix this…" He pitched the tin forward, showing a different pen inside. "And this…" he continued, "you get the best of both worlds."

"No," Miriam croaked again.

"You'll have bliss and acceptance, and I'll have willing and submissive silence. Of course, it doesn't affect the outcome." Butcher's concentration didn't stray from Sam. He patted her bloody cheek above the muzzle, like one might stroke a favored pet. "So, what will it be?"

Sam's eyes locked on to the pen in the tin.

"Oh, you'd like that, wouldn't you?" he teased. "No, we

can't have that, unfortunately. You've already taken too many of my men."

He spun the pen in his fingers again. "But this and a little prick of that…" He tilted the thin box.

He wanted Sam docile but alert. Paralyzed but aware.

"You're sick," Miriam spat, though the words emerged slurred and thick.

"Consider this my gift."

He gestured, and the other Heretic jerked Sam's head to the side, exposing the soft line of her neck. Sam fought the hold, muscles quivering, but Miriam saw her expression change, saw her try to mask the conflict burning behind her eyes. Sam's resolve was struggling.

Then Butcher depressed the pen into Sam's neck.

Miriam's breath hitched. It was Altered drugs, too potent for humans. Possibly too strong even for a heavy user like Sam.

Through it, Sam's eyes never left Miriam's, and in them lay a confluence of guilt, shame, and relief.

The effect wasn't immediate, but Miriam prayed it was enough to send Sam to sleep, or better, for her to overdose. It'd be a better death than whatever these Altered had planned for Sam.

"That's better," Butcher said, pleased. "I have glorious plans for you, Sun-Killer. You don't know how long I've wanted to find you. And now…this is even better. Who is she?"

It was rhetorical as Sam couldn't answer. Her head drooped, her brows pinched with emotion as her body sagged.

"Not one of yours," Butcher said as he looked over Miriam's dirty outfit. "And to think I was going to make it quick; we already have enough roach UMF footage. But for you, Sun-Killer…" He forced Sam's chin toward Miriam. "She means something to you. So we'll take our time."

He pressed his fingers into her cheeks, then wiped the blood on his fingers onto her shirt. "We do have to move soon, but this—this is important. If we must run, Skala can bring her corpse. Or just the fun parts." He looked up at the room. "Head or body, boys?"

All the Heretics tittered, except for Skala, whose head tipped, his nostrils flaring.

Monsters.

A hand fisted Miriam's hair again, sending pain through her neck. The Heretic behind her stared down, multicolored eyes gleaming, then whispered in their language. He stroked his rough knuckles and then the dagger across Miriam's cheek. She tried to twist away, but his grip held, and she whimpered.

"So much fire," Butcher mused. "I can see why you like her." He glanced at the large Altered behind him, whose posture shifted. "Shall we knock her teeth out now? Let the boys play?"

Sam choked behind half-lidded eyes.

His right-hand man mumbled something again, but Butcher dismissed him with a flick of the wrist and positioned himself behind Sam. He jerked her head up again and aimed her face toward Miriam like a camera being repositioned. "Don't fall asleep now. That won't do."

And before Miriam could yell, the other pen jabbed into Sam's neck. But only a prick. A lower dose? Miriam's hope—that the overdose might spare Sam—evaporated.

"I want you to feel every second of this," Butcher whispered loudly into Sam's ear. "This is your show, dear Sun-Killer. For every brother you stomped into the earth."

Sam slumped forward, her shoulder hitting the floor. Her eyes rolled white, then settled.

Miriam spat threats that her swollen jaw mangled. A gag buckled over her mouth; sour metal flooded her tongue. She fought against it, screaming into it, breath coming too fast, too thin, but she didn't have time to adjust as something cold kissed her throat, testing the soft skin there. Her whole body froze, then shook.

The Heretic behind her used her hair like a leash to

straighten her. Miriam's focus locked with Sam's—eyes unblinking, frozen wide by whatever mix kept her suspended, a shell in a narcotic paralysis. Sam was still there, still seeing, trapped. A low sound emitted from Sam like a groan caught underwater.

At her side, Miriam crept her left hand up as far as she could. She signed a lie because it was the only mercy left. IT'S OKAY. IT'LL BE OKAY.

A lie. But excusable. Acceptable.

Sam's irises shot down, then up again.

For a second that stretched for a lifetime, those eyes connected with Miriam's, a bridge of everything they had missed together, every mistake, every misunderstanding, every apology, every word unspoken and spoken passed between them, every emotion and moment they could've had in the space of a breath.

And then it was over.

Miriam shut her eyes.

Her fingers curled as the blade bit in.

32

———————

SENTENCE

IT CAME like an icy sting with an overwhelming and terrifying force. Miriam's eyes clenched at the pure agony of it. Before she could register it fully, a white-hot light exploded across her closed vision, a burst so violent it obliterated sound and air alike. Her ears popped with the force of it, and a wave slammed through the room. For a long, suspended moment, the world dissolved into pain, sparks, and ringing silence.

She didn't know if seconds or minutes passed before the edges of shapes bled back into view. Black figures swarmed in streaks and shadows. Shouts rose and fell but reached her thick and distorted. Her head spun and her body remained fixed, knees aching, trembling beneath her.

Her vision swam with spots as her thoughts blinked in and out like a faulty circuit. Flash or concussive, whatever devices had gone off had shattered her equilibrium. Her body knew it had survived, but her senses lagged behind.

Footsteps thundered outside the house. Too many to count. Another shout boomed nearby.

Miriam blinked again, forcing her eyes upward. A figure loomed, raising an arm, gesturing orders to others unseen. His face resolved just enough—square jaw and dark eyes. Not Butcher. Not the Heretics.

None of it made sense. These were humans. Reinforcements? But they weren't in uniform. Not UMF. Not SRAF. Charonites?

Then the torment in her neck surged back, a pulsing burn that radiated out, a reminder of what had just happened. Her breath caught as her left hand flew reflexively to her neck. Warmth seeped through her fingers.

She pulled it away, and the amount of color stunned her. Too much, too bright. The pain exploded a hundredfold, as if her receptors and mind hadn't truly realized it until she saw the proof, that she was actually bleeding, had actually been stabbed.

Shit.

Sheer terror flowed through her. Carotid? Her jugular? She couldn't see, but there hadn't been a spray, at least she didn't think so. Then what structure was impacted? Her trachea? Every scenario and treatment sprinted through her mind, trying to outpace the panic.

Failing.

Miriam clamped harder, tried to apply more pressure with her palm, but it didn't feel enough. Her hand was weak, strength long drained from her muscles. She wobbled.

At her side, movement stirred. Someone crouched near her, nudging her broken arm. The shift sent pain lancing through her limb and body and she whimpered, but they didn't notice. Hands tugged the muzzle from her face, and a voice spilled over her in urgent words she couldn't follow. They meant nothing through the haze of her own unraveling breath.

Her execution had been thwarted. Relief was short-winded and brief, overcome by the amount of pain she was in, but Miriam still turned, searching.

Sam.

The woman wasn't where Miriam had last seen her. Blond

hair caught the light across the other room, closer to Boy Scout's covered body. A man bent over her, weapon trained on her prone form. Panic seized in Miriam's chest—the glimpse of Butcher, the execution—but this one was different. Not Butcher. Not a Heretic. This figure was smaller.

Sam lay paralyzed, her eyes open, locked forward, and impossibly wide. From the angle she lay, she could only see the sliver of action—if the mixture of Altered drugs were allowing her to process any of it at all.

The man's stance shifted.

No.

Miriam lurched forward, a boot forced out from under her, ignoring the lightning that shot up her body, the way her arm, neck, and face blazed in agony. "No. She's human." The words tore out, hoarse, just above a croak. She stumbled onto her knees again, hand still clutching her throat as she struggled for volume. "She's human," Miriam repeated, slurred but louder this time. The strain in her trachea was already growing.

The man turned, and others repositioned at the brink of her vision. One stepped forward to support her, but she flinched back hard, pain brightening her sight again.

"She's human," Miriam forced again.

The man hesitated as Miriam's words registered, and he lowered his rifle. A breath left her, relief like a noose slackening.

"Are we sure? That arm—"

Another voice cut in before he could finish. "Found something!"

More bodies moved into the other room where the sound of fabric dragged and plastic shuffled. Boy Scout. Expletives rang out. Either at the body or his size, Miriam couldn't make sense of it.

Willem.

The name jolted through her. A warning climbed her ruined throat as she remembered: her, Sam, and Willem all might still be contagious. But she hadn't infected the Charonite from earlier, not that she knew of. Nor had Butcher and the Heretics succumbed. Whatever had hurt Willem and Sam after the facility, it didn't hold sway anymore. The logic twisted, fraying against panic.

"The place is clear! The fuckers ran!" someone shouted from the imploded window in the next room.

"Any of ours give chase?"

"Yeah, they're on 'em."

The responding individual didn't seem optimistic. "Tell them to pull back. Don't go too far. Don't overstretch!"

Voices echoed from outside, overlapping instructions and reports. Miriam tuned it out. None of it mattered unless it meant extraction, getting her and Sam out of there.

"Let's get a move on. Get 'em out!"

Someone helped Miriam to her feet. Her legs quaked, and she held her broken arm against her ribs, her left hand pinned to the open wound at her neck, holding it like she was strangling herself. However, she bit through the pain, refusing to move until she saw Sam lifted into an old UMF mobile litter. The pair managing her muttered about the door and window; Miriam wanted to tell them to knock the drywall down—the same section that Chapel had moved in front of the door—but she was already ushered forward, nudged toward the window through which she had previously tried to escape execution. This time, her exit was more careful.

Miriam tried to stay close, to look back, but a firm hand guided her out. Beyond Sam and the others, she caught the briefest sight of Willem's boots and legs, the carpet she'd used to cover him now stripped away.

"What are—"

"Come on," the individual behind her snapped. "You heard the boss. They might come back."

Miriam didn't argue. By some saving grace, her death had been interrupted. She and Sam had been found and rescued.

It was happening. For real. No false resolution this time.

The world expanded when she stepped aside. The same street she'd gotten used to was now filled with people moving and positioned in what passed for a security perimeter—sloppy by UMF standards but disciplined enough. She caught hints of dark, boxy tattoos on skin. Confirmed Charonites. But these weren't the ragtag children who'd been sent with them before. She saw mercenaries mixed in, some lightly armored, others not. They had kits, supplies, and a chain of command. This was oddly coordinated.

But real.

A gentle hand pushed her to a crumbling curb. She sat, dizzy and suddenly cold. She counted approximately two dozen people, only one or two issuing orders. Everything flattened together underneath the bright sun. She felt the bitter twist of contradiction. Her distrust hadn't softened, but alleviation cut through anyway. They weren't Heretics or the Apostates.

"Get Baby Doc over here!"

She had thought about relief too soon.

A boy no older than sixteen, still round in the face, trotted forward. Alone. "Yes, sir," he said, his voice cracking.

"Help her out."

He hesitated, staring at what must've been the sheen of blood spilling between her fingers. He was green, far too young, and clearly out of his depth.

"Compression. Bandage," Miriam rasped with a pained grimace. Her throat was swelling. She wouldn't have much time left for more words. "Gauze. Do you have?"

He fumbled through his pack and pulled out a roll, but it was narrow. Too narrow. It'd be useless in this situation, possibly doing more damage to her existing wound. She didn't know the extent, but considering she was still standing, she reassured herself it wasn't an artery.

She stopped short of shaking her head, the pain too immediate. *No,* she mouthed instead.

He remained there, his hand still outstretched, the healed ink on his forearm glaring up at her.

She needed to pack the wound. Her mind moved to the clean outfit from the facility. Her stay had been brief—it had been less than a day—but it felt like weeks had passed since.

"Sack. Inside," Miriam said, her voice faltering with a gesture. Lightning shot through her nerves, and she gasped. She really had to stop moving her neck. She tried to nudge an elbow toward the house, to the bag of provisions she had discarded.

And then she waited, trying to maintain heavy compression while the teenager left, only to return a bit later. He held it out and looked curiously at her.

"Clothes," she whispered. Her voice was all but gone, the swollen muscles already pushing.

He pulled them out, confused. His finger tracked a smudge against the white fabric.

"Rip," she rasped.

He gave her a questioning look before he understood and tore it into strips.

Miriam chanced her hand off the wound and snatched the shirt pieces. Her broken arm bent at the elbow, weakly assisting with pressed fingertips supporting her neck. With her left hand, she found the wound, the single vertical slit where the dagger had entered, and braced herself.

An inhale—as much as she could.

And then she shoved the end of one of the fabric strips inside her. Her body tensed, protesting the foreign invasion. She would've screamed if not for the placement, nearly blacked out as her motions became automatic, packing and packing the wound, fabric down toward her heart. Each motion racked her in agony, her fingers steady despite her entire body shaking uncontrollably.

Until she couldn't anymore.

Tears ran down her face as she stopped. She grabbed the

remaining cloth and bunched it over the slit. Only then did her hands start to shake. Every muscle in her body was on fire.

She took another shallow breath. "Wrap," she instructed silently, lifting her broken arm as much as she could with a grimace.

And together, she and the boy guided the narrow bandage into place, using the facility clothes to buffer its width. It hooked under her armpit and around her neck, across the makeshift gauze. When it was cinched tight, Miriam eased her right limb down. Pain seared, but the pressure held. Now with her left limb available again, she manipulated her shirt into a support, raising her right arm diagonally across her chest.

With the most pressing issues addressed, Miriam turned stiffly as Sam was maneuvered out of the same window she'd come from.

"—then why're her eyes open?"

"Then close them!"

"I did. You said she was out!"

Careful, Miriam mouthed. *Please.*

No one heard. She looked around, grimacing, taking more in, realizing the absence now. There were no vehicles. No prowlers or airships. Shit. The Charonites had come on foot. Orders were shouted from inside the house, and then a voice down the street called something back. Fragmented instructions passed around.

"Can you walk?" the teenage medic asked.

Miriam's first impulse was to nod, but she caught herself. She tried to force a noise of affirmation instead, but the inflammation had already progressed in her neck and everywhere else. Her head throbbed now that the adrenaline was coming down, and her broken arm surged in time with her heartbeat.

"Meds?" she rasped.

"Don't got much."

She waved a bloody hand, grimacing, trying to work

through the pain. He swung the pack around, and she dug through it, finally pointing to an old-model jabber. UMF-issue. Leftovers that the military had provided as aid. It'd have to do.

He handed it over, and she bit the cap off with protesting teeth, then stabbed it into her thigh with no hesitation.

"What about her?" the teenager asked, gesturing at Sam, who had been set down beside them.

No, Miriam mouthed. She gave the woman an apologetic look, though Sam lay turned away, unaware. The mix in her system was Altered-engineered. A mystery. There was no telling what damage more chemicals would do—what line would be crossed that her body couldn't return from.

And then relief unfurled over Miriam slowly like warmth through a blanket. It tempered the ache in her face and softened the edges of her pain and vision. Pumping blood no longer rattled through her head, just a slight radiating discomfort. But she didn't relax. She watched the perimeter. Despite the activity, it was too still, too open.

Her pulse quickened. They needed to leave. What if the Heretics came back? What if they attacked with mortars or airguns or small arms?

The panic built again, slower under the medicine, but rising all the same. She wanted to get out. She had only finished the thought when someone snapped a command and the group mobilized.

Four Charonites passed with a large black bag between them. Willem? Then a smaller group followed with another black bag. Miriam stared after them, stomach hollow, but her attention shifted when Sam's litter lifted and moved past. She got up and followed automatically. The steps hurt, but her body moved anyway.

She fixed on the sky in the distance. The colors felt too vivid and brilliant. Miriam didn't think it was the jabber's medication, but rather the consequence of survival that had made everything look different now. Seconds ago she'd been kneeling with a blade to her neck. It didn't seem real.

"We're not fancy like you grunts," someone said, trotting beside her as she limped along. "No airlift. You sure you can walk?"

She didn't bother looking at whoever was talking to her. She managed an affirmative response, although she wasn't sure if she actually could. If she collapsed later on, she hoped they wouldn't leave her behind.

So Miriam kept moving, carried forward on fumes, on legs that no longer felt her own yet still obeyed. Moving. She didn't look back once.

Let it rot. The guilt, the debt, the weight of the past could collapse, crumble, and be buried away with the ash and ruin. She was happy to leave it all.

33
____

DYSPHORIA

MIRIAM REMEMBERED LITTLE of the way out. Her focus narrowed to the motion of her boots, one step in front of the other, following the two Charonites carrying Sam's litter. Everything beyond that was a buzz of static. Her limbs were numb, her thoughts fogged, and her instincts compromised from exhaustion. She longed to sit, to lie down, to let the clamor of what-ifs bleed out of her mind.

What if the Heretics followed them? What if they were ambushed or there was another trap?

She had nothing left to give.

But nothing came. No sounds of pursuit, no clicks underfoot, no gunfire. Only the crunch of boots on ruined concrete and the whispers of wind between the broken bones of the towns.

When the buildings gave way to barren land, Miriam's eyes lifted. A convoy waited at the wrecked margin of another town, prowlers and rhino vans flanked by figures posted around them. Someone familiar broke into a run toward her.

Her knees buckled, and the rhythm of endurance vaporized. However, before she could hit the ground, the figure braced her under the good arm, a firm hand at her hip.

"Tal—" she whispered.

"Oh, hell, it's really good to see you, Tan," Talwar said.

She mustered a crooked smile. "Not afraid of infection?" she managed, uncertain if the words left her at all.

Talwar glanced at the Charonites around them, then back, and his expression flickered. She could see the answer, even if he didn't say it.

Ahead, Hino's scowl softened as she approached. Durmaz and King were behind her, their presence grounding Miriam more than the meds. Gentle touches and supportive glances met her as they accompanied her to the first of two large UMF vans. She didn't question why Gumede wasn't there. She didn't care.

At the vehicle's open door, she resisted. She tried to turn, searching. Sam. She had lost sight of the litter with her team around her. She needed to stay with her.

Hino's face contorted. At first confused, she glanced about, then pointed toward the second van. "They're loading them into the vic behind us. Look," she said. "They're safe. You're safe."

Miriam caught the trace of pale hair in the back of the other vehicle. She tried to back up, move toward it, but Hino kept a firm hand at her back.

"You're safe now, Tan."

"Just—make sure—" Miriam tried, but her throat gave nothing more.

"Come on, let's get you home."

Hands prodded her forward, and as she took a seat, Miriam didn't challenge the motion. She wanted to be done with the North, with the Heretics, with the endless pain.

She wanted home.

Sleep caught her on the first transport, exhaustion overtaking adrenaline and medication, now surrounded by teammates. She stirred once, hazily aware of her transfer into an aircraft, barely a glance to wherever they were, just the visible assurance Sam and the large black body bags were loaded into the accompanying UMF ship. She resisted again at the separation, but a waiting medic jabbed her with something stronger, and the world receded again.

The next time she woke, the aircraft was landing and the sky outside was dark and gray. Convoy lights shimmered beyond hangar doors. Ursus? Station? Miriam wasn't sure. She tried to sit up, her body stiff and sore. There was no sign of Charonites, only UMF uniforms. Miriam found the other ship behind them and exhaled.

Hino had jumped out of the ship with Durmaz, already awkwardly moving the short distance toward the wide building with a casted leg. Miriam could make out the second's voice as she followed, aided by Talwar and King.

"Where the fuck is MED? They said they'd be here. Durmaz!"

"Already on it," came the reply.

Inside the bay doors, another familiar face was waiting. Krill's face dropped when he saw her. "Shit."

If Miriam hadn't been so groggy, she would've laughed. The marine didn't normally swear. She also knew she probably looked like hell, dried blood across her entire front. "Looks worse than it is, boss," she rasped.

He didn't reply, only steadied her on the convoy's running board, eyes tracing her injuries. He stepped as if to embrace her, then stopped. She couldn't have returned it anyway.

"Miriam?"

Emma.

"Miriam!"

The woman barreled toward her but stopped short, eyes wide and brimming with tears. She reached out a shaking hand and restrained herself from wrapping Miriam in a hug as well, but she touched her face sweetly. Held it carefully. Miriam grimaced under the tender pressure.

"I'm o—" she tried, then stopped. She wasn't okay, but she was glad she was back.

Emma trembled. Behind her, guilt swam in Krill's eyes.

"Finally!" Hino shouted on the other side of the bay doors.

Durmaz arrived jogging ahead of a MED-marked vehicle. Another followed behind it.

"Get Tan situated!" Hino shouted, already motioning to the approaching medics.

Miriam opened her mouth to protest, to say she was fine or at least functional, to aid Sam first, but the words caught behind her teeth as the ache in her jaw flared. The lingering medication dampened it, but the movement still sent a shudder through her neck. She didn't resist when one medic took her. It was easier to let them lead her, easier to concentrate on staying upright as they guided her into the back of the first MED transport.

And she sat, rigid on the narrow bench, as they peeled back the wrap and cloth from her neck. The air stung where blood clung to skin. One muttered something, but she wasn't listening. Her eyes had already drifted over their shoulders, past her team and Emma, searching.

Two marines were already moving Sam's litter toward the second vehicle parked parallel. Miriam straightened as much as her body would allow, pushing past the medic's restraint to get a better view. Sam was still unmoving, and Miriam wasn't sure whether to be relieved or terrified. How long did the Altered drugs last?

A light shone into Sam's open eyes, the individual testing her pupils. Another leaned over and muttered something Miriam couldn't catch.

Then came the sound—the thump of something heavy hitting the ground. She flinched and twisted. The motion nearly blinded her, pain blooming immediate in her neck and arm, but she saw it. The large body bag. Willem. The black shape had slipped off the other one in the airship and now lay crumpled, indecent, as if even in death he was being mishandled.

"No," Miriam rasped, trying to stand.

But they held her down, and her attention shifted as the doors to Sam's vehicle closed. Miriam tried to push off the bench again. Her pulse pounded in her ears, each beat a jolt of fire behind her eyes. The separation was too much.

"Miriam," Emma said, trying to calm her.

"Wait," she grated out. "Hold on—just wait."

But the other vehicle didn't. The engine kicked to life, and the vehicle rolled forward.

"She's going to hurt herself," the medic beside her muttered. Before she realized what was happening, he had already administered a jabber into her thigh. It bit through the fabric, a sting. "You need to stay calm, ma'am."

Miriam jerked in response, but the sensation was already fading. She tried to follow the other departing vehicle with her eyes, but the medic caught her shoulder again, steering her down. She rounded on him with what little strength she had left. "Where are they taking her?" she tried to enunciate with her lips.

"To the hospital," he said, calm, as if that answered everything. "Like you. We're going now."

Emma's voice rose as she reached for the back of the transport. "I'm coming with—"

The other medic blocked her.

"I'm with her."

The words hung in the air between them, unwavering, but the medic didn't flinch. "Protocol. We can't make exceptions."

Emma's face pinched in frustration, but she stepped back. "I'll see you there, okay?"

"Greg—Yuri's tracking. He'll meet you, Tan," Krill said. He reached out, trying to pat the woman's shoulder.

"I love—" The words slipped in just before the doors shut.

Miriam wasn't sure if she had dozed off again. It was the first time in hours that she'd gone fully prone, and her body, sedated by painkillers and exhaustion, had slipped into a half-conscious state. When the vehicle came to a stop, she blinked awake, her eyes drifting to the small window near the back.

The buildings outside were familiar but also not.

She pushed herself up slightly, blinking against the light overhead. She waved a hand at the individual next to her, whatever medication they'd given her already alleviating the pressure in her throat. "Where are we?" she rasped.

"The hospital," the medic said beside her.

But something was wrong. She didn't recognize the facility. And she knew Station General. She knew its shape, its color palette, the logo on its side. It was her parents', after all. And this wasn't it.

"This isn't General."

"No," the medic admitted.

Miriam's heart climbed in her chest, trying to fight against the meds. It didn't make sense. Station General was the primary for UMF in Station City. It was standard protocol for medical evacuations and other serious injuries that couldn't be handled at the clinic on base.

"You need to stay down. The meds—"

She shrugged off his hand, the motion too slow for what she intended. "Where are we?"

"Whoa, stay calm." He held his hands out. "We just take you where they tell us."

The rear doors of the transport opened, revealing the double doors to a plain building. It was a hospital or a clinic, but it wasn't the one she had been expecting. Miriam ignored the strain in her arm and neck and looked past the driver's seat. They were somewhere in the medical sector, that much she could tell from the buildings nearby, but her orientation was off.

"Why—" She stopped. Her throat still hurt, as if she'd had a terrible allergic reaction, and she knew she was pushing the limits, but she continued. "Where's Sam?"

The medic frowned, confused. "Who?"

"The woman I was brought back with. The blonde, the one with the—"

"I don't know," he said, not unkindly. "But we're here. You really need to stop moving. They'll get you sorted out."

Miriam tried to sit up fully, and the dizziness came fast. She grabbed the rail beside her. None of this made sense. "My commcuff—" She didn't have one. "I need to contact some—"

"Whoa, okay. Let me know who, but let us do our job, okay? You're safe now."

Safe.

The word rang false in her ears. It bit into her.

She tried again to get up, but the grogginess had crept up too thoroughly. The jabber they'd given her before—she'd thought it had dulled, but now it dragged at her limbs like sandbags.

Something wasn't right.

"Wait—" she said, voice slurring, trying to fight the rising weight in her head.

But the bed beneath her was already moving, guiding her through the facility doors. The brisk air swept across her skin as they entered just before sleep embraced her again.

34

INCONGRUITY

STRANGE, *amorphous shapes stared at her, faceless beings behind reflective masks. Straps pinned her to the bed while blood pooled under sterile partitions. Needles went in, then again, tugging crimson in measured pulls. She tried to lift a hand once, then twice, but the shapes stayed silhouettes, whispering through layers of transparent walls, their words drowned beneath a relentless murmur.*

A door clicked somewhere beyond Miriam's awareness. She thought she had heard it before—opening, closing, opening again—but the hours had blurred so completely, she couldn't pin sound to time. Sleep had dragged her under and spat her back out in ragged intervals, and she hated that her body had surrendered at all.

The crinkled gown scratched against her skin whenever she shifted, a constant reminder of the room's sterility. Miriam didn't consider herself modest, but the draft creeping across her bare back and lower half left her tender and exposed. This place had been designed for observation, not for comfort or healing. She picked at the lip of the rigid cast above her elbow, trying to ignore the grinding saw of pain along her neck each time she swallowed.

The ambient thrum fractured. Muffled shouting pierced

through, faint at first, distorted by glass and partitions. Miriam told herself she was imagining it, that it was another echo conjured by her exhausted mind, until the volume swelled and a crash rattled the wall. Boots hammered tile in quick succession, voices colliding in anger.

"You aren't allowed back here!" someone shouted.

A deeper voice cut through, furious and familiar. "I don't give a fuck."

Her chest compressed. She swung her legs over the edge of the small bed, trembling with the effort. "Yuri?" The name rasped from her lips, too weak to reach anyone but herself inside the glass box.

The sliding doors to the exterior room shuddered under a violent shove. A figure converged in the frame—an attendant in a pale coat—but it was Yuri that broke through, his rage burning hot enough to sear the air. She had never seen him like this.

Miriam pushed herself forward, the strength in her limbs draining. Yuri's fury dissipated when his focus found her, replaced by something carved deeper: grief, determination, and then a reignition of anger as he looked around at the sterile glass prison that held her.

"Let me in," he growled, each word soaked with threat.

An attendant stammered, fists clenching and unclenching at his sides. Yuri repeated himself, his voice dropping lower, colder, until the man wilted beneath it. The attendant fumbled out his commcuff. The lock hissed, and the partition slid open. The man backed away at once, fleeing down the hall in search of reinforcements, leaving the smell of his fear hanging in the air.

Miriam stepped forward without hesitation, her bare feet sticking to the cold tile.

"You look terrible," Yuri said.

Miriam huffed. "Shit. Thanks."

He crossed the threshold, but she took a step back,

suddenly uncertain. "Wait." With the introduction of a friendly face and her wits about her, doubts rushed in at once. Maybe something really was wrong with her. Why else would they have gone through all this fuss, partitions, sealed doors, restricted access? If she had been dangerous, what had that meant for Krill, for Emma? The thoughts tangled until Yuri swept in and folded his arms around her. His embrace was careful, mindful of the bent cast and bandages but firm enough to anchor her.

The hesitation bled out. Miriam let herself sag into him, let her forehead rest against his breast. For the first time since she had gone north, she felt ground beneath her feet again. She tried to return the embrace, her left arm trembling with the effort.

"What—where—" she managed at last, pulling back. Her throat bobbed painfully, tugging at the ache in her neck. "What's going on?"

"Emma showed up at General," he said. "When you never arrived, we rang the alarms."

"Did she—did you bring her here?"

Movement stirred in the doorway, pulling Miriam's awareness to a hulking shape. She flinched, a flash of colorful eyes and foreign words whispering in her ears, but then she blinked.

"Fox?"

Her other former teammate strode forward and pulled her into an embrace, rougher than Yuri's. Pain flared in her arm and ribs, but his presence outweighed the hurt.

"Emma wanted to come," Yuri went on, shaking his head. "But it didn't feel right. Just in case. I didn't want her to—"

"No." Miriam's whisper was hoarse but resolute. "Thank you." She tried to look past the open doors. "Where are we?"

"Meridian."

"What?"

"Meridian Health Institute." Yuri's voice hardened. "It's a

small clinic, more research, but it doesn't matter. It's not Station General."

She had known it wasn't General in her waking moments, but she frowned. The name meant nothing. A small clinic? None of it made sense. "And they let you just walk in?"

Yuri shook his head at the same time Fox flexed an arm.

"Muscle," Fox said.

To Miriam's surprise, Yuri didn't roll his eyes. Instead, his eyes traveled the room. "They really make you feel like a lab rat here, don't they?" His eyes dropped to the floor. "Tan, I didn't know. You never responded to my messages. I knew you were on mission, but I didn't know. Everything—"

"OpSec," Miriam whispered. It wasn't his fault; it wasn't like she could've told her friend, her former teammate, any of this.

Yuri winced. "So I would've found out when it was live on the network? My best frie—" His voice broke before he could finish.

Fox's shoulders drew taut.

Miriam bit down on the correction. It wouldn't have been live—prerecorded, and if the Charonites hadn't stepped in, Butcher might not have broadcast her execution anyway—but she didn't tell Yuri.

Footsteps thundered down the hallway and four figures appeared. The same attendant from before was flanked by two private security guards and another man in a white coat. Yuri and Fox stepped forward, instinctively shielding Miriam.

"This is absolutely unprofessional, Mr. Gregov," the new white-coated man said without preamble, his tone clipped.

"You kidnapped her," Fox snapped, striding closer, his size blotting out the rest of the group.

Yuri pressed a hand against Fox's back. "UMF protocol is to send injured marines to General. This was a mistake, and it's quite ridiculous that your systems didn't have her logged.

Thankfully, a friend in Center was able to assist with the city's camera systems, follow the UMF transport here."

The white-coat straightened. "Well, you're out of the loop. UMF's policy changed. She was never Station General's patient."

"Bullshit," Yuri muttered. "You know that's not how the agreement works."

"You can't just come in and take—"

"Why all these locks? All this secrecy? She's not a patient here." Yuri scowled and shook his head. "None of this matters. Tan, get your stuff. We're leaving now."

"We advise against that—"

Yuri made a show of looking over Miriam before he snapped back to the white-coat. "You've done the basics, I see. But it hasn't been a day. Why isn't she still in a MedJet? General can take over."

"Yes, but—"

"Tan, do you want to continue your stay here?" Yuri said without looking back.

Fuck, no. "No," she said instead.

"Would you like to be transferred?"

She started to nod, then forced her throat to work. "Yes."

"But she can't just—"

Yuri bristled. "She can't what? Is there a reason you're holding her here? Is there a reason for why she's not in a proper recovery or treatment room?"

Fox moved again, his frame filling the opening in the partition. The guards faltered, their retreat toward the sliding doors less a choice than an instinct.

"We'll be taking Ms. Tanner back to Station General. Where she belongs," Yuri declared. "Now where is her stuff? Tan, do you need anything before we go?"

"No," she said, not bothering to look around. She already knew the room was devoid of any of her belongings, and what had those clothes and items been, anyway? Her sullied uniform? Whatever was in its pockets? She didn't want any of it.

Yuri held his hand behind him, and Miriam took it. Using Fox as both shield and battering ram, they drove the group into the corridor. The guards' resentment lingered on Fox, but they stepped aside, while the white-coated man said nothing, only followed them with a watchful, clinical gaze.

No other words were exchanged. Yuri and Fox boxed Miriam in as they moved down a series of hallways. When she risked a glance back, the staff trailed them at a distance, but she exhaled anyway, the presence of her teammates steadying her.

She realized she had stopped believing she was contagious. Whatever she'd been exposed to, it hadn't passed to anyone she'd come in contact with. The lack of distancing from the attendant and the white-coated man before was another confirmation.

Outside, the sky widened above the city's towers, impossibly bright after the confinement. The lack of ruin was jarring, a sudden contrast from the last place she had consciously been. Heat radiated from the pavement into the soles of her bare feet, but she welcomed it; it was better than the chill of imprisonment inside.

Yuri leaned closer, his concern plain. "You okay?"

"I need you to order blood work on me when—"

His face set.

"Just in case," Miriam whispered.

A final confirmation. He nodded but didn't ask anything further.

Her next breath caught, a sudden crack in the tenuous calm she'd been trying to cling to. The question had been buried under pain and disorientation, but now it surged, urgent and insistent. The skin at the back of her neck prickled.

"Tan?"

"Sam."

Yuri's brows creased. "Valk?"

Before he or Fox could stop her, Miriam stormed back inside, her hospital gown fluttering behind her. "Where is she?" she demanded.

The four individuals from earlier had paused in the middle of the corridor in their own heated discussion. They turned, but none answered. Fox's and Yuri's steps resounded behind her as they caught up.

"Sam Ryan," Miriam pressed, her voice straining as it rose. "The blonde. The Seraph. She was with me. Another ambulance."

The white-coated man raised a hand. "No one else arrived today, Ms. Tanner."

Miriam staggered a step closer. "Bullshit. Don't you dare lie to me. Where is she?" Each word landed like it wanted to draw blood.

"I assure you, you were the only one who arrived at Meridian from UMF."

The response fell on her, heavy as concrete, and her heartbeat hammered in her ears. She barely registered Yuri's hand bracing her elbow.

"She wouldn't have been UMF—"

"No one by that name is registered here," the attendant interrupted.

"*Ms. Tanner* wasn't registered here either," Fox growled behind them.

Yuri's grip tightened.

Miriam's eyes bored into the attendant and the white-coat, memorizing every line of their faces. If she found out they were lying...

She glared at them for a second longer, then spun away. She didn't care that the breeze teased her bare legs, lifted the back of her gown, didn't care about the indignity. Fuck them.

Palm on her back, Yuri followed. He murmured instructions to Fox, who jogged off ahead to fetch the vehicle.

Outside again, the sun was harsher than before, slicing at Miriam's vision. She propped herself against the building. Every sound felt too loud, amplified. Doors slamming, a car horn, a stranger's shoes tapping past. Another pedestrian glanced at them and looked quickly away. The motion and energy was the most she'd spent since she'd been back, and she was already lightheaded again, sweat breaking out.

"Valk was there too?" Yuri asked.

Miriam rubbed at the lower rim of her cast just over her knuckles. "Do you think they were lying?"

"I don't know. I don't think so." His hand settled on her shoulder again, warm and gentle.

"Sam. Is she at General?"

His silence was answer enough.

Miriam's stomach turned. If not here, if not General, then where? They were back in Station City. She had seen Sam before they'd been separated into their own ambulances. They were supposed to be safe.

"Let's get you back," Yuri said firmly. "I'll feel better once we get you looked at. Properly."

Miriam nearly protested—she had planned to—but when she moved to shake her head, pain bloomed through her neck. She flinched, and the cycle of it stole the fight from her.

"That's not a request, Tan. We're going to the hospital, the right one. Shit, what were they doing to you in there?" He glanced at her arm. "I know I'm no doctor, but seriously, just the basics!"

She didn't argue. Not because she agreed, but because she needed space to think. Her mind was already racing, circling possibilities. What had they done with Sam?

"We were supposed to get coffee," Yuri whispered.

She looked up, surprised by the guilt etched into his expression. "I know." Her voice cracked. "Sorry. I was a bit stuck."

Yuri laughed quietly. "Do you—do you want to talk about it?"

"No." She stopped short, and her hand automatically went to the bandage on her neck. "Not yet. But I should."

His fingers squeezed gently on her shoulder. "Coffee when you're patched up?"

Miriam tipped her chin, eyes fixed somewhere distant as tires screeched around the corner.

The route back to Station General was short and only familiar once they neared. When they took the side entrance toward Yuri's office, the lighting and faint antiseptic bite in the air struck her, but this was a different feeling. She knew this medical center.

Miriam waved away the staff that met them with a mobile chair and gurney. She felt weaker than before, but she could still walk. She could still control that. So Yuri grudgingly led her into a separate wing, one Miriam knew wasn't meant for the general population. Private treatment rooms.

When he opened the door of one, Emma was already inside, curled on the couch. She sprang up the moment they entered, crossing the room in three bounding strides.

"I'm okay," Miriam began, but Emma's arms were already around her.

It wasn't a careful embrace. It was fierce and frantic, the kind that came with the question neither asked aloud: What if she hadn't come back? Emma drew her cheek against Miriam's, one hand cradling the back of her head, like her grip could erase the damage, as if touch alone could will Miriam whole again.

And for a moment, it almost did. Miriam let herself fold into it, her face against Emma's shoulder, breathing in the faintest scent of her apartment—of her bed, of soap, of a world that hadn't collapsed. Her throat caught without warning. The warmth, the familiarity, the desperate certainty in Emma's touch—it all carved a hollow through her. But it didn't reach the center.

Something else stirred in the space. A flash of blue eyes in a dank cellar, the rasp of her name spoken through blood and dust. Sam's face rose unbidden, overlaid atop Emma's shoulder. Miriam pressed her eyes shut, guilt snapping like a wire through her. She tried to focus on the warmth and realness around her. It was everything she thought she'd fought to return to, and despite that, something in her recoiled. Not from Emma, but from herself, from the part of her that knew this wasn't enough to hold her together anymore. That the gravity in her chest had shifted.

She forced her eyes open. "I'm okay," Miriam whispered again, but this time it came out quieter. Less sure. Something she hoped would become true if she repeated it enough.

Emma didn't let go. "She was there then?" she asked as she turned to Yuri without pulling away.

"It took some strong-arming," he said with a glance at Fox. "But yeah."

"Those bastards. I get you back, just to lose you again? Is this a new UMF thing? I thought Station General was primary—"

"It is," Yuri and Miriam said in unison.

"They didn't have her in emergency or the usual wings," Yuri continued. "They had her in some—"

"Observation room," Miriam finished with a whisper.

"Like a fuckin' lab rat," Fox added with a scowl.

Emma's expression hardened. Miriam recognized the look: Emma stacking details in her head, turning them over.

Yuri glanced at the door. "The doctor's on the way—"

"I'm okay," Miriam repeated. She pulled back. "What happened?"

Emma's eyes flicked to her then down, her expression sobering. She was the first to shake her head. "Krill dropped me off. We lost sight of your vehicle, but I thought we got

caught in traffic. When we got here, and *you* weren't here..."
She waved her hands. "We searched for you for hours, Miriam.
Yuri, he called Fox, and Fox, well—they called your friend
Kai—"

And they had found her. Her girlfriend, her friends had
turned the earth over looking for her. But who would do the
same for...

"Sam. We need to find where she is."

Emma nodded. She had been prepared. "Yuri, I hope you
don't mind, but I took the liberty to check into some things
while you were out."

He raised a brow. "What things?"

"When we were leaving Station, I remembered—I thought I
saw the other ambulance. But I didn't think of it then. I
thought it had already left ahead of yours." Emma paused.
"There are several UMF medical transports, right? But why
would I see it again *inside* the base? It would've left out of the
main gate. For General, or Meridian, I guess?"

"What are you saying?" Miriam asked. "You're saying you
saw..."

"I don't know if it was the same one she was in, but why
would there be another transport driving around at the same
time? Unless there was another emergency..." Emma exhaled
slowly. "I don't know. I reached out to Krill, since he'd gone
back to the compound, but I haven't heard from him since. I
thought it was maybe just a coincidence, but if you're saying no
one else was at Meridian—"

"Emma. What do you mean?"

"The other ambulance. It was still on base."

"The medics said we were going to the same place." Miriam
sank onto the armrest of the couch, already tiring. "Where
were they going?"

Emma hesitated. "Last I saw, it was toward the other gate,
the north one? The outer ring. Where we met—"

The annexes. The exterior sections where access was more

flexible to non-UMF personnel. There had never been a clinic out there, but there had been temporary offices and warehouses. Legion had used them once when their new alliance and collaboration had started. It was the same quadrant where the advisor from their mission brief had been based. It was where the Pit was.

Miriam's stomach turned.

"And Krill hasn't responded?" Yuri asked.

"No," Emma replied. "Not yet."

Miriam set her jaw. "When did you message him?"

"An hour ago?"

"Try him again."

"Miriam."

"Try him again. Or we go back. I'm not sitting here while she's—" Miriam lurched to her feet too quickly. The world tilted; her vision darkened briefly as her knees buckled.

"Whoa. Okay, Tan." Yuri raised a hand. "You need to get fixed up. Whatever they did over there…"

Her healing had been second priority from the start.

"No, I need to—" She tried to shove his hand away, but he didn't budge. Fox had already stepped in front of the door.

"You need to get better," Yuri said.

"Miriam, he's right," Emma added softly.

Irritation shot through Miriam, but her body betrayed her. She was too weak for any of this.

"I'll call Krill, okay?" Yuri added. "Everything will be fine. If she's still on base, Valk's safe. It's one of the safest places she can be."

But Miriam's chest only grew heavier. She had *just* felt safe, and it rang false. Something was wrong; something was off. She just didn't know what it was now.

35

RECONCILIATION

"CAN WE TRUST HIM?"

Across the room, Fox's face ignited with confusion and surprise. "Whoa. That's a jump. It's Krill."

Miriam limped to the side of the bed, her steps tight with restless energy despite her protesting body. Her right arm stayed close, cradled as if that might keep the bones from grating. She knew she shouldn't have been up, but sitting still for two days had driven her half-mad. Lying down had been worse.

She touched the bandage at her throat, and the throb in her neck returned, a lit fuse of pain threading down her arm. The MedJet's first treatments had kept the swelling down, enough that she could speak without grimacing, but the strain lingered. Every swallow felt tight; every turn of her head dragged at the healing tissue. The last dose of medication was fading, but she didn't want to risk being knocked out again. She also couldn't afford to be fogged or slow when Sam was found.

"He works for Command now," she said. "And Command sent us on that mission."

Fox didn't respond right away, but the lines around his mouth tightened. "He wouldn't do that. Are you really…"

Miriam winced, but the doubt still pooled. Every terrible possibility was alive in her blood, and it gnawed at her ribs and carved through her chest.

"I can't believe I'm the one sayin' this, but patience."

She didn't meet his eyes. She hated that she'd said it out loud. Krill was her friend. He'd been her trusted teammate and lead. But the world had slipped off its axis, and if everything else had shifted, what made him an exception?

"Emma and Yuri are working with Krill," Fox said, rubbing the back of his neck. "They'll figure out where Valky is."

"And what? You're babysitting me?"

He shrugged and folded his arms. "Someone's gotta."

She eased back a step and leaned on the bed frame, pretending it was casual. The truth was her leg had begun to tremble from bearing her weight. She tried to hide the wince as her ribs ached, and the muscles around her throat clenched, a warning and reminder she hadn't given herself enough time to heal.

He huffed. "You went through shit. A lot of it. We've been through this before, yeah? What's the point in goin' through all of that, makin' mistakes, and not learnin' from it?"

She held his gaze, the spark of fight there, but relented. "I can't—I have to find her, Fox, I—"

"What can you do that the others aren't already doin'? You've got friends, a team, support. Tan, we'd move mountains for you. Let us help."

Miriam exhaled, but it didn't ease the load on her. The voices in her head were louder than his, louder than any logic.

"Do you want to talk?" he asked. "You know you can. With me."

She looked at him, her jaw tight, a tremor under her skin. Her lips parted, then shut again.

He raised his hands. "If you don't, it's okay. Really. Talk with Yuri. Emma. She's been freaked out ever since word came back, Tan. She's out there right now, helpin' find the Valkyrie. You've got people."

Emma.

Miriam flinched. In the storm of exhaustion and survival, she had shut Emma out. The guilt struck fast, a cold hook through the gut.

"You've got us," Fox said.

"I know." Her voice came out low. She added a whisper of thanks. "I thought—"

The door opened. Emma stepped inside, and the room changed with her. Miriam straightened, heart skipping. The motion sent a cramp through her ribs, but she masked it, holding her breath until the pain dulled. For a beat, she and Emma only looked at one another, and Miriam tried to pack every unspoken thing into that moment. *Thank you. I'm sorry. I'm not okay.*

Fox fidgeted. "I'll come back later—"

"No," Emma said firmly. "We're going to need your brawn, Benjamin. Think you can amp up that intimidation of yours?"

He cocked an eyebrow and tilted his chin, a smirk dancing on his face.

Miriam stepped closer. "Did Krill—"

Emma nodded.

"Told ya," Fox said. "I knew fearless leader'd come through. He isn't as much of a boy scout anymore…"

Boy Scout.

The words hit harder than they should have, especially since Fox didn't know who Sam's SRAF teammate was. Willem. The legionnaires. Perun. Hadeon. Miriam's stomach flipped and guilt hammered into her. How had she forgotten them so fast?

"The legionnaires?" she blurted. "Does UMF—does Legion—"

Fox's eyes fell. "We know. Legion knows. There's a vigil this week. Their sector."

So the Heretics *had* televised Hadeon's execution. Perun's

body may have been there, too, in the background. Had their bodies been recovered? Was there anything left to retrieve?

"We'll get them," Fox said. "We'll hunt them down."

The Heretics. The Apostates. She wanted justice, but it no longer sat at the top of her priorities. She also didn't want to go back to the North, to be the one delivering that justice. It all felt endless. Like every mission only made room for another. More violence, more injuries, more names, and more death. She was so very tired.

Emma rocked back on her heels.

Miriam shook her head, then regretted it as her muscles strained. "What now?" she asked. "What did he find out?"

Her girlfriend's eyes flicked over her, concern written on her face. She hesitated but replied, "Krill sent a location. He hasn't been able to check it out, but it's on the compound."

Miriam pushed herself away from the bed frame. "UMF's doing this?"

Emma's mouth twisted. "I don't know, but Miriam—"

"What?"

Emma flinched but didn't answer.

Miriam frowned, impatient. She took a step toward the door. "It doesn't matter. We're wasting time. Let's go."

"No," Emma said, lifting a hand. "Fox and I will go. Don't look at me like that, Miriam, you can barely stand."

"I'm fine." The words came out too barbed, too quick. She'd felt them slice out, and she felt the guilt immediately after, but she repeated it again, softer.

Emma wasn't convinced, giving her another look. "Look, I don't know what this building is, but I've been looking up stuff, and I think I may know who…it is." When neither Miriam nor Fox said anything, she continued. "I think it's Vertex or one of their liaisons. It's their on-site facility."

Miriam froze. Vertex had worked with UMF to send the SOG and Legion teams to their damn facility.

Fox glanced between the two women. "Isn't that where Nas works? Kai mentioned it before…"

"We can check with him, too—if he knows anything," Emma said.

"The tech company? For Valk's arm?"

Yes, but no. The wrong division. A subsidiary.

"Axiom," Miriam whispered.

Emma's eyes widened. "How do you know about Axiom?"

The two triangles. Miriam's spine went rigid, and a chill moved through her.

"Axiom?" Fox's face scrunched. "Why is that familiar?"

Miriam had already turned toward the door. "We have to go."

"That mission." Fox's eyes widened. "Underground. The stims. Stims?"

"Is Krill going to meet us there?" Miriam asked.

Emma shook her head. "He's caught up in another engagement, but he told us. I have access, too. Yuri got pulled away, but he said he'll check back in."

Miriam paused as something lodged in her throat. She faced Emma. "Did you know?"

Emma blinked, and then her mouth opened, incredulous. "No. No. Miriam. Are you serious?"

"Whoa, Tan." Fox took a step back, awkward and unsure where to stand.

"I swear," Emma said. "I didn't."

"You work for them," Miriam muttered.

Emma stiffened. "GenTech was bought by Vertex, Miriam. And *worked*. Past tense." Her voice dropped and went brittle. "Are you really accusing me right now?"

Miriam squashed her fingers into her scalp. "No. Fuck. Sorry. No."

But it was already too late. Emma winced, her expression closed. What was Miriam doing? First Krill, and now her own girlfriend. She was agitated, frustrated. She knew she was lashing out.

"I'm sorry."

"Let's just go," Emma whispered.

Fox turned for the door, and Miriam opened it for him. She made to follow but stopped when she realized Emma hadn't moved.

"Emma."

The woman inhaled but didn't speak. Then she brushed past Miriam without a glance.

"I'm sorry, Em."

No answer.

Fuck.

"You're sure this is it?" Fox asked gruffly.

The three stood before the long gray annex. It looked like every other UMF structure on the street, another copy of a copy, stripped of character. Miriam scanned the row of mostly empty warehouses where Legion had once assembled before moving farther out to the airfield. Her insides cramped with the reminder of Hadeon and the legionnaires. She made a mental note to check on Legion. Somehow. Without Hadeon, she wasn't sure how.

Emma lifted her handheld, and Fox leaned over her shoulder. "I guess it is," he muttered. "Doesn't look like much. Is there anyone here?"

Miriam tried to ignore how tight her chest felt from the drive and subsequent walk through the compound. Every step had pulled against half-healed bruises and cuts. She felt the bandage on her throat stretch as she glanced down at herself, at the plain civilian clothes she'd been given at the medical center. Emma matched her—civilian, out of place. Fox was the only one who belonged, his black SOG T-shirt and UMF grays marking him as official. The imbalance made her uneasy, but it wasn't enough to stop her.

She ignored the concerned look from Emma and crossed the threshold like she was bracing for a blow. The double doors parted, and the lobby beyond wore the same generic furnishings and color palette as every other annex. Still, something in the air was wrong. It was too staged, too managed. She tensed before she knew why. Her skin crawled as she tracked the surveillance units tucked into corners. Most angled toward the front doors, but more than one remained on the reinforced door beside the counter.

Not the usual UMF-issue. It was both familiar and not. Her pulse hammered, and for a fleeting moment she thought her body might betray her.

"What is this place?" Fox mumbled.

A low murmur carried from the small side corridor, and two marines emerged from a passage behind the counter, their conversation stalling mid-sentence when they saw they had company. The shorter one blinked, caught between confusion and calculation.

"You're early," the taller one said, eyes flicking lazily over them. "Shipments go to the back. Door's already open. I can meet you there in a sec."

"Dumbass," the short one muttered, eyes narrowing. "It's not them."

"Oh." A pause. "How can we…help you?"

"You're UMF," Miriam said flatly.

"Yes," the tall one drawled, stretching the word like a question. His attention skimmed over her, wavering on the cast and bandages along her arm, neck, and body.

There was no clean way to handle this; she had no patience left for games. She gestured at the reinforced door. "You have someone back there who shouldn't be."

The shorter marine stiffened, and then his hand slid beneath the counter. Fox drifted forward, his posture set.

"We're just Division clerks, okay?" the taller one said quickly, an uneasy eye on the large SOG marine. "They rotate us through here. Just doing our jobs. No trouble here. We take shipments, let the white-coats in."

White-coats. Researchers. Scientists. The casual way he said it scraped at her. Complicit.

Miriam's teeth ground together, and she ignored the pain lancing out in her neck. "You're letting them hold another marine against her will."

And in UMF's headquarters, no less.

"Well, she ain't no mar—"

A kick under the counter cut him off.

But it was enough confirmation. And it touched a live nerve.

"Not a marine?" Her focus hardened. "Not a marine." Miriam's laugh cut. "Do you know who she is? Sam Ryan bled for UMF—more than most of this fucking organization. She's been in since she was a kid, since before you were probably even relevant. And now that her contract's done, you just hand her over like fucking surplus?"

"Whoa. We just follow orders," the short one said, his face pale now, his own recognition of the SOG diamond tab on Fox's collar clear. "I've buzzed our ranking officer. He stepped out for a 'synth break, but he'll be back soon. He can answer whatever questions you have."

Miriam didn't want another gatekeeper, but she didn't have to wait long. The doors opened behind them, and a black uniform strode in.

"SOG," the officer said as he looked over Fox. "You've got no authority here."

Fox gave Miriam a small nod. The flick of his wrist told her he'd already pinged Krill.

"She's UMF," Miriam said, stepping in. "She's a daughter of Ursus."

Literally. Even if Sam hadn't renewed her contract, she was practically born and raised UMF.

"How are you allowing this?" Miriam's voice cracked on the words, and she hated the sound of it.

The officer's eyes raked over her as he moved closer. She didn't budge, her own glare on his name tag. *Cunningham.*

"You're out of line, *marine.*"

She nearly laughed and rolled her eyes. Oh, good. He'd clocked her as one of them despite the civvies. The days of deprivation, of blood and dirt and burned skin, of running for her life, starving, and nearly having her throat slit, her head severed, all of it crowded in. She didn't give a shit what this officer thought of her. What did *out of line* mean after all that?

"I know she's here." She jabbed a finger into his breastbone. "Do you just give up your own?"

He scowled.

Her heart thundered and her vision pulsed. She moved despite Fox's angling movement. Beside him, Emma's face knotted.

"You're letting them hold her prisoner." Miriam's voice pitched louder. "What if it were you? Or one of yours?"

"Hey," Fox said quietly.

She shoved his hand away. "Don't touch me."

"Go outside, Tan. Get some air."

"Miriam—" Emma started.

"No. Fuck you, *Cunningham,*" Miriam snapped at the officer. She turned before Emma could reach out. "No. Stay and try to appeal to these fucks. I'll see myself out."

The officer shifted as if to block her exit.

"Come near me," she said, finger up, "and I'll break you. I don't give a shit who you are. Do your actual job. Protect your people." She stormed out with another mutter. "Fucking lapdog assholes."

♟

Miriam rounded the building, the concrete biting under her shoes. When she was out of sightlines, she slipped along the windowless wall, arm aching and neck pulling, but adrenaline propelled her forward.

At the back, she paused. There had been surveillance inside the annex lobby, and now as she scanned the vicinity, there were no guards, just another system watching the door. She hoped Fox and Emma were sufficiently distracting the three marines inside, and before she could change her mind, she approached the door. If they saw her, they'd send people, but not if she moved quick enough. She held a hand over the door panel, afraid it might be locked. If it were, she'd be forced to go back like some desperate supplicant begging for permission.

She engaged the console, and the door opened. The highest security was nothing if there was a weak link. And humans were always that link. Her knees sagged with relief, but she forced herself across the threshold. She didn't bother fully shutting the door behind her.

Inside she waited, listening for footsteps, for murmurs, for anything beyond the hammer in her ears. A long hallway ran between closed doors. She crept forward. It didn't look like the brig or prison; the rooms weren't barred cells, but when she passed each one, they all had the same one-way transparent, window-like door.

She picked up her pace, moving past empty room after empty room. She only slowed nearly halfway in when she neared a cart in the hall, trays on top of it. A jabber gleamed. Her right hand reached out before she could stop it, and a hot spike of pain unspooled down to her elbow despite the cast. The heat was a contrast to the cool metal that wobbled beneath her fingers. Something ugly surged in her.

"What are they doing to you, Sam?" she muttered.

The next window showed nothing.

The one after—

Her breath caught.

Sam had folded herself into a corner, arms cinched around her legs. Her blond hair was disheveled, sticking out over her forearms. Something inside Miriam, some braced bit of herself that had not yet broken, finally gave.

And then, steps pattered in the open area beside her, and Miriam spun, her body reacting before her mind. Next to her, a white-coat with a music device in his ears froze, startled.

Unarmed. Harmless.

But in her state, nothing felt harmless.

He plucked one device out of his ear. "What—who—how'd you get back here?"

Miriam lunged back toward the cart and the jabber, grabbed it, and thrust it out awkwardly.

The white-coat skirted back flush into the opposite corridor wall, his music device falling with a plink to the ground.

She craned her neck but stopped short, the motion too much of a strain. Keeping him in her sight, she stepped into the small nook she'd missed, realizing it was an open supply closet and work area, a smattering of equipment and kits on its counters. No one else. She'd been lucky. She stepped back out and jerked the lightweight cylinder toward one of the empty rooms opposite Sam's. "Open the door."

He blanched and shook his head.

Her hand trembled. "Open the fucking door."

"I can't. You—" His finger gestured at the console next to her.

She nudged the access with her casted elbow and the door opened.

"Move."

He stepped back into the doorway, and she moved with him, forcing him back past the frame. She raised the jabber higher. "What did you do to her?"

He shook his head again but didn't answer. Only a helpless shrug.

Useless. Another link in the chain pretending they weren't

complicit. Miriam was tiring of the lack of answers. She extended her right arm as far as she could, and the door shut between them. Another careful nudge and the partition frosted over, erasing him from sight. His fists thudded on the partition a moment later, but she ignored it. She pocketed the jabber and moved back to the clear door.

To Sam.

A tap to the panel opened the door, and Miriam carefully stepped in. The room's cooler air raised a shiver along the base of her neck as she studied Sam's figure. The woman had been scrubbed, the filth and blood erased, but scabs and colored bruises littered her body. Her fingers hovered at her neck, scratching as if the skin itself itched from the inside, but she appeared unhurt overall. The outfit she wore wasn't clothing so much as packaging: a crisp, paper-like shirt and pants. Something that said specimen more than patient.

"Hey."

No reaction. Not even a flinch or the tip of a head in her direction. Had they sedated Sam, or worse, had they caged her with calmers? Was any part of her awake?

Miriam edged in, cautious because her muscles remembered violence in every movement. She still anticipated pain, still winced from the chance of surprise and failure. Her heartbeat thudded unevenly, and she felt her own breath catch in her throat. Closer now, she crouched and touched Sam's forearm with two fingers. The warmth of skin undid her.

Then, at last, a voice. "Mir?"

It was so quiet, it barely reached her, but it shattered her. That name. Not Tan, not Tanner, not Miriam. Just *Mir*. A name from a previous life, only said by one person. And each time she'd heard it from Sam, it'd cut straight through her.

Sam's face lifted slightly, and the fabric—if one could call it that—crinkled at her shoulders. In the harsh light, she looked smaller than Miriam remembered, drawn, underfed, and hunched into herself like she were trying to make her own body disappear. The bandage on her cheek stood out like a brand, harsh against pale, sallow skin. She looked worn to the bone. Not gone, but close.

"It's me," Miriam said, her voice tremulous despite her best efforts.

"I didn't think I'd see you again."

"Now why would you say that?"

Sam didn't answer. Blue eyes held on her face before they dropped to Miriam's neck, then fell away.

Miriam glanced toward the open hallway and the unsecured path out. "Can you stand? We need to go."

With effort, they rose together. Sam's movements were careful, not stumbling, although it was clear they cost her. Miriam hovered close, ready to catch the woman if she fell, if she staggered, if it was all too much.

She sighed in relief when they exited the room and stood in the hall—still no one there. For a moment, Sam stared. She seemed so frail, like she had wilted, shriveled back to an insecure childhood. She whispered a thank you.

Miriam only set a hand on the small of Sam's back and prodded her toward the back exit. "Are you okay?"

The woman shook her head. "No." And her body shook with it. "I—I need help."

Miriam's heart squeezed. She managed a soft "okay" and offered her left shoulder and arm. The added weight lit up her shoulder, but she bore it, jaw set against the flare.

They shuffled down the hall together until the exit loomed ahead, spilling brilliant white daylight through its open lines. Sam stopped short as Miriam nudged the door open with a foot. Her posture remained rigid, her breath irregular. Sam didn't step farther. Instead, her eyes scanned the outside world as though it were something foreign, something she hadn't thought she'd see again.

Miriam understood. "You can do this," she whispered both to Sam and herself.

They had somehow survived. They *could* do this. And together, they stepped outside and moved along the rear of the building, pausing at the corner. Sam's gaze swept the row of buildings neighboring the annex, over UMF's compound wall and the buildings in the near distance. Her eyes landed on the figures on the adjacent side who hadn't seen them yet, not at this angle. Emma, Krill, Fox.

Miriam caught the sliver of movement—Krill, posture tight, facing the same officer from the lobby. No audio reached her, just hands cutting the air, Krill's palm flat in emphasis, the officer's own responding gestures to the insignia on his uniform. It was a silent picture of argument drawn in stiff motions.

She inhaled, bracing herself for the pending confrontation—she could feel the irritation unbridling—but turned back when she realized Sam hadn't moved. Her face was raised to the sky, eyes closed as if trying to find the sunlight in the shadow of the building, as if she wanted it but couldn't make the step away to grant herself access to its warmth.

"You'll get through this," Miriam encouraged. "We'll get through this, S—" She stopped herself. This was Sam, but what if the woman didn't want to be *Sam?* "Fu—"

"No." The woman didn't look at her. "Please don't call me that."

Miriam's heart kicked painfully. Her mouth opened, then closed.

"I don't want you to call me that," Sam repeated, quieter.

The name hung there, unspoken.

Sam.

Without giving herself time to hesitate, Miriam wrapped her arms as best as she could around the woman. Sam stiffened but didn't pull away. She didn't melt into her either, simply endured it, arms at her sides.

But then, just as Miriam withdrew, hands drew her back. And held her there. Miriam's chest constricted. The embrace deepened. Became something else. Not just comfort, not just acknowledgment. It became a tether, solace, understanding. And need.

It was a rejoining, a return, but also a goodbye. There was longing and sadness, over three years of loss, remorse, regret within it. Once lovers, a point in time come and gone. But at that corner, just out of view, they were safe and nothing else mattered.

Miriam buried her face into Sam's shoulder, her cheek against the fabric of her shirt. The sob tore free before she could stop it—not that she tried. It surged up her throat, and the pressure behind her eyes broke. The tears came hot and fast, smothering into Sam, carrying everything said and unsaid.

She let it happen, let it all come apart.

Not just for herself. For Sam.

For everything.

For the mission, the horrors she had witnessed, for the ones she couldn't save. For Herrera, Willem, Perun, Hadeon, for every person she'd lost. For every wrong choice and every echo of silence that had followed. For what it meant to still be standing when so many others weren't.

She clung to her. To the fragile hope that it was over, to the impossible idea that something better might still exist on the other side. To a future she had stopped believing in. And to the woman—worn and changed, but still there—who, after everything, also held on to her.

PART 3

INTENTION

36

RECLAMATION

MIRIAM LOOKED up at the house. Her own childhood home, her parents' place, was only a block down, tucked into the same strange patch of the city where the vertical skyline gave way to sprawling single-family dwellings. It unsettled her, the sudden absence of upward ambition, the grotesque sprawl that claimed far more space than it needed. Even the city's towers looked down in quiet judgment, yet everyone knew who held the actual power. It was the people who could afford to waste the air above them.

Yuri had never seemed as bothered by it. He shared her views on the absurd wealth gap, but practicality had outweighed principle. After taking the management role at Station General, he'd moved back into his parents' secondary suite. It was closer to work, closer to care. When his father had passed, he settled into the main house to keep his mother company.

He met Miriam near the gate where a fence divided the large home from the smaller outbuilding behind it. "It looks better," he said, gesturing at her face and neck.

She rolled her eyes and scratched at the new flexcast on her forearm, the light polymer warm from the sun. "Helps when you've been forced to sit in the MedJet for far too long. There are protocols, you know."

He shrugged. "Parents worry. Your *friend* worries. When you've got the connections, use them."

She hummed indifferently as they walked slowly into the backyard. She glanced at the one-story accessory dwelling unit. "Thanks for taking her in."

"What, leave Valk on the street? Not a chance. It was either mine or Fox's—it was an obvious choice." He rubbed the back of his head. "Although Fox has been here as much as possible. He's a surprisingly good influence." He huffed. "Who'd have known?"

"Is he around? I want to tell him thanks."

"You didn't get the update?"

"What update?"

"You should really check your messages, Tan. Or at least somehow keep in touch. He got pulled in, mentioned something ramping up—SOG's been busier as of late. Vague, but if I had to guess, it must have something to do with the wunbies. They messed with you, and, well, when you mess with one of us..."

Miriam scoffed. Yuri hadn't been in UMF in a while, but SOG was still part of him. Not the whole identity, but it had definitely been a part of it.

His tone softened. "And Valk? We've bled together. That makes us family. She'll always have a place here."

Miriam gave him a smile. "I'm surprised her team hasn't come looking."

His eyes darted sideways.

"Yuri."

He shrugged. "There might've been an angry Seraph stomping around General the other day."

She straightened. "Chapel?"

"What?"

Miriam shook her head and let it go. She hadn't asked

Talwar or Hino about the others: Chapel, Bretner, the legionnaires. Aside from the mandatory debrief UMF leadership had forced her into—a panel of officers and specialists—she'd avoided the compound and, indirectly, her own team. The guilt bubbled for a brief second; her mind had shut it all out in the aftermath, and though it was a relief, it also felt wrong.

"How did they find—what did you tell them?" she asked.

"I didn't lie. I'm not going to keep her from her team. I mean, it's *still* her team."

We're her team, Miriam wanted to say, but were they, really? Echo wasn't Echo anymore. Krill and Fox were in UMF, but they had moved on. Kai, Nas, and Yuri had also gone their separate ways.

"They left," Yuri said. "But they'll probably be back. I don't know if it's the right thing to do, though, you know? She's trying to get clean."

The meaning was clear. SRAF wasn't built for sobriety.

"But in the end, it's her choice."

They stopped at the guesthouse's wide-paneled window. Inside, Emma and Sam sat in quiet conversation, backs turned. Sam's hand rose, thumb smoothing once along the side of her neck, then fell.

Yuri glanced at Miriam.

"Spit it out," she whispered.

"It's not weird?" He wagged his finger in Emma and Sam's direction.

Of course it was, but Miriam only inhaled.

"Emma—"

"My *girlfriend*," she said. "We've been together a year. She's been there for me."

Yuri raised his hands. "I didn't say anything." He gave her good shoulder a comforting pat, then knocked delicately on the glass.

Emma looked up, and Sam turned. The weight of both gazes

found Miriam, and her chest contracted. When Emma moved for the door, Sam looked away.

Outside, Emma greeted her with a kiss on the cheek. "How'd it go?"

Miriam shrugged. "Hino says hi. Scolded me for going in."

"Well, good. You're on admin leave. We can thank Krill and her advocating for that later. But only if you actually use it."

"No, I am."

She *was* grateful for the break. It was a relief to be away, despite the actual reason. They were all worried for her, concerned about what near-execution by Heretics did to a person, but the old routine of nightmares hadn't returned. Not yet.

Plus, she'd only gone back on base because she wanted to see what Krill had dug up on the mission and Vertex—why Sam had been held there. To her frustration, the little information he had garnered from file searches, soft inquiries around the compound, and whatever Nas had sent on wasn't much.

"So how's Valk doing?" Yuri asked.

Emma sighed. "Surprisingly well, all things considered. She wants to lower the dosage faster than anyone would normally recommend. Hell, I bet she'd have gone cold turkey and just risked it. I'm no expert on this, but I talked her out of it, I think."

Miriam scoffed while Yuri chuckled. That stubbornness hadn't changed.

Emma's face lilted. "Oh. Not surprised? That's good. At least we know it hasn't significantly changed her then."

"Actually, speaking of that, I wanted your opinion," Yuri said.

"Hm, that's dangerous. Shoot."

"The hospital ran Valk's blood work, but there's something inconclusive."

Miriam's eyes flitted to him.

"Nothing dangerous. Or unhealthy," he continued, "but the

lab guys figured it's tied to the stim use, or maybe the tech she's got in her body, I don't know. It's not really our wheelhouse, and, well, I pinged Nas about it, too. Haven't heard back from him—busy, I guess. I hate to bug you, but seeing that you're in the field and know..."

"I'm in between jobs right now, Yuri. I'm happy to help, but..." Emma quirked her mouth. "I don't have the resources anymore."

"My home is yours. Of course, if you have the bandwidth and time."

She checked her handheld. "It's actually good timing. I can head over now, if they're ready. Have them send me the initial panels."

"Yeah?" Yuri nodded toward the door. "Let me check in with Valk, and I'll go with you." He patted Miriam's shoulder and she winced, not from real pain but from the idea of it. "Some of us have responsibilities." He slipped inside.

Now with just the two of them outside, Miriam fell into step beside Emma as they walked toward the gate. "I thought we were getting dinner?"

Emma gave a sideways glance. "You're supposed to be resting. I didn't think you were serious. I figured you were going stir-crazy, that the compound was close enough to the apartment, but I didn't know you were going to come here as well."

"Oh." Miriam bit the inside of her lip. "I'll go with you to General. Keep you company?"

Emma stopped just outside the fence. "No. You're supposed to be resting. At home." She sighed. "But you're here now. You might as well stay."

"I'm really okay. If you want, I can walk you—"

"No. Stay. Plus, she could use more familiar faces, really all the support she can get. This is a crucial stage of *her* recovery right now. She's holding herself together, but I can tell she's hurting."

Miriam didn't say anything. They were talking about Sam's withdrawals, she was pretty sure.

Emma stepped in close and wrapped her arms around Miriam, who folded into the embrace. Miriam's hands rested flat against her girlfriend's back, fingers twitching once. When they parted, Emma tucked a loose strand of hair behind Miriam's ear.

"What's going on in that head of yours?" she whispered.

Miriam didn't know how to answer that simple yet complicated question.

"I love you," Emma said after a moment.

Miriam's focus slid to the small guesthouse, where Yuri stood in the doorway, a parting farewell behind him. "I love you, too," she replied. She tried not to react to Emma's study of her as Yuri rejoined them.

"I forgot to mention," he said. "I asked Kai to look into things as well, but she's been buried in 'oversight review.' If City Center's is anything like our audit and inspections at General...woof." He squeezed Miriam's shoulder and headed through the gate.

Miriam said nothing to that. Oversight, audits, it was all Kai's world of politics. She wondered who it really served. She tried not to scowl and leaned in to kiss Emma. "I'll see you at home?"

"Yeah." Emma paused, took one last look, and then rounded the corner with Yuri.

Miriam stayed a moment longer, the warm air brushing the places Emma had touched. She watched the empty street, listening to the fading footsteps down the sidewalk.

Her fingers rose to her lips, but the warmth didn't hold. She meant the words—*I love you, too*—yet they felt oddly distant, like a line from a part she no longer played. It wasn't that she didn't love Emma—she did—it was just that something inside her hadn't caught up. Or maybe it had—and that was the problem.

She laced her hands together and turned back, ambling outside the small house's door, dissecting the previous conversation, and the conflicting feelings afterward. Maybe Yuri had engineered the errand, fabricated an excuse to leave her and Sam alone. She wasn't sure if she wanted to be alone with Sam. Not yet.

Miriam smoothed her fingers along the frame, and went inside. Sam sat on the coffee table, hunched forward, her fingers twisting while one leg bounced against the floor in a nervous stutter. She didn't look up.

"How're you feeling?" Miriam asked.

Sam gave a quiet harrumph, neither welcome nor dismissal.

Miriam moved farther in and rested a hand on the nearest armchair, her fingertips splaying against the worn fabric. The silence stretched. After she broke down in Sam's arms less than a week before, they hadn't really spoken. Not alone. Not like this.

"She's great, you know."

Miriam looked up, surprised.

"Emma," Sam clarified.

"Oh. Yeah. Emma's amazing."

"I like her."

"Yeah." Miriam offered a weak smirk. "I like her, too."

Another silence bloomed between them, heavier this time.

"You—"

"I—"

They spoke at once, overlapping, then stopped. Sam pressed her lips together, gesturing for Miriam to go on.

"You look better."

Sam gave a humorless chuff. "I look like shit. I *feel* like shit." She rubbed at her neck once, caught herself, and stilled.

"It'll get better," Miriam said, unsure if she believed it and wanting to anyway.

"Yeah."

"Trust me."

She wished she believed that, too.

"Yeah," Sam repeated, then added, quieter, "I know—I know it's the right thing."

Miriam gave a slow nod.

"Are you… How's it healing?" Sam motioned toward Miriam's arm, her eyes dipping toward her neck before snapping away like she'd touched something hot. She wouldn't meet her eyes.

"It'll get there," Miriam replied, touching the bandage at her throat. "I'm in no rush to get back to work."

"Is MED…" Sam didn't finish. Her eyes fixed on the far wall.

"UMF's short on medics," Miriam said. "MED would clear me now if they could, but Krill and Hino—Echo's second— they've been blocking for me."

"Who's covering in the meantime?"

Miriam shrugged. Sam hadn't asked it seriously, and the truth was, Miriam didn't care. Sam picked at a stitch on her pants, fingers restless. Miriam's hand traced the chair's curve.

"Kuan-Lin reached out," Sam said, eyes still elsewhere.

"Oh?"

"Guess she cares a little." The laugh came dry.

"She cares a lot," Miriam corrected. "What did she say?"

Sam shook her head. "I didn't—" Her mouth snapped shut.

Miriam waited.

"I didn't respond." Softer now. "I'm—I want to leave, but I can't."

She was all over the place. But she was talking.

"You're not trapped here," Miriam said.

"No, I know. It's not—I don't mean it like that."

Quiet again.

"Sam. You can talk to me," Miriam said, fingers skimming the chair's worn fabric again, this time with more purpose, like outlining a shape she couldn't quite name.

Sam looked up. At last her eyes met Miriam's, piercing but

uncertain. Her mouth opened, but whatever words had been there dissolved before they could surface. She tried again. "I'm not good with words." Her hand climbed halfway to her neck and stopped, curling back to her lap.

Miriam huffed. "Neither am I." Her mouth tilted at its corner. "If we were, maybe we wouldn't have ended up here. Maybe we could've avoided all of this."

Sam folded her arms, but to Miriam's surprise, a hint of a smile curved her lips. "Yeah, I guess." Her alloy fingers dug into her bicep.

Miriam's new handheld buzzed in her pocket. She ignored it.

Sam rubbed the back of her neck, fingers slipping into her hair. Her leg bounced again. "All I can think about... I—" Her hands balled in her lap. "You don't want to hear this."

"I do." Miriam leaned forward. "I really do. But if you don't want to tell me, it's okay. I'm sorry, I'm—I'm not trying to force you to talk. Shit."

"No. It's—I don't. I'm—" Sam faltered. "Fuck." She held out her trembling left hand. "I did this to myself." Her voice frayed. "I'm weak."

"Sam."

"And I'm scared. I'm scared I won't stop. That I can't. That I've already—" She swallowed. "I know Scott would hate me. Our father—I'm just like him." The words tumbled out. "Fuck, and he had a kid, and I—" Her shoulders lifted and fell. "I don't want to ruin this. And I don't know. I'm scared I'll disappoint; I'll hurt him. I'm not good. I messed things up, and I hate that all I'm thinking about is when and how to get my next hit, and I hate that, I hate that I'm weak, I hate—"

Miriam stepped around the chair and reached out, her hand on top of Sam's, flesh and alloy meeting in a shared tremor.

"I hate what I've become," Sam whispered. "I hate that you're afraid of me. I hate that I've lost—" Her voice cracked. "I hate that I've lost you."

Miriam wrapped one arm around Sam's shoulders, and Sam's breath stuttered into her neck as she turned into the hold.

"I'm so sorry," Sam said, muffled.

Miriam didn't answer, only held on. Her handheld buzzed again, but she paid it no mind.

"I'm sorry," Sam repeated.

Miriam eased back enough to see her face. "*I'm* sorry."

The woman shook her head, face lowered. "Back there... Before..."

"We don't have to talk about it now. It's okay."

"You said you love—*loved* me."

Miriam went still. Past tense. Not present.

It had been in the moment. A confession under fire, when everything was falling apart. And yet—it had been true then, and it was still true now. But they were no longer at death's door. It wasn't just *them* anymore. They were back in a different reality, *actual* reality.

She had thought they were going to die.

Sam pulled back, attention diverting. "It was..."

A successful failure, Miriam thought, but she didn't say it.

"It's not fair to her."

"Emma," Miriam said. "No, it isn't."

Sam's jaw feathered, but she only nodded. After a moment, she shifted away, and Miriam's arm fell back to her side.

"Thank you," Sam said. "For staying."

Miriam bit the inside of her lip. Sam had dragged her back into the airship when they were crashing. She'd fought the Heretic when Miriam had been caught off guard. She'd crushed —killed him. "You would've done the same."

Sam grimaced. "I don't know. Before..."

Miriam waited, giving her space.

"I thought—I thought I lost you," Sam said at last, ragged. "And I couldn't do anything. The drugs—they felt so good and I wanted it—I hate that I wanted it." She dragged her hands over her face, fingers pressing hard into her skin. Blond strands jutted between them. "I couldn't do anything but watch. I just watched."

Miriam didn't speak, but she remembered the cold edge of the blade at her throat, the pressure, and the way she'd lost her breath. She swallowed and only then noticed she was gripping her own wrist, crescents where her nails had bit in.

Silence settled, neither heavy nor gentle.

"I want to see Scott's son," Sam said. She lifted her head, eyes distant. "My nephew. I want to be someone who can…be there and do something." Her voice held steadier than days ago, though her hand still shook. "I know I need help."

Miriam kept her expression even, afraid anything she'd say might matter too little or too much. And for a moment, neither moved. So much had come out. It'd been as if some knot had been untangled, and with it, a sincere rambling of words, thoughts, and truths had come out. It was another scar, but rehealing as it opened. A paradox.

They both flinched as a soft chime broke the stillness, like a warning bell. A mechanical click followed, and Yuri's voice filtered in through a speaker nearby.

"Valk?"

Sam cleared her throat. "Yeah."

"You know an angry short guy?"

She sniffed. "Scar?"

"Multiple, yeah."

Sam's mouth clamped then reopened. "Why?"

"I'm heading back. I don't know how, but I think he's on his way over there."

Miriam turned to the window, her heart rate already climbing. Outside, a figure had emerged at the fence, followed by someone much taller. An Altered. For a second, Miriam's fists clenched instinctually. But it wasn't who she thought. Not the orange eyes. Not him.

Instead, it was a man with a compact frame, storming gait,

and a scar splitting the bridge of his nose. The same one she'd seen before with Willem. Behind him, a former legionnaire with leaner features.

The ache in Miriam's neck flared as she straightened. She glanced at Sam, who watched her teammates approach. Whatever quiet they'd tried to build was already starting to crack.

Miriam exhaled raggedly. "They're already here."

37

LAPSE

"YOU WERE AT THE SITE." Recognition sparked across the man's face, warping it into something between accusation and disbelief.

Miriam didn't flinch. She filled the threshold and held it, spine locked. His pupils were wrong. Too wide. Stims. She caught her lip before it curled.

His finger jabbed the air. "You're the bitch who fucked up our exit. Where's the other bitch boy?"

"Alph," Sam warned.

"Y'know, I shoulda known when I saw you. Boy Scout shoulda let me shoot ya—"

"Alphabet." Sam's voice sharpened. "Stop."

He ignored her, still staring down Miriam. "Ya really gonna try to keep us from our teammate?" He spat to the side, a sour mark on the stone ground.

Behind her, Sam moved in, hand hovering above Miriam's shoulder. But Miriam didn't budge.

Sam said her name, quietly. The potency of it did what the untouching hand didn't. It stung, a stab of betrayal, but Miriam reminded herself that she wasn't Sam's teammate. Not anymore. It was another reminder they had lived very different lives in the past three and a half years.

She hesitated, then eased back to let Sam pass. The moment the air broke between them, Alphabet's hostility deflated. He thrust out his forearm, and Sam didn't hesitate, clasping it.

Varya—or Vengeance, as the others called her—followed with a nod and a low murmur Miriam couldn't catch. Sam stepped toward the former legionnaire, and for an instant Miriam's breath snagged. Varya was Altered, the first Altered Sam had touched since the UMF annex. Miriam knew there hadn't been any impact with the Heretics—or at least from the time they'd had before they'd been rescued. But what if whatever they'd been exposed to hadn't completely cleared? She was still trying to figure out why they'd held Sam in a separate facility. Sam's hand settled on Varya's arm, skin to skin, without a flinch.

They were fine, Miriam reminded herself. There was nothing to indicate otherwise—other than everything else, of course. She stayed to the side and watched, the reunion softer and more intimate than she'd expected for a bunch of SRAF operators.

"Didn't think I'd see you again, you fuck," Alphabet said, studying Sam. "You look like I shat you out." He cut Miriam a glare. "You're not gonna invite us in?" The words were coated in mockery. His eyes swept the little structure, then the main house. "This is some bougie setup. Got friends in high places, Fury. You holdin' out?"

Sam met Miriam's eye, then tipped her head toward the path where Yuri approached. His pace smoothed into something casual, like the moment hadn't needed defusing. His posture settled into a calm that Miriam didn't share. He gave her a small nod, and she stepped aside without a word. Soon after, Varya ducked through the door. Alphabet followed but lagged just long enough to pour another look on Miriam, thick with disdain.

"Don't make a mess," Sam called after him.

"Why d'ya constantly think I'm the messy one?" he grumbled.

Sam glanced once at Miriam and Yuri, gratitude flickering, then disappeared inside.

Miriam made to follow, but Yuri eased the door shut, his hand light but decisive.

"Give her a minute," he said, already moving for the patio. He took a stool at the outdoor counter.

After a long hesitation, Miriam trailed him. Through the window, Varya sat oddly stiff on Yuri's couch, legs braced as if unsure of how to inhabit the space. On the other hand, Alphabet had already sprawled across the cushions, his feet tossed up like a claim to territory. Varya nudged them off with a boot of her own.

"That was particularly frosty," Yuri murmured, elbows on varnished wood. "What did I miss?"

Miriam didn't answer at once, her observation clinging to the small house. "Where were they when we needed them?" The words slipped out, pitched at the glass rather than Yuri.

It wasn't entirely fair, though. Echo had left her and Talwar, too. It hadn't been personal. The environment had been wrong, and the risk was bigger than any one life, but distance salted the wound. Part of her wanted to ask why Sam's team hadn't tried to find her sooner. Although that, too, would have been rhetorical. Maybe she was more irritated that they *were* there now.

Yuri let it pass.

"This was why you were called away?" she asked instead.

He tapped his finger against the bar. "More of a coincidence. I wanted to give you two space. You both needed to talk."

Her thumb found the lip of a coaster and traced the groove, round and round.

"So...did you? Talk?"

A shallow nod. Miriam kept her eyes down. If she looked

up, her body might betray her. "Is it smart letting them near her right now?"

"I think they've been looking for her, Tan." Yuri paused, his tone evening out. If he noticed she had fled one subject for another, he didn't show it. "They're her team."

Silence tilted.

He rolled a wrist, a shrug of bone. "Am I thrilled I've got two—well, three—Seraphs under my roof? Not particularly. But who knows, it might help me. Ever since General floated the new collaboration with the Royals, the neighbors are sniffing for gossip. Hell, perhaps the Sandinos will stop calling me the block's bachelor failure."

Miriam didn't bite. Through the glass, Alphabet had moved to Yuri's vanity table and started rummaging as if drawers were communal.

Yuri sighed. "Krill confirmed she didn't renew with UMF. Valk wasn't even in the system when those marines held her."

Miriam's throat squeezed. "They scrubbed her?"

"Archived or redacted, possibly. But that's the quickest dismissal I've heard of. Perhaps something to do with SRAF. There isn't much insight on that relationship."

Distancing? Or something else?

"So she's staying with SRAF?"

He lifted a shoulder.

"She can't. She'll relapse. She—"

"She might," he said gently. "But it's her choice, Tan. Those people in there? They're her teammates, her family. You understand that better than most. Look at how we were. Echo."

Miriam winced.

"We went our separate ways, but we're still us. That won't shake off. We're all kinds of messed up, but our ties? Those hold. That won't change." He gave her a brief and tired half smile. "They probably think the same of you the way you're thinking of them. That woman is loved, even if they've got a weird way of showing it."

Her jaw set.

Yuri let the quiet stand, then edged a different question. "Are you and Em—"

"Did she say something?"

"No?"

Miriam braced her forearms on the counter, the cast sliding before she caught it.

He waited.

"After everything… I'm not—I can't do that to her."

His attention prickled, and she fidgeted under it.

"I won't hurt her. I just need to make sure Sam's going to be okay, and then, well, Emma—"

"She loves you."

The line landed low, and guilt bloomed under her ribs. Emma did love her, and Emma was good, reliable, and true. Sam's return didn't change or erase that. Miriam wasn't going to hurt Emma the way she had hurt Sam before. She blinked against the sting behind her eyes.

In the window, Sam's shoulders lifted and locked. Blue eyes found her through glass, and two more intense stares followed.

"What now?" Miriam muttered.

Sam came out fast, stride unyielding, Alphabet and Varya in her wake. She stopped in front of Miriam and Yuri.

"Boy Scout."

The name punched the air from Miriam's chest.

"What happened to Boy Scout?" Sam asked.

Heat surged. The memory of blood slick and hot between her fingers. "He's gone. I tried, it was too fast—"

"No." Sam's voice dropped, hoarse. "His body."

Miriam blinked. "What?"

"When they came for us. In the transport, there were two bags, two bodies next to me. One of them—was it him?"

Miriam combed through the jumble in her mind, fingers trembling where she'd dug them into her arm and cast. "I think so. There were two…" The words stalled. She hadn't thought about Willem for days. Guilt daggered in. She had been more concerned about Sam, about herself. "I don't know. I didn't see anything at the facility either—there were a lot of rooms, but I don't remember. I didn't check."

She had stopped when she'd found Sam at the halfway point in the hall. Would she have found more—something else—if she hadn't? UMF should have returned Willem to SRAF or Legion. Someone on the Altered side, someone who knew what rites to send him to rest and where he belonged. But now that assumption was broken. She had no confirmation, no chain of custody. Had it been her responsibility, and she'd dropped that as well?

Beside her, Yuri's mouth compressed. "We never received any of you. Station General's apparently been blacklisted."

Miriam frowned, eyes narrowing.

"We can check with Krill, with the others, if there was someone else," Yuri said. "I'll reach out. There's got to be a trail."

Varya's shadow lengthened as she stepped closer. "We can elevate this to Sky-Eye."

Alphabet's response came hot, a crack of teeth behind it. "If they forgot 'im, I'll find 'em. Tear their spines out."

Miriam looked hard at him. It wasn't a threat, but a promise. SRAF kept violence just under the skin. This was exactly the crowd Sam didn't need.

"He deserved better," Miriam said, more to herself than the ground between them.

"We'll help," Yuri added.

Sam still hadn't spoken, hadn't moved.

Alphabet tipped forward, voice gone iron. "Fine. When you're good to go, Fury, we go back out. Keep the count running."

Miriam's nails bit her palms.

"They're still out there. We'll make them pay." He spat the next words like gristle. "I'll eat their fucking hearts."

A list of targets that never ended.

Pain flared along Miriam's neck as she clenched and breathed through it. Sam hadn't told her teammates. She hadn't mentioned it was exposure in a human facility that killed Boy Scout—Willem—not the Heretics' blades. Miriam searched her face for any flicker, but the woman didn't meet her eyes. Maybe she didn't remember, or maybe the stims and blood loss had chewed that part to mush.

Alphabet's fury rolled off him in waves, and it chilled Miriam more than the words themselves. She remembered the Royal's words from what felt like ages before. SRAF had little to no leash, no oversight. SRAF's power wasn't in contracts, but in creed. If they were convinced the Heretics, the Apostates, were behind all of this, they'd keep hunting.

But what would happen when they discovered it hadn't been the Heretics? What would they do when they learned it'd come from a human lab?

"You got a shitter?"

"Fucking hell," Sam muttered.

Yuri pushed up with a weary breath. "I'll show you—"

"And a drink of somethin'?"

"Alphabet," Sam said with force. She caught his arm and steered him back toward the small house. Yuri excused himself, muttering about drinks for everyone, and slipped toward the main building, leaving Varya and Miriam alone on the patio.

"I apologize for my colleague," Varya said once the others were gone. "He lacks refinement."

Miriam let out air between her teeth, too pointed to be amusement.

"But he is loyal."

The note underneath carried emphasis and a trace of judgment. Miriam held still. She didn't know how much the woman or Sam's team knew about her, their history, or if Sam had kept it to herself. Years had passed, but the scar hadn't faded. Especially not for Miriam.

She turned her hands, fingers brushing the opposite forearm in a small, fixed pattern.

"Chapel," Miriam said, pulling on a different thread. "Did he…"

Varya nodded. "He was delayed, but he escaped. Found us."

So that was why they stood there now. The others must have regrouped once they had their teammate back.

"I'm sorry about Hadeon," Miriam said. And Perun. And Willem.

"She did not deserve that death."

"No." The word snagged in Miriam's throat. She had tried to cloud her memory of the last seconds of Hadeon's life, the scream too vivid, but it surfaced now, unbidden.

"You were there."

Neither question nor statement.

Had she been so obvious? Miriam nodded. "She was a teammate. A friend," she corrected.

"A good leader."

Miriam held still. "Path to glory."

It was a whisper. It wasn't for her to say, yet it rose anyway. But Varya only inclined her head. The words suspended between them, dust that wouldn't lie down. A ritual echo, a small monument of breath.

Miriam looked back through the window. The room was empty. Sam and Alphabet had moved deeper, toward the one bedroom. Out of sight. Out of reach. What if Alphabet was offering her stims? Calmers? Her stomach knotted.

"You're worried," Varya said. "For her."

Miriam pulled her focus back to the former legionnaire. "I'm worried…" She lifted her chin. "I'm worried what SRAF will do to her, what it'll pull her back into."

She braced, expecting a retort or an angry expression, but none came.

"She didn't renew with UMF," Miriam added, lower.

"SRAF has no contract," Varya said, gazing down at her. "But we are bonded otherwise."

Miriam flexed her fingers into her skin. "How long will you be here for?" She was waiting for the answer she didn't want to hear.

"The others are resupplying. Our squad is down, but we can manage this next mission. Once we receive a replacement..." Varya trailed off with an assessing glance. Had the woman heard her and Yuri through the closed door? With Altered, especially legionnaire designs, she was never sure.

"She's safe here," Miriam said, quieter than she meant to.

It was verging on a plea.

"With Kartik and Beric gone, new lieutenants rise," Varya said. "We are glad to chase them, but the tide is changing. Our people tire of these Apostates. It is an embarrassment it has taken this long."

"And Butcher?"

"Quiet, for now, but we will find him all the same."

"He had a former legionnaire with him."

"We will find them all."

Miriam nodded and let the quiet settle. Varya seemed comfortable in it.

"This is a fuckin' palace!" Alphabet's voice cracked across the yard, loud and graceless.

As they came back, he thumped Sam's back hard, and she took it without swaying. Miriam scanned Sam's face, her body, the tension at the corner of her mouth, trying to read what she didn't want to see, but there was no dilation. The tremor was still there, slight. Miriam's jaw loosened, and a tiny exhale leaked out.

"Fuck, you've gone soft, Fury. A bed? An actual bathroom? I hardly recognize ya."

Varya tipped her head, a silent warning.

Alphabet grunted. "What?"

"We should return to the airfield. X-Ray and Chapel are waiting."

"And miss all this luxury?" He spread his arms as if surveying a kingdom as Yuri returned, drinks and a bowl of colorful fruit in hand.

His brow crept upward, and his eyes swung toward Miriam nervously.

"Well, what about Fury?" Alphabet asked, already lifting a bottle from Yuri's tray.

Varya gave Sam a long look. "She will be here when we're finished." She set a small rectangular switch into Sam's palm. A new embed. "Here. Let us know." Then the woman turned for the gate, casting one last glance at Miriam and Yuri.

"Wait—seriously?"

But the woman was already around the corner.

Miriam was taken aback as well. She hadn't expected that, hadn't known what to expect.

"Well, fuck." Alphabet pocketed a handful of fruit, snagged another bottle, shoved it into his armpit, then started after the Altered woman. As he passed Sam, he flicked his fingers in a lazy farewell. "*You're* getting a long-ass holiday, aren't you?"

"Alphabet," Sam said curtly.

He left.

Sam's fingers folded around the embed, but she didn't attach it to the groove behind her ear. Instead, she sat on a patio chair behind Yuri, then tucked in her hands, face scrunched like she was holding a thought in place.

Miriam glanced at her and chased a memory. She had seen the black bag. The Charonites had carried Willem's body. And she was quite sure it had been transferred to the aircraft, but she had been delirious at the time, in and out. Had the exchange at Ursus happened? She couldn't pin it. The harder she tried, the murkier it got.

"UMF took custody. I—" She looked up at Yuri. "Krill can figure this out, right?" She reached for her device.

Yuri lifted a palm. "Are we sure it's not a clerical error? SRAF procedures aren't exactly UMF procedures. Could the body still be in Ursus? He's neither UMF nor Legion."

"After what happened to us?" Miriam asked. After her in Meridian and Sam in the annex facility?

"I'm just making sure we're asking all the right questions, including the stupid ones. You found her on base, right?" Yuri's eyes darted to her. "Do you trust Krill?"

"I trust him," Miriam reassured. She wasn't proud of her doubt and insecurity back when they'd returned to Station City. "I trust you and Echo, *our* Echo."

She studied Yuri and his tightened expression. *He* wasn't sure about UMF. Neither was she, but it weighed heavier to see her friends and former teammates also casting their doubts.

"I already asked my team to pull numbers," Yuri said. "After you, it was bothering me. I won't be able to confirm until I see the data, but we've seen fewer UMF patients. I chalked it up to less engagement up north, but recently…now I'm not sure."

"What do you mean?"

"I thought it was because of the new partnerships and agreements with the Royals, but we haven't announced it officially yet. Of course nothing stays under wraps in this city… but this goes further back. I don't know."

"Yuri."

"Let me confirm it first. I'll check with Kai, too. It's nothing you have to worry about now. Try Krill, but perhaps not on UMF comms."

Miriam lifted her handheld out of her pocket, and its display engaged. She stared down at the UMF-issued device. "I guess it's still work hours. I can find him on base." She sighed; she'd just come from there.

"I'll go with you," Sam said, standing.

"No." Bitterness rose in Miriam's throat, but not at Sam. It was the thought of returning to a compound that had tossed one of its own aside so fast. "You should rest."

Sam frowned. "I'm not sitting on the sidelines." She straightened as if to make a point. "He was my teammate."

Miriam and Yuri traded a look. Stubborn. If Miriam knew anything about this woman, the decision was already made.

"Fine," she conceded.

Blue eyes met hers, then dipped down to the bandage on her neck. Sam turned for the small house. "I'll change," she said. As she moved back, her left arm shook. Tremors. They'd started again, but Sam hid it by angling away.

When the door closed, Yuri faced Miriam. "*You* should rest. Admin leave is rare for UMF. Whatever Krill and Hino pulled, SOG doesn't just hand that out."

She waved him off. The guilt of forgetting about Willem chewed at her again.

"Tan, are you okay? No, don't answer that. I *know* you're not okay."

Did it matter? Would the world stop until she somehow felt a semblance of control or normalcy?

"I need to do this," she said.

There were so many questions left unanswered.

"Be safe," Yuri whispered.

Miriam scoffed. After everything she'd weathered? She was absolutely sure nothing could surpass that hell.

38

———

ONSLAUGHT

"WE CAN TAKE A PEOPLE-MOVER BACK. I'm sure Yuri would be fine with us taking one of the cars, but I'd rather stay on his mother's good side."

Especially now, with a recovering addict and SRAF operator living on the property. Miriam might have offered her own parents' place once, but that would've required favor she no longer held.

Sam kept pace until the narrow streets gave way to the broad sweep of the main boulevard, vertical space returning to walls of climbing concrete and steel. She slowed at the corner and stopped short at the crosswalk. The shuttle blinked across the way, yet she didn't step off the curb.

"Sam?"

Sam turned but stayed rooted. Her chin tipped toward the Altered Sector. "Would Kuan—would the Royals know? Boy Scout was one of them, one of theirs."

Miriam's brows knit. "Kuan-Lin isn't involved." At least she didn't think so. There was a tenuous tie to SRAF, but nothing more.

Sam's jaw locked, the muscle trembling once. Miriam knew

that look. The way her shoulders held, the way her eyes slid away. Sam wanted something else.

Miriam exhaled. "Yeah, okay," she conceded. "It's on the way."

It wasn't. She knew it wasn't. And part of her warned this was a mistake. The last time Sam had set foot in the Altered Sector, things had spiraled. But another part of her wanted to believe this pause, this flimsy excuse of a detour, meant Sam was aiming for reparations, that she wanted to do better. That maybe this was her clumsy way of making amends. And the selfish part of Miriam wanted that for herself as well.

"Thank you," Sam whispered.

Miriam only nodded.

They'd made it a few blocks, their steps monotonous, slowed by Sam's dragging rhythm. Miriam let the silence sit between them, but she tracked every small shift: the clipped way Sam pulled air through her nose and the tightening of her shoulders as if bracing against more than just withdrawal. Miriam adjusted her pace without saying anything, falling into step beside her. It was instinct—habit—and Sam let it happen without acknowledgment.

The city shifted as they went. The wide streets fell away into thinner lanes, the hush of shuttered stoops giving way to the restless grumble of stores and vendors. Pedestrians shouted over the hiss of street kiosks, and vehicles whined around them. And then it all quieted again as they neared the Altered Sector.

Sam's gait changed first. Her spine stiffened. Miriam sensed the crackle in the air before she spotted it.

Half a block ahead, the praetorian stood, tall and unmissable. His mirrored shades caught the sunlight but didn't hide the glint of alert and unnatural-colored eyes. He wasn't alone. An older woman in pristine clothes—a Royal, no doubt —fussed beside him. She batted at his arm with indignation, refusing to be steered. It wasn't Kuan-Lin, just another member of the old governing family the bodyguard was in charge of. Another relic of blood and privilege, too softened by entitlement to recognize danger when it crept close.

And danger had already crept close.

"Wait," Sam whispered. Her hand brushed out, then fell, as Miriam slowed into it.

The street was too quiet. Too vacant of normalcy. Then, shadows thickened in side alleys and doorways until figures bled into view. Black caps. All twitching. All watching.

Charonites. Not the same ones from the North, for whom Miriam had somehow found a splinter of sympathy. These were Station City Charonites who seemed to have no strong reason for their violence and hatred.

Dmitri had perceived the threat, too. Likely long before Sam and Miriam did. She recognized the subtle tilt of his head, a pivot of his stance as he placed himself between the oblivious Royal and the street.

He'd tried to maneuver her away without spooking her, but now she'd begun to sense it. Too late. Her own resistance, her own failing. The Royal's golden eyes and poise unspooled with every backward glance. Panic hardened her stride but still she didn't run, instead hastening off at a graceful pace.

Dmitri stopped, blocking off the group from his principal's exit. The black caps halted, holding just out of reach. It was a standoff. But they weren't focused on the woman as she disappeared around the corner. They were watching Dmitri. He knew it. And they knew he knew it. Whoever their target was, he was the threat that had to fall first.

Miriam worked her fingers into her pocket, her handheld, sending a silent call to SecTeam, but she already knew how this would go. The praetorian was buying time, buying space, buying the Royal's escape. And no matter how many Charonites there were, the ensuing fight would end long before backup arrived. If it ever did.

As she expected, weapons emerged, steel, blunt, jagged,

glittering in the sun. The front wave split. A few held back, uncertain, eyes fixed on Miriam and Sam, who hadn't moved from their own position.

Anyone with sense would've bolted from this situation, bailed by now. But no one did.

Miriam's heart hammered. "They're stimmed." She murmured the obvious. Her body wasn't ready for this. Neither was Sam's.

Shit magnet.

Then the Charonites lunged. Three rushed the praetorian, one with a cylinder in hand. Familiar, but Miriam couldn't place why.

Dmitri didn't move. Not at first. Then he did. He snapped into motion like a whip uncoiled. One Charonite swung high, the other jabbed the canister forward, but Dmitri slipped between them, faster than thought. The third stabbed low. Dmitri turned with the blow, let it pass, then caught the wrist and twisted in the same motion. Fluid. Inevitable.

Miriam had witnessed Sam square off with him once. Fighting Dmitri was like fighting a current. His opponents could swim, could push, but they'd drown.

Sam stepped forward, then staggered. Her hand shook. Miriam darted to her side. Sam's pupils were blown wide, but not from stims. Withdrawal. Her body curled inward, knees starting to give. The prosthetic braced, slamming then digging into the ground.

Poor timing.

Miriam gripped the woman's elbow, attention split. "Sam—"

"I've got it," she hissed. A lie. Sam's muscles spasmed, then slackened under Miriam's hold. Her body shuddered as if tearing itself apart from the inside.

Miriam shifted forward, shielding her, though most Charonite eyes stayed locked on the praetorian.

The rest of the black caps surged, and Dmitri met them

alone. He didn't block, didn't counter. He redirected. Each movement was a precise dance, a violent calculus. One man collided with another. A knee shattered a collarbone. An elbow caught a temple. Steel and metal missed him again and again, hitting pavement, wall, each other. More than one cylinder thrust forward, more coordinated this time.

Then came the cracks. Bone. Teeth. Screams.

Not Dmitri's. He was nearly untouchable.

A pipe swung at his head. He stepped into it, wrenched it back, broke a rib, drove the snapped end into a kneecap. Blood sprayed. Someone howled. His strikes could've been killing blows, but they weren't. A restraint Miriam suspected wasn't his, but rather a Royal's order, leashed him.

He moved like instinct clad in genetically engineered flesh. And still they came. He smashed a man's skull into the concrete, leaving a smear of blood and hair. Another leaped, wild and desperate. Dmitri caught him midair and hurled him into a second. Both dropped like sacks of meat.

One tried to grapple him. It didn't last.

It was a ballet of agony. Transfixed, Miriam couldn't look away, move, even if she wanted to. The black caps on the flank also froze, spellbound, torn between awe and terror.

Yet the attackers drove on, stimmed and relentless. Whether by orders, zealotry, addiction, it didn't matter. They continued. It was pure idiocy, but idiocy en masse finally broke ground.

A machete sliced low.

"No—" Miriam uttered, too late.

Dmitri pivoted, but not fast enough. The blade kissed his ribs, and it cut, red arcing out. It wasn't much, but it was a crack in the dam. He staggered.

The praetorian was genetically engineered, designed to be a lethal weapon. Except this weapon was bound by a Royal's order. And he was still a man. He still bled.

For the first time, his expression transformed into a sneer. It was as if someone had placed a hot poker on both him and the animals around him. He tore the machete free from the attacker's hands and slammed its blunt end into a face. Cartilage and blood burst, and the man screamed. But the others advanced, encouraged.

A palm strike folded another in half. But Dmitri's respirations had changed. Deeper. Strained. His motions faltered as if his limbs had become leaden.

He slipped. Blood underfoot. Not his, but it was just enough. A blade carved into his thigh. The praetorian snarled, more beast than man. He spun, demolished tissue and bone, but the wound had rooted him. Slowed him.

The Charonites felt it, and they surged. One jumped onto his back while another dove for his legs. A third went low, blade-first, punching into his side. Dmitri dropped to a knee.

Miriam gasped, her neck knotting, ignoring the pain that came with it. Sam surged up just as Miriam lunged forward, skirting past the nearest black cap.

He reached for her. Too slow.

Miriam collided with a different one, driving him down. Her cast struck his ribs on impact, and the bruising throb of pain shot through her body. Another swung his club wide, but she ducked. The air split past her cheek.

In her periphery, Dmitri rose. He seized an attacker by the throat and lifted him. Before the body went slack, he hurled it into another. Both crumpled.

Miriam stomped the one beneath her, hard in the groin. The crunch jolted up her leg. She had meant it and more.

Dmitri turned, shoulders heaving. Though he wore all black, the blood showed in dark wet streaks soaking his side. But he was standing. Somehow, he still stood.

The last Charonites faltered, fear and a gram of intelligence catching up. Their eyes darted between Dmitri, Miriam, and Sam.

Then they broke. Some scrambled to drag their fallen with

them, but most scattered. The street was strewn with unconscious and squirming bodies, blood, and the wreckage of a fight that should've been theirs.

When they had mostly cleared out, Miriam inched closer to Dmitri, careful not to startle him. His shoulders had begun to lower, his breath gradually leveling, but when he turned, she glimpsed his parted lips.

He had no tongue. Not that she could see. His mouth closed again, as if she had seen something she'd had no permission to. He drew long inhales through his nose, red eyes never leaving hers.

She scanned his tall and rangy frame, upright despite wounds that should've leveled him. Her breath caught as she noticed the powder on his clothes. The canisters. Another acid attack? But Dmitri looked unbothered despite his exposed skin already blotching red. The wounds were the greater threat. The toughest legionnaire would've been brought to their knees by now. Stimmed Apostates may have stood their ground, but they'd be dead on their feet. Yet the praetorian endured. Dmitri stood as if he had just taken a marathon at a sprint.

"You need to get this looked at," she said softly, keeping her distance.

He was bleeding. A lot. But Dmitri did nothing. Just watched her, unreadable.

Miriam hesitated, then started moving her fingers. You need to get this fixed. Can you move?

Dammit. He was nonverbal, not deaf.

But he didn't respond in sign either. He stood there, whether by sheer will or some inhuman graft of muscle and instinct, she couldn't say. And then his hand lifted. Slow. Too slow. His motions were inhibited, as if his limbs and body were dragged down.

Miriam turned, trying to gather herself. "Sam, we need to get him to Station General. It's not too far."

There was no response from her either. Sam wasn't where

Miriam had last seen her. Instead, she stood a few paces off, frozen near one of the fallen Charonites—dead or unconscious, Miriam couldn't tell. The woman's nails dragged absently along the side of her neck as if pulled by instinct. Her gaze was locked on the ground.

Miriam followed it. A tin. Open. White pills. A jabber.

Her breath hitched. "Sam," she said, taking a step closer.

The woman didn't move, didn't blink. She scratched harder now, as if she could scrub the want out of her skin. She stared at the objects, transfixed, like they already had their hooks in her.

"Sam," Miriam tried again, quieter this time. She tamped down the fear, the urgency, and forced her voice steady. "I need you."

Blue eyes slid up, full of hunger, guilt, and shame in that brief second, then away.

Miriam extended her hand. "Please. I need you."

A hesitation. A pause.

But Sam reached out and took it.

39

ANOMALY

MIRIAM LINGERED IN THE DOORWAY, shoulders drawn and throat dry. It had been a little more than a week since she and Sam came back, and despite the length of time in MedJets and recovery, her body complained at the sudden demand and abuse.

However, her pain had to be nothing compared to the praetorian's, who was sitting inside the hospital treatment room. He had refused the bed, choosing instead to sit rigidly in the chair beside it, shirt off with his back braced against the rest like someone expecting another attack. It was the first time Miriam had seen him out of his usual black garb, and his frame was just as wiry as she had expected. Under the clinical lights, his skin took on a gray cast, drawn over muscle and bone like silk over steel.

An Altered physician cleaned the wound along his side with brisk, unruffled efficiency. Dmitri hardly blinked, his watch skirting Miriam, fixed on the corridor.

She followed his attention. Medical staff moved through the halls and connecting wings in quick flows, and more than a few eyes cut her way. Maybe they recognized her, or maybe it was the bandage at her neck. Maybe she simply didn't belong there.

If not for her connections, she and Sam wouldn't have clearance or access at all.

She'd spent more time in Station General in the last two months than in the last several years combined. The rhythm of the place was familiar—the constant shuffle of staff, the low murmur of clipped conversations—but it did nothing to settle her. Unease collected like deafening static. What if the Station City Charonites had followed them? What if any of their injured were admitted there? But they'd been there for a while now, and she hadn't seen any of their ink or black caps.

"Tan."

Miriam turned too quickly and grimaced at the pull in her neck. Yuri stood behind her, eyes narrowed with something more than concern. His tone held that cautious tilt he only used when there was more beneath the surface.

"You were right," he said.

She touched the seam of the bandage, muscles sore. "Which part?"

"Both." He angled her toward the nurse's station and pulled up a tablet, diagnostic overlays stacking the display.

"This is his?" she asked, keeping her voice low despite the bustle of the space.

"Yeah. This just came back from our labs. It's that dimethyl sulfoxide agent again. And if I'm right..." His fingers flicked to another file for a side-by-side comparison. "I think I *am* right—it's the same synthetic signature as that stuff you got off the kid Royal."

First, Kuan-Lin's nephew, Longwei, and now her not-guardian praetorian. The Royal threaded them both. But Dmitri hadn't been with Kuan-Lin, nor was he assigned to her anymore. He had been with a different Royal altogether. Was it a coincidence? Or was it just a case of a small Altered population in a concentrated city?

"It's a lot of DMSO," Yuri said.

Miriam looked over the back of her hands and exposed

skin, but there was nothing. She had seen the canisters but hadn't seen how they were applied. She'd seen Dmitri's irritated flesh when they half dragged him to Station General and had been careful not to make direct contact. It just seemed reckless for Charonites to be using something they didn't understand in such close proximity. Was it worth the possible collateral?

"He was still on his feet," Miriam murmured. "Unless they didn't account for his biology." She glanced back. Dmitri hadn't moved.

"You're sure they were Charonites."

She nodded. But certainty didn't bring clarity. The human supremacists' tactics had shifted and evolved. She still didn't understand how their capabilities had advanced, how they'd gotten their hands on this kind of weapon and substance. It was dangerous. A bad precedent.

"And General's intake data?" she asked.

Yuri opened a new window. "Trend confirmed. Our UMF case numbers are down. Not drastically, but it's been consistent. Our contract with the military isn't up for another six months, but this drop predates any renegotiation."

She frowned. "But nothing's changed with UMF."

"Unless there's been some Center policy update. If anything, with the recent push for stim aids in UMF, you'd think we'd be seeing more."

"Talya had said usage is up," Miriam said.

"I can believe it. The cases on the street have been spiking."

"Unless you think regulation's gotten better?"

Yuri raised an eyebrow. Neither thought that.

"This doesn't prove UMF's diverting medical care, though," Miriam said. "Management could argue they're diversifying, sending cases to other clinics and centers."

Yuri nodded. "But it's fishy."

"It's fishy," she agreed.

"I'll ping Krill." He chucked his head toward Dmitri's room.

"I never asked. What happened? I thought *you* were going to find Krill."

"We were." She exhaled slowly. "We got...detoured."

He gave her another look but didn't press.

Another Altered physician passed them, bright-eyed and concentrated, slipping through Dmitri's door. None of the human staff reacted.

Miriam muttered, "I'm a shit magnet, remember?"

He huffed. "You ever consider that the shit comes to you to be fixed?"

"I've got enough broken pieces on my list."

Including herself.

"And I'd prefer it if I wasn't dragged into things I *definitely* can't fix." She scanned the corridor and wing. There were noticeably more colored eyes milling about, including the two Altered physicians she had counted. "This is new," she said with a twist of her finger.

Yuri looked around before it registered. "Ah. Well, UMF numbers dropped, but Altered ones increased. The collaboration is young, but it's moved fast. The agreements have been signed, and I'm now pushing the board to designate a space, perhaps a wing, just for the Altered. Dedicate something permanent. What do you think?"

She gave a tired shrug. "Progressive."

He studied her. "Yeah, it is. We could use the help around here. *I* could use some help."

Miriam hummed noncommittally.

"Maybe it's time to be done with UMF. Have you figured out your contract yet?"

"I don't know."

He waited.

"I don't know," she repeated. "Emma's deciding on which assignment she wants with the new org. They offered her a placement up north, and...it might be easier to stay with UMF in Ursus if I can transfer."

Her mouth dried. She hated how the words tasted.

The lines on Yuri's forehead bunched. "You'd renew? With SOG?"

"I don't know," she said again, wincing. "But I'm tired. I'm getting too old for this."

Maybe Talya was right to switch to BigMED. After everything, Miriam wasn't eager to step back into the field. Admin leave, the lack of action and stress, had been a reprieve. A change of pace she hadn't known she'd needed. Plus, she had only stayed this past UMF contract for Sam. For the chance— however faint—that the woman might return. And in a wild succession of events, she had. Sam *was* there…

Miriam's chest constricted. She was with Emma, and she couldn't hurt her. They'd been together longer. Emma had been consistent, patient, good for her. Miriam hoped she'd been the same in return.

"Well, if you two stay," Yuri said, "there's always a place for both of you here."

She managed a smirk. "Are my parents speaking through you now?"

"Your mother, perhaps." He waved it off. "But no, I'm speaking for myself. I miss working with you."

She didn't answer. Her gaze drifted down the hall. Sam sat on a bench outside the recovery wing, a coffee cup in hand. Her metal thumb rubbed against a metal index finger in a quiet loop. Miriam watched that gesture. It was a minute motion, but it was something of the Sam she knew. Something quietly vulnerable.

Sam had faced temptation—that tin of stimulants on the ground. She had nearly caved, but the important thing was that she hadn't. She hadn't relapsed or crossed that line. That counted for something. It mattered more than Miriam could admit.

Yuri followed her line of sight. Before he could comment, Miriam asked, "The embassy. Have they been notified?"

"Yeah. The reps already reached out. Both embassy and Center."

"Is Kai coming this time?"

Yuri shook his head. "I don't think so."

"Because he isn't a Royal," she said.

Just another body. A meat shield. But one superior in genetics and reaction. She wondered how differently the war might have gone if they'd had a dozen Dmitris on their missions. Or worse—if the Apostates had them.

"I thought legionnaires, Apostates... I thought they moved fast," Miriam murmured. "But not like him. Not like that."

"Specifically crafted. One could say they're the most 'pure' and resilient designs, along with the Royals," said a new voice, uneven steps scraping the floor. "I assume you're talking about the praetorian."

Miriam and Yuri turned.

"Each series is a little different," Nas said as he reached the patient window across from the nurse station. He grimaced as he dragged one foot closer to the other. "NG-C5s, NG-A3s, and the very special NGXs..." He bent his head toward Dmitri through the glass. "Each runs their own profile; all designed differently. Legionnaires, Royals, praetorians, and the K-series, what they called the black-market Altered, what we know as the general Altered class. Most are patchwork, cut corners. But the praetorians..."

"Nas," Yuri greeted him.

"Hi, guys." Nas leaned the better part of his weight off his left leg. "These damn legs," he said with a rueful grin. "It's good to see you again." His eyes dropped to Miriam's cast. "Kai mentioned—well, I'm glad you're alright. You seem to have bounced back. Still UMF, at least, yeah? Let me know if I can help in any way."

Miriam glanced away, then at the braces along his lower limbs while Yuri clapped his shoulder.

"What are you doing here?" she asked.

"Yikes," Nas said, wincing. "That good to see me? What am I, a stranger now?" He raised a hand. "Don't answer that."

"No, sorry. Hi." Miriam gave him a cautious hug, mindful of the metal bracers that hugged up his waist and torso. "Are you still in pain? I thought you were doing better. The medication you'd been on before—"

"Never gonna stop trying to fix me, are you?" He laughed. "I can actually take care of myself, you know?"

She gave him an uncertain look. When he was on Echo, he'd never been great at taking care of his injuries. She'd had to prod him several times on his treatment—*nagged* if anyone asked Nas.

"But no, I had to stop the dosage. It messes me up too much...up here." He tapped his temple. "I've needed a clearer head lately." His attention slid down the corridor. "Valk?" he called. "Hey there!"

Sam looked up. Her nod was faint, more reflex than greeting. A bead of sweat clung to her temple, glinting under the hospital lights. Miriam caught the way her eyes skittered elsewhere, already retreating behind their usual guard.

"Wow," Nas continued. "Didn't expect to see her here. I'm digging the haircut." His eyes widened, and he placed his fingers against his head. "And the embed."

Yuri cleared his throat. "It's good seeing you, Nas, but what *are* you doing here?"

"Tan's gal pal reached out, and I was already in the area. Then I heard you had a praetorian, and—come on, it's a praetorian. I've always wanted to see one." He smiled, more boyish than sly.

He craned to see into the room. One of the Altered physicians had stepped out.

"Who let you back here?" Yuri asked. "This isn't a public area..."

"Oh, you know. Confidence. Walk like you belong, or in my case, hobble convincingly." Nas grinned, but the joke didn't reach his eyes. He winced a second later and shook it off.

Yuri rubbed his forehead. "Hell, our security is abysmal."

"Think he'd chat with me?" Nas asked, nodding toward Dmitri's room.

"I doubt he'll be here long," Yuri said.

And Dmitri couldn't speak anyway.

"Frankly, I'm surprised he's still here—ah." Yuri checked his tablet. "He might not have his full motion back yet. Regardless, their doctors are with him now. Between Altered genetics, their expertise, and the newest stuff they're sharing, our turnarounds are faster. Actually, Nas, I figured you'd be interested in that."

"Oh, sure. Sounds fascinating." Nas took a step toward the room.

Yuri's hand rested lightly on his arm. "How's Vertex treating you?"

"Good, good. Busy and boring, but it's no SOG." Nas chuckled. "I've been looking into what you asked me before, but it's pretty locked down. I sent over what I could to Kai, nothing deep, just briefing packets, summary sheets on UMF liaison work. Nothing out of the ordinary from what I can see." He lifted one shoulder. "Sorry, I just don't think I'm in the lane that you want for this stuff."

Yuri touched his fist to Nas's shoulder. "No, we appreciate it, though."

Nas answered with another sly grin. "Hey—did General run a panel on the praetorian?"

"Standard intake," Yuri said. "Given the circumstances, we didn't want to miss anything."

The second Altered physician returned, now followed by familiar figures: Kuan-Lin and behind her another tall Altered woman in Legion white. The Royal's gold eyes swept the hall, catching each of them in turn. They lingered on Sam farther down.

Sam stood, barely, but didn't approach.

Without a word, Yuri gestured toward Dmitri's room, although the physician was already walking in. Both Kuan-Lin and the legionnaire disappeared inside. The door shut.

"Damn. Missed my chance." Nas rubbed his neck. "I'll have to catch him another time."

"You can stick around," Yuri said. "Did you find Emma?"

Nas said nothing, watching the room's window before the transparent glass engaged, misting into an opaque texture.

"You said she asked for you," Yuri prodded.

"Hm? Yeah, right."

"I can bring you over to where she's settled if you'd like." He nodded at Miriam. "Both of you. Or if you want to hang out more, we could catch up. Hell, wrangle everyone for another dinner at Tsutsumi's."

Nas nodded absently. "Tempting, but I should run." He glanced down at his legs, then chuckled without humor. "Can't really commit to anything these days. Busy, you know. I'll go track Ms. Dubois down so I'm not in the way. See you when I see you?"

Without waiting for a response, he gave a small salute and turned, his steps uneven on the tile. Yuri and Miriam watched him limp down the corridor until his heels disappeared and the sound of his shoes faded.

"That doesn't look good," Miriam murmured. "It's like he's regressed. He looks worse than before."

But who was she to talk? The same could be argued about her.

Yuri folded his arms. "Would rather bear the pain than lose his edge, I guess."

"Hell."

SOG marines could leave UMF, but their stubbornness remained.

They stood in silence as the hospital streamed around them, a current moving over stone. Miriam's attention drifted, unfocused, her thoughts stretching until the moment unspooled and ceased to hold. She flinched when Yuri lifted a hand.

Emma approached from the corridor Nas had gone down, steps brisk and expression set. She looked to Miriam, then to Sam, the corner of her mouth turning. Miriam leaned in to meet her for a greeting kiss.

"Everything okay?" Emma asked.

"Yeah. No," Miriam replied. "Slight change of plans."

Emma nodded slowly. Her stare roamed over Miriam's shoulder to Sam again, then back toward the closed door.

"Shit," Yuri said. "Nas. Did you see him? He just went to find you."

Emma shook her head. "I didn't. We must've just missed each other."

Yuri's brows furrowed.

"It's alright. He's probably on his way over to the labs. I wanted him to look at something I found. His opinion. But Yuri mentioned you were here."

"Oh," Miriam said. "What did you find?"

Emma's chin tipped toward Sam. "I ran her blood work again. I'm not surprised your techs were confused, Yuri. It's a pattern I caught back when I was at GenTech, mostly in heavy stim and calmer users."

"Like what?" he asked.

"It's a recent progression, if you can call it that. When Vertex bought out GenTech, the meetings—they didn't seem to care when I flagged it—long-term effects and studies aren't really their priority, I guess, but we don't really know what this stuff does to people over time, especially with excessive use. It's still relatively new."

Miriam glanced at Sam, but the woman's focus was fixed on the room behind her. She squeezed her eyes shut; the pressure behind them pulsed.

"Every pharm org has a signature," Emma continued. "And

though Vertex doesn't officially have a branch or subsidiary on the books—they prefer to be known for their practical tech—we all know they do have a pharm arm." She chuckled at her own rhyme. "This one looks a lot like Vertex's, from what I've seen. I don't know how or why Sam's got their compounds, but it's in her blood and system. The signature doesn't lie."

"Vertex supplies UMF," Miriam murmured. Talya had mentioned something about Sam taking her stash of trial stims. Sam's prosthetic arm was a Vertex prototype as well.

Emma tipped her head. "Sure. But there was something else. Another anomaly. I isolated it, but I don't know. It's not his specialty, but I was hoping Nas could look at it, help me cross-check with whatever he has access to and confirm. I'd need higher-grade equipment to be sure, but it's...odd."

"What do you mean *odd*?"

"Well, its behavior seems to be attracted to specific cell structures. Proteins. This is all speculation, of course."

Miriam glanced at Yuri, whose stare had fallen into the middle distance. Her own thoughts pulled inward. She tried to concentrate and replay what her girlfriend had just said, but the words swirled, not settling. It wasn't that she didn't understand—or maybe it was.

"What's going on over here?" Emma asked.

"Charonites attacked another Altered," Yuri answered. "Again."

"Is the—are they okay?"

"They chose the wrong target," Miriam muttered. But as she said it, doubt rippled beneath her ribs. Dmitri wasn't just any Altered. He wasn't just a target of opportunity. He'd been protecting another golden-eyed Royal. Were the Charonites going after them? And why? A bold statement?

She looked up to see Sam approaching, drawn by the same invisible current that had tugged at her thoughts. Her regard remained locked on the sealed room.

Kuan-Lin. They *had* been on their way to see the Royal.

"Did they? Choose the wrong target?" Yuri asked. "From what you said earlier, there were plenty more assailants. They might not have been winning, but they got that substance on him, that DMSO. It would've been a matter of time."

"Dimethyl sulfoxide?" Emma's mouth pinched together. "From Charonites? Why would *they* have DMSO?"

"That's what Tan said."

"You have those results? Can you send them to me?"

"You think this has to do with Sam?" Miriam asked.

The woman hesitated, watching her. "No. I just...I want to check something." She took a breath. "I'm going to find Nas."

"Wait. Em." Miriam followed, leaving Yuri and Sam. Voices murmured behind the glass as she passed the patient room.

But Emma didn't slow. Her gait was clipped, shoulders taut, not abnormal, but more controlled than usual. Guarded.

"Em," Miriam said, catching her elbow. "Is S—"

Emma stopped, exhaled, and turned with her face composed. Guilt rose hot in Miriam.

"What are you doing here, Miriam? You should be home. Or, I don't know, back at Yuri's. What are you getting mixed up in?"

"I didn't exactly go looking for trouble. We—I was going to UMF, and—"

"You're on admin leave. You're supposed to be healing."

"How am I supposed to sit around while—"

"Why do you have to be the hero?"

Miriam stepped back. "I'm sorry, are we fighting? What is going on?"

Emma's cheek shifted like she was grinding her teeth. But whatever reply she considered, she bit it back. Her breath let out. "I just wasn't expecting to see you here. With her."

"I—you told me to stay with her."

"I know." Emma's expression folded for a heartbeat. "I didn't mean to come at you. I've just been...feeling off."

Miriam set her hands on Emma's waist. This was her fault somehow. She knew it. "Are we okay?"

Emma nodded.

Miriam pressed her lips against a soft cheek. "I'll come with you."

"You'd die of boredom," Emma said, a small smile returning. "And then you'd annoy me."

"I'll behave."

"No. We're okay. I'm—I should go find Nas. I don't want him to wait."

"Yeah. You'll want to make sure he hasn't put his nose or fingers into anything," Miriam said.

Emma brushed her knuckles along Miriam's jaw, and Miriam leaned into it.

"We'll have that dinner another night."

"Tomorrow," Miriam said.

"Tomorrow," Emma echoed. She turned, casting one last glance over her shoulder before heading toward the lab wing.

Miriam crossed her arms, the cast turning the motion awkward. She felt like she was slipping. She was back in her regular life in the regular world. And despite Sam being back, being around her, Miriam had already moved on. What she'd said to Sam in the North was an exigent circumstance. It had been desperation. The verge of death had a way of simultaneously sharpening and smearing the truth. That was their reality then, but it wasn't how it was now.

She sighed and circled back toward Yuri, Sam, and Dmitri's room. As she rounded the mouth of the hall, she slowed. They hadn't noticed her; their focus had pulled inward, into a private exchange, but she was close enough to see the shape of it. Sam's and Yuri's hands moved between them, the rhythm too precise to be idle. A silent conversation, laid bare to anyone who understood.

Miriam stopped, tucking back behind the corner, caught in place by a situation she hadn't expected. She understood just enough to follow. It felt wrong, like an invasion. She shouldn't be watching. It was eavesdropping, and she knew it, but she didn't move. She'd learned to sign for someone she thought she'd lost. She'd kept the language anyway. And now it opened a door she wasn't sure she wanted it to.

Sam glanced down toward her, and Miriam angled her shoulders, pretending to study her handheld. When she looked up again, the quiet conversation had resumed. Miriam crept forward and acted naturally, her head ducked, eyes flicking between her darkened display and the silent words unfolding before her.

HE ISN'T HERE, BUT HE WOULDN'T HAVE WANTED YOU LIKE THIS.

Sam flinched. She looked up at Yuri.

BUT YOU'RE GETTING BETTER. YOU CAN STILL MAKE THIS RIGHT.

I MADE A PROMISE TO HIM—

YEARS AGO, Yuri replied. IT WAS A PROMISE HE NEVER WOULD'VE WANTED YOU TO MAKE.

Sam's shoulders dipped.

I'M GLAD YOU'RE ALIVE, BUT YOU'VE GOT TO GET YOUR SHIT TOGETHER. MAKE IT RIGHT. He made a motion toward the room.

Kuan-Lin. Ren.

Sam hesitated, then stepped to the door. Her fist hovered, knuckles inches from the surface. She inhaled, once, then twice, before she knocked.

The door slid open, and she stood in the threshold, frozen for a heartbeat. A voice called from inside, and she crossed through. The door sealed behind her.

Miriam let out a breath and lowered her device. She scuffed the floor just enough to be heard. Yuri turned.

"Hey."

"What was that about?" she asked.

He gave a dry exhale. "Told her to pull herself together if she wants to stay in her brother's—in her nephew's life."

"Shit, Yuri."

"Was I wrong?"

She paused. "No, but still—shit."

His breath caught in something halfway between a huff and a laugh.

"You're not her brother."

"No," he said, quieter. "But she needed someone to say it." His awareness drifted. "All good with Emma?"

Miriam sighed. "Yeah. I think."

"Oh?"

Miriam watched the room's door and opaque window, trying to hear for anything, any movement. The silence felt neutral, not tense. She took it as a good sign.

"She sees you and Emma," Yuri said.

Miriam's head whipped toward him, and the pain and throb of her neck followed. She swallowed a curse.

"You've changed, Tan. Arguably for the better, I'd say. I told her perhaps that's why you have what you have with Emma. Because of everything you went through with her. You're not the same person. I mean, you are, but not entirely. You've grown. I think we all have. So has she."

"Oh."

"What are you going to do?"

"About what?" Miriam gave a hollow laugh. "The Charonites? The DMSO? Willem's missing body? I don't know why any of this is happening."

She was supposed to be on admin leave. She was supposed to be recovering. Resting.

Yuri shook his head. "No. What are you going to do?"

She narrowed her eyes at him. "What do you mean?"

He shrugged and tipped his chin toward the closed door.

And Miriam understood. She just didn't have an answer.

40

<hr>

REDRESS

BY THE SECOND MORNING, Miriam woke to find Emma already dressed, already halfway out the door. She'd kissed Miriam goodbye, quick and light. Not cold, but not quite warm either.

By the third, they orbited each other. Meals became scheduled rituals, shared out of habit and as attempts to remediate something rather than out of hunger. Evenings passed in the stasis of dimmed lights and the network murmuring in the background. When they spoke, it was about blood panels or medical updates or Miriam's growing frustration. Every avenue they pulled led to nothing. No answers about what she'd been exposed to, where Willem's body had gone, or who had signed off on it. It was never about them. Never about what came next. They both knew they needed to talk, to fix it. But for the first time in a long while, neither reached across the growing distance.

By the fourth morning, Miriam stood at her window, staring at the slip of ocean between the skyline. The glass was warm beneath her fingertips, but the sensation barely registered. She had kept away from Yuri's house and away from Sam. She had tried to rest, to recover as ordered, but the stillness grated against her skin. At least the nightmares she'd expected never came, although the anticipation was its own irritation.

Her flexcast itched beneath its layer, the advanced weave stiff but light enough that she could rest her arm against the sill without pain. The tech inside was doing its work, but the reminder of her mending bones was constant. Her fingers tapped a restless rhythm as a city transport passed between buildings. Her handheld buzzed on the counter.

She let it vibrate a few more times before crossing the room.

N. TALWAR: You free?

Miriam read the message again. It wasn't the first time her teammate had reached out. Hino had checked in, too. Durmaz, once. But Miriam had kept her responses short. The last time she'd seen any of them had been during the mandatory check-in with MED on compound. They'd found her at the clinic, unplanned. She hadn't intended to return to the SOG team room, not even to figure out the forms for all her gear she'd left behind in the North. She didn't want the reminder.

But four days inside the apartment, limited walks outside and to Station General, had begun to wear thin.

M. TANNER: Yes.

She knew Talwar had been pulled into debriefs like her, likely not long after he returned to Ursus Outpost. She hadn't asked him what he said. Hadn't wanted to. If he'd sold Sam out somehow and was the reason why the woman had been abducted into a windowless cell, she wasn't sure she could forgive him.

N. TALWAR: I know you're on leave, but you
should swing by. You'll want to see this.

Miriam grimaced. She had no intention of going back to

base and for anything short of answers she wanted. Echo had returned to the rotation; SOG had already assigned her temporary replacement. The last time she'd been summoned to UMF a couple days after her return, the debrief had felt like a trial. Faces she didn't know, or couldn't remember, had taken notes while asking the same questions in different ways. She had danced around Sam and Willem; the pain meds and ache in her neck had been convenient shields.

> N. TALWAR: Bring your friend.

She frowned. What did he mean by that? After Miriam and the others had broken Sam out of the annex building, UMF and Vertex hadn't come again for the woman. Not yet, at least. She was thankful for Krill in Command and Nas in Vertex for helping look out, at least providing them with any semblance of warning. Just in case. But she was still on guard. She'd restrained herself from asking for constant updates from Sam, from Yuri. She was trying to make things work with Emma, and she knew she was doing a terrible job of it.

Her fingers hesitated before she responded.

> M. TANNER: ???

Nothing.

> M. TANNER: Where?

> N. TALWAR: Annexes.

Her chest constricted. She thought of the windowless buildings and the rooms inside them, the kind that consumed and disappeared people.

> M. TANNER: No.

No reply. And then—

N. TALWAR: Hino says Pit.

That gave her pause. Hino was with him? Why wasn't Hino messaging her directly? Why use Talwar?

N. TALWAR: It's safe.

But the words didn't settle anything. The Pit *was* in the outer ring—less fortified, more flexible in access—but so was the Vertex liaison building. Both were on UMF ground. Still too close. She didn't trust it. Not anymore.

Another ping.

N. TALWAR: Bring your Foxtrot friend if you
need. I'll be there, too.

She exhaled slowly and stared at the display. Her curiosity and restlessness outweighed her suspicion. She sent a short reply, then another two messages, each through separate channels.

As she dressed, she input one more and sent it to Emma.

♟

Sam wore a slightly oversized T-shirt and loose pants that tapered at the ankle. It was odd to see her in civilian clothes. Different, but pleasantly so. Miriam had seen her in casual wear before, but she was used to seeing the woman in uniform, or, more recently, the utilitarian black and olive green worn by the SRAF. This was neither.

It felt like more time had passed than it really had. She hadn't avoided Sam, not exactly, but the days had drifted by, slow and heavy.

As Sam approached, she shrugged. "I had no say. Yuri did the shopping."

Miriam smirked. "No, you look great."

Different, but still her.

Sam tugged at the hem, then glanced toward the UMF gate. The new embed glinted through blond strands behind her ear. "What is this about?"

"I don't know," Miriam admitted. "But thanks for coming."

"I had time before—" She hesitated.

"Before?"

"I've got something in an hour."

"Oh?"

Another shrug, and a shoe shuffled against pavement.

"You didn't have to—"

"It's okay," Sam said. "I wanted to."

Miriam studied Sam's face; she kept the rest to herself. Across the small loading dock, there was no sign of Fox. She had sent a message, but he had actual duties, actual responsibilities like the others. Still, he had requested she share her location, and she had. She'd added Yuri, too. It wasn't much, but it gave an extra measure of security she didn't want to admit she needed.

Without a commcuff, Miriam used a secondary access point. The process was slower, and the sentry gave her a long look, then cleared her. She kept from touching the bright pink scar on her neck, but the moment she stepped into the UMF compound, the weight settled back on her shoulders. She knew it was only in her head, but the air tasted like carbon and stale condensation. A young first-contract pounded past on concrete at a shouted order. It felt like slipping into dirty clothes.

Behind her, Sam followed, but the terminal blinked red. She touched her embed.

Miriam frowned. "She received pre-cleared access."

The sentry muttered, worked the terminal, and tried again. Another denial. Sam's jaw flexed, and her hands balled. Miriam stepped back out to join her, relief sneaking through. She messaged Talwar and Hino from the side, visible to the gate but out of earshot.

Meanwhile, Sam said nothing. Only the small twitch of muscle under the new scar across her cheek. UMF had shut Sam out. They'd cut the line and turned their backs. Sam had been raised a marine, molded in youth, shaped to be of use. They'd *used* her and wrung her dry. And now when she was done, *they* were done. Miriam couldn't tell if it was withdrawal or fury that made the woman's fingers tremble.

"How's today?" she asked gently.

"Shit," Sam said at last.

Miriam gave a quiet huff of amusement.

Sam's mouth pulled into a slanted, tired smile. "A bit better. But for every good day, there are at least two bad ones."

"You didn't need to come."

"No. This is a distraction," Sam said. "A good one. If I sit still too long…"

Miriam nodded. She understood too well. She caught herself leaning in and shifted back a step.

"Emma alright?" Sam asked.

Miriam hesitated, then nodded. It wasn't a lie. Emma was fine. They were fine. But the word felt like a formality now, a placeholder. She'd spent the past few days sitting and sleeping beside Emma, saying everything and nothing, watching their orbit widen degree by degree. And yet, standing here beside Sam—on the brink of everything she was supposed to leave behind—she felt steadier than the last weeks.

When Hino arrived, the tension in Miriam's shoulders eased, but only slightly. The team second met them at the back gate, face open and kind, which helped.

What didn't help was watching Sam go through visitor processing. It was strange. Wrong. Miriam had never seen her on that side of the line, and even if Sam hid it, Miriam knew the woman. Being a visitor to UMF stung.

While the system churned, Hino turned to Miriam. "You look good. Better."

"So everyone keeps saying. Talwar—"

"He's waiting inside." Hino fidgeted with her gloves. "I'll let him tell you. I don't know what happened out there, but he's been…different. Not bad. Kind of in a good way? Regardless, I hate to admit it, but he found this first."

"You can't just tell me?"

"I promised." Hino sighed. "But it's worth the trip, Tan. I swear."

Miriam narrowed her eyes. "Sure."

Hino's fingers curled. "I…I'm so sorry."

"It wasn't your fault."

"No, but Gumede… If I'd said something sooner—"

"Hino. You tried. It's okay."

That path of what-ifs went on forever. She knew that trail. She'd walked it for days in the North.

"What happened to him?" Miriam asked.

"Transferred to SOG-B. LOGS, you know."

With Gumede's connections, he'd probably received a slap on the wrist and reprimand. But his reputation would be tainted in the ranks of the SOG teams.

Miriam scoffed. "That won't last. I'm sure UMF'll promote him to Command tomorrow."

To her surprise, Hino chuckled unevenly. "Yeah. No shit."

"So, you're lead now?"

Hino scanned the low industrial skyline. She gave a single nod.

"Contract?"

Another nod.

"That's good. You were the de facto lead, anyway. Who's taking your place?"

There was a pause before Hino looked back at her. "I was hoping you'd consider it."

Miriam lifted her brows, then let them fall. "No." She laughed at Hino's lack of surprise. "I'm honored, but hell no."

The team second-now-lead smirked, but it faded fast. "You're not coming back, are you? Your contract?"

Miriam didn't answer right away. She glanced over at Sam by the sentry, the woman's finger scraping absently along her thumb. "I'm waiting on what Emma decides. But no, if I stick around, it won't be SOG." She blew out a breath. "I think I'm done, Hino."

It was strange saying it out loud. She'd been thinking it for a while now, but she'd actually said it to her own teammate. The shape of the words, the idea, strengthened.

The sentry waved Sam through, and Miriam and Hino straightened as if returning to formation.

"I thought so." Hino gave Miriam a long look. "Echo will manage. We'll miss you—I'll miss you—but we'll be fine. This isn't goodbye, though. You still have to check in, you know. We got your leave extended, but that doesn't mean you vanish."

Miriam smirked. "Yeah. Sure." Her handheld buzzed in her pocket, but she ignored it.

When Sam joined them, shoulders squared, they followed the narrow strip behind the annex blocks. It was unfamiliar ground for Miriam; she'd rarely entered the compound this way. It felt like trespassing into her own past, the wrong angle on something she once knew.

The buildings ahead were bland, gray slabs interrupted only by ventilation grates and sealed doors. She wouldn't have recognized the Pit if Talwar hadn't been pacing outside. He spotted them, hurried forward, then stopped short, too quick to hide the awkward burst of motion. It looked like he wanted to reach out, maybe hug them, maybe shake hands, but couldn't decide. His eyes flicked down to her neck before they moved back up. He settled for a clumsy pat on Miriam's shoulder.

"Talwar."

"Tan."

He glanced at Sam. "Hi. Is Chapel—"

Sam nodded back. "He's with the team."

"That's great." He rubbed his neck. "I never told him thanks. Could you…"

Sam nodded again.

Miriam stepped closer to her teammate. "What's going on?"

"Uh, not out here," he said, grinning with a nervous twitch. "Let's get inside."

That unease tugged at her. The questions, the suspicions she'd banked flared again.

"Talwar."

"Tan, it's okay," Hino said, stepping beside their teammate.

Miriam raised a hand. "No. Before we go in—whatever this is—what did you tell Command?"

Talwar blinked. "What? You mean the debrief?"

She waited. Sam and Hino hovered nearby but said nothing.

"I told them what happened," he said.

Miriam pulled him aside. A few paces brought them near the side wall, out of easy hearing. "And the facility? Willem? Sam?"

"Everything happened so fast, Tan. I told them I wasn't a good source. I didn't recall much."

Her eyes narrowed.

"Do you really think I'd sell you—sell them out?" he asked, voice tight. "They saved us. Chapel. He—when we left you, there was a point where I fell behind. I thought I was done. He saved me. He didn't have to." He shook his head and sighed. "Whatever happened in that facility, we were set up. I know I'm an ass and I'm green and new, but I'm not stupid. I think we were supposed to fail."

She studied him another second. "Then what are we doing here?"

"You won't believe it until you see. Come on."

They rejoined the others, and Talwar led them into the

building. The front-desk marine barely asked a question, just glanced between the four, recognition sharpening his posture. Miriam quickly deposited her handheld into a lockbox and moved on.

Beyond, the corridor was lined with the same empty holding cells. Miriam's breath shortened. She hadn't been back since Jace and Hino. Her heart beat faster despite her effort to control it. Sam tensed beside her. Neither spoke.

At the end of the hall, two geared-up SOG marines stood. Spartan team, but she couldn't remember which; she vaguely recognized them from gym rotations and training exercises over the years. Talwar clasped one by the forearm.

The control room opened past them. Three figures huddled around the central console, two standing, one seated and hunched over his work. Talwar and Hino paused at the threshold.

"Go ahead," he said.

Miriam eyed them. "What is this?"

Neither answered.

One of the figures pushed off the console and turned, gait slightly uneven.

"Jace?"

"Good to see you two," said the intelligence officer. He offered a hand, but when neither Miriam nor Sam took it, he dropped it. "I'll take it from here."

Behind, Talwar and Hino nodded and stepped back, each giving Miriam a light touch before retreating past the other marines.

Miriam opened her mouth, but Jace broke in. "Come on, we've been waiting for you."

She followed him in with Sam close behind. The spoke of rooms branched outward in all directions, most empty except one. The open door pulsed with artificial light, too bright and sterile. Miriam squinted as they approached.

Inside, four SOG marines surrounded a man on the floor. A

deafening sack covered his head, and his hands and ankles were bound.

"What—" The words scraped her throat, too rough to finish. Her throat worked once. "Who?"

Jace passed her a tablet, and she looked down at its holodisplay. A face confronted her—orange eyes and sunken cheeks. Unmistakable.

Butcher.

Her skin tightened, her breath catching in her ribs. Pain sang along her neck, and she forced the nausea down. She glanced at Sam, who could see the display and face as well. Her expression had gone stony.

Jace made a low sound and gestured. Two marines stepped in; one yanked the sack free.

Miriam flinched.

The Altered man, the Apostate, the Heretic, blinked at the light, disoriented, then locked eyes with each of the nearby marines in turn. A muzzle was strapped across his face, nearly identical to the one he and his band had used on Sam. Below it, the collar of his uniform sagged, and Miriam glimpsed it—the same brand carved into his neck, triangle and ring scorched into scar tissue, but uneven, the strike-line cut twice. Crude and cruel. His gaze landed on Jace, then Miriam. Recognition flickered before it slid past to Sam. His bright eyes lit up.

Behind her, Miriam felt the tension in Sam's body, saw it in the slight tremor at her side. But only for a heartbeat.

"How?" Miriam whispered.

"Don't know if you've been following everything going on over in Altered territory, but the Heretics have been pissing off more than just us and Legion. Suicide bombers? Executions? *Children?* It wasn't just marines and Legion. They've been infighting with the other factions of Apostates—crying over whose methods and doctrines are right. The Altered caught in the middle despise all of them. Shit, the Heretics and other factions have been trying to police towns. Actions have consequences. They let something loose that they couldn't control."

Miriam shook her head. She didn't understand how it had led to this.

"The people had enough. It was too much. You'll have to ask the Titan team that brought him in, but the Altered just gave him up. Who knows, could be he tried running back and they finally grew a pair. But we found him before the Charonites did. Lucky us. The transfer process, the secrecy, it's been a clusterfuck of twenty-four hours—used up a third of the SOG teams scouring for others and security along the way. We would've never known this one was captured or dead if that hadn't happened. Doubt the Children of Charon can tell one from the other."

"What happens now?" Miriam asked. "What will UMF do with him?"

Jace's mouth twisted. "Whatever City Center decides. Hold him, put him on trial, probably. Personally, I'd say skip all that noise. He doesn't deserve it. None of them do."

"And Legion? The Royals?"

"What about them?"

"He didn't just torture and kill marines," Miriam said.

Hadeon, Perun, Willem, how many more?

"They should know. Have a say."

Jace shrugged. "Maybe the Royals already do. But I'm not in that loop. As I said, it's whatever Command and City Center want."

"Command knows?" Miriam asked, looking to Sam, whose prosthetic fingers dug into her other arm.

"Someone does. Everyone? Probably not—not yet, at least."

"So why is he being held here?"

"Confirmation."

"It's him," Miriam said, handing the tablet back.

"Of course it is." Jace glanced between her and Sam. "Credit the new Baby Echo. RUMINT works in strange ways. Someone talked." His glare swept the space, although he didn't focus on any individual Spartan marine. "And here we are, although it wasn't too hard to be convinced."

The realization settled.

Jace gave a dry smile. "Consider it a gift. Some of us figured you'd want a little time face-to-face. Before the handoff."

Miriam's neck muscles flexed.

"Titan passed the target to Spartan team, but they didn't indicate his status. Don't know if he's dead or alive," Jace added with a nonchalant stare at Butcher. "Boys."

The four marines lowered their rifles and filed out. Each nodded to Miriam and Sam as they passed. The room felt larger without them, but colder, too.

"I've got to hit the head," Jace muttered. "Bladder's been a bastard. This fucking war. You know how it is. Might take a while." He stepped out.

The others were already drifting down the hall.

At the second door, Jace turned, one hand on the frame. "Oh, and be careful. Engineers have been poking at the power grid. No eyes in this area right now. So if he tries something—shout."

The door eased shut behind him.

For a time, neither woman moved. Butcher sat, glowering up at them, bound and muzzled, and yet the mixture of rage and amusement in his eyes had lost none of its heat. The capture, the restraints, the cell, the protocol—it hadn't dimmed the fire. It was still a show and performance to him. He'd never stop. Hatred and spite like his didn't die without a cause; it metastasized. It found new ways, new justifications. And Miriam could see it in his eyes. He was already rewriting his options, trying to figure out how to hurt them more.

She wanted to hit him. Wanted to wipe that look off his face and grind it into nothing. But her body held.

And Sam moved first. She stepped forward and knelt. Miriam opened her mouth to warn her she was too close, but her neck muscles constricted and her voice failed her. Sam's fists clenched, metal and flesh both tight enough to tremble.

Miriam braced. She wouldn't blame Sam, but this was a different relapse, one into darkness and rage rather than stimulants and depressants. It rolled off Sam's body, and Miriam stiffened, scared. She cursed Talwar, Hino, and Jace for bringing them here, but the curses were shallow. She ultimately cursed the man who deserved it. She wouldn't blame Sam.

Sam raised her hand, metal digits pressing into Butcher's cheeks just above the muzzle. The pressure deepened, and Miriam watched the indentations swell in the man's skin. Her throat burned, and she looked away.

But the crush of bones and flesh never came. To Miriam's surprise, Sam drew back. Her prosthetic hung in the air a moment longer, fingers twitching as if the urge still ran through them. Then she exhaled, slow and measured. Her breath fell into rhythm as if they were being counted.

Without a word, Sam stood.

And suddenly, *she* broke. Miriam's own fury surged from some place buried deep. All the nights she'd spent staring at the dark, thinking of Herrera's blood on her hands, Willem's blood soaking into her clothes, Perun's face, Hadeon's cries. Sam's body, crumpled and torn. Every beat, every gasp, every name she hadn't been able to save. She didn't remember crossing the space—only the sound of her boots and her own breath, ragged and rising.

She was on him, grabbing the front of his plain prisoner's uniform and yanking hard. Her forearm cast smashed into his throat, and he rocked back. Butcher's eyes stretched wide, and though he couldn't speak, the snarl behind the muzzle thrummed. Miriam struck him once, then again, fists hammering a rhythm that wanted no end, no reason, just release. Someone shouted—maybe her. The old pain lanced back through her neck, but it didn't matter. Nothing mattered but the impact of her hands.

And then arms wrapped around her. Sam.

Miriam fought the hold, struggled against it, but Sam didn't let go. She hauled Miriam back so they were both on the floor, grunting with the effort. She held on, full-bodied, her strength both anchor and barrier.

"Stop. Stop," Sam whispered again and again, the words low in her ear. "You're okay. You're here. You're safe. You're safe."

Miriam thrashed once more before the fight drained from her. She sagged into the floor, into Sam, who adjusted her grip behind her, arms banded across her shoulders and chest. The metal of the prosthetic was cool where it met skin, but Sam's body was warm. Grounding.

"I've got you," Sam murmured.

Miriam's breath came shallow and fast. Her eyes burned. She forced down the sob clawing up.

Across the room, Butcher laughed—or tried to. The sound was strangled, caught behind the muzzle, but the intent landed. He'd broken her before, and he watched her break again.

Sam tightened her hold, then shifted, placing herself between Miriam and the man. "I'm here," she whispered.

Miriam didn't answer. They stayed that way, drawing breath together. Sam's chin rested lightly against Miriam's temple.

When Miriam stood, Sam rose with her. Miriam exited the room without another word, her eyes never returning to Butcher or his orange irises. Sam followed, and the door closed behind them. In the central room, Miriam took in deep gulps. The air felt lighter but still unclean.

"I'm going to see my nephew," Sam said, voice rough. When Miriam didn't respond, she continued. "We're going to a museum. Human history or something."

Miriam turned.

Sam scuffed her shoe, then looked up. "Do you want to come? With me?"

Miriam paused. The adrenaline hadn't washed out

completely. Her arms shook, but Sam was watching her—not pitying, not pushing. Just there.

"It's okay if you don't want to. Or if you're not free, I just thought—"

"Yeah," Miriam said. "Yes."

Sam bit her lip, but the corners of her mouth turned, mirroring Miriam's.

41

PRIVATE MESSAGE
[E. DUBOIS TO M. TANNER]

E. DUBOIS: Running late. You okay with a later dinner?

E. DUBOIS: Babe?

42

RESTORATION

THE MUSEUM WAS A SMALL PLACE, tucked underneath a series of apartments between a shuttered bookstore and a municipal storage building. Miriam wouldn't have known it was there if Sam hadn't led her to the door. There was no signage beyond a tarnished plaque and a keypad.

She brushed her knuckles and winced; one of her strikes had landed too close to Butcher's muzzle. The skin was tender. Miriam shoved the memory aside and steadied her breath. The walk had drained her, yet something steadier pushed through. Not energy exactly, but a second wind made of friction and quiet resolve.

If not for the track lighting inside, she would've assumed the place had been closed for years. Sam dithered just outside, rocking from heel to toe. Her face carried that pale, pinched look again, as if any sudden motion might break her in two.

Miriam leaned on the wall, arms crossed. "Talk to me."

"I should be looking for Boy Scout," Sam muttered. "Or be with my team. Not wasting time here."

"It's not a waste."

Sam glanced sideways.

"Is this important to you?" Miriam asked. She already knew the answer, but the question wasn't for her.

Sam's nod was nearly imperceptible.

"Then the rest can wait."

"It doesn't wait for others," Sam whispered.

"No," Miriam agreed. "But we've earned a breath, don't you think? We have a moment. It'd be worse not to take it."

Sam didn't answer but didn't argue either. She fidgeted, her fingers tapping at the seam of her pants. "Are you okay?"

Miriam met Sam's eyes. Her thoughts were scattered, looping back to Butcher, to Emma. "I'll figure it out."

Movement drew their attention. Kuan-Lin rounded the corner, her pace slow but composed, her pantsuit simultaneously hugging and flowing around her. At her side, young Ren walked with his arm raised, hand tightly in hers. The same legionnaire from days before trailed a few steps behind. The boy slowed as they approached and ducked behind his mother's legs.

"Apologies," Kuan-Lin said. "Any timeliness I once had has been hijacked by this little rascal. He refused to be carried. Had to walk on his own, of course." Her stare settled on Sam and held a fraction longer than courtesy required.

"Thank you for coming," Sam said carefully. She tugged at the bottom of her shirt and glanced at the tall Altered behind them. "I'm clean, I promise."

Kuan-Lin's mouth bent toward a smile, though her hand stayed on Ren's head, thumb slowly combing his light brown hair. "I see," she said at last. Her eyes moved over Sam, pausing at the hollows beneath her eyes and the way her stance rested unevenly. Then they softened, minutely. She turned to check on the boy. He had wrapped himself tighter around her knees, his face nestled into her pants.

Kuan-Lin looked up at the modest facade. "Scott told me about this place once. I thought he made it up."

Sam managed a grin. "He wanted to bring me here before... We never got to it."

Kuan-Lin's nod came slow, her fingers never leaving Ren's hair. "Shall we?"

But no one moved for the door.

Sam knelt, trying to catch Ren's eye, but he tucked farther behind his mother. Her shoulders sagged. "He's afraid of me," she murmured.

It wasn't said in bitterness. The first and last time the kid had seen his aunt, it'd been a mess. She'd been rageful, broken, barely human.

"He's a bit shy," Kuan-Lin said. "Aren't you, Ren?"

One gray-and-gold eye peeked out from the crease of her trousers.

The Royal moved her fingers in front of her where her son couldn't see. HE'LL WARM UP. YOU UNDERSTAND.

From a step back, Miriam gave the boy a quick wink when he peeked again. He grinned crookedly.

Inside, the museum opened larger than it appeared, its footprint disguised by the modest exterior. Light hummed in the walls, guiding them through sparse halls and archival displays. Dust motes hung suspended in amber light. The air smelled of old paper and something else, perhaps preserved fabric or old glue. Shelves held relics of life from generations before.

Sam paused near a display case, her fingers sweeping the surface. Inside was a rusted toy, a battered holoreader, and a row of bound books, their spines cracked with age. The woman's gaze drifted to Ren, who had let go of his mother's pants, transfixed by an animated short projected onto the far wall, bright and archaic.

Kuan-Lin moved with intent, giving each display its due. Sam shadowed her, posture rigid, attention boomeranging back to the boy. Watching. Hoping.

As Ren leaned closer to the animation, Sam eased nearer, not quite beside him, not quite distant. The awkwardness was raw and palpable, but so was the want.

Ren's fingers twitched, mimicking a gesture from the cartoon. Sam's eyes roved over him, taking him in. Even Kuan-Lin's attention had turned back.

Sam lowered herself to the boy's height. "Hi."

He turned, wary. A small sound left his throat, more a murmur than a word, but something close to a greeting in response.

"I'm...Sam," she said. "What's your name?"

His eyes searched for his mother, but when he found Kuan-Lin, she only inclined her head. Ren whispered his name.

"Hi, Ren." Sam's voice wavered. "Did your mom name you that?"

He nodded.

"My brother—your dad—he named me." She offered a tentative smile.

"Okay," he whispered.

Miriam's eyes widened as the boy reached out to touch the ends of Sam's blond hair. The woman froze, then a quiver took over her mouth. She bent ever so slightly forward so he could keep petting, his small hand so close to her face.

When he drew back, Sam sniffed and cleared her throat. "I've got something for you." Her hand dug into a pocket and came back out.

The boy leaned in. His fingers touched her prosthetic fist. Sam peeled her alloy digits open to reveal a silver chain pooled in her palm. Ren glanced down, up to his mother, then to the metal on metal.

"Your...dad would've wanted you to have this," Sam said. "It was his. And before that, *his* mom's. He wore it every day."

Ren's fingers splayed as he traced the links. And then he looked up at Sam as if realizing how close he'd gotten and curled back into himself.

Sam nudged her hand forward. "It's yours. I've just been... holding it for you."

He hesitated, then took it, clutching it in his fingers, and scampered to Kuan-Lin's side.

"What do you say, Ren?" Kuan-Lin murmured.

"Thank you," he said, peering back at Sam before lifting the chain to show his mother.

Sam stood slowly with a hand braced on her thigh. Her expression folded inward. Ren moved on to the next display, the necklace in his grip.

"Give him time," Kuan-Lin said. She turned to Miriam. "If you don't mind, I'd like to speak with Sam. Alone."

Miriam nodded and drifted after the boy, who had ventured deeper to an animal exhibit in the corner. Faded placards and half-working holo-tags labeled domesticated pets that humans had once had the luxury to keep. He reached for an ancient approximation of a small dog, its synthetic fur matted and abraded in patches, worn to the weave by generations of curious fingers.

Ren ran his hand over its back, slow and fascinated. Miriam paused. The instinct to stop him, to caution against germs or the questionable cleaning cycles of a public museum, rose and faded. He was too engrossed, too present in the moment. And maybe, years before, Scott had once trailed a palm across the same model.

Her knees cracked as she crouched beside him, and she winced at the echoing sound, but Ren didn't startle. He remained absorbed, flowing the chain between his fingers like it was part of the display. His lips moved with some private narration.

From her crouch, she glanced toward the far end of the room. Sam and Kuan-Lin stood in a narrow alcove. Whatever they spoke about hadn't spoiled the moment. If anything, it looked close to tender.

Ren held the necklace out, eyes bright with joy. A small

dimple curved in his left cheek, lopsided and shallow, oddly asymmetrical for a Royal, but maybe that was the human part of him.

Miriam grinned back. "Do you want me to put it on you?"

He shrugged, passing it over without a word. She took it gently, looping the chain around his neck. The motion was clumsy; the cast made her grip less certain, forcing her to work slower. Her fingers brushed the nape of his neck, warm and soft. "Pretty sure this is a choking hazard and your mom's going to kill me," she muttered.

The chain settled loose on his upper chest, and he dipped his chin down to inspect it.

Miriam folded her arms over her knees. "You're lucky you're cute."

"Thank you, Miriam."

She blinked. Kuan-Lin had approached without a sound. Ren barely noticed, busy tipping the links back and forth so they caught the light. Behind them, Sam loitered near a display of ceramics, cracked, but beautifully repaired by a bright metal. She wasn't reading the placard; her eyes had gone unfocused. Whatever she and Kuan-Lin had said clearly left her steeped in thought.

"Everything okay?" Miriam asked, straightening.

"It will be."

"She's trying."

"I see." Kuan-Lin fixed on her son. After a quiet beat, her eyes returned to Miriam. "And how are you?"

The question took Miriam aback—she'd been asked several times by her friends and teammates, but this caught her harder than she expected. She said nothing, rubbing her tender knuckles. She meant to deflect, to answer with the perfunctory *fine* that would have ended the moment, but the word stuck.

"Adjusting," she admitted at last, though the response felt inadequate. She rubbed the end of her cast with her thumb.

After seeing Butcher? After each monotonous day where she felt like more of a stranger with Emma than she'd ever been? And now she was in a museum of human history, tucked in a fold of Station City. She was standing between lives she didn't know how to live. But that wasn't anything she felt like broaching right then and there.

Her attention moved toward Sam before settling back on Kuan-Lin. "I'm afraid she doesn't have what she needs here. The environment—the stim use, it's too rampant. She has too many reminders."

"And other reminders?"

The Royal's tone was deceptively light, but Miriam caught the substance beneath it. She frowned.

"It's interesting you say that."

Miriam glanced at her, waiting, but Kuan-Lin didn't elaborate. The Royal stroked Ren's head, her expression softened, though something guarded remained in the set of her shoulders.

Ren lifted the chain.

His mother smiled. "Go show your Auntie Sam."

He hesitated, but when Miriam gave him a subtle flick of her chin, he ran off, his feet whispering over the old tile. Ahead, Sam's attention was pulled from whatever thoughts had clouded her.

Kuan-Lin turned to Miriam. "You're surprised?"

"A bit."

"You were right. She's his family," Kuan-Lin said, quiet but strained. "And with what's coming...he'll need all the love and support we can give him. It's important for Ren to see everything. The good, the bad, the mundane. Of course, as a mother, I need to—I want to protect him. His existence holds a lot of significance, but it's my position not to let that inhibit or shape him. At least not yet."

She straightened, spine tall with the grace of someone

designed and trained to wear power like posture. "I'm not perfect. None of us are. I can't control the world around him, nor can I control what he ultimately decides. But I'll be there for him. Whatever, whenever."

Miriam nodded slowly, absorbing the Royal's conviction.

"For now? He's a child. I want him to have a real childhood. It's a luxury in wartime, but I see the end looming, Miriam. I want him to have that—before the world tells him who to become."

An actual childhood before politics subsumed him. Before Ren became a symbol, a bridge, a pawn. Miriam studied Kuan-Lin's expression, tight at the corners, drawn not by calculation but by the crush of impossible responsibility. The Royal looked conflicted, not because she didn't care, but because she cared too much. Caught between diplomat and mother, she was trying desperately to be both.

"We're going back."

Miriam's head lifted. "To Arshangol."

"Yes."

"Is it safe?"

"Is anywhere safe in this world and age?" Kuan-Lin frowned. "My people are now enraged with the Apostates, especially the Heretics. It's an opening, an opportunity, and we have to use it. I think I'll emancipate Dima. My nephew, Longwei, wants to return as well. His mother's indecisive as ever, trying to keep him sheltered—insulated. But with Longwei's sister, Xiaoling, staying, it might be good for a change of scenery. After that attack, he needs a break."

Her attention drifted. "But it's a balance, as you know. He's experienced trauma and the hate that comes with it. At his age, that pain doesn't fade. It rewires the mind, everything. One wrong push and it hardens."

Miriam had seen it before, how grief and rage bled into ideology. How quickly vengeance, wrapped as protection, spread like rot. The Charonites were examples of that. The

Apostates. UMF. She thought of the kid she'd come across in the North, in the store. She wondered if he'd made it out—if she could have made a difference in his attitude, his beliefs, or if she had made things worse.

"You think Arshangol will be better? Won't *not* being around humans make it worse?"

"Not if he has the right people, the right influences."

"You're one person."

"There are more of my family who have softened toward your city and kind, more than you'd expect. Many plan on returning to Arshangol to work on our future. After these years, we want to rebuild something better."

Miriam looked across the room at Sam, who had knelt to hear Ren say something she couldn't make out. "Does she know?" Miriam asked.

Kuan-Lin dipped her head.

"What did she say when you told her?"

The Royal paused. "She wants Ren to have the chance to be a child. That whatever else I or the world wants to make of him, he should at least have that—an ordinary childhood for as long as possible."

Miriam nodded.

Gold eyes leveled with hers. "I asked her to come with us. To help me protect that for him."

"Oh."

Kuan-Lin's statement landed like a shift in pressure. Miriam hadn't expected it. She thought Sam might be given time, space, some trust, but not like this. Her chest locked with something complex—relief edged in fear, hope, or envy. She couldn't name it.

"But only if she's clean. If she's willing to stay clean. There's no quick solution or fix. She and I are grateful for what your friends have done, for what your partner has helped with, but it'll take work, and she has to fight for it."

"She's strong," Miriam whispered. The ache in her throat

grew. "But what about the enemies she's made? What if your people turn on you again?"

"They might. We face the consequences of our actions, and so do they," Kuan-Lin admitted. "Where do we come together? Compromise? And can we? Perhaps we have to make that first step, temper our pride, and work to earn their trust." She sighed. "Some of my family and peers believe we can return to how things were."

"And you don't."

"No." Kuan-Lin's voice was low. "Power insists it's keeping the peace, even when it's the one setting fires." She glanced at Miriam. "And the people are fickle, but they want a voice. Representation. Some of us have ideas to make that happen."

"Progressive," Miriam murmured, not unkindly.

Kuan-Lin gave a dry laugh. "What's the point of continuing things as they are? We must break the cycle, no?"

"And their views on us?"

"It'll take work," she said, her eyes settling on Ren.

Miriam followed her line of sight. Sam's hands rested on her knees, listening intently to whatever Ren was saying. The boy had already begun to incline toward her.

"But nothing worth doing is ever easy," Kuan-Lin added.

The Royal was too forward-thinking, too progressive for her own family and people. Change would demand strategy and sacrifice, the right people in the right places to redraw what had once been etched in stone.

As they looped back toward the entrance, Sam and Ren rejoined them at their own unhurried pace. The exit waited ahead, framed by aging posters and a plaque with faded lettering. The legionnaire stood squared where she'd last stationed herself beside the door.

Just before stepping outside, Kuan-Lin extended an invitation to visit her apartment, her voice gentle and genuine.

Sam gave a small nod, uncertain but eager. Her fingers grazed her prosthetic as though grounding herself. "I'm not sure why Scott was so excited about this place," she said. "But it's very...him, I guess."

"It has its charm," Kuan-Lin replied.

Sam scoffed, but the sound dissolved into a faint chuckle.

Kuan-Lin paused. "Sam?"

Sam's brows raised in silent question.

"Thank you." The Royal smiled. "I'm glad we did this. Perhaps next time—"

"Something more thrilling for a toddler, I know."

"Well, no." Kuan-Lin placed her hand on Ren's head. She shrugged. "But sure."

Sam managed a lopsided smile.

"Ren," Kuan-Lin prompted. "Say your see-you-laters to your Auntie Sam and Auntie Miriam."

Ren slipped his fingers to the chain around his neck and tilted his head up, eyes squinting with feigned shyness. "Bye, Auntie Mim-mim," he said, tongue poking at the corner of his mouth. Then he turned to Sam. "Bye, Auntie Sammy."

He giggled, full cheeks lifting, before bolting into the legionnaire's shins. The Altered soldier hardly reacted, stone-faced as ever, but her chin tipped a fraction, a subtle acknowledgment. Ren raised his arms, wordless in his request. At Kuan-Lin's nod, the soldier lifted him easily with one hand.

"Oh, now your legs are tired," Kuan-Lin said with a laugh.

Miriam lifted her hand in farewell, watching them go, warmth unfolding through her. The boy was deeply, impossibly loved. Or maybe just stubborn enough to bend the world into loving him.

"Cheeky kid. A sunbeam," Miriam murmured. She turned to Sam, voice light. "A joy magnet."

But Sam didn't answer. She hadn't moved. Her eyes followed the boy's figure down the street, the curve of her shoulders too still.

"Sam?"

Sam's breath shuddered. She turned at the sound of

Miriam's voice, slow, as though surfacing from somewhere far deeper than the museum floor. Her eyelids lowered, then lifted again, heavy with the effort. A soft radiance bled through—bright blue—as her gaze met Miriam's. Sam gave a small shake of her head, but her mouth fought against itself, trembling, tightening, then creasing into a fragile smile.

43

———————

RENUNCIATION

THEY HAD LEFT the museum in silence, the conversations and words echoing in both Miriam's and Sam's heads. When they separated at the intersection toward their different sectors, Miriam glanced back at the silhouette of Sam in the wash of the sunset, rooted where she stood. For an instant, the woman looked lighter, as though some invisible burden had been pried off her shoulders.

Sam had Ren. She had a home again. A center of gravity and purpose. Miriam didn't know what she had. Guilt. And a decision she didn't yet know how to make.

Twilight stretched across the street by the time Miriam reached her neighborhood. Shadows leaned long against the buildings, the air smelling of dust and warm, baked pavement. She shoved a hand deep into her pocket. The ache in her knuckles and the memory of Butcher had eased, but something else hadn't. Sam's smile, the way her eyes lit up when Ren said her name—those lingered like fingerprints pressed to the inside of her chest.

She didn't know why it had hit her the way it did. The softness in Sam's face when the boy clutched the chain. The way Kuan-Lin, protective to her core, still allowed the moment.

It was stability offered in place of ruin. A flicker of something that wasn't regret.

When she turned down the block, she had the message half-drafted. A poor apology, a vague excuse and explanation. Takeout from one of Emma's favorite restaurants was the best she could manage. A peace token. She didn't want to go back to the apartment, but she did.

Emma was there when Miriam opened the door, the food containers sweating in her hand. The air was warm with the scent of soy and citrus, sesame and heat. Something simmered on the stove, but the smell didn't hide the tension wound through Emma's posture. She stood at the counter, back to Miriam, shoulders taut, motioning with more force than needed.

"You got my message?" Miriam asked, setting the containers down.

Emma nodded but didn't turn.

"Sorry," Miriam said. "The day just got ahead of me."

"I figured."

Miriam wrapped an arm around Emma's waist and brushed a kiss against her cheek. Emma pressed into it, but her body was stiff. She stepped away too quickly.

"How was your day?" Miriam tried.

"It was fine. Busy."

Miriam lowered her arm. "I didn't know you were cooking tonight. I brought back noodles from Sugita's."

Emma gave a short sigh, stirring the pot with restless movements.

Miriam reached out and stilled her hand. "Em, what's the matter?"

Emma set the spoon down. She backed against the opposite counter and drew a slow breath.

Miriam's throat constricted.

"You have something good right now. With me."

"I know," Miriam said quickly. Her voice cracked, but she

forced the words through.

For a second, she wanted to believe that was the end of it. But that would be a lie. Miriam knew what was coming. She just hadn't wanted to admit it.

Emma's eyes searched hers. "Do you love her?"

The question landed like a blow. Miriam's chest tightened. Guilt bloomed, and her lips parted—but Emma raised a hand.

"I know you love me. I'm asking if you love *her*." Emma's voice strained at the end. "Or do you just feel guilty about what happened before?"

Miriam closed her mouth. There was no clean answer. Not anymore.

"She has a hold on you—"

"I—"

Emma closed her eyes and sighed. "You hurt her, I know. But you don't owe her anything more."

Miriam swallowed hard. She knew that. It wasn't about debt or owing anymore.

"I feel like we—I feel like..." Emma's voice shook. "I don't want to be where we are now. I'm not going to be your backup plan, Miriam."

"You're not." Miriam shook her head. "I love *you*."

"I know. I love you, too." Emma reached for her hand. "But I think you love her, too. And I'm not blaming you for that, I've known—you've mentioned her before." She looked up at the ceiling, eyes glistening. "I thought I'd be okay. I thought you finally found some closure. I told myself I could wait while you worked it out—"

"Em—"

"But I don't know, Miriam. This could be—hell, I can't believe I'm actually saying this—but this could be the right time. I'm taking the job up north. This might be a bandage I just need to rip off." Her hands twisted together restlessly. "I don't know if I can be your second choice."

Miriam shook her head fiercely. "What are you talking about? I'm choosing you. I chose *you.*"

Emma stepped back. "It's breaking you, and it hurts. And *I* don't want to hurt you, I don't want to be what holds you together just enough to keep you from falling apart. That's not...love, not really. It's like we're just surviving, but it's actually killing both of us."

Miriam clamped her palms against her eyes, and her voice cracked. "Please stop."

"If we stay together, you'll resent me."

"I won't."

Emma's look shouted her disagreement.

"I wouldn't," Miriam whispered again. "She's not staying here." She heard herself blurt it, even as something inside shrank. The thought stung, hard and sudden.

Emma exhaled painfully. "I don't want to feel like I held you back."

"Em, this is so stupid."

"It's not. Listen to me."

"I *am* listening. This is stupid." Miriam's hands dropped. She already knew—she'd lose, no matter what.

"If you stay with me—"

"I *am* staying with you—"

"Part of you will always wonder. I don't want to be your safe bet, Miriam. I want to be your first choice. And I know you'll smother it, try to prove something, but then here I am, and I'll always wonder if I held you back, if I really *am* your first choice." Emma's voice gave way to a whisper. "That's no way to live. For either of us."

"I—"

"Don't. I know what you're going to say. You can't promise me that."

Miriam took a deep breath, but it burned. "I don't want to lose you."

Emma steadied herself, face tightening back into resolve. "I want someone to look at me the way you look at her. I know, I know you love me. But I want you to look at me the same way."

"I do."

Emma gave her a long look, quiet and devastating.

Miriam shook her head. "I would never—"

"I know you wouldn't. And I trust you, I do. But I also know you're not over her, and you won't be until you find closure. And to do that, I have to let you go." Emma took a shaky breath then let it out slowly. "But I know what I deserve. I want you, but I know what I deserve."

"I want you, Em," Miriam whispered. She stepped forward again, her hands reaching desperately. But as she moved, the words, the motions didn't feel right.

"I think it's better if we just have a clean break."

"Em—"

Emma stepped close and embraced her. "I love you. I'm letting you go," she whispered, the words vibrating against Miriam's shoulder. Her breath hitched, damp and uneven, and Miriam clutched her back in return, desperate, greedy for the warmth she knew she was about to lose.

They stayed locked together, neither moving, the silence filled with the sound of the simmering pot and Emma's heartbeat thudding against her breast. Miriam buried her face into the curve of Emma's neck, inhaling the familiar scent of citrus as if she could brand it into memory. The longer they stood, the more it felt like grief disguised as comfort, a tether fraying strand by strand.

When Emma tugged away, the separation was slow and reluctant, her fingers tracing along Miriam's arm as though memorizing its shape. She wiped at her eyes with the heel of her hand, then reached back, cupping Miriam's cheek with a gentleness that burned. "We'll be okay," she affirmed, though the tremor in her hand betrayed her. A hollow smile bent her lips. "I'll let myself cry over you for a day." Her voice cracked, but she forced a laugh through it. "Maybe two days."

"Oh. Okay." Miriam sniffled and tried to smile back, but it was empty. She laughed once, but it broke halfway.

"Three days. Tops." Emma slipped her hand into Miriam's. Her fingers trembled. "I want you to be happy. I hope we can both be happy."

She turned back to the pot, though she didn't reach for the utensil. She stared into the bubbling surface, eyes wet and shoulders set.

Miriam stood, staring at Emma's back, at the curl of steam rising from the stove, at the takeout cooling on the counter. All insignificant now. She wanted to hold on. She didn't want to let go. Emma was safety. Emma was the first light after she'd fallen, and fallen hard. They had something good.

She didn't want to let go.

But Emma already had.

44

PRIVATE MESSAGE
[UNKNOWN DEVICE TO M. TANNER]

DEVICE-02: Thanks for coming with me. It means a lot.

DEVICE-02: Yuri's mom invited me to their dinner. Are you coming to this?

DEVICE-02: Hey.

DEVICE-02: Is everything okay?

45

———————

SUBTERFUGE

DAYS HAD PASSED since Emma left. The apartment felt quieter now—not only in sound but also in presence. The air itself had lost its shape. Her girlfriend's—*her ex-girlfriend's*—belongings were gone. Empty pockets where shoes had been at the door, abandoned half-folded laundry by the bed, the lack of datapads charging on the counter. What was left behind only made it worse. The ghost of her scent on the blanket. A sketch and silly note still crooked on the fridge. Miriam hadn't touched it.

She'd thrown herself into motion instead, reorganizing the closet, rereading the files and results Yuri had sent from Station General, scrubbing old UMF layouts and annex maps Krill had provided, and cross-referencing messages for any hint of Axiom or Vertex, any whispers on the network. Every message was kept professional, only about Willem's body or the purpose of the facility they'd infiltrated. She read scrubbed deployment logs and combed through UMF contracts, anything to distract herself from the absence that waited in every corner. She tried to find explanations for the drop in UMF cases at Station General and her own transfer to Meridian.

Sam's embed had pinged her more than a few times in those

days. Each time, Miriam had begun to reply, typed a few words, even full lines before deleting them all. She told herself Sam didn't need the added weight or the drama. But she knew it wasn't only that.

Now she sat at her kitchen counter, forearms pressed to the surface, head bowed, eyes tracking the flashing cursor of a blank comms window. Above it stacked Sam's unanswered check-ins. She closed every window and leaned back in her chair.

Her gaze swept the apartment again. It was hers, but it no longer felt that way. It was like something had been plucked from her. She noticed how empty the rooms looked without Emma's things, and yet somehow it wasn't enough space. Sam might be gone soon, too, and Miriam's own admin leave was nearly over. Her injuries had healed, skin closed with fresh scars, and her pain and medications tapered. There was no valid excuse left to stay sidelined—not physically, at least.

Soon, she'd return to UMF, to SOG, and to Echo, where Command would probably squeeze another mission or two out of her before her contract officially ended. Not that she'd sent her confirmation yet. There was still the chance of transferring to Ursus. She could follow Emma, try to prove the breakup hadn't been final, prove she could fight for them.

But that meant staying with UMF, and even if she left SOG and transferred elsewhere, she still had the chance to be in the field. Still subject to wherever Command wanted her to go, the same hands pulling the strings.

She exhaled shallowly.

Emma's voice returned, quiet and merciless in her memory. *I don't want to be what holds you together just enough to keep you from falling apart.* The words ironically circled like a rope pulled tight. Miriam winced at the thought that followed, automatic and reflexive.

Sam.

Do you love her?

Miriam shook her head, though no one was there to see it. Denial from guilt, not certainty. She tried to redirect her mind, tried to refocus on the mystery she'd spent hours and days on, but instead, her thoughts turned to that same day at the museum. Ren's toothy grin. And then Kuan-Lin.

Power insists it's keeping the peace, even when it's the one setting fires.

The words echoed.

Kuan-Lin.

Emma.

Two different women. Two different truths.

But maybe they were the same, too.

She closed her eyes and lowered her head against her handheld, its surface cool against her skin. The device was filled with all the files, reports, and fragments that refused to align. UMF, Station General, Meridian, Apostates, Heretics, Charonites, City Center, Royals, it was too much. There were too many threads, too many names. Maybe nothing connected, maybe it was all coincidence.

Or maybe that was the point. A manufactured clusterfuck. Maybe there *was* a through line. Maybe that was what whoever was orchestrating this, whoever was behind the facility, the mission—Vertex, UMF, others—wanted. Just enough confusion and calm to stop anyone from looking too closely, pulling at the real truth.

She retraced her thoughts, a mixture of before and after. The Heretics had captured and killed UMF marines. The same unit sent to evacuate Vertex scientists from their hidden facility in the North—the same facility Echo and Charlie had been ordered to secure or destroy. The Heretics had arrived, havoc following in their wake. And afterward, it was northern Charonites who had pulled her and Sam from the wreckage, returned them to UMF, where they were split up, her to Meridian and Sam to the Vertex annex.

She thought of UMF's aid to the Charonites. Of their

waning presence and interaction with Station General, the same medical center she had walked through too often in the past months. First after the attack on Kuan-Lin's nephew, then again with the praetorian. Both times, the same compound. DMSO. A chemical that Charonites should not have had access to. And she remembered the Charonite advisor who spoke so easily with Kai.

Once, Kai would've despised men like him, tried to challenge every argument with compassionate conviction and hopeful idealism. Now she met them in quiet halls, speaking their language with a diplomat's patience. Pragmatism, maybe. Or something colder. Miriam couldn't tell.

Her jaw tightened as she thought of her former teammates. She'd leaned on Yuri like old times, and he'd given her what he could. Krill, too. And Nas, through the others. Fox was less connected and integrated, but still supportive.

That left Kai. The one who had changed most, though arguably not by choice. Sometimes Miriam wondered if the bright and kind woman she'd known had died in that northern trap and blast. She shook the thought and the phantom pain in her abdomen away. It was cruel and unfair. Kai was alive, and though Miriam thought her coolness unsettling, it was probably the aftermath of her injury.

She opened a private channel. No answer. Maybe Kai was buried in City Center work. Maybe it was the surgeries, the recovery, the shift Miriam couldn't quite name. Still, there had to be a common line in all of this clutter. Something Kai, from her position, could see.

Miriam reminded herself that not everything connected. Not every coincidence and overlap meant conspiracy. She knew that. But when they bunched together like this…it was difficult not to imagine a larger hand pulling the strings.

Miriam pushed back from the counter and stood. If Kai wouldn't answer her messages, she'd go to City Center herself.

Miriam sent another message on the private channel. Like before, there was no reply, but that was fine. She was already en route. She took a people-mover, choosing one of the early lines before the full crush of morning commuters. She didn't want to be reminded that the city hadn't paused, that life kept moving, indifferent.

At her stop, the government blocks rose in bland planes of concrete and glass, engineered for function over grace. All straight lines and clean facades representing security and stability. She'd never visited Kai's office, never had a reason to stand inside the administrative core of Station City. As she climbed the steps, aides and clerks streamed past, each sealed inside the orbit of their own work. This wasn't Miriam's world, but she needed the person who did live in it.

She checked her handheld again. Still nothing.

Miriam bypassed the front counters and skimmed the directory panel by the back of the atrium, closer to the middle courtyard. There were no names except the most public ones, but she found the Office of Integration on the third floor, memorized the office number, ignored the sprawl of the spiral staircase, and stepped into one of the lifts with several others. She caught a black cap pulled low in the corner, but on second glance it was only dark hair under a hood. She scoffed at herself, thinking momentarily back to the Charonite council member talking with Kai. Projection and paranoia.

Upstairs, the halls were narrow and dim. The ceilings loomed low, and the windows were stingy with light. The corridor smelled of old carpet and ozone from overworked servers. It felt like UMF's older buildings, only flatter, airless. She passed individuals in pristine suits, people who, judging from their posture and breathless pace, had not lived in the outside world in years. How could they set policies for a world they barely walked?

She deposited her handheld into a small wall of lockers and waited at a booth until someone she never saw buzzed her through. Inside, the receptionist didn't look up. "You here for the Honorable Patterson?"

"Er, no," Miriam said. "Is Kai—is Ms. Wester in?"

"Do you have an appointment?" the woman said, engrossed in her own terminal.

"No, but I'm an old friend."

The receptionist barely stifled a sigh. "She's in a meeting."

"I can wait."

A finger flipped toward a sparse row of chairs.

Miriam sat. The broadcast feed on the wall ran silent, a familiar anchor mouthing outrage on a main city channel. Even without sound, the posture carried enough venom to tighten her back. She watched, waiting to see if there was any news about Butcher, the Heretics, or the North, but the flavor of the hour was two anchors arguing about crime in the city—either Charonite- or Altered-based.

A door opened down the hall. Kai's voice came out first. "I just don't understand why these contracts were awarded in the first place."

An older man followed, hair tinted the wrong shade of youth. "It's contingency planning, Ms. Wester. You're former UMF. You of all people know preparations are necessary. Especially after what happened with Mr. Patterson's son."

"Yes, but this predates that incident—"

"How long have you been in this role?"

"Two years this—"

"Infancy." He gave a short, condescending chuff. "Your parents may have gotten you a seat in the chair—"

"I worked my—"

The man tutted. "But you're a junior. This is how it is. You'll come to understand how things run when you've gained more experience." He turned away.

Only when his back vanished did Kai's polite mask slip. Then her eyes found Miriam. "Tanner?"

"Tan," Miriam reminded her as she rose to greet her former teammate. "Who was that?"

She caught herself before the next question—if he was another Charonite shill—and let it die. After everything, she couldn't scrub the image of the Charonite councilman-turned-advisor looming over Kai at Station General, but this wasn't how she wanted to start. Instead, she gestured toward the hall. "What an asshole."

Kai let out a chuff, almost a laugh, but she only glanced toward the receptionist, who still hadn't looked up. She motioned Miriam along, and they stepped into a small office tucked around the corner. The walls were bare, the shelves nearly empty. Not a sign of someone who had just moved in, but someone who had never unpacked.

Kai closed the door but didn't sit. Instead, she hoisted herself onto the rim of the desk, fingers loosely on the surface. "That man has never done anything outside these halls. Twenty years in City Center, and this is the only world he knows. I only had a couple years in SOG after high university, but the audacity…"

"A couple years of what we went through was enough," Miriam said, still standing. The only other chair in the room was piled with a wrinkled jacket and a clutter of devices.

"I thought I'd serve out my contract with UMF, transfer here afterward. It was all mapped out." Kai's voice caught. "I didn't finish the contract. This wasn't my plan."

"Of course not."

The former engineer hadn't asked to be blown up, to have most of her skull reconstructed.

Kai nodded once, the smallest gesture, and looked up again. Shadows deepened under her eyes. "You think I've changed. Since then."

"Brain surgery or not, we all have."

"And somehow not at all," Kai murmured, arms crossing. "I'm glad you're here, though. I don't get many friendly faces here. You *are* friendly?"

Their last conversation had been in Station General's corridors before a Charonite advisor stood too close.

"I shouldn't have lashed out at you," Miriam said.

It wasn't that her views had softened on the Charonites; it was actually the opposite. But after being in the North, fighting against the Apostates, the Heretics, there was a vast trench of nuance between the Charonites there and in the city. Up north, it was a daily struggle, a constant immersion where that was the entirety of life. Ruin, violence, and fear. In the city, she couldn't find any excuses for the group.

"It's been a lot."

"I heard." Kai's eyes dipped to Miriam's neck, to the fresh scar there. She stood, and for a second Miriam thought she saw a glimpse of her warm, bubbly teammate. That she'd reach out, pull her into an embrace. But Kai cleared the chair instead.

Miriam inhaled and lifted a hand. "Don't. I won't be long."

Kai straightened and watched Miriam as if she were trying to gauge the slight shift. "I'm sorry. For what happened to you. And Valkyrie. Is that what this is about?"

"Did the others tell you about her labs? Her abduction? *My* transfer to Meridian?"

"They did."

"I've been going over what I can," Miriam said, fingers twitching for a handheld she'd locked away. "But I don't know what I'm looking at anymore. I was hoping you might have some other insight."

"What exactly are you looking for?"

For all of it to make sense. She couldn't talk freely about the Axiom facility they'd come across in the North; UMF and SOG operational security had its procedures, but Kai was also former SOG, a former teammate. She'd indicated she knew about Sam's stay in the Vertex annex, and Miriam didn't know how much information Krill and Fox had passed along already. She took a breath. She'd start with something that she'd received *no* answers to, something that she was still unsure of with her hazy memory.

"Will—" She corrected herself. "An SRAF operator's body went missing. A former legionnaire." She hesitated. "Beyond that, I don't know. I'm looking for something to make sense. That's the problem. Everything feels too messy, but the more I try to wrap my head around it, the more it feels like it's all the same thing."

Kai frowned but didn't interrupt.

"It's been in the news. We know the Heretics executed UMF marines who'd been left behind in the North."

"Yes," Kai said. "After they were sent to escort Vertex staff in the North."

So Kai knew more than she'd expected.

Miriam drew in a breath. "Yes. The same Vertex staff from a facility that had the same logo you and I saw in that…that underground facility years ago. Axiom."

Kai's expression tightened.

"UMF sent us to retrieve something from that same site—or destroy it, I don't know. It all went to shit, but Kai, we were exposed to something. A friendly Altered died. Sam—Valk—she almost died. And when we were rescued by Charonites, she and that Altered just disappeared."

Now that she'd verbalized it, the Charonites coming to her and Sam's aid was fortunate. She was grateful, of course; they had stopped her execution, but standing in someone else's office and not in her own space and head, she saw how odd it was. How *convenient*.

Her thoughts spiraled. And what about Echo, Charlie, and Legion's position *at* the lab? Where had the Heretics come from? What had the Charonites shot at? She had maybe chalked it up to the inexperienced youth at the time, but were there truly visuals on the attackers, or had they created noise to draw them in? The chaos and mess bore down on Miriam. She inhaled then exhaled. Verbalizing it had helped clarify things, but it'd also hurt her head with more questions.

She looked up when Kai cleared her throat.

"The Royals have been complaining about Altered disappearing in the city as well."

Miriam narrowed her eyes. She'd witnessed two attacks, but she hadn't been fully aware of what else was happening. Neither woman said anything for a few seconds.

"I don't know what's going on. Someone's pulling the strings," Miriam muttered. "And it just feels like no one is trying, questioning, or looking."

"You think this is all orchestrated," Kai said.

"If it isn't, then it's a series of coincidences so fucking convenient, it might as well be."

Kai exhaled through her nose.

"You're here. You have a different view; you see more than any of us." Miriam studied the woman's even expression. "None of this is a surprise to you."

"Some of it." Kai flexed her fingers and hesitated. "But not all. The contracts between UMF and Vertex. City Center has something similar—parallel instruments, contingency policies, and shadow clauses that were implemented before my tenure. I started looking into them, but the more I dig... I don't—I don't trust many of my colleagues. There're too many ears, too many mouths in the wrong places."

"Is this all Vertex?"

"I'm not certain. Nas is helping where he can, but this sits above his level." Kai's mouth flattened. "And I can't endanger him or risk flagging it from here. I'm one person."

"You have us."

Kai shook her head. "This is an entirely different beast. There are too many players, too many agendas."

"So what? We wait for the next 'coincidence' and pretend it's not connected?"

"I really don't know." Kai shut her eyes for a moment. "I do miss us. Echo. UMF, even. As terrible as it sounds, things were easier there, I think. At least there, the problem shot at you and you were allowed to shoot back. Here, the rules are different. I don't get that…luxury."

Miriam pressed her back into the cool wall. "So what does this mean?"

"It means we keep going. We keep trying to find a connection. A solution."

"But to what?" Miriam asked.

Kai didn't respond.

Restless irritation grew in Miriam's muscles. That wasn't enough. She'd come here for answers, and she'd only gathered more questions. They stood in the hush of the small office.

"I'm glad you stopped by, Tanner, but I have another meeting soon," Kai said at last, pushing off her desk again. She stepped closer as if to touch Miriam's arm, then opened the door beside her instead.

A low sound lifted in the air. Something familiar and faint, but there. Miriam stilled, her neck muscles straining. When neither Kai nor the receptionist reacted, she let it go. Probably nothing. Maybe nerves or imagination.

But then it came again. A susurration that rose from the building's bones. This time, Kai paused, attention narrowing, her body language sharpening without a word. Miriam's skin prickled. The air shifted like a breath before a breach, a sound before the inevitable zip.

She didn't hear the explosion. She felt it, a soft invisible force folding the atmosphere inward, pushing through bone and skin like a slight change in gravity. The room stuttered, a heartbeat suspended in the grip of silence. Then came the shuffle—chairs scraping from within offices, bodies rising, voices murmuring, eyes tilting toward the scant windows and doors. Instincts atrophied by routine and disbelief. Curiosity over protocol. Stay away from the windows and doors. They all knew that, and they all forgot it the moment something real cracked through the veil.

"That was—" someone began.

An Altered airgun.

Not an accident.

Another attack in Station City. At City Center? It didn't make sense, but it didn't need to. Not yet.

Miriam's body had already moved, muscle memory overriding thought. "Get back! Get down!" Her voice whipped out, slicing through the confusion with command. The room froze mid-motion.

"Tan!" Kai snapped.

Miriam's hand reached instinctively for weapons she didn't carry. The arm cast checked her movement, reminding her of its limits as adrenaline pulled her. No rifle, no sidearm. Just the echo of experience and training thrumming in her bones.

Footsteps pounded past the main doors.

Miriam tried to keep her breath even. City Center had its own SecGuard division. If they were worth anything, they were already reacting.

Kai stepped toward the door, a glint of old reflexes, an old persona surfacing. Miriam slotted in behind her.

"SecStation?" she whispered.

"Basement," Kai breathed. "What about these people?"

"Not until we know what we're dealing with."

Sheltering in place was protocol, the smart and sensible option. But neither of them had ever been good at waiting behind closed doors or standing to the side. It wasn't the SOG way.

Miriam turned to the receptionist peeking out from beneath her desk. "Do not open this."

The woman's lips cracked open, but Miriam didn't wait for a response. Kai had already cracked the door and slipped through. Miriam followed without hesitation.

Outside, a silhouette crossed fast and disappeared around

the far corner. A second shape lagged a pace behind. A glint and outline of a weapon caught the light at its hip, its grooved cylinder and grip somehow familiar but not. Miriam blinked, and the corridor was empty again.

She and Kai moved low and fast, eyes sweeping.

Then they saw it.

The far end of the hallway was gutted. Ruin stretched where polished decor had stood; splintered paneling now lay scattered across the floor in chaotic fragments. A ragged hole had been punched through the wall, scorch marks spidering outward in sooty arcs. Smoke drifted from molten seams. Gnarled metal rebar jutted like broken ribs from the opening, and the acrid sting of wiring clung to the air.

Footsteps rang down the hall. A SecGuard sergeant slid into the alcove across from them, sidearm out. "Shelter! Get back inside—" She stalled. "Ms. Wester?"

"Luna," Kai hissed. "How many? Who?"

"I—I don't know! Maybe two! I only saw their backs. Dark hair? Hats? I didn't see anyone else!" She pointed toward the ruin. "Where did they go?"

Miriam shook her head. They'd heard the whine, felt the pressure, seen the damage, but there was no sign of the attackers, no visible path, no sign of where the strike had come from.

Another concussion rumbled through the building, followed by another. Multiple floors. Coordinated and fast. How many attackers were there?

Miriam glanced at the SecGuard's sidearm.

Then a louder boom rippled—more a vibration and zip that rolled past like a wave. The windows along the corridor quivered. Somewhere nearby, crumbled plaster cascaded from the ceiling. The clatter of debris came from outside.

"That was in the courtyard," the sergeant breathed.

"Shit," Miriam muttered. "Did you call for reinforcements?"

"Someone must have called it in," she replied.

"Luna," Miriam said, level and controlled, *"you* call it in. Now."

She gulped. "Yes, ma'am." The SecGuard fumbled with her transponder and tried to raise the SecStation, but nothing came back.

Miriam stepped to the side and scanned the openness of the hallway. There were too many doors and angles. Kai did the same, eyes narrowing as she swept their lines of sight across the remains of the outer corridor, checking for attackers.

A voice bled through the sergeant's comm, garbled and thin. And then gunfire broke outside in the courtyard. A short burst of automatic fire. Then nothing.

Kai moved for the atrium stairs, but Miriam caught her arm. It was too exposed.

"Service stairs?" she whispered.

Kai paused then nodded toward the end of the hall. They strode in that direction, the SecGuard trailing close, speaking clipped commands into dead air.

At the corner, Kai cleared and pushed into the stairwell where concrete threw their steps back at them. On the base landing, she stopped short.

Miriam braced herself behind the woman. "What—?"

Kai pointed. Miriam followed her line—and felt the bottom drop out of her stomach.

Beneath the main atrium staircase, tucked where casual traffic would never look, sat a device. From the service side, its edge was visible. A fist-sized core was lashed to a pack of gravnades and something else. Enough firepower to crater the entire atrium if someone wandered close. They could pass it and save themselves. But someone else might not. They couldn't just leave it. Not now, not after seeing it. They owned the responsibility now.

Kai stepped forward, and Miriam lifted a hand out of reflex.

"You don't have the tools," she breathed.

Nor the practice. Not for years. When was the last time Kai

had touched live ordnance or refreshed on explosives training? Kai was bright and intelligent before she'd gone through reconstructive surgery, and she was still bright and intelligent, but Miriam didn't want to rely on memory held together by scar tissue and medical-grade alloy. But what other choice did they have? There was no one else.

"Knife?" Kai said to the SecGuard.

The sergeant's hand trembled as she fished a compact blade out of her belt and passed it forward. Miriam took it before pressing it into Kai's palm. She looked back at the sergeant, pale with her firearm lowered. Without asking, Miriam reached over and turned off her comms device. She shook her head. The SecGuard nodded and held position.

Miriam fought her instincts and moved forward. "Legion?" she asked as Kai settled and examined the bundle.

"No. Not only. There are disc grenades in here." Kai's voice dropped, all tension folded into cold precision now. She leveled the knife, eyes tracking wire.

Now that she mentioned it, Miriam could see the shape of the pucks. UMF standard? An older model that had been out of the rotation for ages. Possible surplus and repurposed?

"You might want to step back," Kai murmured.

Miriam eyed the charge again. There were too many gravnades, the same kind that she'd seen the legionnaires and Altered use. The kill radius would wrap the whole area. She would need angles upon angles of wall and concrete to escape the blast. And she wasn't leaving her teammate behind.

Kai leaned in. She cut carefully and pulled back a flap of tape. A tangle of leads bared its tendons.

"Crude," Kai muttered.

Miriam's throat worked. "Can you—"

"I think so."

Footsteps echoed above. Behind them, the SecGuard pivoted, weapon raised. Two figures bent over the mid-landing rail then ducked away. For a split second, Miriam thought the sergeant would fire.

"Stay there! Do *not* come down!" Miriam called out before she ducked back under the stairs where Kai crouched under the device, body contorted, eyes narrowed, tongue to one corner of her mouth. She inhaled slowly, and Miriam mirrored it without thinking.

Kai's fingers hovered, then slipped the blade through the mass, easing between filaments.

And then a metallic snap. A slight hiss bleeding off. Followed by silence.

Miriam did not breathe until Kai did. Kai rested back on her heels and hands, collected herself, then slid free of the stairwell's throat.

"Is it over?" the SecGuard stammered.

Miriam looked around. There hadn't been more explosions or gunfire since.

"Luna, you should stay here," Kai said. "Don't let anyone come by."

She nodded. "Is it—?"

"I pulled the detonator, but it could still…" Kai let the rest hang.

The sergeant gulped.

"Luna."

"Yes, ma'am."

Kai didn't wait. She pushed past and through the back courtyard doors. Miriam followed.

The space was a broken shadow of its former self, once a serene civic garden, now a scatter of stone and ash. Dirt blanketed the tiled ground, mingled with shards of pale flagstone, broken and tossed like teeth from a busted jaw. The colonnade that had ringed the small square was riven, its columns blackened, walls pocked with bullet holes and spiderwebbed glass. The fountain at the center gurgled weakly, though its basin had split down the middle, leaking water in a slow, relentless trickle. A statue stood in the pool—barely. The right side had been blown off, the head sheared cleanly away. Benches lay splintered and overturned, but it was the object at the fountain's base that drew Miriam back, then forward.

It didn't belong. A dark casing nestled just under the rubble, buzzing, its surface traced with cables that snaked like veins. Scorched along one end, the device looked half-imploded, as if the blast had turned inward, devouring its own source. It looked inert, but she skirted the border of the courtyard, eyes locked on the thing, just as a pair of SecGuards pushed in through the northern breach.

Miriam heard them before they emerged, one with a rifle, the other with a sidearm, weapons raised, fingers already on their triggers. She raised both hands immediately. "Friendlies! Blue blue blue!"

Kai moved slower, one palm open, the other gesturing toward herself. "Unarmed," she reassured, her voice curt but calm. "City Center official. Kai-Ming Wester."

The nearest SecGuard hesitated, and his eyes flitted around the courtyard space. His weapon lowered, and he nervously ran a free hand through his hair. "Fuuuuck," he said.

The other followed suit, his own sidearm dropping. "What is that?"

"The fucking idiots!" the SecGuard with the rifle spat. "It blew up in their own faces!"

Miriam cast one last look at both before she breathed out in relief. With the SecGuards now taking in the destruction, she stepped closer to the fountain. Near the rubble's edge, the curve of a black knit cap lay half-buried in the tossed dirt, damp from the spray of the shattered fountain. Her eyes caught on it for a breath, evidence of someone who had been there and gone in haste, before a glint of pale broke through the debris. She stopped cold.

A hand. Gloved in scorched white. Still attached to an arm.

Boots crunched loudly nearby.

"Wait," she whispered. She repeated it louder.

But the SecGuard with the rifle didn't. He moved forward, angling around the rubble until he could see.

A body.

A legionnaire.

They were half-armored, limbs sprawled unnaturally, and one side blackened up to the closed helmet. Had they been caught in the blast? And what the hell was a legionnaire doing here in the middle of City Center? In the middle of an attack?

"Shit! I've got another one here! This one's huge!" the SecGuard shouted.

Another one? More legionnaires?

"What the fuck is going on?" the second SecGuard muttered as he hurried over. He stopped short when he saw the dark casing nestled at the fountain's base. Wariness pulled him back a step.

"Holy shit! Their own bomb cooked them!"

Miriam didn't answer. She couldn't. The world narrowed to the wreckage in front of her. There was something wrong, something off balance in a way she couldn't yet name. She did something against her instincts, as if drawn forward in a magnetic pull despite the unnerving possibility that the device was still engaged.

"Wait," the SecGuard with the rifle called out, reaching to stop her. His hand grazed her shoulder, but she leaned away.

She crouched beside the large body and found the scorched helm clasp. It was Legion-issue; she had disengaged enough of them with Hadeon's crew to recognize the make. The latch opened with a crisp click, and she tugged at it.

A gasp clawed its way out of her. She lurched upright.

After a moment, she turned to find Kai moving closer to the fountain, her eyes on the wired device.

"Is it alive?" the second SecGuard asked.

Miriam ignored and pushed past him. "Kai," she said,

hoarse, trying to make her voice obey. "It's not Legion. Not the Altered."

"They're legionnaires," the second guard said.

Yes, the right armor, the right eye colors, the right build. All yes, and no.

Miriam shook her head.

Voices filtered into the courtyard from the building, distorted by stone and debris. An all-clear was called. And then more orders followed, distant and useless in Miriam's ears.

She ignored it all and turned to Kai, pointing at the body. "That one," she said, breath catching. She looked again to be sure she hadn't lied to herself.

She stared at the skin, what remained of the face. Wrong. All wrong. She couldn't explain any of it, couldn't explain how there was no decay, no further rot than what she would've expected. It was nature, no matter how genetically engineered a being could be. And this, this was unnatural.

"Tan?" Kai's voice was cautious now.

"I know him." Miriam forced the words out. "He was with me." Her voice faltered. "He died. Weeks ago."

46

———————

HOMECOMING

"I DON'T FUCKING KNOW HOW," Miriam said. "I swear, Krill. I watched him die."

Fox's commcuff glowed across the patio bar, throwing pale light into her scowl. On the other end, Krill looked distracted, probably perched outside his windowless Command office. Willem's body had been under plastic and torn fabric for days—however long she and Sam were trapped in that war-torn house.

"Yuri said the labs are analyzing it," Fox told Krill. He wore the usual SOG black tee and gray pants, forearms braced on the counter. "And Valk's on her way back from there." He slid Miriam a look, apology tucked behind concern, as if asking whether she was still in one piece.

She ignored it. After Kai had vanished into post-attack procedures, after her own round of questioning by SecTeam—who she was convinced had missed every relevant clue and useful angle—Miriam had ensured Willem's body was handled properly. She stayed until the Station General transport took him. Her handheld had been left behind, locked inside a City Center box, forgotten.

Yuri had then kicked her out of the medical center the moment the body was transferred, promising her it would be turned over to the right people afterward. He'd frustrated her more by forcing her to wait for Fox, citing something about her lack of comms.

"Decomposition, the smell, none of that?"

"Krill," Fox warned.

They had all been around their fair share of dead bodies. But Miriam *hadn't* thought about the smell. She tried to think back on her time in the North. Had her senses just blunted so far, she stopped noticing? She didn't recall Willem's body putting off any other odor other than the usual bodily fluids and excrement; she had been distracted by other pressing issues. She also hadn't been in the same transport with the body bags. Did Altered, did the legionnaire class *not* break down the same way as humans?

"No, I'm just trying to understand. The network's been spotlighting the Altered attack—"

"It wasn't them," Miriam said.

"I believe you and Kai. But no one, not even Command, is saying what you're saying. It *is* too early for anything concrete—"

"I don't know. It doesn't make sense."

"Greg also said the alty had a brand on his neck—"

"It had to have been done after. I don't know. It isn't his."

"Okay, but he didn't have any other markings than the legionnaire bars. The Seraphs all have tattoos—" Krill began.

"I already told you," Miriam said. "He didn't have any. That's why he was called—"

"Boy Scout."

The voice came from the corner of the house. Sam stepped into view and joined them at the patio bar. Fox drew her into a quick side squeeze, and Miriam met Sam's eyes—the first time since the museum, since before Emma.

Sam didn't hold the look. It slipped away, and Miriam didn't chase it. Fox and Sam traded a few words with Krill; their voices ran together. Miriam watched instead.

With the days' distance, Sam looked different. Not only physically— the healthier weight gain was already noticeable— but also in the way she stood. She hadn't pulled away from Fox's touch. His hand rested loosely around her, casual and protective. Maybe he was holding her there, anchoring her, but it didn't feel forced. Before, Sam would have recoiled or shied away. But Fox wasn't a stranger. Yuri had mentioned that he'd been around, supportive and checking in. That he had stayed close. They were all different now.

"Hold on," Krill said. "Kai's calling. I'll connect her in."

Miriam turned back to the holodisplay as Kai's face flickered into view, the bare walls of her office behind her. "You're still at Center?" Miriam asked.

"There's work to be done," Kai replied.

Miriam might've protested in a previous life, but she didn't now.

"Did anything else come up?" Krill asked.

"It's trickling in, and I'm juggling several things right now. This media coverage—"

"A shitshow," Fox interjected. "The main channel's already spinnin' it as a wunby infiltration. Sayin' they're embedded in Legion, possibly the Royals behind it. Not even twenty-four hours, and shit, full-on conspiracies."

"How does that make sense?" Miriam muttered. "Some of the Royals are already heading back to Arshangol." Her eyes tipped to Sam again, but the woman didn't look up. "Kai, this isn't another coincidence. You have to believe me."

"I do," Kai answered quietly. Her expression remained inscrutable, but the cool certainty in her tone set Miriam on edge. "I think I know who staged it."

"You do?" Fox asked.

"The Charonites," Miriam said.

The black cap she'd seen. Possibly even the Charonite marshal with the revolver, although she couldn't be certain.

But Kai inclined her head as if she had come to that conclusion herself. "Center will have to address the Children of Charon issue one way or another, but this is the least of it right now."

"Charonites?" Krill asked. "So it wasn't the alties?"

Fox grunted. "Tan said it wasn't Legion."

"I wasn't saying it was them," Krill corrected. "I meant the wunbies. You're saying this wasn't another outside attack? UMF's QRF has been geared up and ready for hours."

"That's why I was calling *you*," Kai said. "I've already sent liaisons to confirm the Quick Reaction Force is stood down, but I need you to look into some of the clauses and files I've sent."

"Clauses?" The lines deepened across Krill's forehead. "Okay…"

"Wait, Kai," Miriam said. "What about the other body in the courtyard?" She had seen it from afar, SecTeam already cordoning it off, but it had been in similar legionnaire armor. Scorched and torn apart, worse off than Willem's body, but she hadn't gotten a good look.

Kai exhaled. "It took a while with the remains nearly unidentifiable, but the embassy just confirmed it was one of theirs."

"Fuck," Fox muttered.

"Legion?" Miriam asked.

"No, this is where it gets complicated." Kai took another breath. "An envoy. The embassy said she was an attendant, an aide. But she'd been reported missing for weeks."

"Defected?" Krill asked.

Kai shook her head slowly. "SecTeam and the embassy are battling over custody, so we can't fully confirm. I had to dig my heels in, and I barely got *this* information. But SecTeam reported an Apostate brand on her neck."

"Another mark."

Miriam shot a glare at Krill's displayed face, but it was Sam who hissed out, "Boy Scout wasn't one of them."

He raised his palms.

But Kai only continued, voice clipped. "Yes, and I have to check with Yuri, but I think we all have our doubts. I didn't see it myself, but my source says there's something odd about the scarring. It's too clean."

Miriam stilled. When was a brand mark *clean*? They'd all seen what the branded Apostates looked like, had fought against them more than once to know. A memory sliced through her of Butcher and the others. None of their modified Heretic triangle, circle, and line scars had looked perfect or uniform. No two marks had ever looked the same.

She didn't say it aloud, but the shape of the truth had already formed. Kai had nearly confirmed the attack had been staged. Devices cobbled together from Altered explosives and UMF disc grenades. Bodies in legionnaire armor for the camera and network. A neat package, a narrative prepared for anyone watching.

Fox scratched his head. "Kai, how the hell is this the least of our problems?"

"I'll explain more later," she replied. "I need time to verify and confirm details on my end. Yuri, Nas, and I have been running another line, trying to fast-track autopsies and cross-check results. But we'll need a secure space to discuss after."

"A secure space?" Fox asked. "What details?"

Kai ignored his question. "Not at City Center. Not UMF either. And not anywhere public."

Fox started, Krill broke in at the same moment, and Kai overrode both of them.

"We'll talk more later."

Did Kai think UMF was compromised? She clearly trusted Krill, but Kai was also speaking to Yuri and Nas separately. Compartmentalizing. The questions went unspoken, but it hung as Miriam glanced at Sam, at Fox, then back to the holodisplay. Was it strategy or something else?

"How about here?" Fox offered with a shrug.

No one volunteered a better option.

"Someone tell Yuri." He grunted. "It ain't gonna be me."

It wasn't going to be Miriam either. She didn't have her device, and with the clutter of media probably on-site, she didn't plan on going back to Center to retrieve it. Especially not as the day was already coming to a close. The only people she'd want to communicate with were around her, and as long as she stuck close to one of them, she'd stay in the loop. Being off the network suited her fine. She could imagine what was being broadcast—lies and exaggerations dressed up as breaking news, half-truths served with hysteria.

Kai signed off first, and Krill followed soon after, promising to look over the files and ping if anything shifted. Fox latched his cuff back onto his wrist and looked between Miriam and Sam.

"I'm gonna check on Kai," he said.

Miriam nodded. Whatever leads Kai was chasing down, there was a slight possibility there'd be risk involved—either professionally or personally. Especially if they pointed toward something much larger, if they unraveled the truth behind a frame job or unearthed the wrong evidence. The Charonites or whoever was orchestrating this had more complexity than she'd imagined. This was already something more than smoke and mirrors.

"What about Foxtrot?" she asked.

"My team'll understand," Fox replied. "What's UMF gonna do? Suspend me again? Been there, done that." He shrugged. "You'll be alright here. Valk, holler at me with that head doohickey if you need." He gestured at Sam's embed and headed for the gate. He glanced back once more before rounding the corner, and then he was gone.

Miriam and Sam stood in the quiet that followed, the patio

still underfoot. The air held the day's warmth and the scent of fake grass and city dust. Neither of them turned fully to the other. Sam's gaze skimmed Miriam. Scanning.

"Were you hurt? City Center. Are you okay?" Sam asked.

"The more I think about it," Miriam said, avoiding the question, "I don't think there were any actual attackers."

Sam hummed.

Miriam turned away. She hadn't planned to end up alone with Sam. The guilt had already come creeping in, ambient. Emma wasn't there, and yet her words echoed. She'd been right—Miriam knew it, but she felt awful about it. She should've excused herself, should've said she needed to get back to the empty apartment, but her feet planted, and instead, she asked about Ren, about Kuan-Lin.

Sam nodded once. "They're good."

Short and flat. A statement, not comfort.

"That's good," Miriam said. "And Varya? Your other *friend*? Did their mission go alright?"

"They stopped by again the other day. I'm actually..." Sam paused as her fingers worried the shirt's hem.

Miriam held her breath. Sam was going back to SRAF.

And like she'd read her thoughts, the woman shook her head.

"You're going to Arshangol," Miriam said. The realization came simultaneously as the words spilled out. The Royal had mentioned that she'd offered Sam the option. And Sam had accepted.

Sam nodded again, slower this time.

"Oh," Miriam whispered. "That's...good."

She'd expected it, but that didn't mean it didn't hurt. Arshangol wasn't Ursus, it wasn't the North. It was far, too far.

"When?"

Sam didn't answer. Not directly. Her hand kept moving, a nervous current with nowhere to go. Soon, then.

"Oh," Miriam whispered again. And this time, it stung hard.

"I wanted to tell you. You haven't been—"

"I know." Miriam drew a breath. "I'm sorry. I meant to respond, but I've just been…" She stopped. She hadn't told anyone about what'd happened between her and Emma, not officially. Yuri probably knew from his own recent interactions with Emma, but he hadn't brought it up, hadn't forced it into daylight.

Miriam cleared her throat. "I should probably get back. It's getting late…"

The tension caught again, like cord snagging between them. Sam's shoulders stiffened. Miriam hated that, hated how easily they could fall back into silence and blame and guardedness. Especially now. Especially if this was the last time. She didn't know what she wanted to say—only that it felt wrong to say something, *not* to say something.

"Yuri said you should stay," Sam said quickly. "In the big house, I mean."

Miriam shook her head. She searched around for her things, realized she hadn't brought anything with her, and took a step off the patio. Her cast bumped a chair in passing, the knock sending a muted vibration up her arm. She took another step, as if movement alone would push her past this—past whatever this was.

Sam's expression shifted, but she followed, trailing a few steps behind. "I'll walk you back," she offered.

"No, it's okay. Really."

But Sam continued after her, closing the space. By the gate, she tried again. One word and name. "Emma?"

As if that were a reason and answer for many things.

"Yes," Miriam whispered.

It had been easier, somehow, to keep her distance from Sam after the breakup. Like it was a protest of Emma's statements, a denial of the truth there. Like space might disprove what she hadn't been ready to fully face. That she couldn't keep a relationship, keep a commitment.

"She left," Miriam said.

"North."

Miriam placed her palm on the gate. "Yes. No. We—we're not together anymore." The words landed more gently than she'd expected. No explosion of hurt. No echo.

Behind her, Sam's step faltered, the sound a brief catch on the ground. Followed by stretching silence.

Miriam opened the gate and passed through. Sam came after. It wasn't a matter of first or second choice. Or was it?

"But you two—you're happy," Sam said. "You can get her back."

Miriam stopped at the property line. She rolled her head up, looking into the amber wash of cityglow. "I—"

"Go get her."

Miriam sniffed, then swallowed the ache behind her teeth.

"I didn't—" Sam hesitated. "You're not okay. You deserve to be happy."

A door slammed down the block. An engine turned over.

"I'll be fine," Miriam said at last. "I'll come back tomorrow when the others—I'll come back."

It was meant as reassurance. A compassionate gesture that hurt at the same time. A closing door.

"Mir."

"Stay," Miriam said, her voice quieter. "I'll really be okay." She stepped into the street without looking back. Behind her, shoes scuffed, then stopped. She heard the sound of Yuri's gate open, then close.

Her legs carried her another few paces before she paused. She stood for a few seconds as her mind spun, then stilled itself. The habit of retreat. Was this what she always did? Run, justify, let fear decide? If she kept walking, she could tell herself it was easier than admitting what she still felt. And if she stayed, she might say the wrong thing. Or the right thing. And both would cost her, have her betray the ghost of one person, for the ghost—*no*, not the ghost—the actual person.

She turned, her body obeying something other than instinct and thought. Her stride quickened back to the gate, drawn like a tide pulling toward the moon.

She shoved it open.

And nearly collided with Sam.

Sam—who had only stepped just inside, as if she, too, had done the same exact thing as Miriam—turned back, retraced her steps by the same impulse.

They froze, barely a breath between them, two bodies suspended in impossible gravity. Twin poles of the same magnet, straining against the want, the pull.

Then it snapped. They fell into each other. Sam's arms locked around her, fierce and sure. Miriam answered with equal force—not to crush, but to hold.

To keep.

Anchor.

Stay.

They fit.

Not like they once had. Not clean nor easy. They were warped things now, fractured and re-formed, but the pieces clicked, all the same.

Miriam felt the rise and fall of Sam's chest, the solid press beneath lightweight clothes, the tremor in her own hands. Her eyes burned. Her throat tightened.

Sam buried her face in the curve between Miriam's neck and shoulder. She spoke against skin and fabric, "Did you mean it?"

Barely sound. Almost broken.

"What you said before?"

Miriam turned her face toward Sam's, their breath meeting in the narrow space between them. The scar carved Sam's cheek—flesh pink and crude where *I love you* had been scrawled and stitched into skin. Ugly and beautiful.

"Yes," Miriam whispered.

She didn't know who moved first—maybe they both did. It was a surrender. Mouths finding each other, breath bleeding into breath. Miriam tasted her. The want, the need, the grief and memory. It was desperate. As if this moment was all they were allowed. As if the future might vanish by dusk.

They parted only long enough to breathe. Sam's eyes were dark—too dark. Her hand caught Miriam's, and they stumbled across the narrow stretch of lawn, the small house looming just ahead.

The door had barely slid shut behind them, and Miriam hardly registered the sound before her back struck the wall. Cool surface. Short gasp. Sam's weight leaned into her, hands at her waist, mouth tracing rough and hungry against her throat. They weren't going to make it to the bedroom.

Fingers fumbled, and Miriam's pants came undone. She reached for Sam, but the woman pushed her hand aside, filling the space herself. Sam's palm slid between fabric and skin, and Miriam's head tipped back, another gasp on her lips, her body arching, hips chasing rhythm and friction.

Sam inhaled sharply, a growl low in her chest. She turned Miriam with startling force, and Miriam caught herself on the wall, breath catching in a shiver. Sam pressed against her from behind, her mouth climbing the line of Miriam's spine, kisses wet and urgent at the base of her neck. It was too much and not enough.

Miriam panted, heat flooding, body trembling with sensation. Hands roamed higher, curling beneath Miriam's shirt, cool fingers possessive along her ribs. The others slipped lower, impatient and hunting. She adjusted her stance— offering angle, offering space, access, all of her.

Then—

A cold edge kissed her neck.

Everything inside her shattered.

Her breath caught—no, vanished. Her lungs seized, and she was gone—ripped back through time. Back on the ground.

On her knees.

A blade against—into her throat. Hands, restraints, the

pitch-black undertone of a voice she could no longer bear to remember. And pain, so much pain.

She gasped—but there was no air. Her diaphragm spasmed.

The knife bit again. Her body remembered what her mind begged to forget. Her heartbeat thundered in her ears, dull and wild as the room spun.

Not here. Not now. Please.

She crushed her eyes shut. Hands shaking.

She wasn't on her knees. She wasn't back there. She tried to feel around her. A table. An edge. Cool surface. She was standing. She wasn't there. Her fingers gripped against hard material.

A breath in. A breath out.

Again.

Miriam forced her eyes open, chest heaving, still desperately trying to find itself. The room had changed. Sofa. Armchair. Window. Walls. Yuri's home. Not the North. Not the dead city or the husk of a house.

A breath in.

A breath out.

Again.

Here.

She was safe.

She was safe.

She was safe.

Sam.

Miriam shook as she turned, trying to find her. Sam stood across the room, stricken and motionless. Her body suspended, as if some unseen wall, some partition separated them, held her back. Why was she so far?

Miriam extended a shaky hand. "Sam. Come here." She swallowed thickly. "Please."

"I'll hurt you again," Sam said, voice brittle.

"You didn't—" Miriam's body gave out, knees dipping.

And Sam was there, catching her before she fell. Miriam

clung to the table's line, supported by strong arms. She shaped each inhale slowly through parted lips, trying to count them, lengthen them, hold them—but they caught halfway. Her body trembled.

Sam spewed apologies, endless and frantic, but Miriam could only focus on her eyes. Blue. Wide with panic. The moment Miriam steadied, Sam stepped back. Her stare fell to her prosthetic, her alloy arm, her expression twisted with horror, revulsion creeping into the corners of her face. But Miriam didn't want distance. Not from Sam. Not now.

"No," she said. "Stay."

"I'm so sorry."

Miriam reached for her hand, laced her fingers through its coolness, and held fast. They stayed like that, Miriam hunched over, trying to still the shudder in her limbs, and Sam close and motionless, uncertain.

"I'm okay," Miriam said, quieter, as if saying it made it more true. "I'm okay."

She knew she wasn't.

"Mir, I'm sorry."

"Stop apologizing."

"You're not okay."

She inhaled, slower this time, and met Sam's eyes again. "I know. I'm not."

It was like the nightmares all over again, only more compressed. Worse. Her mind spiraling, her body screaming. But she'd survived those, she'd clawed her way out. She'd learned her lessons, was better, stronger now.

"But I'll be okay."

She meant it.

"I lost you."

"You didn't. It's okay, Sam."

"I hurt you."

Miriam shook her head. "No." She pushed herself upright.

Sam flinched. "If I hadn't—when we were up there... Before

they—when you didn't come back that night, Mir, I—" Her voice broke. "I thought you'd left, I thought you were gone. I was about to go out—"

"You couldn't have. You could barely stand."

"But I—it didn't matter." Sam pulled her hand away and flexed it, staring at the fingers as if they belonged to someone else, to a traumatic memory. "You came back, and I—"

"It's o—" Miriam stopped herself, caught the reflex in her throat, and softened it. She didn't care; it didn't matter to her anymore, but it mattered to Sam. Whatever guilt she was carrying, whatever guilt Miriam was carrying, they were both damaged. "We'll work on it."

"I... Scott... My father..."

The words stalled, and Miriam frowned. She didn't follow, but she turned, reached out, fingers brushing the scar that cut across Sam's cheek, raised and uneven. A memory branded into flesh.

Sam leaned into the touch. "You thought we were going to die," she whispered.

That was true. But it didn't invalidate Miriam's words either. They had been her truth, were *still* her truth.

Sam's head bowed. "What are we doing? What about Em—"

Miriam set a finger on Sam's lips, and blue eyes bored into her.

"I meant it, Sam," Miriam said. "I love you."

A breath slipped between them.

"I loved you. I love you. I will always love you."

Doubt quivered in Sam's eyes, fragile and vulnerable. "I'm not who I was."

"I know."

"I'm broken."

"We all are."

"No, Miriam. I'm not—" Her voice cracked. "I'm really broken."

"I know."

It wasn't denial. Not dismissal or deflection. Just truth and presence. She waited, letting their words hover then settle.

Sam hesitated. "Are you choosing me?"

"Yes."

"Why?"

Miriam closed the last bit of distance between them. "Because it's you. It'll always be you. I'd choose you every time." Her hands found the backs of Sam's arms, and she held her there, planting both of them in place, as if it could stop the tilt of the world. "Any other questions?"

Sam didn't answer.

Miriam kissed her cheek, just over the mangled scar. *I love you.* She didn't rush. She waited for Sam to exhale, making sure everything was okay. She kissed the other cheek, and Sam's eyes fluttered closed. A quiet tremor passed through her, soft and full of surrender. Acceptance for both of them.

With a feather-light touch, Miriam tipped Sam's chin with a thumb and laid a kiss to her crown—a quiet benediction, an imprint of memory, of mourning, of things survived. Sam's eyes stayed shut, her respirations slower now. Miriam took in the familiar scent of her—fresh linen, clean skin, something achingly hers. Years lay between them, fault lines never truly sealed, but now, something was mending.

Her fingers traced the line of Sam's jaw, reverent and slow. Then—finally—their lips met. Not with heat, not with haste, but with the stillness of a held breath. Gentle and drawn out. As if the moment itself needed time to remember how to begin again.

It was different now. Not like their first kiss in Duncan's, which had burned raw. Not like the one fevered after months of uncertainty. Not even like earlier—just minutes before—sharp with need and hunger, an urgency after all the years and distance. This kiss was none of those things.

It was something quieter. Deeper.

A return. An apology.

So many things left unsaid and then said, finding motion.

When Miriam took Sam's hand and led her to the other room, they moved without hurry. And when they came together, it was with a tenderness born of knowing what it meant to lose, and to choose again anyway.

47

HALLOW

MIRIAM ROLLED ONTO HER SIDE, pressing her forehead into the back of her hand where it rested against the mattress. Her shoulders lifted and fell in short, uneven breaths until they smoothed, a rhythm that lulled her toward sleep. The drag of it was slow and heavy, pulling her down by degrees. She didn't know how much time had passed—only that the living room beyond the doorway lay dark.

Content. She was content.

Her eyes closed.

The bed shifted as Sam rose, the rustle of bare feet carrying her across the floor. In the en suite, the faucet opened. Miriam drifted nearer to sleep, but the sound persisted—not the steady pour of washing, but a staggered gulping, the water taken in long, desperate pulls.

Her body tensed. She blinked toward the shadowed doorway, meaning to form a half-hearted joke, but the words caught. In the dimness she could make out Sam, braced against the sink, shoulders rigid, hands clamped at its corners. Miriam sat up.

The faucet shut before she could move. "It's okay, Mir." Sam's voice wavered.

She returned to the bed and perched on its edge. When Miriam reached for her, Sam neither recoiled nor leaned in. Her skin was hot beneath Miriam's touch, damp with sweat. At her throat, marks were faint in the darkness, but the contrast was there, angry enough to see where restless fingers had dragged. Miriam moved closer, and Sam held stiff for a breath. She exhaled, some of the strain loosening. Not all, but enough.

Withdrawal.

Sam was holding herself together on the surface, but beneath it she was fighting. Years of dependence gnawed at her. Still at war, still relentless. And though she'd done well in sobriety, this was something that wouldn't go away instantly. For a long time. If ever.

"Talk to me," Miriam whispered.

"It's late."

Miriam stayed quiet, only rested her chin on Sam's bare shoulder.

"I just want one moment," Sam murmured, "where I don't —" She broke off with a rough exhale. "I keep thinking I'm okay, and then I think it'll *be* okay. Just one last time, just another hit, and then I'll stop, I swear I'll give it up for good."

She sounded so tired.

Miriam's fingertips traced the lattice of scars and ink across Sam's back. She'd seen some of them before—tended to them when Sam was half-conscious and fading. But they were different now. Context changed everything. A bullet wound, a blade, shrapnel? So many maps and stories etched into flesh. Her relationship with stims and calmers entwined throughout.

"Everyone's moving forward," Sam said, no louder than a breath. "And I'm stuck. I'm trying. I swear I am."

Miriam tenderly turned Sam's face, coaxing the woman to meet her eyes.

"I'm trying, Mir."

"I know."

"I'm a mess."

"You are."

Sam's mouth twitched.

"But I am, too," Miriam added. "We both are, but I'd rather be a mess with you than not."

Silence followed, stretching long enough for Miriam to return to her slow tracing of the Seraph tattoo, the geometry of wings and watchful eyes. She didn't like what the ink signified, but it belonged to Sam as much as the scars did.

"This is real," Sam said at last. Not quite a question, not quite a statement.

"Yes."

"I'm scared."

"So am I."

The words hung between them.

"I'm scared this is temporary."

"What? Me?"

"Whatever this is." Sam's voice frayed. "I keep thinking maybe this is something it isn't. Maybe it'll fall apart outside this room, these walls. That you'll leave. Or I will."

"If you need space—" Miriam began, the words tasting wrong as she said them.

"No." Sam shook her head hard. Her hand moved behind her to find Miriam's skin. "I don't want you to leave."

Miriam searched her face, dark shadows catching in Sam's lines. "I meant what I said," she murmured. "I'm here."

Sam hesitated, dragging the words behind her breath. "Before this. Before we—" She stopped and started again. "Ren. I told Kuan-Lin I'd go with them. I said I'd be on their flight."

Miriam's chest seized, and she froze. "When?"

"Tomorrow."

The word struck like a deep blow. She had known, in the abstract, that Sam would leave, but not so soon. Panic and regret corded through her spine. She'd wasted days keeping her distance. Avoiding this, avoiding Sam. And now—

"I don't know," Sam admitted. "I don't want to go. Not if it means losing this. Losing you."

Miriam pressed her hand to Sam's shoulder, then sunk her forehead against it.

"I don't want to lose you," Sam repeated into her hair.

And with that truth hung between them, everything else waited—distant reverberations of what came next. The meeting with their old Echo, the reckoning, the coming questions and answers that hadn't ended.

"We'll figure it out," Miriam whispered.

"What if you get bored of me?"

"I won't."

"What if I scare you away? I keep thinking just one more time. I know I can't, but—what if I break? What if I can't stop?"

"Sam." Miriam cupped her face, both hands firm.

Sam shifted as if ready to retreat but didn't. "Mir," she whispered, her voice cracking. "I'm afraid."

She carried enough darkness to drown in. Trauma with density, violence with memory. So much pain and grief bound up inside her, stitched shut but bleeding beneath.

Miriam couldn't promise anything. She didn't want to lie and give false hope. What could she promise? Life was uncertain, cruel, and already had taken more than its share. But in this moment, she could give what mattered most. She bent, lips caressing the seam of metal and skin at Sam's shoulder. A kiss like a vow.

"Me too," she breathed. "But I'm not going anywhere. I can't promise it'll be easy. I can't promise I won't get frustrated, but I'm here. I'm staying. We'll get through this. Together."

It didn't chase the shadows from Sam's eyes, but something in her frame softened. They sank back into the sheets together. Miriam felt Sam's warmth against her body, the rise and fall of breath evening out until it brushed steadily over Miriam's collarbone. She stayed awake a while longer, counting, letting the darkness hold around them—different this time—like a shield. The silence felt borrowed, a small note held in a storm, precious because they didn't know when or how it would end. Outside the room, outside the walls, the city and world moved uncontrollably, but there, together, despite its flaws and cracks, was a brief sanctuary. Miriam smoothed her fingers over the woman next to her, memorizing heat, curves, and weight. She held the silence like something divine.

This was sacred.

48
———

RITE

"SHIT, Yuri, it's bougier on the inside."

"Fox, that's my mother's. Don't…don't touch anything."

The man raised both hands in mock surrender, grinning as he circled the large space. "I knew you lot were fancy, but damn, not even an invite to the parties here?"

Miriam leaned against the table, arms crossed. She didn't bother rolling her eyes at her two friends this time. The room felt too bright after the night, its warmth and calm already ebbing. She closed her eyes and held the quiet from the hours before.

"Surprised you could get away," Yuri said to Krill.

"Used Elly as an excuse." He shrugged like it was nothing. "Pregnancy helps."

"Hope she's doing well."

"She is." Krill let his gaze travel the high ceilings and the restrained finish of Yuri's childhood home. "So, what's the plan? Or the explanation? Any of it." He rubbed a knuckle along the table's edge, impatient.

"Kai's on her way," Yuri said.

"No one's gonna ask how I got away from Foxtrot?" Fox spread his hands in mock offense as he drifted along the room's circumference near the kitchen island. He plucked a fruit from the bowl there and tested its weight.

"Do you want us to ask?"

He made a face. "Probably not. Plausible deniability, right? Or to get our stories straight…" He scratched his jaw, unbothered. "Anyway, I get why Krill's here—Command, UMF shit. Yuri's tied up in hospital shit." He pointed at Miriam. "And you got dragged into this fucked-up shit. So why am I here?"

Miriam didn't blink. "You're morale."

His eyebrow climbed.

"And the muscle," she added.

Fox settled, satisfied. "Alright." He waited a beat. "And Valk?"

Miriam glanced toward the window and the small guesthouse outside. "She'll be back."

Relief prickled. Sam had gone to spend time with her nephew, to tell Kuan-Lin and Ren she'd meet them in Arshangol later, although Miriam wasn't sure what that meant. She hadn't asked her to do that, and she felt selfish, albeit relieved. She looked around the room. Had the others known Sam was leaving? Would Sam have said goodbye if last night hadn't happened?

Her attention settled on Yuri. Sam would have told him, at least. He gave her a look and opened his mouth, but his device buzzed. He stepped away, returning moments later with Kai on his heels, hands full with three devices.

She didn't greet them, just moved toward Miriam and the kitchen table with purpose. The rest rose as if on cue. At the head, Kai set down a tablet and a handheld. She held out Miriam's device, and Miriam took it.

"Thanks for letting us use your place," Kai said, still standing.

"You're not usually the paranoid one," Fox said, dropping into a chair and tossing a small fruit into his mouth.

"I don't know who to trust," Kai replied.

Miriam pocketed her device and stepped closer. "Are you okay?"

Kai waved her off. She wore the same clothes from the day before. Miriam had managed to change just before, slipping away while Sam left for the Altered Sector, in time to come back and pretend like she hadn't spent the night meters away.

"It was a ruse," Kai said, taking stock of who was in the room.

"That's not what the network's sayin'," Fox said.

"It was a frame job," Miriam said, certain. "There were no Altered attackers."

"Do *they* know that?" Fox asked.

"I'm handling it," Kai affirmed, "but it isn't the pressing issue. This is all distraction."

"What?"

Kai paused. "Sloppy," she said at last. "The best-laid plans fall apart at their weakest link. In this case, the human link that cuts corners. Such typical short-term thinking."

The kitchen door slid open, and heads turned. Sam stepped in. Surprise flickered across her face as she took them in. When her eyes found Miriam's, the corner of her mouth tugged. Miriam's own lips mirrored before she caught Yuri and Fox watching.

"Valk," Kai said with a hint of surprise in her voice. "It's good you're here."

Sam nodded and slipped toward the kitchen island. She braced there, composed.

"Kai, wait," Fox said, gesturing. "Everyone's here except wonderkid." He shrugged. "I might be the muscle, but I know he's the brains. Some of the brains, at least."

"No, you're right," Kai said. She turned to Yuri on the other side of the table. "We didn't want to alert his employer, and Nas agrees it's better that he stays in the office. He knows what's going on—we've been talking. He's trying to track something down right now and should get back to me soon."

"His employer? You mean Vertex?" Krill asked.

"Tracking what?" Fox said at the same time.

"Yes. Vertex," Kai replied.

"No, I get that, but why wouldn't we want to alert—" Fox broke off. "Nah. I don't get it. I thought the theory was that it was the Charonites behind the attack."

"Yes, but not alone. They aren't organized enough for this scale."

"That's what we said about the wunbies at the beginnin'."

"I understand, but no." Kai shook her head. "This is something else. Something worse."

"Sorry? Somethin' worse than the wunbies?"

"Axiom."

The double-triangle sigil burned at the back of Miriam's mind. Her stomach squeezed, memory tilting toward the North.

"I thought we were talking about Vertex," Krill said.

"I thought we were talkin' about the COCsuckers—the Charonites," Fox added.

"Axiom is a Vertex subsidiary," Kai said. "It's not general knowledge. The buyout was quiet, years ago. But Axiom's behind the stimulants, I think—and I think they have something worse now."

Miriam pictured the northern facility. It was definitely something much worse than stimulants.

"Stims?" Krill asked. "The stuff's not exactly new. It's been around for ages."

Miriam shook her head. "Not this kind." She glanced at Sam, who hid her left arm behind her back. "Remember that underground facility near the radiation zone? We captured Apostates for them..." As she said it, realization sparked. She sat up straighter, eyes widening. "They wanted live Altered... specimens." Miriam's focus returned to Sam.

To her side, Kai nodded slowly. Yuri remained quiet, while Krill's and Fox's expressions contorted.

"I remember that, but how is this all relevant?" Krill asked.

"Stop. Wait," Fox said, waving a hand. "So this Axiom group used stimmed-up wunbies to make...their own stims?"

"Reverse-engineered, maybe. But it's the same stuff circulating on the streets, or at least diluted copies of it. The same ones that UMF's contracted with," Yuri said, arms crossing tighter. He shot a look toward Sam, whose eyes had dropped.

The room quieted.

Miriam digested it with the others, but her blood ran cold. "Yuri. Sam's blood work. It was inconclusive. On what panel?" She pressed on before he could answer. "Were there Altered signatures as well?"

Eyes slid to Yuri, then to Sam. Miriam wished she were closer, wanted to close the distance, to steady the woman—or *be* steadied.

"Emma said it was Vertex's signature, but—" He inhaled. "I wouldn't be surprised."

Miriam's throat knotted at both the name and the admission. She tried to swallow and partially tuned out the undercurrent of side talk as she ordered her thoughts and emotions.

"Shit," Yuri breathed. "That could explain why UMF cases dropped after the collaboration with the Royals..." He shook his head. "No, that's not right—we were already trending down before..."

"General never aligned with Vertex," Kai said.

"Well, no. They had a clause we didn't take. Things petered out after the prosthetic prototypes—"

"Krill," Miriam cut in.

The others stopped. Even Sam looked up, quiet this entire time.

"Why were we sent to that facility? Echo and Charlie."

Lines deepened around Krill's mouth.

"Who insisted Hadeon—the legionnaires—be with us?"

His silence and expression were answer enough.

The Vertex advisor mentioned at the brief. The annex in UMF's compound. *Live Altered specimens.*

The magnitude of it settled. Had Hadeon and the others been sent in for exposure and death? Had they evaded some intended fate only to be captured and executed another way? But there had also been a dozen ways that plan could've failed. What if they'd isolated themselves like she'd done with Sam, Willem, and the others? If they'd done that, there might've been a few casualties, but not what Vertex or Axiom would've intended. Had they underestimated UMF and Legion? Or were they looking for something else?

Her temples throbbed with the tangle of it.

"Okay, so Axiom. Or Vertex. One and the same," Fox said. "Playin' UMF *and* the Charonites? With what? Stims?"

"Funding, maybe," Yuri responded.

"So what was their plan *if* the Charonites hit Center, *if* Vertex was behind it? I love a good conspiracy, but these are a lot of ifs." Fox shrugged. "And the frame job was sloppy. You picked it apart pretty fast."

"That's what happens when you involve variables and conditions you can't control," Kai said, readjusting the devices in front of her. "I don't think they expected the Altered to turn on the Heretics, for that rhetoric to change. I don't think they expected the Royals to announce a return to Arshangol either. I also don't think they realized how inconsistent the Children of Charon can be, depending on which faction you work with." She glanced at Miriam. "The patchwork explosives. So many cut corners. There're too many variables. The idea itself wasn't flawed, it was the execution. That's what makes it dangerous."

"Okay, wild cards." Fox shook his head. "I still don't see how this connects."

"It's a jump," Kai admitted. "But everyone has their own

agendas. They might align momentarily, but then they drift. You can't control what people do or believe." She slid her tablet forward, its holodisplay blooming as she flipped through windows. "A lot of this is speculation and conjecture, but I've been tracking regulations and policies as they slip through. Emergency clauses and contingency protocols filed under Altered crisis planning. A lobbying effort." She looked up to Miriam.

The Charonite council member hovered at the fringe of Miriam's thoughts. Advising. Softening language. Moving thresholds. Helping orchestrate? A puppet master being puppeted?

Kai continued, "All pointing to Vertex."

The others gawked at her, unsure of what she'd introduced.

"It gives them control."

Fox and Yuri folded their arms at the same time, but Fox spoke first. "Control of what?" He looked around. "If I'm understandin' this right, you're sayin' we gave them somethin' like a nuclear option?"

"Something like it."

Krill straightened. "That's a massive oversight. No one would just hand that over. UMF? Are you saying someone at the top is working together on this? That the medical sector, tech companies, research whatever, they're all complicit?"

"Media, too," Kai said. "I don't know, but I don't think it's that coordinated. I do think people have stayed in their lanes so strictly that no one's seen the whole picture. Complicit, perhaps. But it's more likely *indirect* complicity."

Krill's jaw feathered. "So how are we—*you*—seeing the big picture?"

They watched Kai. She stared at her handheld for another second before she lifted her eyes. "Yuri? Would you like to start?"

Yuri tipped his chin toward Sam. "Your teammate. The autopsy and blood work. Some of it matches what we found in your panels. After this conversation, I guess that's no surprise now."

"What about the decomposition?" Miriam asked. The lack of it.

"Some tissue preservative," he said. "Possibly synthetic. There's evidence of processing, possible cryoprotectants. But more than that—bioanomalies. Altered-specific proteins bonded to carriers, a delivery system."

Fox frowned. Krill crossed his arms tighter.

"And there's a common denominator," Yuri added.

"The COCsuckers," Fox muttered.

"DMSO," Miriam said simultaneously, the word bitter on her tongue.

Yuri glanced at Fox, then gave Miriam a short nod. "Dimethyl sulfoxide, a carrier solvent that drags whatever it's mixed with straight through skin and into the bloodstream. It's the same compound and signature we found used on the Royal kid and the praetorian. The effects were different; the ones used in Station seemed to have inhibited motion. Different preparation, same signature."

"And the acid effects?" Miriam asked.

He shook his head. "Cruelty? It's the Charonites. I don't know."

Fox squinted. "So, Charonites."

"Kai believes someone's been using them, steering them."

"So, Axiom?"

"Vertex," Kai corrected. "I think they've created—as you said—a *nuclear* option."

A hard pressure seized Miriam's gut.

"More drugs?" Fox asked.

He hadn't caught the most important part yet.

"A bioweapon," Miriam said, her voice thin, shredded raw from the inside.

The room stilled. Five pairs of eyes found her, a single beat of silence stretching tight. Fox made a sound between a huff and a grunt.

Kai nodded once. "Genocide."

The word settled like dust in the lungs, fine and invisible, impossible to cough out once it took hold.

"Xenocide, whatever you want to call it."

"Okay. Fuck." Fox threw up his hands. "This…is a lot."

"Labels don't change the fact that it's a solution some are prepared to use. But I'm afraid I've made a mistake," Kai whispered. Her shoulders sagged, then squared.

"How?" Fox bent closer. "This is good. If this is all true, we expose them."

"I don't know what the Charonites did," Kai said slowly. "But I think they mishandled something. Their plan at Center didn't go as intended. Those bodies weren't meant to be found, let alone examined. Perhaps they thought Valk's teammate would be discarded or they didn't know he wasn't a legionnaire. Perhaps the charges should have destroyed the evidence."

Miriam folded her arms and braced.

"By involving Station General, by bringing in the Royals, by letting his body reach Altered partners, I may have set off a chain of events. I think the schedule—whatever it is—moved up."

Fox narrowed his eyes. "Meanin'?"

"Vertex knows General has Valk's teammate. Which means the Altered know," Kai said. "Or they will, once they follow what's in Valk's teammate."

"A bioweapon," Krill said, low.

Fox blew out air. "That can't be stuffed back into a bottle."

"How sure are we that it actually works?"

Miriam clenched her jaw. Whatever they'd encountered in the northern facility had been a test run. "It works," she whispered. Willem's eyes flashed in her memory, lifeless and open.

"It was one alty," Krill said.

Miriam's head snapped up, a retort cold and ready.

"Not just him," Yuri cut in. "Valk's blood work showed anomalies as well."

Every head turned to Sam. She didn't flinch, didn't blink.

"What does that mean?" Krill asked. "A blood-specific weapon?"

The room hushed again, sound deadening like it had been drawn through gauze. He'd answered his own question. Tension knifed through Miriam's shoulders.

"Can City Center sanction them?" Krill said after a moment. "Send SecTeam in."

Kai shook her head, mouth pinched. "Who can we trust? We don't know who's in Vertex's pocket. And I've already asked Nas for help. I'm waiting on what he can provide. A delay, access…"

Their inside man.

Krill looked from Miriam to Yuri to Fox. "What about the Royals? Legion?"

Miriam glanced at Sam.

"That might make it worse," Yuri muttered. "Is there time for that?"

"How far does Vertex's reach extend?" Krill probed. "How would they deploy something on this scale? Just Station City? It's not close to Altered territory."

Something else was missing.

Miriam stepped in. "Why did you call us here?"

Kai met her eyes. For a moment, something passed over her expression—a remnant of the woman Miriam used to know, one who laughed too easily and carried sentiment like it was strength. It was gone as quickly as it came, replaced by composure. "We were Echo once."

Krill balked. This one he caught immediately. "You want us to storm Vertex?"

"We've faced worse," Yuri said. "And with Nas on the inside…"

Blightbringers, maybe. Suicidal odds. But this—a bioweapon? This was not a terrain they could fight through. This was a weapon built in labs, built for genetics and bloodlines, not battlefields. And they couldn't effectively fight it, guns blazing.

"We don't have weapons," Krill said.

Fox crushed his hands together. "Three of us are still UMF. We can get some." He gestured to Sam. "Let's get the Seraphim to help. They're alties. They've got chips on the table."

"No," Kai said. "No UMF. Checking weapons out will require records. It invites questions."

"Not SRAF," Miriam whispered, surprising herself.

Sam's blue eyes cut to her.

Let SRAF off the leash and they'd never get the leash back on. Wasn't that something Kuan-Lin had said before? And half of SRAF was Altered. The others were probably like Sam was before, addicts. They could fight, but they couldn't fight effectively against exposure.

"Vertex is full of scientists and civilians. Office administrators," Kai said, tracking the same thought.

"So what do you expect us to do?" Fox scoffed. "Show up and charm them into a confession? Surrender? The goodness of our hearts won't protect us."

"I think it's more complicated than that."

"No shit."

"Do we know how to stop this?" Yuri asked. "This is all out of our realm of expertise. What kind of plan is this?"

"It's not. Not yet. I've been working sanctions, trying to stall with inquiries and investigations, but all that buys is time. Eventually someone makes a harder choice. Until then, we have Nas."

"Sanctions, Kai?" Krill said. "After everything we've just said? And Nas, I thought he works the tech field."

"Yes, but he's inside. He's working on access now."

"The kid does get his nose into places he shouldn't..." Fox muttered.

A chime sounded on Kai's device. They all looked over.

"Speak of the devil?" Fox murmured.

Kai didn't look at him. She answered the device and extended its display. "Nas?"

"Hey, you were right," he said. "I dug into some back files and found a few logistics reports."

Kai ignored the looks around the table. "Can you see what they were?"

"I skimmed them. Standard materials and parts with a Center signoff. Why? What'd I miss?"

A muscle jumped on Kai's neck as she thought. After a moment, she looked back at her device. "Nas, can you get us into the building?"

"Uh...like the cafeteria? Probably."

"Nas."

"I like my job, Kai."

"Nas."

He sighed. "Emergency time?" A pause. Then another resigned breath. "Tell me when."

"Soon. I'll let you know."

"Okay. See you when I see you."

The call cut out. The silence that followed wasn't quiet. It held the churn of thought, the bloat of a dozen more questions no one knew how to ask aloud. They were all catching up, trying to fit what'd been discussed and laid out on the table. Coincidences that weren't all coincidences. How it all made sense.

Miriam's attention drifted back to Sam. The woman hadn't moved, but something in her posture had drawn tighter, like a wire pulled to its limit.

"Don't we need a better plan?" Krill asked, careful now.

"No further briefs?" Fox added mockingly, although it fell flat.

"Do we even have a plan?" Yuri said.

"No weapons, but..." Fox rubbed his knuckles together. "Muscle?"

Yuri exhaled loudly, then motioned toward the foyer and hallway beyond it. "I've got one."

The others turned to him.

"You what?" Krill asked.

"Muscle?" Fox added.

Yuri gave him a look. "Gun."

Fox pushed out his lower lip and nodded, impressed. "Okay, we have one weapon. Dibs."

Kai didn't react. "I have more calls to make. I don't know what we're walking into, but if we fail, someone has to know what happened."

"The Royals?" Miriam asked.

Kai hesitated. "Yes, and others. But I have to be delicate."

"You think there's a chance you're wrong."

Kai gave a single nod. "After the missing Altered, this attack now, everyone's on edge. One misunderstanding, one spark, and everything ignites. And what? We all end up with the same results."

Miriam didn't ask how she would manage that when trust had reduced to a thread.

"Shit."

Everyone turned to Krill. The man rarely cursed.

"One last mission as Echo?" he said.

Fox forced a grin but couldn't hold it. "Well, fuck. I hope it's not my last."

49

BREACH

THE VERTEX LOBBY was too immaculate. White surfaces gleamed under natural light, high ceilings leeched sound, and the architectural emptiness felt designed not for comfort but for spectacle. Nas met them just beyond the second checkpoint. He wore a long white lab coat that made him seem as though he belonged there—not simply employed, but integrated into the structure itself. The coat masked the exo-frame bracing his legs and spine, though not the imbalance of his stride.

"That was easier than I expected," Kai murmured, her eyes scanning the area with habitual calculation. "What did you tell them?"

"City Center inspection. VIPs." Nas's grin widened as he gestured at them. "We're all together again. Fuck, this is so cool."

The words struck something nostalgic, awkward against the sterile lobby yet stubborn in their resonance. For a breath Miriam could see and hear their younger selves like they'd been transported back into Echo's team room, laughter spilling over half-cleaned gear and nutrient bar wrappers. The newest additions, the Baby Echoes, Nas and Kai, inseparable from the start. Nas forever pilfering chocolate bars from the dining facility, swiping snacks from briefings without shame. Kai's laugh cutting through long nights of training, bright and unguarded, often sparked by Nas and Fox's banter. Her amused disgust at Fox's crudeness, his idioms decades out of use. Yuri with that unhurried, disarming smile, leaning close to share a quiet joke with a nudge of the elbow or an arched brow. Krill, still only the team second back then, struggling to be taken seriously while they teased him, though they'd trusted him more than he knew. All of them crowded in a scout cruiser's homey galley, their company enough, mugs of steaming coffee warming their hands.

They had been a family. Respect given as much as it was earned, trust hard-won yet absolute. Until that one mission that changed everything. Miriam's own turning point. The introduction of Sam and Scott, the Golden Twins, as Fox had terribly dubbed them. One sibling gone now, the other battered but alive, standing there beside her. The same woman she'd fallen in love with, lost, and somehow found again. The same woman who had postponed her own departure, a new life with her reunited family, to be there. With Miriam. The thought made her ache to reach out and lace her fingers through Sam's, but she held herself still. This was Echo. Her team. Her friends. Her family.

She wasn't the only one folded into the memory. She noticed the contour of a smile touch Yuri's mouth. Even Krill's rigid posture loosened. Kai's arms dropped from their folded guard. Old rhythms stirred, stubborn things. They had fought and bled together, and for a fragile beat, the shape of who they'd once been reassembled.

Nas studied them with boyish awe, gaze slowing when it reached Sam before sliding on to Fox, the last in line. His grin faltered by the smallest margin. "Fox," he said.

"Nas."

"Surprised you showed."

Fox's reply carried weight but no bitterness. "It's all of us. Together again."

Nas's smile brightened, quick and eager. He opened his mouth, faltered again, and took in the man's black T-shirt. "Couldn't dress the part?"

Fox didn't answer. The silence that followed wasn't pointed, but heavy—an old scar left beneath years of distance, something unresolved and buried. Things between the two had come to a head once, emotions and aggression crashing together until they'd snapped. Miriam felt it in the way Fox shifted from one foot to the other, one shoulder sloping lower, his frame less squared.

Nas looked as if he might continue, then let it go, turning to lead them deeper. "Crazy what happened at Center, huh?"

No one answered, but he didn't seem to mind.

The halls narrowed into gleaming corridors with glass walls and polished surfaces that babbled with quiet, mechanical life. Behind transparent panels, sleek devices ran silent cycles. Some mirrored Sam's prosthetic arm in design; others diverged, chasing something alien, technology racing to mimic or outpace the Altered. Staff receded as they passed. Doors slid shut with softened finality. Their avoidance wasn't fear, but protocol.

"No one likes dog-and-pony shows," Fox muttered behind Miriam, then scoffed. "Nosy Nas was right."

If others heard him, they didn't react.

"Is there a control center?" Kai asked.

"Like a tactical ops center?" Nas gave a short laugh. "This isn't the military."

"Nas."

He sighed, shoulders lifting in reluctant concession. "Not like what you're imagining. Not manned, but yeah, there's something like a command and control room."

"Can you take us there?"

He hesitated with a stagger to his step. "You're asking a lot."

"You said you received access," Kai pushed. "With the promotion."

"I did what I could, yes."

Miriam caught Yuri's brief turn toward her, silent question etched in his brow. Promoted? She gave a slight shake of her head. Emma had been right; she hadn't been keeping up with her old friends, and now she was trying to readjust mid-stride, piecing together fragments of a life she'd let drift. The thought of Emma stabbed under her ribs. She checked on Sam.

The woman walked several paces back, eyes roving the halls. She carried herself as though expecting trouble at any movement. Her steps slowed as her focus fixed on a recessed display behind glass, and Miriam followed her line of sight. Inside lay a curved module, cradled in foam. Its familiarity unsettled her. Sam's shoulders tensed, but she said nothing.

At the next checkpoint, Nas swiped his hand over the reader. The scanner blinked, and he glanced over his shoulder, catching their attention on the display. "Good eye, Valk," he called, smile widening. "Looks like your embed, doesn't it?" He gestured at the device behind Sam's ear. "The next leap after visors. Instant comms, full neural input. Doesn't matter if you're sedated, paralyzed, or restrained. As long as the brain's going, you're online. That's the project I've been championing."

Miriam frowned. "The Royals shared this with you? With Vertex?"

Nas gave a playful scoff. "Give us some credit, Tan. It's *our* science, too." He swept back the curls of his dark hair to reveal the identical implant set behind his ear, its rail barely visible against his scalp. "Perks of working here. Immediate prototypes. None of that waiting-in-line UMF bullshit."

"Nas," Kai interjected impatiently. Her voice pulled like a tug on a leash.

"Right, right." But his eyes gleamed with a proud intensity. "This way."

He led them forward to where the gloss of the outer levels

gave way to stricter corridors, darker paneling, and cold-lit labs. The shine and tech displays disappeared. So did the windows. Steel doors and numbered observation ports lined the hall, buzzing with unseen machinery. This wasn't for the public.

Nas checked the empty passage, then pulled a small terminal from his coat and handed it to Kai. "Limited access," he said, watching the device pass to Yuri. "But you'll see the outgoing manifests I mentioned before."

Yuri's fingers skimmed the display, brows pinching. "Mind if I try a deeper pull?"

Nas shrugged in neutral permission.

They moved on to where the halls branched into labs separated by glass bays, and inside, pallets of sealed metal canisters and crates were stacked with obsessive precision. Many of the containers lacked labels entirely. The ones that did have them bore codes she didn't recognize—alphanumeric strings with no glossary. The temperature dropped perceptibly. Miriam inhaled and caught the sterile tang of ozone, cold metal, and antiseptic.

"Here," Yuri said, working on the move. "Three packages went out." He slowed, and his voice lost momentum as he scrolled. "Tagged this morning."

The group halted with him.

"Bioform freight."

"Bioform?" Kai doubled back, peering over his arm, her expression hard. "It says bioform?"

Yuri nodded. "Three shipments. All logged as delivered, transferred, and loaded. Two through cargo," he murmured, swiping again. "One through a passenger ship."

Miriam heard Sam's breath stall beside her. Her posture locked like a system error.

"When?" Sam asked. Her voice pared to razor-thin control. "The passenger ship. Air? Sea? Which one?"

Miriam's stomach hollowed, and her throat dried as a rush of cold flushed her skin. The way Sam stood rigid, trembling with some internal voltage, struck like a flare in the dark. Miriam moved instinctively closer, drawn by a gravitational need to protect.

"I don't know—today? Yeah, today." Yuri's fingers quickened. "I can't imagine anything slower with the time frame we're looking at, so it has to be by airship. That's the only option that'd make sense."

Sam's expression gave. Her brows pulled down in arcs, mouth parted as though in protest, though no sound came. She touched her embed in a quick motion. When she didn't get the response or engagement she wanted, her teeth clenched against a hiss.

Nas lifted a hand toward the rough ceiling. "It's the shell infrastructure. Dampens signals. No comms in or out unless you're on the Vertex line."

"Fuck." Sam's voice was barely audible. Her eyes locked on Miriam's, urgent, then darted behind them, back the way they'd come. Her shoulders rolled forward, weight shifting like she was about to break into a sprint. "I have to go."

"Wait—" Miriam's voice broke off. "Yuri, are you sure?"

He didn't look up. "It says it right here." He angled the terminal so they could see. Beside him, Kai had already pulled her own handheld out, fingers navigating with precise, economical motions. Her face was a mask of concentration, and from the set of her mouth, Miriam could tell she wasn't getting a signal either.

Sam's breath came faster. Something primal in Miriam's brain registered that ragged sound and that tremor that had nothing to do with withdrawal and everything to do with panic. Sam was already backpedaling, her fingers jamming against her embed as though force alone might punch something through.

Miriam followed, closing the gap, not touching but near enough to catch her if she broke. Sam halted just past the reinforced threshold that separated each section.

"Sam—"

Sam tried again. This time, her face lit up and her voice hardened. "Sky-Eye. No, not later—I need you to patch me to the airship that left Station City earlier." She paused. "Yes, today. I don't know—the last one. Yes. That one. I don't care. Get me someone. Anyone."

"Sam?" Miriam's voice softened.

Sam flinched as if struck, face contorting with pain. Her hand ripped the modular rectangle from its rail. "Fuck!" she hissed, then thudded her forehead against the cold doorframe. "Something's jamming me. Come on—" A beat later, she snapped the unit back into place and tried again, words tumbling quick. "Hello? Did you get—okay." Blue eyes darted to Miriam. "This is Fury with SRAF. Emergency connection priority. Listen. There's a Royal on your ship. She's traveling with a child. A young boy. I need you to find her and put her on this connection—now."

Silence.

Miriam's heart struck once, slow and heavy, echoing through her ribs.

Sam looked up, and in that single glance, stripped of everything, Miriam understood. The manifest. One of the passenger ships bound for Arshangol, capital of the Altered territories. *The* passenger ship that Sam was supposed to be on.

She was already turning, already moving. "Nas," she called. "The bioform canister. We need to send instructions. How to stop it."

Behind her, the reinforced doors slid shut with Sam on the other side.

"Wait—" She spun. Lunged. Her fingers scraped at the seam, but too late. She snatched her hand back before the seal crushed her bones.

The security mechanisms clacked as they engaged inside. And then, a dull thud. Another. Metal on metal, muffled through the barrier. Miriam threw her palms to the door then skimmed the side panels in frantic search of a release. A third impact rang out.

Sam.

She turned. Yuri, Fox, and Krill were frozen, shocked. Kai stood a step apart, watching the door seal with narrowed eyes, her face inscrutable in the light. Miriam spun back to the console, frantic, but it only blinked its quiet refusal. No handle. No override. Nothing.

She whirled to face the group. "Help me open this." The words rasped harshly in her throat.

But no one moved.

"Yuri. Kai." Her eyes then found Nas behind them.

He held her stare, and then his lips parted and formed around the word. "No."

50

IMPOTENCE

YURI'S VOICE WAS QUIET. "Nas. What did you do?"

"She can't interfere," he said.

There was no triumph in it. No venom. Only a calm, unshakable certainty, which landed worse than anger. It settled like ice in Miriam's core and spread.

She stared at him. "Open it."

Nas turned from them and crossed to a separate entrance at the far end of the section, its panel flush with the steel-paneled wall. Overhead, the lights seemed to buzz louder, as though they understood what none of them had spoken aloud.

Miriam stayed where she was, one palm on the sealed hatch Sam had vanished behind, listening for anything—breath, impact, a voice—but the other side held its silence. "Nas, open the fucking door," she growled.

"No," he said again without turning.

The new door in front of him labored open with a mechanical groan, revealing the largest chamber yet: a command nexus. It was a tiered atrium lined with matte graphite, the floor descending by concentric steps into a low-set station ringed with rails. Screens hovered in soft blue halos above the console. Several displayed diagnostic overlays and comm routing windows, while others rotated through facility schematics. No guards. No techs. Just darkened alcoves and the whir of servers hidden underneath the grates.

Yuri's voice turned brittle. "You said you didn't know what was going on."

"I didn't," Nas replied. "Not all of it. Not at first."

Fox moved. "You smug little shit—"

Kai's hand caught his arm. Nas didn't notice or look back. He was already walking through the widening door. And they followed because there was nowhere else to go. They had been shut in, and there didn't seem a point to go farther down the corridor.

Miriam spared one last breath for the seam behind her. She willed something—anything—to break, that Sam on the other side would somehow get through. But there was nothing. Not a rattle or a knock, only pressure systems syncing somewhere deeper. She turned and grudgingly joined the others.

"Is it a virus?" Yuri asked.

Nas let out an exhale, neither heavy nor light. Simply tired. "Not in the way you're thinking." He walked down the steps into the well, white coat catching the diffuse glow. "No liquefying organs, no contagion. It's selective. Precision-engineered." He stopped with a foot on the last step, braced above the console railing. He looked first to Kai, then to Yuri, then to the rest. "It only binds to Altered genomes."

The room muted itself around the hum of the machines.

"You've seen what the K-series—what the wunbies are capable of," he continued. "What the neogens are doing. Even now. You think this war is over because the Altered on the other side tired of yesterday's freedom fighters? What happens when a new faction rises? When the Royals crown a new Sovereign and calls their reign of terror a new order?" He came down the final step, fingertips grazing metal. "It's the same old, just a different day."

Yuri's voice thinned. "Virus, bioweapon or not. Semantics.

You're talking about unleashing death on the masses. It's genocide."

"No," Nas said. "I'm talking about survival. About immunological superiority. An advantage. About futureproofing our species." He turned to Kai, slower, his expression softening and hardening somehow simultaneously. "I'm talking about never watching a friend bleed out because something built in a lab, an *abomination,* needed to prove a point."

Miriam swallowed the heat rising in her throat. "Is this what you're telling yourself?" Her voice scratched as if it had traveled too far. "You think this—this is protection?"

He met her eyes, gaze gentle, not apologetic. "It's the only way to break the cycle. To end it. *You* came back from that last mission, our mission, broken. Like me. Like all of us. And you know what I saw in every one of you? The same thing I saw in myself."

The blue spill from the displays drew hard angles across Nas's face. At the console, he looked framed, like he was on a stage. A pulpit.

"We keep hoping someone else will make the hard choice," he said. "That someone will draw the line in the sand. But then we call it mercy when the tide comes and erases them. We redraw and just watch them wash away again and again. We're doomed to do this over until someone makes the choice to end it. To make that final decision."

He looked at Kai. "You showed me the pieces, and I saw what you were trying to show me. The more I dug, the more it made sense. You were right, Kai. This is our moment. *Our* choice."

Yuri dropped one step, scanning the portable terminal.

"You're letting emotions blind you. You can't do anything from there, Yuri," Nas said kindly.

Yuri ignored him. "Three canisters. Loaded onto separate transports." He bounded past Nas into the well, hands flying over the displays and controls. "Two on supply craft and one on a passenger shuttle."

The one that Sam was supposed to be on. The one with Kuan-Lin. With Ren.

"How much time do we have?" Krill asked.

Miriam thought back to what Sam had relayed earlier in the day, before she'd gone off to talk to Kuan-Lin, to spend some time with her nephew. "A couple of hours, maybe less. They would've left a while ago."

Krill's mouth set. "So they cross into Altered airspace within, what, an hour?"

"It doesn't matter," Nas said. "Don't you see? We're just as clever as they are. They're not more intelligent, not superior to us."

Krill swore, disbelief narrowing his eyes. "Why bring us here?"

Nas's heavy brows knitted, a wince tugging at the corner of his mouth. "Because we're friends. I wanted us to be together when the cycle finally breaks. We all deserve to witness it." His attention dragged across their faces and hit quiet air. He faltered and blinked. "Was I wrong?"

He found Miriam again, and his voice became gentle. "I'm sorry about Valk. I didn't know she'd be here. She's too integrated with them, and she's stubborn. She'd try to stop it. I know she wouldn't understand. She'll be hurt, but if you talk to her, I'm sure she'll come around. This is so much bigger than all of us."

Krill's jaw flexed. "But you can…stop this?"

"Yes," Nas answered, baffled. "But why would I?"

Miriam's throat was dry. "What are you talking about? Nas, this is wrong. You know it."

"Wrong?" He canted his head. "Wrong. Right. What do those even mean?" He took a quick breath. "They're flexible constructs! I don't understand, how are Kai and I the only ones who see this? The neogens were engineered by us. They were meant to serve human survival. This correction *is* human survival."

Miriam looked desperately at Yuri, hoping he'd figured something out in the control system. She wasn't sure why they were in this room or what could be done from there, but his face had gone ashen, his focus somewhere in the middle distance. Her stomach lurched.

Nas swung to them, his arms up in earnest, pleading. "The world didn't end; it was reframed. The summits, the treaties, integration—all of it is surface. Beneath all that, the Altered are still controlling the rules, still manipulating us. They grow unchecked."

"You sound like them," Fox muttered.

A breath caught between them. The media broadcasts. The Charonites. Axiom. Vertex.

Nas flinched. "Sound like what? The truth?" He lifted a finger and pointed it behind them into the corridor. "This is the right thing to do. The Altered were never meant to exist, to become this second species. Vertex's solution corrects a mistake, a misstep. We rebalance the equation so we can return to what we were."

"What were we?" Miriam asked, cold.

"You think this is leveling the field?" Krill said.

"It's mercy," Nas replied.

Miriam's mind flashed to Willem—Boy Scout—blood webbing out through ruined clothes and armor. "It's not mercy." The muscles in her neck suddenly ached. "You haven't seen what it does."

To Vertex, to him, to Center, UMF, even Station City, casualties were just bodies. Numbers and lines.

"Our science made them, and our science can unmake them, too."

"But when does it end?" Miriam asked.

"Now. It can end now."

"How?" Her voice rose. "How do you guarantee a different outcome?"

"I can't," Nas said plainly. "No one can. Vertex never acquired every sample and strain to maximize efficacy rate—that was an obstacle—but we don't need every Altered type. You remove seventy percent of the threat and the remainder can be contained."

The casualness of it made her stomach turn. "Seventy percent," she echoed. "Seven out of ten dead, and you think the rest will just forgive us? That they'll bury their dead and let this pass? What about the incubation, the exposure distance and period? None of this is confirmed, it'll kill millions, but—"

"Axiom, Vertex, they adjusted. They set other factors."

"That haven't been tested!"

"It'll do the job. We don't have the time."

Miriam shook her head. "It'll only cause more anger and violence, Nas. You can't just flip the board—it's still the same game. It'll never end."

"It *will*. We might not get all of them, but we'll handle the rest. UMF has the reach, the power—"

"You're talking like they're vermin," Krill interjected.

Nas lifted his chin. "They think we're pests. What's stopping them from doing the same thing? Sanctions? Peace summits? It all comes back around. We have to make the move first."

Miriam's nails dug half-moons into her palms. "What about all the people, the stims? You haven't seen what it did to Sam. *She's* human. It doesn't stop at Altered—"

"Collateral. Unfortunate, but necessary."

The words broke like glass beneath skin. Miriam felt the slow, creeping pressure already in her muscles. "Did you know Echo—did you know I'd be on that mission in the North? That *trial run*?"

Something tugged at the corner of his mouth. He didn't answer.

Bodies. Numbers and lines.

"Who are you to decide?" Her voice shook. "You're playing god."

"We need a reset," he said. "You know we do."

"Releasing those canisters won't fix anything."

Behind Nas, hunched over the terminal, Yuri groaned. "*Is there a way to stop this?*"

Nas touched his embed. "Precautions exist, but with things already shutting down, sanctions, investigations, leadership has already removed files, data. They're cowards. When this breaks, all momentum, all the advantage is gone. The Altered will know; they'll move first. Which is why I had to step in." He turned to Kai. "When you sent me those leads, I saw what you were warning about. The console here offers control, but I helped restructure the pathway."

Yuri's grip whitened on the terminal. "You routed command through that device."

"Well, a bridge. A loophole and a back channel. But it *is* a failsafe." Nas flexed his fingers.

"And it's all legal."

Miriam flinched at Kai's voice, flat and detached.

Nas shrugged. "Yes, but we all know war and survival don't care about that."

"Nas," Miriam said, pulse kicking. "Please."

He half turned, palm lifted. "We're saving humanity. I don't understand why you're not seeing this. Look at the pattern. How long does this farce in Station City last? Ten years? Twenty? We tried humility and called it coexistence. What did that buy? Cities burned, people kidnapped, violence escalated, friends turned into footnotes. Blood remembers, and it's not evil to prefer survival. It's simply math." He closed his hand in frustration. "The Royals are returning to Arshangol. They'll consolidate, and the pendulum swings back. They come again. We can end the swing, the cycle."

"By xenocide?" Krill asked. "Listen to yourself. This isn't you."

Nas didn't look at him.

"What about the innocents?" Miriam said.

"No one is innocent."

"The hybrids? The children?"

The pulse in his neck ticked. Then he shook his head. *"No one* is innocent. Their pride, ego—it all stems from their blood."

"You don't have to do this," Miriam tried.

He only whispered the same words again, as if repetition carved certainty and truth.

Silent and still the entire time, now Fox moved. He ripped Yuri's sidearm from underneath his shirt and leveled it at Nas's chest.

Nas peered at the pointed barrel and stepped closer.

"Don't." Fox's knuckles paled and trembled around the pistol's grip. "Please don't make me do this."

"Do it. Shoot me. You've already made me the villain."

Fox's mouth opened, but nothing came out. The weapon dipped just barely.

Nas scoffed. "You've grown soft."

Pressure thickened the air.

"Fox," Kai whispered as she stepped in. "Put it down."

He didn't move. Her fingers touched his forearm. A breath. Then another. His arms slackened, and the pistol sagged to his side. Fox hung his head.

Nas scoffed again. "I thought you were strong. I looked up to you once."

Kai eased the weapon from Fox's grasp and turned it in her hand. "You're wrong on that part, Nas. He *is* strong. But these decisions were meant for people like us. *We* can look past the emotions to the logic. *We* can make those hard decisions." She looked up at Krill and Yuri. "What did they tell us in UMF?"

The former team lead and second only gawked at her in shock, along with Miriam.

"The worst decision is no decision."

Miriam's heart stalled. "Kai."

The woman didn't look over. She nodded, just once. "This whole time, we've been chasing smoke, pretending there's something left to salvage. But there isn't. He isn't wrong about the cycle, about what inevitably will come next. We're trying to hold back the tide with our bare hands."

"Kai—"

"Let me speak," she told Krill as he started. She faced Nas, the gun hanging from her hand, unraised. Her expression softened, a mix of acceptance and affection. "You're not the villain."

Nas's shoulders eased as if a spring had uncoiled inside him. He stood taller and looked, for an instant, younger. He looked less like a man on the verge of atrocity, more like the teammate they all had trusted.

Kai stepped closer. One pace, then two. No one moved to stop her. "There *is* logic to it," she murmured to the others. "It's brutal, but it's a solution."

Nas smiled softly at her like she was a tether thrown into the open sea.

Miriam's gut twisted, and the taste of copper rose in her mouth. She searched faces for refusal, for someone to cry out against the two, but Fox's head remained bowed, shoulders folded in on themselves, his eyes fixed on the floor like it might open beneath them. Krill was caught between steps, lips parted but no words emerging, and Yuri's expression had gone flat, but his focus cut to Miriam and held. In that flicker of connection, she recognized it. A plan forming.

How could they stop them both? A distraction?

Yuri's hand flexed at his side, just out of sight of the others. Rush them?

Would Kai turn the gun on her own team, her own friends, if they tried? Would they be fast enough to rip control from Nas before he triggered the command?

Nas's smile tilted, weary at the edges. "This is good," he said, voice rising enough to fill the chamber. "We end the cycle together. We stand on the winning side."

Krill took a step and halted when Kai's arm shifted, the weapon rising slightly. "Kai," he said. "This isn't you. You know this isn't right."

But maybe the Kai they all knew had died in the North, in that blast.

Yuri's fingers spun at his thigh. FOLLOW MY LEAD.

Miriam tried to catch Krill's eye, but he was too far forward.

Kai's lashes lowered. She angled her chin toward Nas. "Sometimes you have to get your boots dirty."

Nas's hand found her shoulder; he squeezed, a small intimate triumph. "It really is a better view from here." He turned toward the console, his back to them.

Miriam's skin prickled.

Now, Yuri signed.

She inhaled, matched his stance, and let her muscles prime. Yuri moved. Miriam followed. It'd be two on two, maybe three if Krill understood.

Kai lifted the sidearm. Her arm straightened. And Miriam could only watch as she pulled the trigger.

51

OBSEQUY

IT WAS a cruel illusion of memory. Miriam saw the moment unfold as though she were back in that dark cellar with Sam. But this time no one had missed. The gun was too close, the distance too point-blank to falter, the chance for interruption gone.

The shot bloomed red, and Nas fell.

For a breathless instant, the world was stripped bare, silence ringing through the chamber, heavy and absolute. Something had been broken in a way that could never be undone.

In that instant, Miriam didn't see the man collapsing, but her teammate who had once slipped chocolate bars into his pockets and into Kai's, her colleague who grinned wide as Fox cursed him over another lost hand of cards, her friend who smirked slyly when he stole into depots to glimpse new tech. She saw the young man who had laughed until he couldn't breathe, whose bright eyes had turned to her for reassurance before his first deployment. The memory cut, sharp and fleeting, gone before she could hold it. Miriam stared as the blood spread across the floor and into the grates.

To her side, Kai lowered the gun by a few degrees, as if her body had only just understood what it had done. Her gaze fixed on the space her best friend had occupied, refusing its final resting place on the ground, the body itself. After a moment her arm stuttered, then dropped to her side. There was no expression left on her face, only the spatter freckling it. She turned her head away from what she'd done, what she'd ended.

Fox reached her a second later. He eased the sidearm from her hand, slow and careful, as though disarming a wounded animal, and pulled her against him. She didn't resist or respond. Her limbs hung limp, head tilted into him, eyes open and empty.

"I didn't—" she whispered. Her eyes dropped to the crimson edging toward her shoes. "I'm sorry. He—I never meant for this to happen."

Fox hushed and turned her fully, shielding her from the sight. She let him.

Miriam sank beside what was left of their friend. There was nothing to be done. His eyes were already filmed over, his pulse already gone. Her hands trembled as she maneuvered his head and matted hair to extract the intact embed from just above the bullet's entry point. His skin was soft and leeching warmth by the second. Her lip quivered as she readjusted his head so that the ruin was hidden. She rose slowly, breath catching on the taste of metal flooding her nose and throat.

"The bioweapon." Krill's voice caught. "Did the command go out?"

Yuri glanced between the body and Miriam's hand, then moved back toward the console. "It didn't," he said after a moment. "I think I can cut the execution path now. I can try to quarantine it here."

The human link—the immediate threat—had been addressed, but the danger still shadowed the air.

"I'm sorry," Kai said, her voice flat and scorched. "I had to."

She didn't have to say it. They knew. They all knew. If she

hadn't pulled the trigger, the command—a war, a genocide, worse—would have been released. It would have swept through most of the Altered on those ships, killing and breaking a fragile balance that had taken years to build. Sometimes there was no negotiation, no other angle or option. Sometimes the only answer, the only resolution was violence. A final choice and decision.

"What about the canisters?" Krill asked.

"They still need to be disengaged manually," Yuri said, working. "But without that contingency override, it should be manageable. The code's here, but I've cut off its route to the network. It can't propagate without being rebuilt from scratch. I'll see what I can find on disengaging the local devices once I'm done."

Miriam clenched her hand around the little embed. How could something so small hold so many lives hostage? How could one person decide the fate of so many? She looked down at Nas again. He was one of them. The old Echo. He was their friend. Their family. They had trusted him.

She stepped away from his body. The smell of blood was already overpowering, making her throat constrict. The chamber pressed in; she wanted out. The shell of a friend lay at her feet, and she wanted out.

"The doors," Miriam said, backing up. "Can you get them open? We need comms, and Sam can help with the ship, the containers—" She balled her fist more, the embed digging into her palm.

"I'm working on it. One thing at a time." Yuri's hands flew. The console's glow shifted, lines rearranging. "I think that's it. I've burned the bridge, at least what I can. That loophole's been quarantined for the time being."

Miriam's stomach turned. Was isolation enough? Vertex had already pulled back, but that meant its existence was still there. "So it's just contained. That's not the same as destroying it."

"It's the only option we have right now."

Krill's jaw tightened. He looked at Miriam, then at Kai in Fox's arms. "What's stopping Vertex from erasing their tracks? Biding their time? Can't they just rebuild it?"

"What do you suggest? That we burn the place down?" Miriam snapped. The words came worse than she had intended, but the thought itself revolted her. Fire and ruin were what they had long been offered as solutions. It was destruction dressed as closure, annihilation passed off as an answer.

Her words died in the stagnant air, buried under the purr of machines that carried Nas's fingerprints. The chamber smelled of scorched metal and blood, and all she could think was how easily it could become another grave.

She wanted out. Not because the danger was over—it wasn't—but because she couldn't stand another second in this place where her friend—traitor, but still a friend—lingered in blood on the floor and betrayal within the walls. She needed air. She needed life. Proof that something still lived, that something still mattered, something still worth saving.

"We'll figure it out," she said, quieter, though the words tasted like ash. "We always do. Yuri, get us out of here."

This was Nas's truth. But it wasn't theirs. It wasn't hers. And if she stayed a moment longer, she feared it might seep into her bones the way it had seeped into his, the way it had poisoned others. She feared it might make her believe there was no way out but through fire.

♟

Sam wasn't outside when the last doors opened, but the corridor beyond had changed. As all of Echo—but one— retraced their route toward the main atrium, the air felt crowded, taut with motion. Vertex workers clustered in uneasy knots, voices pitched low. SecGuards lined the walls outside, their presence too stiff to be mistaken for routine. There was no media, no spotlights, no recording devices, no theater. Not yet.

Whatever Kai had set in motion before with City Center had held, even if none of them could yet grasp what it meant. Everything that had happened was buried beneath the surface, shielded from the city and its fleeting interests. To an outsider, it would read as paperwork, contracts, a lack of oversight. Boring. But boring had teeth, and boring had nearly smothered them all.

The sound reached Miriam first—a quick patter of shoes over polished tile. She knew before she looked.

Sam.

Even before she saw her, Miriam *felt* her. Sam's eyes swept the crowd, frantic, and Miriam lifted her hand. The distance between them vanished. Sam cleaved the space with single-minded velocity. She reached Miriam and wrapped her arms around her with such force that the breath left Miriam in a startled gasp.

She didn't resist. She let herself go, lost and found. The scent of Sam's skin hit her like something remembered, something that meant home. The absurdity and horror of the past hour—the betrayal, the near-catastrophe, the lives upended—spilled out of her in the form of a broken laugh into Sam's shoulder.

Sam pulled back just enough to search her face. Miriam opened her mouth, but the words never formed. Sam's lips found hers instead, fierce and desperate. The kiss was heat and hunger, and Miriam surrendered to it utterly. Once, she might have worried about appearances, about propriety, about public displays of any commitment. Once, she might've held back. But that belonged to another life. Here, now, this was all that mattered.

When Sam drew back, Miriam's breath was uneven. Sam's hands framed her face, thumbs caressing her cheekbones, as if she needed to prove she was real. "Are you okay?" Her attention flicked toward the others, where Kai was already pulling the remnants of herself together.

Miriam couldn't answer. Not yet. She held Sam's eyes instead. The fresh scar across her cheek, the older scar beneath her mouth, the blue that had steadied her in darker hours.

"What happened?" Sam asked at last. She repeated it, softer, when Miriam didn't respond.

Miriam's eyes dropped to the side, and a ragged exhale broke free. She wanted to tell Sam everything, but it was too much right now. "Did you reach Kuan-Lin?" she asked instead.

Sam nodded. "They'll do what they can—an emergency landing, but the command—"

"It's stopped. For now." Miriam hesitated, then opened her hand to show the embed lying in her palm.

Sam blinked at the small device, confusion flickering across her face. And then she looked up, trying to find the others, counting, before her focus dropped to Miriam's hand again. Her shoulders sagged with a whispered "oh."

Miriam swallowed.

"So it's over?" Sam asked.

Miriam shook her head. "The command's cut, but the weapon's still there. The plans are still there." She glanced across the atrium, where Kai stood surrounded by SecGuards and officials, Fox at her side like a shield and guardian. Kai's mask was already back in place, but Miriam could see the blood dark on her shoes. Kai looked like she'd shed the weight of the control room like another uniform, yet some stains couldn't be hidden.

"She'll push Center on sanctions, oversight," Miriam muttered. "It might slow Vertex, but it's not enough. They'll bury this while bureaucracy drags and committees argue. They'll try again when the timing comes around."

"What are the other options?"

Sam and Miriam turned to Yuri, who looked raw, his eyes bruised with fatigue.

He shook his head. "We go to the network? They'll spin it until truth doesn't matter. Kai will put on a brave face, push with whatever she can, but she knows City Center can only do so much. Everyone has their own motivations, their own agendas."

"The Seraphim?" Sam whispered.

SRAF. Miriam felt her chest constrict. Another weapon. She shook her head. It'd be unleashing more violence, more swing to the pendulum, even if it came from a joint force of human and Altered. Every path, every option led to violence, and Nas's words echoed: cycles repeating, only broken when someone made the ultimate decision.

Yuri frowned, his attention flicking between them. "You said something earlier, Tan. About flipping the board, the same game."

Miriam's brows knitted.

"The Altered know," he pressed. "They have the evidence in their hands. Why not bring them in? Force both sides to the table."

Miriam's throat tightened. "I don't know about that. They'll be furious, if they aren't already—"

"They *should* be. They have that right. But they have to also realize that we're all playing the same game. And that game, this conflict and division, requires that one side win and another lose. What if we both agree to…not play? Why does one side have to win? What Nas said is true. It'll never end until someone makes the first move. But they'll never trust us until they know we *didn't* choose Nas's truth. What if *this* is the first move?"

An ideal. Possibly naive. Impossibly difficult. A what-if. But wasn't that what the future was? What life was? And the worst thing they could do was not make a choice.

"We tell them the truth and hope they trust us," Sam whispered.

Truth. Hope. Trust. All words that sounded too fragile, too foolish. But what else was there?

"What is the truth?" Miriam muttered, her fingers closing around the embed in her palm.

But she knew.

The truth was that in war, there were no winners.

52

ECHOES

TSUTSUMI'S RAN WARMER in the back corner, the way it always had. The space was tight—tables crammed close, the clink of cutlery and hiss from the kitchen constant—but it smelled of onions and bread and memory. Of rituals carried forward, of traditions that lingered. Of a time before any of them had understood what it truly meant to bleed for something.

Miriam sat in her usual seat, thoughts folding in on themselves, until Fox shouldered through the door with that familiar, lumbering confidence.

"Kai?" she asked as he approached.

He dropped into the chair beside her and shook his head. "Still at Center. Krill's pickin' her up today."

Miriam raised a brow. "Did Foxtrot let you off the leash?"

"Won't matter in a couple days anyway," he muttered.

She tried not to smile and failed. "Hino reached out." It wasn't a question.

He didn't answer right away, only met her eyes. "Did you do this?"

"Do what?"

The look persisted, more serious than she was used to, but he finally let it go.

"Tell me you took it," Miriam said. "She'll be a great lead."

"And me?"

"You've got…potential."

He snorted, but the corners of his mouth tipped up. Her laugh slipped out, startled and soft, and his followed. A crack of lightness they both needed.

"Potential for what?" Yuri arrived behind them, drying his hands on a cloth.

"You're looking at Echo's new second," Miriam said.

"No shit!" Yuri clapped Fox so hard the plates rattled. "Didn't think I'd see the day."

"Yeah," Fox muttered. "Makes two of us." He frowned. "Haven't said yes yet."

"Why not?" Yuri huffed. "Scared of baby marines?"

"Fuck off." Fox lifted a middle finger.

Miriam laughed again. The sound felt good. Safe.

"I'll call Hino myself and accept for you," Yuri said, grinning as he slid into the seat on her other side.

She leaned into the small quiet that settled.

Fox rubbed the back of his neck. "Feels strange, you know? Sittin' here. Laughin'. After everythin'."

"We have to take the good moments when they come," Yuri said. "There's only so many of them, and a whole lot more of the bad. Might as well enjoy the balance while it lasts."

Miriam nodded, reached over, and squeezed Fox's arm. "Speaking of balance, how's Kai?"

"Hard to say," Fox replied. "Can't ever get a bead on what's goin' on in that noggin of hers. She hasn't exactly been talkin' much about it either. Been busyin' herself with all that regulatory shit."

"We're making sure she's not alone, right?"

"I've got her," Fox said firmly.

"You're going to be pretty busy with the new job."

"Won't stop me." His jaw set. "Don't worry. I've got her."

"*We've* got her," Yuri added. And he meant it. They all did. There was a time they would have kept it unsaid, convinced it didn't need saying. But not now. Not anymore.

Miriam's gaze drifted to the window where Sam stood outside. Ren's tuft of light brown hair was a blur on the display of Miriam's handheld.

"Maybe I should postpone," she murmured. "I can stick around, help—"

"Are you kidding me?" Yuri deadpanned.

She smiled despite herself.

"No, seriously. That's what comms are for," he said. "When a Royal offers you a place and a job? Especially with everything that's happened? You can represent us and Station General over there. Keep the channels open, build the future, or whatever fancy buzzwords politicians and higher-ups are throwing around these days."

"Some of us *are* those higher-ups now," she teased.

"Hell, don't remind me." Yuri folded his arms. "Regardless, *we've* got this over here. You'll do more good as a field liaison, an envoy, an emissary, whatever the title is. Go make a difference."

Miriam hadn't asked for it. She wasn't a diplomat or a medical industry expert, and she had never wanted to be either. She was a combat medic who had spent too long in UMF, too long in a war she knew she no longer wanted to fight. But Kuan-Lin had insisted. Medical coordination between humans and Altered. Progress, she'd said. It'd be something different.

"What if—" Miriam began.

"If you can't rise to the challenge, fine," Yuri cut in. "Take the win, sit in a garden, breathe. I'd say I'd be worried about you over there—I will, 'cause that's just how I am—but I've seen what you both can do. You fight and survive. This is just a different challenge, and you can figure it out together."

"Or fight and thrive," Fox grunted with a shrug. He jerked his thumb toward the window. "Who's Valky talkin' to?"

Miriam turned back with the others, catching another glimpse of the little boy on the display. "The real future," she said. Her smile softened as she looked over at Sam. Civilian clothes, metal arm, shoulders looser than they had ever been. She regarded the dark ink climbing her neck, the small node of tech above her ear, the jagged scar across her cheek—an underline to the raw blue eyes Miriam could drown in. Once, she'd thought Sam would never want to be anything but a marine. A weapon. Yet here she was, laughing, waiting, open to something vulnerable, and although not new, still different.

She felt both Yuri and Fox's attention shift back to her, and she let her stare idle a moment longer before she broke away. She rolled her eyes at them preemptively. "It's her nephew."

Yuri smirked but didn't press. "The Royals are doing alright, then?"

"No insurrections, no riots in Arshangol yet. We would've heard from Kuan-Lin."

"No backlash from the Vertex mess either," Fox muttered.

Yuri murmured in agreement. "Valk and Mute certainly chose the right Royal."

Whether it was fate, timing, or dumb luck, Miriam wasn't sure. The choice was what mattered. They *had* taken the opportunity and made something of it.

"She's been a bastion for us with all this," Yuri continued. "Between the connections she initiated with General, and I'm sure the ones with Center and Kai..."

"For now," Fox said.

"What, you think she'll change her mind?"

Fox shrugged.

"Do you think she should've leveraged her child more? For the city? Relations?"

"Now you're projectin'. With everythin' happenin'?" Fox

shook his head. "I don't know, don't got a kid—don't know how anyone can have a kid in these times. But no, I'm not implyin' any of that. It would've put a target on their backs in Station."

"Is it any different over there in Arshangol?" Yuri asked.

Fox made a face, lips screwing together before his expression softened with relief. "Speakin' of havin' a kid..."

The restaurant door opened. Krill stepped in first, Kai behind him, her posture rigid, jaw set in that familiar mix of fatigue and determination.

"About fuckin' time," Fox said, rising. He met them in five long strides.

The three paused, halfway between the door and table, falling into their own conversation.

Miriam felt Yuri's elbow nudge into her. "Are *you* ready for it?" he asked.

"For what?"

"Having a kid."

Her eyes widened, then narrowed.

"Joking," Yuri said quickly, raising his hands as if to ward off the blow.

She gave him another look, but beyond the flash of surprise there was no fear.

He grinned. "No. I meant the big change. Moving on."

She pondered on it. "You said something a while ago. Before."

"I've said a lot of somethings. What did I say?"

"You said war changes us. That we're either dead or broken."

Yuri blinked. "I remember."

"You're wrong."

His brow lifted.

"Well, not completely. But you missed something." Miriam gazed back to Sam outside. "Dead is...well, dead. But broken?

That's not an end state unless we let it be." She took a deep breath, considering. "I broke. I know I did—we all did in some way—but I don't think I'm still broken, Yuri. I...I think I'm a better person than who I was before, and I don't want to be who I was back then. I can't be her again." She looked back at him. "This is a change, but I think the hardest part is behind us."

Yuri gave her a warm smile and draped an arm across her shoulders.

"What?" she asked. "What?"

He shook his head. "I thought I was supposed to be the optimist."

"You can have that role back," she whispered. "It feels weird."

"Nah." Yuri pulled her closer. "It suits you."

They looked up as the others broke apart and gathered around the table, unhurried greetings passing with light hugs. Miriam had seen Krill just yesterday, checked in with Kai not long before that. Still, it mattered. It all did.

No one mentioned the empty chair at the end.

"What's new?" Miriam asked, her eyes lifting as Sam reentered the restaurant. It had only been a couple weeks since they'd been in Vertex's building—since Nas—but it felt as though everything had changed while nothing had at all.

Kai sighed. "Another hearing tomorrow, and the day after. I've pushed for an investigative committee. We need accountability and consequences. It's the first actual step to show the Royals, the Altered, something real. True faith."

Miriam touched Sam's knee as she sat in the open seat between her and Fox. "How much do people know?"

"How much do *we* know? My team's been working with Patterson and others who were raising questions before. We've been processing summons and inquiries, but I don't know if we'll ever fully get the whole picture. And to answer your question with the public—not much," Kai admitted. "We've tried to minimize it on the networks."

"That won't hold," Fox grumbled.

"I can take a page out of Vertex's book and keep things quiet, under close hold for now, but yes, it'll surface one way or another." She glanced at Miriam. "We've already handed the Butcher over as part of the ongoing talks. He won't see a trial, won't get the stage he so desires. They'll put him away, far from any spotlight. But that's just one of many. And until we can figure out this Vertex behemoth, we'll do what's right."

"Those bastards won't do time."

It was bleak, but Miriam didn't disagree. She glanced at the vacant seat. The organization would find a scapegoat, divert the blame, or find a distraction.

"No," Kai affirmed, then sighed again. "Probably not. But we'll get more oversight in place. Stop this before it happens again."

"You think it'll happen again?" Yuri said. He lifted his hands. "I ask the dumb questions. Someone has to."

"And the sympathizers? The Charonites?" Miriam pushed.

"Is there an easy answer?" Kai's head bowed. "Information sharing, transparency, reform, but in what way? More collaboration, more open lines with the Altered? Look at General. Our medical care has advanced in such a short time. There's potential, but people are afraid. How do you change that?"

Miriam thought of Talwar and his own attitude shift. It had taken being left behind and being put in dire circumstances for him to warm up to the Altered next to him. And on the other side, Longwei, Kuan-Lin's nephew, shaped by needless hatred and cruelty. What chance did they have when attitudes and opinions could change so radically with violent catalysts? When it took much longer to deprogram and unlearn?

"It's an uphill battle," Kai said, voice thinning. "And it always will be."

Miriam found Sam's hand on the table and squeezed. Action and reaction. Reaction, unfailingly, lagged behind. What Kai and Kuan-Lin were trying to do was be that first motion, a tide pushing and steering forward. And Miriam and Sam would be a part of it. Indirectly. Minutely. But still, a part of it.

Krill clapped his hands once. "Alright, alright. Enough shop talk. This was supposed to be a break. What, Echo's going to solve the world's problems?" He chuckled.

Laughter flickered around the table at the strangeness of it all. Miriam's gaze moved over them. At Yuri, who she had known since childhood. Her best friend who had been with her through everything, through uni, UMF basic, and then SOG. He had been her steady rock, and to no surprise, the team's as well. At Krill, their friend and leader who said yes when it mattered, who wanted to do right. At Kai, younger but no less scarred. Her idealism had bent but not broken despite being blasted apart. And Fox. The insufferable asshole who'd somehow become so indispensable. A confidant, a shoulder to lean on. He, like the rest, had fought his own battles and come out on top.

And herself. Changed, unrecognizable to who she once was, but not ashamed of it. It was who she was, her journey, and she had made a fair share of mistakes and learned her lessons.

She clutched Sam's hand again, and the woman leaned closer, a question in her eyes. Miriam shook her head and returned a soft smile. Her glass lifted halfway, then stilled, her awareness settling on the empty chair. The others noticed, and the table quieted.

Yuri sighed. "We should say something."

"To Nas?" Kai asked.

Fox set an empty cup at the place and poured golden liquid until it brimmed.

"To who he *was*," Yuri said. "We owe him that much."

Silence hung.

Krill broke it first. "He never let me get through a brief uninterrupted. But when you needed him, he was there."

"Nosy as hell," Yuri said with a fond smile. "But just as brilliant. I hated admitting when he was right."

Fox drummed his fingers. "Everyone knows we didn't always see eye to eye." He shifted. "But I admired him. He watched our six. Got us out of trouble."

"Got us *in* trouble, too," Miriam added with a huff.

Chuckles scattered gently.

"He was a friend," Miriam said, softer.

"He was my best friend," Kai whispered.

They sat quiet.

"But he still chose that," she added.

The weight settled again.

Yuri studied his drink. "If we pretend he was always the enemy, we lose the ability to see how a teammate, a friend like him becomes...*that*. He didn't just wake up and decide this. He got there, however fast or slow. And maybe we should've been there earlier, recognized it, addressed it." He sighed. "He was one of us. And he was also...wrong. Both can be true."

Fox tilted his glass. "To Nas."

The name circled the table.

"And to never letting that happen again," Miriam said quietly.

The group raised their cups. The ones closest to the end clinked their glasses to the lone vessel in front of the empty chair, the sound soft and reverent.

Miriam finished her drink, then set it down. The filled cup remained at the end of the table as conversation shifted to lighter things—naming Krill's coming baby, Yuri's stories from the hospital, Kai's ridiculous coworkers, and Fox's ribbing questions about his new team. Sam chimed in now and then but mostly seemed content to listen. There was no pressure, no urgency. Just a pocket of peace as the untouched cup sat as silent company.

When most of the dishes had been picked clean, Krill patted the table with both hands and glanced at his commcuff.

"Leaving, boss?" Yuri asked.

Krill got up. "I'd stay longer, but Elly's got the cravings." He shrugged. "I've gotta stop by the bodega, pick up some snacks on the way home." His attention moved around the table before settling on Miriam. "You know how to find me."

He was the first to leave—one more hard embrace with Sam, another with Miriam—before he waved to the others. It wasn't a goodbye. Far from it.

"He's going to be a great father," Yuri said.

The others murmured their agreement, too full, or too reflective, to add more.

Kai's commcuff trilled, and she sighed, heavy and tired. "No rest for the wicked," she said quietly, her eyes flicking toward the full cup near her.

"Back to Center?" Fox asked.

She nodded.

"It's late. I'll walk you."

"It's really okay—"

"Let me be a charmin' asshole, okay."

Her mouth closed. She touched his arm and gave the faintest nod. "Fine."

Another round of farewells followed. Fox delivered a squeezing hug that left Miriam breathless before pulling Sam into his arms, whispering something that drew a sheen to the woman's eyes.

Miriam turned to Kai, holding her a little longer and a little stronger. "We're here. You're not alone," she whispered.

Kai gave the smallest nod against her shoulder. A quiet thank-you. When they separated, her focus held on the lone chair and the waiting cup before she turned for the door, Fox behind her like a guardian.

"I guess you should both call it a night as well," Yuri said. He opened his arms to Sam.

She hesitated, then let herself be enveloped. His head dipped close, and Miriam couldn't make out the words, only the quiet exchange. When Sam resurfaced, her eyes glistened more. She sniffed, murmured, "I'll give you two a moment," and slipped toward the door.

Miriam watched her go, then turned back. "What'd you tell her?"

"What she needed to hear," he answered. "I didn't know him long, but I think I knew her brother well enough. It's what she needed to know." He didn't elaborate.

Through the window, Miriam saw Sam pause just outside, face canted toward the sky as if searching for stars and satellites. The city's haze would make it impossible, but they were there. Even if unseen.

"So," Yuri said, sitting back down. "What now?"

Miriam eased into the chair beside him. "That's the big question."

"Aside from the new gig, what are your plans? Settle down? Paint?"

Miriam flicked the condensation from her cup at him. "I..." She stopped. She hadn't thought past Kuan-Lin's offer or, really, the fact that she just wanted to be with Sam. The question dug at her now. The war wasn't over—dwindling maybe, but the violence and division would be there or circle back. For her, if she could help it, she was done. Removed. Separated. Until the cycle dragged her in again, but it wouldn't be her choice or her initiative.

"I don't know," Miriam admitted with a growing smile. "But I don't really care."

Yuri mirrored a grin. This was her best friend. He saw her, knew her, had been there despite the lows and dips. Their friendship wasn't perfect, but it was precious.

Pressure pricked at her throat and behind her eyes. She cleared it away with a cough. "We should probably go. It *is* a weeknight."

He hummed.

She rose, tucking her chair in. When he didn't move, she turned. "Yuri?"

"I think I'll sit a while."

She hesitated, then pulled her chair back. "I'll stay with you." She raised her hand toward Sam, ready to wave her on.

But Yuri caught it and held it before patting it between his palms. "No, you should go. Don't keep her waiting."

Miriam stood there, uncertain, but when he didn't budge, she said, "We'll stop by General before we go."

"Your parents throwing you a party?"

She rolled her eyes. "*You're* throwing me a party."

"Oh, am I?"

Her laugh drew his, and when it tapered off, he rubbed at his face, his eyes redder than before. "You'll call, right?"

He'd barely finished when Miriam wrapped her arms around his broad shoulders. "I have a reminder set," she whispered. "Every day? Too much? Every other day?"

Yuri chuckled, mist brimming his eyes.

"I'll miss you," she said into his shoulder.

He sniffed. "You're supposed to save the tears for the actual goodbye, when you actually leave, you know that, right?"

She dug her chin into his shoulder, then softened, their temples touching.

"I'm proud of you, Tan."

She snorted.

"You're happy. And you're doing what you wanted. Getting out."

"Better late than never. You know you can come over. Arshangol's a big place. Plus, I like seeing your handsome face."

"Well, I've got to *now*." His chuckle rumbled through her chest. "Save a room for me?"

"Always." She squeezed him. "You've always been our rock, Yuri."

He sniffed again, then laughed, pushing her lightly away. "Go. Get out of here before you make me bawl."

She kissed his cheek and let go, moving toward the door.

Outside, Sam nudged the ground with her shoe. "Everything okay?"

Miriam sniffed, tears bright in her eyes, but smiled. "Yeah. Better than okay."

53

THE VETERAN

"IT'S WEIRD, ISN'T IT?" Sam's voice was quiet, nearly lost beneath the churn of the airship's preflight grumble. They stood just outside the boarding ramp, boots on cracked pavement that smelled of fuel and ocean salt. "That out there, shit's still happening," she added, nodding toward the skyline where the buildings blurred into the morning haze.

If Miriam squinted just hard enough, she could make out some of UMF's gray blocks just beyond. Already in the distance.

"And we're not…in it?"

Miriam arched a brow as she turned back. "Are you saying you already miss it?"

Sam's arms crossed, jaw tight. Her prosthetic finger worked one of the straps on her pack. The rising light caught the pink line along her cheek.

"Not at all, huh?" Miriam tried, half-joking.

A shrug. Sam dragged the toe of her shoe against the ground, eyes down.

Miriam smoothed a stray hair from Sam's face. "I'm sure you'll get into scuffles over there."

Sam didn't look up.

"I really hope not, though," Miriam added, softer. "It'd be nice to have something quiet for a change."

"It'll be a lot of change, anyway."

"Yeah." Miriam's voice faltered. Her chest tightened as the burden of what they were about to do pressed in. "It's not going to be easy—"

"No. But I'm expecting that. I think you are, too."

Blue eyes locked with hers.

Miriam smiled. "So, what are you going to do over there?"

Sam hesitated, then smirked. "I don't know. Maybe learn how to cook? Remember those buns in the South? In Matam. I think about them sometimes."

Miriam's grin widened. At her side, Sam's finger worried at her thumb. Miriam tapped her knuckles lovingly against the same hand, and without looking up, Sam shifted and took Miriam's hand in hers. The grip was strong and familiar.

"Nervous?" Miriam asked.

Sam nodded.

Miriam didn't say it, but she was too. Not in the way she'd felt before missions or drops. This was quieter. Deeper. The fear that meant something had begun to matter again. But the two of them had taken on worse. They'd survived when they shouldn't have. They'd been ripped apart and slammed back together. Through every fracture, every impossible, infuriating crack in their story—they had returned to this.

Each other.

She turned fully toward Sam. The words worked up her throat and the back of her mouth. She should have said it years ago, should've said it in that dark pit over and over, said it a hundred times before, said it in that back corridor of Duncan's. And though Miriam had said it several times since, she wanted to say it more.

"Sam, I—"

Sam kissed her, stealing the words before they left her lips. Miriam returned it, both hands fisted in Sam's collar. When they pulled apart, their words came at the same time, tangled over each other.

"I love you."

Sam said it again, quieter, like it hadn't been enough to say it once. It was the first time she'd said it since all those years before.

And like all those years ago, Miriam froze. But this time, it wasn't out of fear. This time, it was from the warmth of surprise. She'd known, of course she'd known, but she had been giving Sam space to find her own footing, the time to figure out her emotions, the capacity to utter the words afresh. The first time Sam had said it, Miriam had run. She wasn't running now. Instead, she smiled.

Sam gestured her head back toward the ramp, but her gaze didn't waver. "We should probably get going," she whispered.

Neither moved.

"Hey! Lovers! You coming or what?" someone shouted from inside the ship.

Miriam didn't bother to turn. She lifted a middle finger toward the voice, then softened it with a lazy wave. Sam huffed a laugh, breath brushing Miriam's lips. They kissed once more, shorter, but no less real. They'd have hundreds if not thousands more. The thought warmed her, melted the what-ifs that had become rampant and haunted her. She couldn't control the conflict, others' rhetoric, or why things happened the way they did—fate, luck, or not.

Only one what-if remained.

"Okay?" Sam asked.

What if Miriam could be content? Happiness was fleeting, she knew. But she could only control what she could—choose where it existed. And this part that she could, was hers to keep.

Miriam nodded. "Okay."

Sam adjusted her pack, then moved up the ramp, but Miriam's feet didn't follow. Sam paused at the top, brow lifting in silent question. Miriam gave a small shake of her head. Just a moment.

And Sam understood. She disappeared into the hold—no carbine rifle, no kit, only herself. And though she carried weight, it was lighter now. No longer dragging her down.

Miriam turned back to the city in the distance. The buildings stood like a receiving line, waving her off through the shimmer of heat. It was her life, her past. But she didn't feel the ache of leaving, just the quiet sweetness of something finished, something done.

This wasn't goodbye. It was the next thing, the next step to the next destination. And for once, she felt a bit more complete, a bit more whole.

"Ready?" Sam's voice called from the frame of the compartment, one hand extended. Not pulling, not rushing. Just waiting like a promise.

And when Miriam Tanner took Sam's hand, she was home.

ACKNOWLEDGMENTS

The first and biggest THANK YOU will always go to Claudia, who supported me through this entire process. Words on paper, words out loud cannot capture the depth of my love and appreciation for you.

Thank you to my alpha readers who endured pure word-vomit: Katie P., who's stuck with me since my first book and through every bout of imposter syndrome. That scene in this book is the spiciest you'll get from me. You're welcome. To fellow authors Ian Patterson and Ian Young, thank you for your feedback, encouragement, and friendship. To my beta readers: Holly T., Nicole J., Christine H., Lauren H., Jessica L. (a particular thanks for your help on the science and Hokkien Taiwanese/Mandarin details), Eric M., LunaB, and Margaret N. And to Liv L.—our unhinged conversations about feasible injuries were a highlight. Anyone eavesdropping at that sushi spot would've been horrified.

To my editors, Allister Thompson and Lee Tipton, and to my friend, colleague, and proofreader, Brett B., thank you for making sure the words did what they needed to. And thank you to Savannah Gilmore, who gave this book its voice in narration. You brought the story to life in a way I never could have alone.

And, as always, to the readers who found connection to this world and characters, thank you.*

---

* If you enjoyed *Of Imperfection*, please consider leaving a review on Goodreads, Amazon, Barnes & Noble, or your favorite retailer—or share with a friend! It really makes a big impact for indie authors.

AFTERWORD

When people ask me if I enjoy writing, my answer is most always no. Don't get me wrong—I love this series and my babies—but did I enjoy the journey? Ha. Still no.

Maybe it's just how my brain works, how I process things. I didn't write these books because I *like* writing. I started writing because of a web series cringe-binge and the idea that fuck it, I could write better than that. Spite is a wonderful motivator. I then wrote *Of Friction* because I couldn't get to *Of Abrasion* without it, and then I couldn't just stop at Book 2 without a Book 3. Spite, so much spite.

For the past three years, I'd rush home after a ten-hour workday, and force myself to draft, edit, and labor over these books until my wife told me to go to bed. I spent every "vacation" and weekend working on this.[*]

Does this all count as spite? Shit. Sure.

But *look*. I did it. I *did* this. Maybe it's hindsight, or the relief and grief that comes after finishing, but I guess I did enjoy it. I enjoy the feeling of accomplishment. Of completion.[†]

----

[*] My wife is the true hero. She tolerates this madness and *still* supports me.

[†] Hey, that could be a fourth book.

As said on each book's dedication, this has been mainly for me, something I've both wanted and needed to do. And now that it's done, I guess I *am* proud of myself. Is it perfect? Absolutely not. But neither am I. I accept that, and I am okay with that.

It is strange now that this story is out in the world, these characters and scenes have stopped playing in my head. Sam and Miriam kept me company for nearly two decades, and through this bizarre exorcism that is writing, it's oddly quiet up there. It's a really weird kind of grief and mourning that I'm still dealing with.

Is this story done? In the trilogy sense, yes. I know there are some character and story threads I left inconclusive and a bit dangling, but they're (mostly) intentional because isn't that how life is? There isn't a why or understanding or closure on everything, and this book is no different.

Is that a shit excuse? Probably.

That uncertainty—the loose ends—is part of life. The world is so big and just like Sam and Miriam, we only see one slice, one perspective, of it. We, just like them, won't know or care about everything. Plus, I like to think those unanswered questions are also what makes a story live beyond its final page.[*]

And yet, that's often when readers close the book and move on. They skip the back matter, the extra bits that might not push the plot forward but hold something quieter.[†]

Before I started writing this series, I never read the back matter of books. They were always just that part—filler and obstacles to the next thing on my never-ending list. So, if you've stuck around this far...

---

[*] Is it still a shit excuse? Sure, but I'm sticking with it.

[†] And if my explanation makes you upset, then it holds something quieter *and more frustrating.*

I admire you, I appreciate you, and I thank you for spending a slice of your life with my characters and this world.

Sincerely,

S.J. Lee

GLOSSARY

Alty—Human slang for Altered in the Station City region

Apostates—Also known as The Promised

AOR—Area of responsibility

Arshangol—The capital city of the Altered; where the Royal Court resides and governs

BigInt—Informal moniker for UMF Intelligence

BigMED—Informal moniker for UMF Medical Services

Carbine—A long gun with a shortened barrel

Charonite—A member of the Children of Charon

Children of Charon (COC)—A prominent human-supremacist group

Command—UMF's leadership charged with overseeing the military's operations

Commcuff—A wrist-worn technological device used to communicate and connect to the network

DFAC—Dining facility

Duncan's—Compound bar in UMF Station

EXFIL—Exfiltration

HUD—Head-up Display

Intel—Intelligence

Jabber—An injection device

Legion—A company of Altered soldiers

Legionnaire—An Altered soldier

LMG—Light machine gun

LOGS—Logistics services

LZ—Landing zone

Matam—Large human population center located in the South (Andean region)

MED—Medical services

MedJet—A large medical support device

MedPort—A portable medical support device

MP—Military police

New Zapala—Southernmost human population center (Andean region)

OpSec—Operations security or operational security

POC—Point of contact

Prowler—A large utility task and terrain vehicle that can carry at least four passengers and cargo

The Promised—A prominent Altered supremacist group

Rabbit—A modular all-terrain vehicle that can carry at least two passengers

Recon—Reconnaissance

Rhino—A vehicle with a boxy shape and a high roof used for transporting goods or passengers

ROE—Rules of engagement

Royals/Royal Court—The governing body of the Altered population; legacy of original genetically engineered Altered

RUMINT—Rumor intelligence

SecHut—Security hut; a SecTeam's office

SecTeam—Security team; a local security force

SitRep—Situation report

SOG—Special Operations Group

SOL—Shit out of luck

Sovereign—The highest authority of the Royal Court

Station City—Largest human population center located in a central location

Station General—A prominent medical center in Station City

Sunali—A small town in the North

Tapetum Lucidem—A reflective layer of tissue in the eye that assists in low light vision

TDY—Temporary duty

Temunco—UMF's southernmost outpost, which overlooks Matam, New Zapala, and other regional settlements; borders Altered territories

Tsutsumi's—A restaurant in Station City

TOC—Tactical operations center

UMF—United Military Federation; the unified human military that oversees the defense and security of the entire human population

Ursus—UMF's northernmost outpost, which overlooks Gould and other regional settlements; borders Altered territories

Visor—A head-worn technological device used to communicate and assist with tactics

Wunby—Human slang for The Promised/Apostates based on their mantra, "one blood, one promise"

Yoomy—Slang for UMF

CONTENT WARNING

This fictional novel is meant for adults only. It contains material and scenes with:

- Profanity and explicit language
- Graphic violence
- Substance abuse and addiction
- Death
- War and terrorism
- Child violence
- Sexual content
- Torture
- Decapitation

ABOUT THE AUTHOR

S.J. Lee is currently in the foreign service and holds a master of science in security and intelligence and two bachelors of science in different business fields. She has lived and worked in Iraq, Mexico, Chile, India, Brazil, Guyana, and all over the United States.

instagram.com/sjleewriter